His f...

"Kate," he gr...

For an insta..., ...
Her entire body awakened to dormant emotions she
never knew she possessed.

The kiss was as hot as it was brief. Sawyer jerked back
with a shattering expletive, directed at himself, she was
sure. Yet his next words canceled any remorse he might
have felt. "I won't apologize."

Her mind reeled beneath the implications of what had
just happened. I . . . didn't expect you to," she said weakly.

He rubbed the back of his neck. "Look, I—"

"I have to go," she said, getting in her car.

"I'll be in touch," he muttered, slamming her car door
shut and stepping back.

It wasn't until Kate pulled up in her driveway that the
truth hit her. She had known that searching for her
daughter would pose insurmountable difficulties. She had
expected and prepared for them.

What she hadn't expected or prepared for was Sawyer
Brock.

*   *   *

"Fascinating, emotionally gripping and sensual, this
book delivers on all fronts."
**—Debbie Macomber, bestselling author of
*Morning Comes Softly***

"Popular romance writer Mary Lynn Baxter makes a
perfect 10-point dive into women's fiction. . . . Ms.
Baxter has constructed a dramatic, riveting and
emotionally complex novel that should land on the
bestseller list."
—*Affaire de Coeur*

"A tender and touching story that strikes every chord
within the female spirit."
—Sandra Brown on *A Day in April*

MARY LYNN BAXTER

Sweet Justice

WARNER BOOKS

A Time Warner Company

Enjoy lively book discussions online with CompuServe. To become a member of CompuServe call 1-800-848-8199 and ask for the Time Warner Trade Publishing forum. (Current members GO:TWEP.)

WARNER BOOKS EDITION

Cover design by Diane Luger
Cover illustration by Jeff Barson
Hand lettering by Carl Dellacroce

Warner Books, Inc.
1271 Avenue of the Americas
New York, NY 10020

.A Time Warner Company

Printed in the United States of America

First Printing: February, 1994

10 9 8 7 6 5 4 3 2 1

This book is dedicated to
my sister-in-law,
Dory Baxter,
for all the right reasons

My deepest gratitude goes to my friend, Susan Ward, whose expertise as an attorney made this book possible.

Special thanks to Dorothy Due, Debbie Pitman and Candice Parke at the Angelina Country Courthouse for their help.

Sweet Justice

One

Austin, Texas. Spring 1993

Kate Colson pushed her half-empty cup of coffee aside after the last sip hit her stomach like a glob of wet cement. She couldn't blame the coffee; she'd just brewed it.

Jittery panic had thrown her body out of kilter, yet she had no choice but to keep this appointment. No matter how humiliating, how stressful, or how threatening to her career, she had to find the answer to the question that had haunted her day and night for years.

Kate stood, then stepped from behind her desk. Her gaze fell on her nameplate: Judge Kate Colson. She stared at it, something she'd done periodically since her appointment.

Did she look like a judge? She didn't feel like one, not today, anyway. Did her features reflect the condition of her insides, which felt as if they were in a meat grinder? No. Her panic subsided. She knew without looking in a mirror that her makeup was intact. Her hair was held away from her face with two combs. Her lavender suit and gold jewelry were subtly correct.

Her conscience, not her appearance, was the problem, she thought with impatience.

Before she could indulge in any more soul-searching, she

1

grabbed her purse and left the chamber to face Sawyer Brock.

"It's a pleasure, Ms. Colson. Please, have a seat."

"Thank you," Kate said in what she hoped was a firm but cool tone, then eased down into the plush chair.

"Would you care for a cup of coffee?"

"No, thank you. I just had one."

"Mind if I do?"

Kate forced a smile. "Help yourself."

"By the way, congratulations on your appointment as judge. You seem to be doing a hell of a job."

"Thank you."

He stared at her for a moment as if he wanted to say something else. Then he turned his attention to the coffee bar.

Kate took a deep breath and strove to get her bearings. She weighed the scene with her judge's eyes. Crystal ashtrays. Persian rugs. Porcelain sculptures. The detective's office was a little too polished to cover what Kate instantly recognized as his rough edges. She shifted in her chair at the same time Sawyer walked back to his desk, his gaze on her.

It wasn't only his office that made her uncomfortable. It was the man himself. His eyes were too penetrating. Kate had anticipated a bulbous-nosed private investigator in a rumpled trench coat the same disgustingly dirty color as his cigar-stained teeth. Sawyer was certainly not that. He wasn't handsome either; his features were too strong and rugged, his dark hair, salted with gray, too thick and too long. Somehow, on him, the excesses fit.

There was something about him that attracted her and she quickly figured out what it was. In spite of the suit tailored to fit his height and muscular build, he looked like a man who would be more comfortable outdoors in jeans and boots, than in a concrete office complex wearing a tie.

There was something else, too. Under his cool demeanor simmered violence. The simple act of lifting his coffee cup to his lips seemed explosive. His type was familiar; she'd grown up with boys who utilized their fists instead of their brains. With Sawyer Brock, she'd have to admit he apparently used both or he wouldn't own one of the best detective agencies in Texas. So what could she conclude from her observation? Sawyer Brock was a man to be reckoned with, a man not easily fooled.

"So how can I help you?" he asked from behind his desk.

"Harlan Moore said that you're the best at what you do."

"Ah, yes, Harlan." Sawyer's large hand curled around his cup as he raised it to his lips and took a sip. "Is he a friend of yours?"

"A business acquaintance, actually."

"I see."

"Is what he says the truth? Are you the best?"

Sawyer put down his cup. "That seems to be the consensus."

Modesty wasn't one of his strong suits, either, Kate decided, but modesty had little to do with talent. Didn't she need a man who was confident in his ability?

"I assume you're also discreet," she added to the mounting silence.

"You are, if you want to last."

Kate heard the impatience in his voice but didn't let it rattle her. She shifted her gaze and, for a moment, concentrated on the mounted fish displayed on one of the shelves in the bookcase. Why hadn't she noticed it before?

"So again, how can I help you?"

"I want you to locate someone; a young woman."

Sawyer lifted his eyebrows. "How long has she been missing?"

"She's not missing in the sense you're talking about. She's nineteen years old, and I want to know her whereabouts." Kate crossed her legs, then uncrossed them. "She was born at the hospital in New Braunfels, Texas, then later adopted, or at least I think she was adopted."

"Go on."

"Well, actually, there's not much more."

Sawyer rubbed his chin. "I'm good, Ms. Colson, damn good, in fact. But I'm not that good. If I'm to find someone, I'll need a lot more information."

Kate moved to the edge of the chair. "Please, just look over this folder, and if you can't or won't take the case, then I'll understand."

"I'm sure I'll take the case, if for no other reason than Harlan would want me to." He reached across the desk and took the folder she extended. He opened it, glanced down, then looked back at her. "Not much here. Any particular reason why the parents' names are omitted?"

"They're not relevant."

"Not relevant. That's where you're wrong. I—"

"Trust me, they're not," Kate interrupted, peering at her watch. "I have to be in court soon." She paused and cleared her throat. "When you study the information I've provided, I think you'll find it's enough to get you started."

Sawyer looked far from convinced, but this time he didn't argue. Instead he tossed the folder on his desk, then leaned back and folded his arms over his chest. "Why do you want to find this young woman? Can you answer that?"

Kate lifted her chin and in her best judicial tone said, "The 'why' is unimportant. Finding her is all that matters."

"Yes, ma'am," Sawyer said in an insolent manner.

Color tinted Kate's cheeks, but she didn't flinch. "I'm not sure of your going rate, but here's an advance." She drew a wad of bills from her purse and pushed them toward him. "If that's not sufficient—" Her voice faded.

He pushed them back. Their hands accidentally touched. Kate withdrew hers.

"I'll bill you," he said.

"Are you sure?" she asked as she stood and placed the money back in her purse.

"I'm sure."

Kate smiled, but it didn't reach her eyes. "I guess I'll be hearing from you."

"Count on it."

She turned and made her way toward the door. His voice stopped her.

"Don't worry, Judge. I'll find her. Meanwhile, I can't promise there won't be more questions that you obviously don't want to answer."

Kate's hand circled the doorknob with a deathlike grip. But when she turned, her features were composed. "Just do your job, Mr. Brock. That's all I ask."

Somehow, she managed to walk to her car before she released her pent-up breath. Her heart raced as though she were on a treadmill.

She had opened Pandora's box, and her life would never be the same.

Brock stared at the picture of Kate Colson on her personal file. Like hell she had to be in court. He didn't believe that excuse for a second. She just wanted out of his office. He tapped his pen against the edge of her photo, then frowned.

Judge Colson as a client? He still found it hard to believe that someone of her caliber would turn to a detective agency for help. But more than that, he was damn curious.

He knew the Colson woman's reputation as a hard-working attorney and now, as a tough district court judge. He'd also seen her on television. Who hadn't? When she'd been appointed to the bench to fill an unexpected vacancy, the Austin news media had had a field day. Thirty-five was an unprecedented age to reach that status. At age forty, he had come a long way himself. But he couldn't match her success.

Thrusting back his chair, Sawyer rose and walked to the window. He had an excellent view of the city park directly across the street from the Brock Building. Sometimes it soothed his mind to gaze out the window at the children playing.

Spring had arrived in full bloom in the Hill Country. From his office complex on the top floor, he could see the hills west of Austin in the distance, covered in trees and a riot of wildflowers, as was the park in front of him.

He turned, eyed the two files pertaining to Kate Colson, and groaned. Work beckoned him—not just the Colson files but others as well.

Lately, he'd had difficulty concentrating, which was unlike him. Work was what he most enjoyed. Work meant he'd never be without money, never be poor again. That ghost had always ruled him, fueled his determination to expand his business abroad. Yet, he procrastinated as if he had nothing pressing.

The knock sounded at the same time the door opened. "Jane said you were here."

On hearing Ralph Hutson's excited voice, Sawyer whipped around. Ralph was his assistant and right-hand man. Without him, Sawyer admitted, the agency wouldn't operate on such well-oiled wheels.

A first impression of Ralph was not in his favor. The thick mane of rust-colored hair and dusting of freckles across his nose were overwhelming. Then there was his stick-figure leanness. However, the minute he spoke, one forgot everything but his quick mind and his ability to get things done.

Sawyer likened him to a toy robot that, once wound up, couldn't be stopped until it completed its program.

"Are you knee-deep in it?" Ralph asked, grinning.

Sawyer quirked his mouth and waved Ralph in. "If you're referring to work, the answer is no."

"I find that hard to believe," Ralph said, crossing to Brock's desk where he peered at Kate's folder. "You've been looking over the judge's file. That's work."

Sawyer sat down at his desk, then leaned back as far as the chair allowed. "That's all I've done."

"So what do you think?"

"About what?"

Ralph snorted. "Don't give me that. You know I'm talking about the judge. She just left, didn't she?"

"Yeah," Sawyer said.

Ralph hitched his pants and perched on the edge of the desk. "So why does she want our services?"

"Wants me to find someone who's been missing nineteen years."

Ralph made a face. "Well, that's a curve I never expected. I figured it would have something to do with the election."

"I've only glanced at the information she gave me, but I can tell you, it's awfully skimpy."

"I don't get it. If she's hiring you, why the secrecy?"

"Beats me. But she was sure in a hurry to get out of here, and nervous to boot."

"That obvious, huh?"

"Yeah."

"Then you think the illustrious judge is hiding something?"

"My gut says yes."

"Mmm," Ralph said, "That's real interesting."

Sawyer didn't respond.

"Well, you have to admit, news-wise, she's hot."

"That she is," Sawyer said. "I saw her on TV just last night." But the only reason he'd paid attention had been because of today's appointment. Otherwise, the scuttlebutt about the woman beneath the robe would have been ignored. Women like Kate Colson didn't appeal to him.

"So, you must've formed an opinion."

"I did," Sawyer responded bluntly. "An ice cube has more warmth."

Ralph laughed.

Sawyer answered with a cynical smile. He preferred his women warm and ready. Personal observation told him Judge Colson was neither.

"You have to admit she's a knockout." Ralph's eyes were narrowed on the photo. "Does she look that good in the flesh?"

"Better, actually," Sawyer said, remembering her delicate bone structure, her skin as smooth as a child's framed by lush blond hair, the tasteful clothes, and a body that was perfection in motion.

"Mmm, sounds like my kind of woman."

Sawyer frowned. "She's cold as well as calculating. Hell, she has to be, if she's involved in politics."

"Don't forget about Harlan. He's the one who sent her. We both know he doesn't play by the rules."

Sawyer couldn't argue. If Harlan Moore recommended a client, he usually took the case himself.

Ralph broke the silence. "Well, as I said, whatever she's up to, it ought to be interesting."

"Yeah, right." Sawyer closed the folder and put it aside.

"You'll never guess who's waiting outside to see you. Someone even more prestigious than the lady judge."

Sawyer lifted his eyebrows. "Oh?"

"Senator Dan Hemsley."

"What does *he* want?"

"Actually, I ran into Harlan and the senator at the courthouse. While the senator left to make a call, Harlan gave me a quick rundown. Of course, he wants *you* to oversee . . . the senator's problem."

"Which is?"

Ralph stood, then shifted his gaze. "Domestic—"

"Damn. Harlan knows I don't get involved in that kind of case."

"I tried to tell him that." Ralph paused with a shrug. "But you know better than anyone that what I said made no difference."

"What is the senator's problem, exactly?" Sawyer asked. "He get caught with his drawers down?"

"No, surprisingly enough. His wife is the alleged culprit here, and the senator knows that if the media gets hold of it, he's up shit creek."

"Great," Sawyer said with black humor.

Ralph grinned. "I knew you'd love it."

"But not nearly as much as you, right?"

"Right. I never liked the squirrely s.o.b. He's too liberal and thinks too highly of himself."

"Name one politician who doesn't. Other than the fact that he can't keep his wife satisfied, what's he up to?"

"Besides campaigning for reelection, he's on the budget finance committee. He's also working with a committee on the rights of adopted children."

Sawyer rolled his eyes.

"Didn't I tell you, a fuckin' do-gooder?"

"Yeah, you told me. But on down the line, he might be able to help us with the Colson case. So you'd better send him in."

A few seconds later Senator Hemsley rushed into the room with his hand outstretched.

Sawyer was struck by how good-looking he was, even though on closer observation, his "pretty-boy" handsomeness made Sawyer immediately mistrust him. He was tall, with dark hair and bronzed skin that Sawyer bet had come from hours in a tanning booth.

His eyes, however, belied his confident pose. Though a brilliant green, they were subdued. If Sawyer read them right, they were tinged with fear.

Sawyer extended his hand.

"I can't thank you enough for seeing me on the spur of the moment like this." Hemsley smiled a plastic smile that thinned his lips.

That's a lie, Sawyer thought with growing contempt. You expected me to see you. He gave Hemsley a cool smile and said, "No problem."

"You won't regret it. If you'll help me with this little matter, I'll return the favor."

"Have a seat, Senator."

"Thanks, Brock."

A senator and a judge in one day, Sawyer thought. Some would say he was living right. The way he figured it, though, both clients could turn out to be more trouble than they were worth.

Two

Four Corners, Texas. Winter 1975

Thomas Jennings, bent like a question mark, peered through a tiny hole in the wall. "Hey, Jackson, you gotta see this. I'm not believing my eyes." He jerked his head around, removed his eyes from the target, then scanned the boys' locker room to make sure the assistant principal, Jim Anderson, wasn't standing in the door.

Wade Jackson transferred his Marlboro to the other side of his mouth. He looked at his companion. "Hey, what the hell you doing?"

Thomas grinned. "Looking at the biggest set of knockers I've ever seen."

Thomas had talked his friend, Wade, into cutting their sixth period junior English class. But before they left the school grounds they had taken a detour to the boys' locker room, where Thomas, two days ago, had found the hole in one of the stalls.

Since then, he'd been back several times to check things out. So far he hadn't seen anything to brag about. But today he'd struck pay dirt.

Wade's mouth gaped open. "You're shittin' me, man." He rushed over to Thomas and shoved him aside. "Lemme see."

The smelly bathroom stall was quiet while Wade gaped

through the hole that exposed a portion of the girls' locker room. "Hot damn, you weren't kidding."

"Move it," Thomas said. "She's my prize."

"If you get caught, you're gonna be old man Anderson's surprise."

"Aw, I'm not worried," Thomas said with false bravado. "Old High-Pockets Andy won't do anything."

"Maybe not to you, not with your old man being a preacher and all. But me, now that's different. Anyway, no tellin' what my old man will do if I get in any more trouble."

"Aw, stop bitching. We're not going to get in trouble. You worry too much."

"Yeah," Wade said, his gaze fixed on the door behind him.

"Have you ever seen anything like those tits?"

Wade took a long draw on his cigarette. "I kinda liked the ass myself."

Thomas flashed him a grin. "That ain't bad either. I'm getting hard just watching her."

"I always thought Kate Colson didn't have anything going for her except more brains than she oughta have."

"Me neither." Wade licked his lips. "But boy, were we both wrong. And would I like to grab a piece of that."

"Dream on. Kate Colson wouldn't give you the time of day."

"She wouldn't you either."

Thomas' perfect features chilled. "Wanna bet?"

"Naw." Wade dropped the cigarette on the cement floor and ground it out with the toe of his scuffed boot. "You'd win, even if you had to cheat."

Thomas turned back to the hole. "Mmm, she's something else."

"Stop hoggin' the show. Lemme look again."

"Why?" Thomas sneered. "Even if you could, you wouldn't do anything about it."

Wade never dated. Thomas figured it was because he was self-conscious about his looks, about the way his cauliflower ears stuck out, which he tried to disguise with his long hair, but couldn't.

Jackson gritted his teeth. "I just might."

"Not until I'm through with her." Thomas' tone was cold.

"God, you're a cocky bastard, Jennings."

Thomas merely shrugged, then said, "Bad as I hate to leave the show, we'd better split. I'm surprised someone hasn't come in to take a leak."

"So you're really going to ask the brain out, huh?"

"You betcha." Thomas grinned a lascivious grin and held his ground.

Wade shifted from one foot to the other. "Come on, let's get our butts outta here."

"Hold your horses, okay?"

Wade lit another cigarette with shaky fingers. "Damn you, Jennings."

"Oh, yeah, yeah. 'Atta girl."

"What's happening?"

Excitement raised Thomas' voice. "She's taking off her pants!"

A section of the girls' locker room filled with the sound of giggles.

Kate acted oblivious to the group of cheerleaders, who were the most popular girls in school. Instead, she groped for a towel to cover her nude body.

The giggles turned to snickers and increased in volume.

"Aw, come on, Katie," one taunted, "don't be shy."

"Dry up, Dorothy," Angie said in an ugly tone.

"You stay out of this, Angie Strickland. This is none of your business."

Waves of scarlet flooded Kate's face. As usual she was the brunt of their jokes. But this was the first time Angie had witnessed their cruelty.

Would her pain and embarrassment ever end? Kate wondered. She longed to lash out, to hurt them, like they were hurting her. But retaliation on her part would add fuel to an already out-of-control fire.

Standing white-faced, Kate glanced at Angie, whose lips were drawn in a thin, mutinous line. Angie was her best and only friend, though they were as different in temperament and looks as two friends could be. While Kate was tall, thin, and fair, Angie was short, with auburn hair and olive skin. Kate wore her hair long and straight; Angie wore hers in a short bob. Kate was quiet and reserved; Angie was outgoing and bold. But both were smart and shared the same interests, such as swimming, reading, and collecting pictures of movie stars.

"Surely you're not ashamed of your—er—over-endowed body?" another quipped, pulling Kate back to the moment at hand.

"I—" Kate got no further as her towel was snatched out of her hand. "Oh!" she cried, and covered herself as best she could with her hands.

Angie tossed Kate another towel. "Stop it. Leave her alone," she snapped at the others. Then for Kate's ears only, "Ignore them. They're just jealous, especially Kathy; her boobs are flatter than two fried eggs."

Kate saw the sympathy in Angie's eyes and wished that she could simply disappear. But since the Lord didn't see fit to bring that about, she bowed her shoulders and jutted her chin. She wanted to cry. She wouldn't, though, not in front of her best friend, not in front of the mean girls. Pride wouldn't let her.

The snickers continued.

"Come on, let's go over there and finish dressing," Angie whispered. "Who needs those creeps, anyway?"

Once the group reached the other side of the room, the popular side, Kate lowered her head and concentrated on dressing, but the effort was almost more than she could handle. Her hands shook so that she added another run in her stockings.

She must have whimpered aloud because Angie stopped what she was doing and looked at her. "Want me to go. beat them up?"

Kate almost smiled. "I wish I had the guts to do that myself, only I'm too chicken."

"They'll all get their comeuppance one of these days. You'll see."

Another round of laughter suddenly rocked the room.

Both Kate and Angie glared at the girls.

When the laughter didn't stop, Kate stiffened her spine.
She still refused to cry as she folded the too-long stocking
twice under the toes to try to hide the holes already there.
She slipped into her worn sweater, long baggy skirt, and
rumpled coat, cringing inwardly. She hated her unstylish
clothes. Often she would sneak magazines into her room and
drool over the pretty things in them, her imagination placing
her in each outfit.

Kate's clothes reflected her home life. Her parents were
poor as well as strict, especially her daddy. Her parents had
had to get married; Kate had overheard conversations in
which that sin was vehemently discussed. And her daddy
never failed to throw it up to Kate that he wouldn't tolerate
her turning into a tramp like her mother.

Emmitt's bitterness, combined with his alcoholism, made
him volatile and dangerous. Kate's mother always agreed
with her father. It was easier, Kate supposed, than suffering
his abuse, both physical and verbal.

"Come on, let's get out of here," Angie said, when she
was dressed.

Kate fought back the tears and followed Angie out the
door into the crisp air that was tempered only by the bright
sunlight. Kate paused a moment and drew the chilly air deep
into her lungs. She felt the lump in her throat start to dis-
solve.

"It looks like you've missed the bus. Come on, I'll take
you home."

Kate frowned. "I hate for you to have to do that."

"Hush your mouth. You know I want to, so come on."

Kate didn't argue. She was too tired and too upset. Besides, she loved riding in Angie's Camaro. It didn't matter
that the car wasn't a new model, especially since she didn't
even have a car.

Kate tried not to envy Angie, but she couldn't help it.
Angie's mother, Roberta, earned a good living as a registered
nurse at the local hospital. She doted on Angie, who, like
Kate, was an only child. Roberta continually tried to make
up for Angie's daddy having run off with another woman.

Kate felt for Angie and wanted to console her, but Angie was loath to talk about her daddy and Kate didn't press. Lord knows, she had enough in her own life she didn't want to talk about—her own parents for a start.

"Why don't you go home with me for a while?" Angie asked, the Camaro in sight. "Mamma got me a Butterick pattern and material for a new miniskirt. I want you to see them."

Kate didn't take offense at Angie's reference to new clothes; none was intended. Angie was astute enough to recognize her quiet pride and respect it. She treated Kate as if she had the same amenities.

Kate sighed. "I'd love to. But I have to get home and help Mamma with the milking."

A whistle suddenly came out of nowhere. Both girls stopped mid-stride. But it was Kate who spun around first. Two boys were several yards behind them: Thomas Jennings and Wade Jackson.

"Oh, me," Kate said in a breathless voice, "it's Thomas . . . and—"

"Wade," Angie finished for her, having turned and looked herself. "That little weasel gives me the willies."

"Me too," Kate said. "I don't think he's ever brushed his teeth."

"Me neither. He sits behind me in English, and every time I turn around he grins at me. All I can see is that rotten hole in his front tooth, which usually has something caught in it, like a piece of spinach."

"Oh, gross."

Angie giggled. "But Thomas—"

The boys were directly behind them now. "Where y'all headed?" Thomas asked, a grin curving his lips.

Kate couldn't utter a word. Simply looking at Thomas Jennings twisted her tongue into knots and made her legs feel like jelly.

"Home," Angie said airily.

"How about coming with us instead? We'll buy you a Coke." Thomas nudged Wade in the ribs. "Won't we?"

"Er . . . yeah, sure."

Angie answered again. "No, thanks. We have to go home."

"Hey, Kate," Thomas said, "what about you? Cat got your tongue?"

Kate licked her dry lips and looked at him. "No," she said breathlessly. "I'm . . . sorry, I can't go either."

Continuing to ignore Angie, he winked at Kate. "Maybe later, okay?"

"Okay," Kate managed to eke out.

Once the boys had sauntered off, Kate turned to Angie, an incredulous expression on her face. "Wow! Can you believe that?"

"What?" Angie asked innocently.

"You know what!"

Angie rolled her eyes. "Will you please stop drooling long enough to get in the car?"

Four Corners was a small farming community in the Hill Country, nineteen miles from the Austin city limits. Because the city was so close, Four Corners had little claim to fame. Even so, the folks took pride in what assets it did have, such as its agricultural resources and Appleby's new grocery-filling station on the main drag.

As the Camaro headed out of town toward the farm where Kate lived, both girls were quiet, lost in their own thoughts. But the radio blared. A song from Loggins and Messina's *Full Sail* album filled the silence.

Angie had reached the farm road when the song ended abruptly and the disk jockey came on the air and announced:

"A top story just in from the Associated News Wire. Patricia Hearst, 19, granddaughter of the late newspaper publisher William Randolph Hearst, has been kidnapped from her Berkeley, California, apartment."

"Oh, how awful," Kate said, sitting up straighter in her seat and listening carefully. She guessed her history teacher would quiz them on the subject tomorrow, since current events was his favorite topic.

As the report ended, Angie shivered. "I can't imagine that happening to me."

"Me neither," Kate responded, then fell silent again, her thoughts turning once again to Thomas Jennings and the way he had looked at her. Even now, she felt her heart trip in her chest.

"Angie?"

"What?"

"You don't like Thomas, do you?"

Angie kept her eyes on the road, but Kate noticed she clenched the steering wheel a little tighter.

"Oh, he's all right," Angie said in a nonchalant tone, then turned and flashed Kate a smile. "Only problem is, he thinks he's God's gift to women."

Kate answered her smile. "Well, he is, isn't he?"

"Yeah, you're right."

They both giggled.

"Did I dream that he winked at me?"

"Nope. I saw him."

"I can't imagine why. He's never even spoken to me before."

"Who knows what those dumb guys are thinking?"

"I wish he'd ask me out," Kate said unexpectedly, with a wistful note she couldn't control.

It seemed as if she'd had a crush on Thomas Jennings forever. He was by far the best looking, the smartest, and the most popular boy in the junior class, if not the entire school. Although he was seventeen—a year older than she was—he acted much more mature than his peers. His movie-star-handsome face, made more striking by coal black hair and smoldering black eyes that reminded her of Elvis, had given her many sleepless nights.

His body more than equaled his eyes. He was tall and well-proportioned and had a breath-catching smile that could charm the pants off the girls, or so the grapevine said. Kate was green with envy, though the thought of "doing it" with him never entered her mind. She intended to remain a virgin till she married. Still, in her dreams they had kissed and kissed.

"I figure the wink was a come on," Angie said, bridging the long silence. "I wonder what he's up to?"

"I wish I knew." Kate's features were glum. "I thought he had the hots for Sally, especially since she made head cheerleader."

"That little bitch. Why, if she had a brain, she'd be dangerous."

Kate swallowed a sigh. "Unfortunately, she doesn't seem to need a brain."

"Well, I don't know what she's got," Angie said cattily. "She sure hasn't got any boobs. And while we're on that subject, I was tempted to yank every frosted hair out of her head back in the locker room."

Kate bit down hard on her lower lip to stop it from trembling. "By the way, thanks for taking up for me. I'm not sure I ever—"

"Hey," Angie interrupted, "you don't have to thank me. You'd have done the same for me."

Kate struggled to control her emotions. "True, only I'm sure I won't have to."

Angie shrugged and didn't say anything.

The silence lingered until they reached the turn to her farm. "You can let me off here," Kate said. "I'll walk the rest of the way."

"You sure?"

Kate couldn't quite meet Angie's penetrating gaze. "I'm sure. It's such a pretty day, I'll enjoy the walk."

Angie looked at her for a long moment, her brows puckered.

Although Kate saw the disbelief reflected in those green eyes, she couldn't bring herself to acknowledge it. Her daddy objected to her friendship with Angie, so to avoid trouble she didn't wave the red flag in front of his face. She'd learned the hard way not to.

"Thanks for the ride." Kate forced a bright smile. "I'll see you tomorrow."

"Ask your mamma if you can spend the night with me tomorrow night."

Kate's brows drew together. "I'll ask, but—"

"I know. Don't get my hopes up."

"You know Daddy."

"Well, so long," Angie said.

Kate drew her flimsy coat closer around her thin shoulders and began to trudge up the muddy road. Although the day was lovely, not a cloud in the sky, the past week had been hideous. It had rained bucketfuls every day.

She dodged a mud puddle, wishing she could dwell on Thomas Jennings and the way he had looked at her. But she couldn't. Her mind was caught up in the misery that dogged each step she took. She hated going home and she hated herself for feeling that way.

Thomas' grin flashed through her mind again. Don't, she told herself. Now wasn't the time to analyze his winks. She'd stash that wonderful tidbit in her heart and drag it out later, after she'd faced her daddy, after she'd done her chores.

Kate had just reached the front yard when she heard a commotion. She stiffened and felt her stomach plunge to her toes. "Oh, no . . . oh, no," she whimpered, and charged up the rickety front steps.

She jerked the door open in time to see her daddy's beefy hand connect with her mother's jaw.

"Mamma!" Kate screamed.

Three

Fear held Kate rooted to the spot. She watched her daddy raise his fist once more with the intention of slamming it into the other side of Mavis Colson's face.

"Mamma!" she screamed again.

Emmitt Colson paused and turned around. "Git outta here, girl, or you'll be next."

"Daddy . . . please," Kate sobbed, "don't hit Mamma."

Mavis Colson finally lifted pain-glazed eyes toward her daughter. "Do . . . what . . . your daddy says. Go on, get out of here," she added in a strangled croak.

Kate couldn't have moved even if she'd wanted to, though she tried to wrench herself free of her self-imposed bondage. Her legs were simply too weak to carry her, and her heart thumped too wildly inside her chest. Her eyes locked on the purplish red swelling on her mother's face.

"You'd best listen to your mamma," Emmitt bellowed, striding across the room toward her. The hulking man, with empty eyes and cruel lines around his mouth, seemed to Kate like the devil himself.

She tore out of the house and didn't stop until she reached the barn. Its cold semi-darkness was a balm to her heated face and body. Sobbing blindly, she fell into a heap on the sweet-scented hay. Her body curled into itself. She was aware only of the pain inside her heart.

"I hate them," she muttered over and over. "I hate them both. I wish I never had to see them again."

Even as the bitter words poured from her lips, she feared God's wrath. She lifted her head toward the heavens and silently begged forgiveness.

She couldn't count the number of times over the years that she had sought solace in this exact spot. This barn had become a refuge seven years before on the day her daddy had delivered the first blow to her mother's face.

She had awakened in the middle of the night and heard her daddy yelling at her mother. She had crept down the short hallway to their room. The door had been ajar. She'd peeked in at the instant he had hit her mother hard enough to bloody her lip.

Both Kate and her mother had screamed, but it had been Kate's scream that gained Emmitt's attention. He had lunged across the room, yanked the child into his arms, and said, "If you ever sneak up on us again, I'll beat you till you can't stand up. Do you hear me?"

"Yes . . . Daddy," she'd cried, hot tears scalding her cheeks and lips.

He'd dropped her then, as though she were a sack of garbage, and turned back to Mavis.

Somehow in that black moment, Kate had ceased to be a child.

During the harsh years that followed, she had plotted and planned many ways to stop her daddy from hurting her mother. She'd pictured herself creeping into their room at night, while he snored unaware, and striking him with a baseball bat. Other times she'd plotted less violent ways, such as tying him to the bed so she and her mother could safely leave town.

She'd done nothing, though, because she was too afraid of reprisal.

Kate felt that same raw panic claw at her insides now. She couldn't function, but she couldn't let the beatings happen again. She would march back inside and defend her mother. *Liar!* she countered silently, and sniffled back another sob.

No way could she stand up to her daddy. Though she admitted her cowardice, she hated herself for it.

She couldn't believe the beatings were starting all over again. For several years, Emmitt had turned from his wicked ways and sought the Lord's will for his life, or so he'd said over and over.

He'd stopped drinking. Every time the doors opened at the small church, he was in the front pew and insisted that Kate and Mavis be there also. Yet Kate had seen no change in his personality, except that he no longer struck her mother. He remained the same cold, brooding man he'd always been. The only difference was that he nurtured the Bible instead of the bottle.

What had set him off, caused him to revert to his old ways? Lack of money? A dispute with the church? Kate didn't know. But one thing she did know: her mamma was too frail to undergo much of his punishment. Maybe this time she would turn him in to the sheriff. Kate brightened at the thought.

If only she could ask advice, but she couldn't share her pain with anyone. No one would understand, not even Angie. Anyway, she was too embarrassed and had too much pride to let the outside world know her family's secret.

She knew they guessed, especially Angie and her mother. The tight, pinched look on Kate's face many a morning and the drab, shabby clothes she wore were dead giveaways that all was not right in the Colson household. Angie's expressive eyes often held questions, but she never pressed Kate for the answers.

Oh, dear Lord, what was she going to do? Kate huddled deeper into the bed of straw and sobbed until dry heaves racked her body, all the while groping for answers that wouldn't come.

"Kate?"

A sob caught in her throat. She lifted her head and blinked several times. Had she heard her mother's voice or had she imagined it? The latter most likely, for she pictured Mavis in her room, in bed with a cold rag on her brutalized face. Besides, she had never come looking for Kate before.

"Kate, where are you?"

No mistake. It was her mother. Kate wanted to sit up, but just trying proved a struggle. Her gut-wrenching sobs had sapped what little strength she'd had left.

"Over here, Mamma." Somehow Kate forced her unsteady legs into an upright position. By the time her mother stood in front of her, she had removed the damp strands of hair from her cheeks and mopped the tears from her eyes.

"Are you all right?" Mavis asked.

Kate didn't answer. Instead she assessed the damage done to her mother's face. Other than the strawberry-colored welt that even the muted light in the barn couldn't conceal, Mavis hadn't changed.

Her dull gray hair pulled back tightly in a bun remained the frame for tiny bird-like features, devoid of makeup. Kate inherited her height and slenderness from Emmitt, who in turn had inherited them from his mother.

The only traits she had inherited from her mother were her deep brown eyes and her oversized breasts.

"I came to get you. Your supper's ready."

Kate swayed slightly. *Oh, Mamma, is that all you have to say?*

"Where's . . . Daddy?"

"At church," Mavis said in a dull tone. "Come on."

They trudged across the mud-spattered yard, barren of anything except a few squawking chickens. Nothing was said. No words of comfort. No touches. Kate shivered, not from the chill in the evening air, but from the desolation.

Once they entered the house desolation turned into resignation. If anything, the interior appeared more dismal than ever. Kate looked at her home as if seeing it for the first time. The fingers of remaining sunlight touched the shabby curtains on the dingy windows, the sofa with its stuffing spilling out of the split cushions, and the linoleum floor, so worn that the color was lost. Her bedroom was worse, despite her efforts to spruce it up with money she'd made babysitting.

Each year the frame farmhouse and the surroundings became more run-down, more dilapidated. Instead of tending to the crops, turning a profit, Emmitt spent his time reading the Bible, hoping for a miracle from the Lord.

In her daddy's drinking days, her mother had worked, taking in ironing. But after her daddy had been "saved," he had refused to let Mavis work, translating from the Bible that it was the man's place to earn the living—only he never earned it.

Kate hated her home, and she hated everything about her life.

"Go wash your hands, and I'll dish up your food." Mavis' voice was devoid of emotion.

"Mamma, we have to talk."

"Not now. You run along and do like I said."

Clamping down the urge to scream, Kate left the room. A few minutes later she returned to the kitchen with scrubbed hands and face, but inside she still felt dirty.

"Mamma, why did Daddy hit you again, after all this time?"

"You wouldn't understand." Mavis stood at the stove with her back to Kate, stirring something in an iron pot.

"Mamma!"

"He's a good man. He . . . he's just having a hard time."

"The man I marry won't treat me like that," Kate responded fiercely, a light in her eyes. "If he does, I'll . . . I'll kill him."

Kate's bitter words brought Mavis around; her eyes were wide and troubled. "Kate Colson, don't you dare talk like that. The Lord will strike you dead."

Maybe he already had, Kate thought, knowing how she felt inside.

"Your . . . daddy loves me. You must remember that. And I know he loves you."

Kate jerked the chair away from the table and plopped into it. "No, he doesn't, Mamma. You're just fooling yourself. He's a monster."

"Don't talk that way about your father." She turned and began stirring again. "There are things you don't know."

Kate clenched her fists. "Mamma, I'm not a child any longer. I'm sixteen years old. Please talk to me."

"You're still a child."

Kate fought the urge to scream again. Better still, she wanted to shake her mother. However, she sat stoically, her face giving away none of her churning thoughts.

Mavis reached an unsteady hand to the back of her head and put a hair pin back in place. "The farm's not doing well and you know how much pride your father has."

"I can't remember it ever doing well." Kate's eyes flashed with suppressed emotion. "I hate being poor. Everyone except Angie makes fun of me." Her lower lip quivered. "I can't wear makeup . . ." For once she ignored the pain in her mother's eyes and went on. She'd kept her feelings bottled inside until she thought she might burst if she didn't say how she felt. "My clothes are awful. I look like an old frump with my long skirts."

"You're no old frump." Mavis walked up to where Kate sat and placed a hand on her shoulder. "You're beautiful." Then in a rare show of affection, she leaned and placed a kiss on the top of Kate's silky blond hair.

"Oh, Mamma, why can't we go away, somewhere where he can't hurt you?" Kate had wanted to ask this question so many times, but her mother's martyred aloofness had kept her quiet.

"Leave your father? I could never do that. Where would I go? What would I do?"

"We could go live with Aunt Milly in Idaho." Kate's eyes flashed excitement now. "I could get a job and so could you. Together we could make it."

"I could never leave your daddy," Mavis repeated, that aloofness back in her pinched features and in her voice. "I only went to the eighth grade, you know. Your daddy rescued me from a miserable foster home and married me."

Only you had to get married, Kate wanted to add, but didn't. Her mother had never told Kate the circumstances of her birth. Kate doubted she ever would. The shame factor kept her silent.

"Before he started drinking," Mavis went on, "he was a good man. Then when he found the Lord and stopped drinking, he was a good man again."

"He never worked, Mamma."

"How can you say that?" Mavis' tone was scornful. "For years he . . . did good."

Kate lowered her head and bit back the angry retort that rose to her lips. She'd never been one to argue with her mother; fear of her daddy kept that urge from surfacing. But she knew with a wisdom far beyond her years that she'd be wasting her time anyway. Her mother was never going to leave her father, no matter what. And that was that.

"I've made beans with hamburger, your daddy's favorite."

Defiance flared briefly in Kate's eyes, then died. They fell silent while Mavis filled Kate's plate and set it in front of her.

"Mamma," Kate said, turning away from the food. "Angie asked me to spend the night with her tomorrow night. I . . . know . . . Daddy doesn't—"

Mavis held up her hand, stopping Kate's halting words. One corner of her lip curved into a small smile. Kate's heart leapt; she was grateful for that one crumb, small as it was.

"You go ahead and go," Mavis said. "I'll take the responsibility."

"But what if Daddy—"

Again Mavis stopped her. "He'll be at the church. They're . . . we're making plans for the revival that starts next week; when he comes home, he'll be in a better mood."

Kate was torn. She ached to go to Angie's house, but she was afraid of what her daddy would do when he found out.

As if Mavis sensed Kate's uncertainty, she said again in a firmer tone, "It's all right, I promise. Everything's going to be all right. You just wait and see."

"Oh, Mamma," Kate said, speaking as softly as a sigh.

"Go ahead, eat your dinner. Then get your bath and see to your homework."

Kate looked at the food on her plate. The hamburger meat stared back at her, a greasy, soggy lump. Her stomach flip-flopped, and she almost threw up on the spot. She pushed her plate aside. "I'm sorry, I'm not hungry."

Mavis sagged against the cabinet. "Go on then, get ready for bed."

Kate watched her mother in alarm. She was so pale, so bleak, so dismal that Kate looked away. Finally she stood and muttered, "I'm sorry, Mamma."

A short while later Kate climbed onto the mattress that was so worn the springs poked into her back. It wouldn't have mattered if she'd been on the most expensive of beds covered in silk sheets. Sleep wouldn't have come any easier. She stared at the ceiling, her eyes wide open, her heart filled with renewed fear.

"Please, God, if you're listening," she whispered into the darkness, her eyes leaking tears, "and if you're not mad at me, please help my Mamma. Please . . . help me, too."

Four

Kate stepped off the school bus and saw him. Thomas leaned against the huge oak tree that draped a portion of the science classroom. As he pushed away from the tree and walked her way, she thought he had never looked so handsome.

Surely he hadn't been waiting for her? Just the thought made Kate's heart race and the saliva go dry in her mouth. She twisted her head around. No one else was in sight. Pretending not to notice him, Kate continued on the path to the cafeteria where she met Angie every morning.

She was almost there when Thomas stopped directly in front of her. Kate pulled up short and lowered her head. She dared not look at him. She felt awful this morning, the events of yesterday having worn her out physically and mentally.

She'd washed her hair and her clothes were clean, but that was her only claim to presentability. Dark circles rimmed her eyes; and her lips, devoid of lipstick, were drawn in a tight line. And her clothes—well, they didn't even bear thinking about.

"Hi," he said.

The sound of Thomas' low voice brought her head up. Kate glanced at him shyly. He wore stylish bell-bottom jeans and a white shirt trimmed in a blue yoke. His hair was slightly mussed and his sideburns needed trimming.

She opened her mouth to respond, but to her dismay, her throat squeezed shut and no words came out.

"Where're you headed?" he asked, his grin widening as if he knew she was awed by his attention.

Kate cleared her throat. "Over there." She pointed to the cafeteria. "To meet Angie."

His eyes narrowed. "You two are pretty tight, aren't you?"

"She's my best friend."

He seemed to think that over, yet he didn't comment. "You going with anyone?"

"No . . . no," she stammered in muffled bursts. Had he really asked her that?

"Good. Want to go out sometime? Maybe catch a movie or something?"

"What did you say?"

Thomas' grin was more than a little cocky. "Hey, come on, I know you're not hard of hearing."

"No, of course I'm not," she said in a quavering voice.

"So you wanna go?" he pressed.

Kate nodded her head for fear that if she tried to speak, her voice would sound like a croaking frog. This couldn't be happening. Could it? The most popular boy in the school didn't ask out an ugly duckling like her.

"Jeez, you're acting weird."

Though Thomas sounded impatient, his smile didn't slip, nor did his gaze. His eyes roamed her body as if he knew exactly what secrets lay beneath her tattered underwear. She blushed when something strange happened to her nipples; they turned into hard pebbles.

"All right . . . I mean . . . sure I'd like to go."

"How 'bout Saturday night?"

"Fine." She only had to look at him to feel his magnetism.

"Lucky you," he said. "My old man sprung for a new car for my birthday. You'll be the first to ride in it."

Kate's eyes lit. "A new car? Wow. What kind?"

"Mustang. All black."

"It matches your hair," Kate blurted.

"Hey, that's what my mother said."

Despite his favorable response, Kate wished she could

chop off her tongue. Normally, she wasn't prone to making such corny comments. But Lord, he threw her whole system out of whack, and she couldn't begin to think straight. Yet she wasn't complaining; she loved every second in his company and wished it would last forever. But then, nothing lasted forever, except pain, she thought.

"I'll pick you up at seven, okay?"

Kate panicked. He couldn't come to her house. She'd die of embarrassment. "I'll be at Angie's," she said, which was the first thing that came to mind. "You can pick me up there."

She thought he was going to reject that idea, but then he shrugged and said, "Whatever."

"I . . . guess I'll see you tomorrow night, then."

"Right."

With that he turned around and ambled off.

Kate was still grappling with the sudden turn of events when Angie bounded up beside her, out of breath. "Was that the one and only Thomas Jennings?"

"It was." Kate's voice was barely audible.

"What's going on?" Angie asked, her eyes following Thomas as he disappeared around the building.

Kate sucked in her breath. "Oh, Angie, you'll never believe this in a million years, but he actually asked me out."

"On a real date?"

Kate's face lost some of its glow. "I don't blame you for not believing me. Who'd want to take me out?"

"Oh, Kate, I'm sorry. I didn't mean it like that." Angie bumped her playfully on the arm. "There's lots of reasons why guys would ask you out, only you've never given them any encouragement."

"That's not the reason and you know it. But I won't argue with you."

"Did you ask if you could spend the night with me?"

"Yes."

"And?"

Kate grinned. "I can."

"Really?"

"Really."

"Halle-damn-lujah."

Kate's grin erupted into outright laughter.

"I still can't believe you're here." Angie was sprawled across the canopy bed with her head propped against the palm of her hand, her eyes on Kate, who sat cross-legged across from her.

"Mamma's the one who said I could."

"Figures."

They had been closeted in Angie's room for the past two hours. Kate loved to visit the Stricklands. Angie's bright domain in no way compared with her dismal one. Cluttered with clothes, posters, photographs, and dried prom flowers, the room had a warm, lived-in look.

First they had listened to records, then watched a couple of shows on television. Now, while the stereo played an album by Chicago, they sat on the bed with a huge bowl of popcorn between them. Two cans of Pepsi sat on the table beside Angie's bed.

"Is something wrong?" Angie asked out of the blue, scrutinizing Kate closely. "You seem kind of quiet." She grinned a knowing grin. "Ah ha, you're getting the jitters about going out with Thomas, aren't you?"

Kate looked away. "Not really."

"Liar."

Kate stuck her tongue out at Angie. A soft knock interrupted their sudden attack of giggles.

"Mamma?" Angie asked.

Roberta Strickland opened the door and walked to the bed, a smile on her face. "Now, just who else were you expecting?"

Kate thought Angie's mother was neat. She wished her mother were like this woman whose smile seemed endless.

She didn't look like her daughter at all, Kate decided, studying Roberta's square face and the raw-boned frame that helped to diminish her large breasts and heavy thighs. But her features were nicely put together, and with the aid of makeup and artificial coloring to perk up her dull brown hair, she presented an attractive picture.

"You girls don't stay up all night, hear?"

Angie wrinkled her nose. "We won't."

"I wish I could believe that." Roberta's smile increased as she turned to Kate. "I'm depending on you to keep my daughter in line. You know what a grouch she is if she loses too much sleep."

"I'll take care of it."

Angie tossed a pillow and hit Kate in the head. "Ha, we'll see about that."

Roberta just shook her head, then quietly closed the door behind her.

"I like your mother."

"Yeah, she's okay, most of the time."

Kate smiled.

"So, aren't you about to bust a gut?"

Kate didn't pretend she didn't know what Angie was referring to. "I'm still pinching myself to make sure I didn't dream he actually asked me out."

"Well, I can testify that he talked to you."

"Hey, maybe we could double date with you and Larry."

Larry Elliot, the biggest stud on the football team, was Angie's latest love. Though good-looking, he wasn't nearly as dreamy as Thomas, Kate thought, still marveling that Thomas had given her the time of day, much less asked her for a date.

Angie shook her head, then averted her eyes. "Nah, I don't think so. Anyway, that wouldn't be a good idea. Larry doesn't like Thomas."

"He doesn't? Why?"

Angie shrugged. "Beats me. But then you know how jocks are. They stick pretty close together."

"Yeah, I guess you're right." Kate wound a strand of hair around her finger. "Thomas likes cars . . . and girls."

Angie grew pensive and she shifted her gaze. "Look, are you sure you want to go out with him? I mean we both know his reputation—" She broke off with a shrug and a flushed face.

Kate pulled on her lower lip with her teeth. "I know. That's what makes me wonder why he's bothering with me."

"But you're still going?"

"Of course. Besides, he won't try anything with me."

"How do you know he won't?"

"How do you know he will?" Kate asked in a teasing tone.

Angie's face remained serious. "I don't, but I've heard things."

"Such as?"

"Oh, you know," Angie said, sounding flustered.

Kate angled her head. "Do you think he does it with everybody he dates?"

Angie shifted her gaze, though her face turned redder. "Why, Kate Colson, I can't believe you asked that. Lordy me."

Kate smiled. "Yes, you can."

"Well, you're asking the wrong person," Angie said in a low, tense voice. "I've just heard gossip."

"Have *you* ever done it?" Kate's cheeks now matched Angie's. "You don't have to answer that if you don't want to," she added on a hasty note. "It's none of my business . . . " Her voice trailed off.

She'd ached to askAngie that question, only she hadn't had the nerve till now. While they had discussed sex in general, they had never shared personal experiences—or lack of them. But her upcoming date with Thomas had prompted the question.

"Of course I haven't done it." Angie said, keeping her eyes averted. "You haven't either."

Kate laughed without humor. "That's the understatement of the year. How can you not be a virgin if you've never even had a boyfriend?"

"Well, you've got one now."

"Pooh. It's a one-shot deal. Anyway, I think he was probably drunk or something."

Angie cut her an exasperated glance. "Oh, come on."

"We'll see."

"Will your daddy let you go?"

Kate's face clouded. "I don't think I'm even going to ask."

"You're kidding."

"No. Think about it. You know how strict my daddy is. Can you see him letting me have a date?" Kate's voice shook with bitterness.

"You're right, but if you sneak off and get caught, you'll be in a heap of trouble."

"He'd kill me," Kate said flatly.

They were silent for a moment.

"So what are you going to do?" Angie asked.

Kate's features took on a determined look. "Oh, I'm going, one way or the other." She paused, "I . . . er . . . told him to pick me up here. Is that all right?"

Angie pursed her lips. "It's okay, only I think you should ask if you can go. After all, Thomas *is* a preacher's kid. Your daddy ought to love that."

"I guess you're right. So, I'll ask, but I still want Thomas to pick me up here."

"Where's he taking you?"

"To a movie in Austin, I think. He said something about *Serpico*."

Angie lunged into a sitting position. "Well, then, we need to get busy and pick out what you're going to wear."

Kate's stomach knotted with embarrassment. "Forget it," she muttered miserably, tears stinging in her eyes. "I can't go."

"What?"

"I said I can't go," Kate wailed. "I'll call and tell him I'm sick or something dopey like that. I don't have anything to wear."

"We're fixing to take care of that right now." Angie bounded off the bed and dashed to her closet. "Mamma bought me a new blouse and denim jacket, both with orange stitching." She jerked them off the rack. "Well, what do you think?"

Kate scooted to the edge of the bed, her eyes wide. "Oh, gosh, they're beautiful."

"I'm glad you think so because you're going to wear them."

Kate dropped both garments as if they were on fire. "No, I couldn't—"

"You can and you are. You have a denim skirt, don't you?"

"Yes, but—"

"These will go great with it. And because we both have boobs—" she paused with a giggle "—you can wear them. So get off your buns and ditch your clothes."

Kate's eyes glistened with tears. "Oh, Angie."

"Hey, don't start blubbering, for Pete's sake. There's something else, too. Appleby's just got it in. It's the new Cover Girl Lip Gloss in little-bitty pots. Remember we saw the ad in last month's *Glamour?* I bought three colors: Melon Ball, Chili Peach, and Coral Smash. Now, you pick which one you want. It's so light, your old man won't even know you have lipstick on."

Without saying a word, Kate grabbed Angie and hugged her tight. "You're the best friend a girl could ever have."

For a second, Angie's features clouded. Then she smiled an embarrassed smile. "Just be quiet, will you, and try this stuff on."

At one o'clock in the morning the room finally fell silent. Angie went instantly to sleep. Kate didn't. She lay in bed, hugged her arms across her chest and rehashed the events of the day. She was actually going on a date. She stifled the urge to giggle out loud, but no way could she keep still. Every nerve in her body felt on fire.

For the first time in her life, she couldn't wait for tomorrow.

Five

The Reverend Paul Jennings paused in front of the oval mirror in the living room and straightened his tie. Once that was done, he smoothed the sides of his dark hair.

Thomas, sauntering down the hall on his way out the door, caught his father's reflection. He paused and watched, his lips curved in a sneer.

He'd bet his ass that his old man wasn't thinking about the sermon he would soon deliver. No siree. Most likely he was thinking about the next time he could sneak off and screw the head deacon's wife.

What a hypocrite, Thomas thought, recalling all the lectures he'd gotten about how he should always conduct himself in a gentlemanly fashion and respect the girls. Ha, respect the girls—now that was a good one, especially coming from his old man. The girls were the ones with the itch in their panties, who made the first move, who went for the zipper. Except Kate, that is.

But he wouldn't think about her now. He'd rather watch his old man primp, making ready for his next conquest. Perhaps the liaison would take place after the service tonight, when his mother was in bed with another one of her headaches. Paul would tell his wife he'd be in his study working late, if she needed him. She never needed him.

Thomas had to admit the first time he'd caught his old

man fondling the deacon's wife, he'd been shocked. He'd never thought of his daddy as the type who would screw around. Reverend Jennings was tall, but slightly stooped, with dark, graying hair and eyes that were partially shielded by silver-rimmed glasses. But he was an impeccable dresser and had a way with words that could charm anyone, except his son. With Thomas, he'd always been detached and disinterested until Thomas did something that reflected on his ministry, good or bad. Then he paid attention.

But one day Thomas had done something that had forced him to stop by the church to talk to his father. He'd had a confession to make, before their neighbor could beat him to it. Thomas' car had jumped the curb and knocked a dent in the rear of the neighbor's vehicle.

The outer office had been deserted, but Thomas had heard a soft laugh. He'd made his way to the door marked PASTOR and found the door ajar. His father had chosen that moment to plunge his hand inside the woman's blouse and squeeze her breast.

Thomas had watched, a triumphant smile sliding over his face. Then he'd tiptoed away, knowing that one day this incident could be used to his advantage.

Now, as he watched his father walk toward him, it did not occur to Thomas to fault him for his infidelity. After all, Thomas was a chip off the old block. Screwing was his favorite pastime, too. Thomas frowned, his thoughts reverting to Kate.

"Where're you off to, son?" Reverend Jennings asked.

"Jackson's coming by and we're going for a ride."

"Remember, I expect you in church and on time, too."

Thomas shuffled from one foot to the other. "Yeah, I know. I'm supposed to pick up Kate and bring her with me."

"Good. She's a fine young lady. Your mother and I approve of her."

"That's nice," Thomas said, eager to escape. "I think I hear Jackson. See you later."

He darted out the door and met Wade Jackson moseying up the walk. "Where the hell have you been?" Thomas demanded.

"Gettin' your grass, like you told me."

"It took you long enough."

A muscle twitched in Wade's jaw. "Maybe I won't get it for you anymore."

"Yes, you will," Thomas said, "because you can't afford to buy it on your own."

Wade flushed, but didn't argue.

"Come on, let's get the hell outta here. My old man's home."

Once they were inside Wade's beat-up Ford, Wade fished inside the glove compartment and whipped out several joints.

"Ah, manna from heaven," Thomas said with a grin, clutching one like a lifeline.

Moments later, both boys were puffing hard, while the deepening twilight shielded them from passersby or curious neighbors.

"God, I needed this." Thomas inhaled deeply, held his breath, then eased it out.

"Man, you're sure uptight. You haven't gotten in her pants yet, have you?"

"Don't worry about it, Wade, it'll happen."

Jackson gave an ugly chuckle. "Maybe not. Damn, but you're slipping lately."

"Drop dead."

Wade snickered.

"Just shut up, okay? It'll happen. It's just taking longer than I thought."

"But maybe it won't. Maybe she's not as crazy about you as you think."

Thomas' lips formed a cruel line. "I warned you not to get any ideas. She wouldn't give you the time of day."

Thomas rued the day he had ever let it slip that he hadn't gone all the way with Kate. Oh, he'd wanted to, on their first date. Kate, however, had shown reluctance, and he hadn't pushed. But now that they had been out several times, his patience was coming to an end.

He'd show Wade. Tonight. Sometimes he wondered why he put up with that fatso, but deep inside he knew. Wade would do anything Thomas asked, twenty-four hours a day—

even buy his grass. There was no way Thomas could take the same risks, not with his old man a minister and his mother on the school board.

Wade had no such problem. He was one of ten children and, like Kate, was dirt poor. He had nothing to risk. Besides, to Thomas' way of thinking, Wade got more out of their relationship than he put into it. Hanging around with Thomas bought Wade respect and acceptance.

And when Wade got too big for his britches, as he was now, Thomas loved putting him back in his place.

"Yeah, Wade, my friend," Thomas drawled between drags on the joint, "you can forget ever making it with a girl like Kate Colson."

"Go to hell," Jackson muttered.

"Me, go to hell?" Thomas said in a mocking tone. "Why, man, with my daddy being a preacher and all, I've got a one-way ticket into heaven."

Wade scowled. "Don't bet your ass on that. And while we're on the subject of Kate, she's nothing special. She don't have a pot to pee in or a window to throw it out of."

"Right." Thomas' grin was leering. "Hell, I don't want to marry her; I just want to screw her. Besides, she's got the best tits I've ever seen."

Just talking about her breasts caused his dick to pound. Getting into her pants was all he could think about. He shifted in the seat. Smoking grass certainly didn't help. It made him that much hornier.

"Oh, and she's smart, too," Thomas added. "Since I've been seeing her, I've made much better grades. She's been helping me."

"Bully for you."

"Whatsa matter?" Thomas taunted with a grin. "You still got your nose out of joint?"

Wade's chest heaved as he glared at Thomas. "One of these days, you're gonna get what's coming to you. I just hope I'm around to see it."

"Never, my friend. My favorite Bible verse is stick it unto your fellow man before he sticks it unto you."

"Jeez. You're sick, Jennings."

Thomas laughed, then said in a bored voice, "I gotta go in and get ready for my hot date."

"You like this boy?"

"Yes, Mamma, I do."

Mavis took a deep breath and let it out. "Your daddy said for me to tell you he'd better take you to our church, then bring you straight home, it being a school night and all."

"We're going to the Methodist church instead, to hear Reverend Jennings preach." Kate's eyes registered her anxiety, for on Wednesday nights, her daddy expected her to be in the front row of *his* church, as he did on Sundays. "Daddy won't care, will he?"

"Don't reckon he will, not as long as you're in church."

Kate didn't respond. She turned and faced the mirror again and began brushing her hair. But instead of concentrating on her own reflection, she looked at her mother. Uneasiness shot through her. Mavis looked worn, with dark circles under her eyes. Her face was bone-white.

"Mamma."

"What?"

"Has . . . has Daddy . . . hurt you again?"

Mavis straightened her shoulders, but her gaze avoided Kate's. "No, of course not."

Kate wasn't convinced her mother spoke the truth. But her mother's tone brooked no argument, and maybe Kate didn't want to know the truth. Right now, she didn't want anything to tarnish her upcoming evening with Thomas.

"All right, whatever you say."

"Then I say you'd best hurry and not be late."

When her mother shuffled out of the room, Kate's thoughts immediately returned to Thomas. *I'm in love,* her heart sang. And he loved her. He had told her that Saturday night after her face and breasts were wet from his kisses. Thinking about the liberties she'd let him take sent the blood rushing into her cheeks. She had no intention of stopping, though. She loved for him to kiss her, and she loved kissing him back.

She just loved him period.

Her time alone with him was precious, and she guarded it as closely as her mamma guarded a penny. She feared that any day now her daddy would stop her from seeing Thomas. In fact she found it hard to believe that he'd let her date him in the first place. But Angie's prediction had panned out. Thomas was a preacher's kid, and preachers in her daddy's eyes could do no wrong.

She and Thomas had been seeing each other for a month now, and her life had changed . . .

Her daddy's gruff voice interrupted her thoughts. "Girl, that boy just drove up."

"Tell him I'll be right there."

"Git on out here; I'm not telling him a damn thing."

Even Emmitt's harsh words couldn't dampen her spirits. With a smile lighting her face and on feet she was sure had wings, Kate raced from the house.

Six

In the far distance, the lights of Austin winked. Closer, a brutal north wind moaned as it whipped around the car.

The couple inside were far too wrapped up in each other to pay attention to anything other than their own needs.

Thomas' soft wet lips broke away from Kate's. He gasped for breath. "Man, this sure beats the hell outta listening to my old man shout fire and brimstone from the pulpit."

Kate didn't know if he expected her to answer, but it didn't matter. She couldn't talk. Her heart was making more noise than the wind outside. The sound of her breathing was nearly deafening. She and Thomas had been kissing and petting for half an hour.

After they'd left the church, Thomas had driven to their favorite parking place, a secluded bluff between Four Corners and Austin. Weather permitting, they sometimes necked on the grass while the stars and lights from the city encircled them.

But tonight was too cold. A blue norther had made its way into the Hill Country, dropping the temperature. In the back seat of the Mustang, however, it was toasty warm.

Thomas reached for Kate again and slammed his tongue deep into her mouth as his fingers roughly fondled a breast that he had only moments before exposed to his eyes and hands.

Moaning, Kate struggled against him.

He pulled back. "What's wrong?" His eyes narrowed in the moonlight like those of an angry animal. "You don't want me playing with your knockers?"

Kate's heart wrenched. She hated it when he talked about her breasts in such a crude way. Yet she dared not say anything, for fear of making him angry.

But then, he'd been angry from the onset. She'd sensed it when he'd picked her up. Throughout the church service, he had shifted restlessly in the pew. When she had looked at him, his eyes had smoldered with dark passion. She had known what had been on his mind, and it hadn't had anything to do with the Lord saving the world. He'd been thinking about kissing her until that warm, unsettled feeling between her legs made her crazy. Only now she was more than crazy. She was afraid. For the first time, he frightened her.

"Nothing's wrong," she finally whispered. "It's just that it's time to go."

Thomas slumped against the seat, his lower lip stuck out like a sulky child's. "I thought you loved me."

"Oh, but I do," Kate said in a strangled tone.

"Well, you sure as hell aren't acting like it."

His words winded her, made her lungs hurt so that she couldn't say anything.

"If you loved me, you'd go all the way with me." Again that petulant ring edged his tone.

"You know I love you," she responded, tentatively placing her hand on his thigh.

"Then why can't we?" His hand surrounded the other breast, and he sank his lips into the fragrant softness of her hair.

"Oh, Thomas . . . I don't know."

"What do you mean, you don't know?" His hot mouth nibbled at her neck. "It'll be good, I promise. I know how to make it good."

Kate clutched him tighter while her mind waded through a myriad of emotions so strong, yet so conflicting, she was terrified. She wanted to do it, but she was afraid.

Her upbringing loomed large in her thoughts. If she and Thomas went all the way, would she indeed burn in hell as her daddy and the church said she would? On the other hand, if she didn't do what Thomas wanted, he would drop her and find another girl. She couldn't bear that.

"Come on, babe," he urged, "open your legs."

Kate wanted to cry no, but she couldn't. She had to let him do as he wanted. Her parents approved of him, didn't they? He was the son of the town's most respected preacher. Her classmates approved of him; he was the student body president. And because she was his girl, they all had come around to approving of *her*. She liked that feeling.

As if he sensed her weakening, Thomas whispered in an urgent, yet cajoling tone: "You know I really love you."

His words suddenly shook something loose inside Kate, made her ache, made her yearn for the love that had been denied her. She moved closer to him and as she did, the wall inside her came tumbling down.

"Oh, Thomas, I love you, too," she whispered, closing her eyes and thinking of love and acceptance.

"Is that a yes, babe?"

She sighed against his lips even as he groped to shove her legs apart, but not before stripping her panties down to her ankles and onto the floorboard.

With bent knees, he raised himself above her. She stared at him, her heartbeat thundering and her eyes wide, while he unzipped his pants. Kate had never seen a man's penis before and the sight of Thomas' thin veined hardness repulsed her. How could she enjoy that being inside her?

Panic gripped her, as he lowered himself over her again and took a nipple into his mouth.

"Thomas . . . I don't think we should." She felt cold, yet drops of perspiration gathered on her skin. "Please . . . stop."

"I can't." His voice came out a low moan. "It's . . . too late."

Kate felt his fingers probe the wetness between her legs. Before she could utter another word of protest, his mouth covered hers, and he thrust himself deep inside her.

Had his mouth not prevented it, she would have screamed

as a hot, sharp pain seared her from inside out. He thrust several more times, while the pain continued, freezing her heart and paralyzing her lungs.

Then, mercifully, the ordeal came to an end. Following another harsh grunt, Thomas collapsed against her. His damp head landed on her quivering breasts. Her entire body shook, raked by tremors. Was what she had just endured supposed to be wonderful and satisfying? If so, something was terribly wrong. His invasion of her body had been neither.

"Wasn't that good?" he muttered, lifting his eyes to meet hers.

Tears washed Kate's face, while pricks of pain continued to steal her breath.

"Ah, shit," he said, climbing off her and zipping his pants. "Why are you crying? Didn't you like it? Man, I thought it was great."

Kate fought to contain the tears, but she couldn't. They rained down her face, scalding it. "I . . . can't seem to stop . . . "

"I don't fool with girls who cry, you know."

She wiped her face with the back of her hand.

"I'm sorry." Her voice cracked. "It's just that it hurt . . . "

"Ah, it'll be better next time." Thomas grinned like a satisfied cat with more than his share of cream. "You'll see."

Kate nodded wordlessly, doubting there would be a next time.

Thomas watched her, something hard in his expression.

"I'll be all right tomorrow," she said at last, desperate to salvage what she could of the situation.

"Sure you will." Following a moment of strained silence, Thomas added, "Come on, let's get back in the front seat."

Somehow Kate managed to retrieve her panties and slip back into them, trying her best to ignore the sticky glob between her legs. She felt numb and slightly sick all over.

Changing places proved to be even more difficult. Kate winced with each move, but she dared not let on, nor did she dare think about what she had done.

Once the Mustang was headed toward the farm, she stole a glance at Thomas. "Will I see you tomorrow?"

"Nope. My old man's making me work to buy gas for my heap."

"Monday, then?"

Thomas jammed the gear shift down and the car shot forward. "Most likely."

Silence fell between them. Kate wanted to scream again as indecision raged in her, and the sobs she refused to release jammed her throat. But she had to ask. She had to be reassured.

"Thomas?"

"Yeah?"

"Do you still love me?"

He turned to her, his eyes shrunk to pinpoints. "Sure, I do, babe. More than ever, now."

Twenty minutes later Kate stepped into the bathtub; the hot sudsy water eased the rawness between her legs. Though her numbed body seemed to have come back to life, her heart hadn't. It lay like a lump inside her chest. She loved Thomas more than ever. Yet she wouldn't care if she never saw him again. Why was she having such mixed emotions?

Feeling another bout of the weak trembles coming on, Kate scrubbed herself with controlled diligence, angry that she hadn't tried harder to stop him. She'd known what was sure to happen the instant he'd urged her legs apart. But she had wanted to appease him, and she'd been excited and curious. Then when he'd pushed halfway inside her, she'd kept thinking he'd pull back, only he hadn't.

What was she going to do? She had to destroy the evidence of her lost viriginity. After she'd told her mother she was home, she'd dashed into her room and immediately peeled off her clothes. She'd been horrified by what she'd seen. Splotches of dried blood had covered the insides of her thighs. She'd turned away at the sight, her thoughts so jumbled, her feelings so disruptive that she hadn't been able to think.

Her parents must never suspect. The thought of them spurred her into action. If she dallied in the bathroom too long, her mother might think she was sick and come check on her. She couldn't risk that.

Quickly she finished her bath, then returned to her room and got into bed. Only after she had the covers pulled up to her chin did she let the tears flow again.

"Oh, Thomas," she whispered into the darkness. "I'm so scared."

She squeezed her eyes shut and felt the tears saturate her cheeks. Everything was going to be just fine, she tried to assure herself.

After all, Thomas said he loved her.

Seven

Spring arrived early, painting the Hill Country in a blaze of color. The trees were littered with leaves, the hillsides with wildflowers.

The weather, however, continued to be chilly. Kate took another peep at the calendar in the back of her notebook, counted, then shivered. The goose bumps on her arms didn't have anything to do with the temperature.

She had missed not one but two monthly periods. She couldn't ignore that fact any longer, especially since her stomach was in continuous upheaval.

Today was no exception. She was studying at Angie's house. Angie had gone to the kitchen to get them some Coke and popcorn. Kate couldn't guarantee she'd keep either in her stomach, but she had to try.

Although Angie hadn't said anything, Kate knew her friend sensed something was wrong. All Angie had to do was look at Kate's pale features.

She had thought about telling her mother that she felt awful, but since she hated the idea of going to a doctor and being poked, she'd kept quiet. Anyway, she knew her parents didn't have the money to pay a doctor, even if her daddy believed her, which he wouldn't. He'd say there wasn't anything wrong with her except laziness.

As usual, he was wrong. Kate wasn't lazy. She worked

hard at anything she undertook, especially her chores and her schoolwork. She loved being in high school. Her favorite subjects were history and English. Spanish ran a close third. She not only had dreams of becoming a lawyer, but she also wanted to travel to other countries.

But now school no longer came first in her life. Thomas did. He even took precedence over her health. Since that night in the car when they had gone all the way, she had thought of him constantly, though she hadn't seen that much of him. At first she'd been afraid she had disappointed him, but then he'd reminded her about his job, saying that claimed much of his free time. Whenever he passed her in the hall at school, he whispered words of love in her ear. These few words kept her going from one day to the next.

She believed him. He wouldn't lie to her. She had to trust him.

If for no other reason than Thomas, she had to get well. Kate feared that if she continued to look half dead, he would drop her for someone else, though she admitted she hadn't liked doing it that much and had dissuaded him from trying again.

For weeks afterward, she'd watched her parents, as well as Angie, to see if they noticed a difference in her. Once the guilt and fear of discovery had faded, she realized that the difference was within. She felt completely grown.

She was reluctant to share her secret with Angie, maybe because she hadn't wanted to share any part of Thomas. She felt he belonged exclusively to her, and she wanted to keep it that way.

She'd rather be dead than lose him.

"Hey, Katie, get yourself in here."

Kate closed her notebook and eased to the edge of the bed. That was as far as she got. The room spun and her stomach revolted.

"I'm waiting," Angie called. "The popcorn's getting cold."

Kate inhaled deeply. The room righted itself, and she rose to her feet. Still, she was none too steady. She waited another moment, then made her way out of Angie's bedroom down a long hall.

Angie's house, with its homey and cheerful atmosphere, boosted her dejected spirits. Deciding she felt much better, Kate straightened her stooped shoulders and passed through the living room, which was sparsely but tastefully furnished with a flowered love seat and two overstuffed chairs. A brass-and-glass coffee table and a fireplace added just the right touches.

"Follow the smell," Angie said, laughter in her voice, "and you'll know where I am."

"I'm coming," Kate muttered.

The kitchen was also bright and airy, with large windows and lots of plants perched on a deep windowsill.

"Holy cow," Angie exclaimed, "you look awful. You sick again?"

Kate responded to the first statement with a forced smile. "Thanks a lot. You sure know how to make a girl feel good."

"I'm just telling it like it is," Angie said bluntly. She peered more closely at Kate. "Seriously, are you sick? Cramps maybe?"

"No cramps, but my stomach does feel kind of funny."

"Sit down and have some popcorn. It'll cure anything known to man."

While Kate followed her advice, Angie set a can of Coke and a bowl of popcorn saturated with melted butter in front of her. The smell wafted to her nose; Kate moaned, fearing she would throw up.

Angie seemed to sense all was not right as she stopped pouring her own Coke and said, "You aren't going to be sick—?"

"I am!" Kate burst out, and dashed from the room.

Angie set down the Coke and ran out behind her.

Kate barely made it to the bathroom before she lost the contents of her stomach. When she reached the dry heaves stage, she felt a cloth against her forehead.

"Hold still," Angie said. "The cold will help."

Blessedly it did, yet Kate couldn't say a word to thank

Angie. She feared if she so much as moved a muscle, she'd be sick again.

"Are you feeling better?" Angie asked after several minutes.

Kate nodded.

"Pray tell, what's going on in here?"

Angie swung around. "Oh, Mamma, I'm so glad you're home."

"And from the looks of things, none too soon, either," Roberta said, looking tired, but still immaculate, in her white nurse's uniform.

"Kate's sick, Mamma."

Roberta cast her daughter a frustrated look. "I can see that." She crossed the narrow space to Kate and knelt beside her. "Kate, honey, can you get to your feet?"

"I . . . I think so."

"Good." Roberta turned toward Angie. "You get one arm and I'll get the other."

Minutes later, Kate was propped against the pillows on Angie's bed, the washcloth still on her forehead. Angie was sprawled on the other side, her head cradled in the palm of one hand.

"How do you feel now?" Roberta asked, concern deepening her voice. She sat at the foot of the bed and studied her patient.

Kate pushed a damp strand of hair off her cheek and let out a shaky breath. "Better."

She was grateful for Roberta's unexpected appearance. Seconds after she'd been helped to bed, Roberta had given her a nausea pill, and it had already taken effect.

Kate faced the window and stared into the sunlight. Outside a squirrel scampered from one tree to another. She watched, mesmerized, for a long moment, and found herself envying its uncomplicated life.

"Kate?"

Roberta's voice brought her head back around. "Angie tells me you've been feeling bad for a good while now."

"That's right, I have." A tear slid down Kate's cheek. She rubbed it away with a knuckle.

"Your stomach?" Roberta's tone was soothing.

"Yes."

"Are you having trouble with your periods?"

"I haven't . . . had a period in two months."

Silence, profound and deep-felt, descended over the room. Angie's mouth gaped. Roberta's tensed.

"Do . . . you think I could have something bad wrong with me?" Kate asked, her gaze shifting between them.

"Yeah, you're probably pregnant," Angie blurted.

Roberta threw her daughter a scathing look before facing Kate and asking gently, "Kate, honey, could you be pregnant?"

Kate's look was incredulous. "Why . . . I . . . don't—" she began, only to have her words jam in her throat, paralyzed by the suppressed, but nevertheless accusing, look in Roberta's eyes. She dared not look at Angie.

"Kate, answer me." Roberta's tone remained soft, though firm.

"Yes," Kate whispered before her voice grew all tight and choked.

Angie groaned, then scrambled to an upright position. "I can't believe you'd be that—"

Roberta glared at her daughter again. "Hush."

Angie fell silent and toyed with a thread on the bedspread.

"Kate, honey," Roberta said, "you just sit tight while I call the doctor I work for. I'm sure he'll see you this afternoon, even if it is getting late."

Kate could only nod, for her mouth and lips were numb with fear. But her chest wasn't numb; its pounding spread to her throat. Pregnant? Noooo! Oh, please, no.

Angie interrupted her thoughts. "Honest to Pete, Kate, how could you have been so . . . so stupid, so careless?" She shifted so that she was practically in Kate's face. "I can't believe you didn't make Thomas, you know, use something."

"Like what?"

"Like what?" Angie's face turned scarlet with anger. "A rubber, that's what. Thomas always has rubbers."

"How do you know that?"

"Well, I don't, not for a fact," Angie hedged, "but I do know that most all the guys carry rubbers. I'm sure Thomas is no exception."

Kate couldn't comprehend. Her brain fought to stay ahead of the fear that threatened to suck her into its black void. Pregnant. No, it just wasn't possible, she rationalized. She couldn't have gotten pregnant by doing it just one time. She struggled upright. Her lungs felt as if they would burst. Tears flowed out of her eyes and ran down her face. She covered her face with her hands.

"Crying isn't going to do any good," Angie said and grabbed a Kleenex off the table and handed it to Kate. "I thought you knew the score."

Though Angie's tone remained blunt, her eyes were no longer condemning, for which Kate was grateful. She couldn't bear it if her best friend shunned her.

It hit her then, like a knife in the stomach. She groaned aloud. Her parents? Oh, dear Lord, her parents. No. She wouldn't think about them now. After all, she might not be pregnant; it could be just a false alarm.

"Kate, did you hear me? Are you sick again?"

The pain in her head made it hard to hear, to think. "No."

Angie sighed. "You were thinking about Thomas, weren't you?"

"I was thinking about my parents."

"But what about Thomas?"

Thomas. She let out a short breath. If she was indeed pregnant, how would he react?

"I don't know," Kate finally said.

"If I could get my hands on him about now, I'd—"

"Don't, Angie. Don't talk about him like that. I'm just as much to blame."

Angie pressed her lips together. "Somehow I doubt that."

"It's true."

"You're just too naive for your own good, that's all."

"I love him."

"You what?!"

"You heard me."

Before Angie could comment, Roberta walked back into the room, her eyes on Kate. "Are you still feeling better?"

Kate nodded.

"Well, then, go wash your face and tidy up. The doctor will see you."

Eight

Unbroken sobs pounded Kate's body like fists. She winced visibly against the onslaught.

"Now, honey," Roberta said in her soothing professional voice, "crying won't solve a thing."

"I . . . know, but I . . . " Kate broke off, another sob catching in her throat. Pregnant. She was going to have a baby. Oh, dear Lord, how could she stop crying when she was sixteen, unmarried, and pregnant? If the situation hadn't been so terrifyingly real, she might have laughed. Hadn't she and Angie snickered on several occasions when one of the other girls in the school had been struck with the same misfortune? They had, and perhaps now God was getting back at her. Her daddy always warned her. *Her daddy*. She rocked forward and moaned again.

"Kate, you must listen to me," Roberta said in a sterner tone. "You'll make yourself sick and what good will that do?"

"Yeah, Katie, Mamma's right, you gotta stop. What's done is done."

Angie's anxious words finally penetrated. With a set to her shoulders, Kate lifted her head and faced her friend. Leave it to Angie to get to the heart of the matter. If only she could stop crying. Hysteria bubbled close to the surface.

"Here, clean yourself up," Angie added, and handed Kate

a handful of Kleenex. "Just what would you do if I wasn't available to supply you with tissues?"

Angie's attempt at humor brought a tiny smile to Kate's lips. It didn't last long. She took a deep, shuddering breath and for a blessed moment, numbness penetrated her body, but not her mind.

Ever since the physician had confirmed that she was pregnant, Roberta and Angie had stayed close to her side.

Now, as Kate sat on the sofa in their living room, they continued to hover, determined to put this tragedy into perspective. Kate wished she could slip away, crawl off into the nearest hole and die.

This empty, hopeless feeling wasn't new to her. She experienced it every time her daddy whacked her mother; every time prom day rolled around and she didn't have a date, much less a new dress; and every time her peers made fun of her because she was smart and plain. Those moments, however, seemed of little consequence compared to what she faced now.

"Kate, honey, I'll agree it's devastating, but it's not the end of the world," Roberta said.

"Yes, it is," Kate muttered, wadding the tissues and mopping her face.

Angie eased back down on the couch beside her. "Sip this 7-Up. It might make you feel better."

Kate took two sips, then set it aside. Nothing was going to make her feel better.

"You know you have to tell your parents."

Silence followed Roberta's statement. Kate opened her mouth, but nothing came out. Her numbness had twisted into a mindless, gripping panic.

"Hey, hey, don't fall apart now." Angie awkwardly patted Kate's shoulder, while her eyes turned to her mother.

Roberta shook her head, as if to indicate Angie should be quiet, then sat next to Kate and placed an arm around her quivering shoulders. "I know how you must dread telling them, but you have no choice."

Kate pulled away and stared at Roberta through tortured eyes. "I . . . can't."

"But—"

"Please, Mrs. Strickland," Kate begged, "please don't make me." The thought of facing her daddy with what she'd done went beyond terror. His fury would be all-consuming. He would more than likely beat her until she lost the baby. Would that be so terrible? she asked herself. Her problem would certainly be solved. Still, she couldn't let that happen. Until now, she hadn't stopped to think about the tiny life nestled inside her. Her hand went protectively to her stomach.

"Have you thought about an abortion?"

Another silence accompanied Roberta's words, deeper and more ominous than the one before.

"Oh, Mamma," Angie wailed, staring at Kate, then taking one of Kate's limp hands in hers and gripping it.

"Kate?" Roberta urged, when Kate didn't respond.

"No, ma'am."

"Perhaps you should. It's an alternative, you know, considering how you feel about telling your parents."

"What . . . do you have to do?" Kate forced herself to ask.

"To get an abortion, you mean?"

Kate nodded. "Does it . . . would it hurt?"

Roberta was quiet for a moment. "Actually, it's not a painful procedure, and it normally only takes five to ten minutes." She paused and took a deep breath. "First, a doctor does a pelvic exam, followed by an injection with a numbing medicine."

"I wouldn't be put to sleep?"

"No, absolutely not."

Kate crossed both hands over her stomach and shuddered visibly. "What happens next?"

"The doctor will use a small plastic tube and do what is called a vacuum aspiration, which, in laymen's terms, means the contents of the uterus are removed by suction."

Kate's breath hitched in her lungs and her eyes widened. "I could never do that. If my daddy didn't kill me, God would."

Roberta looked distressed. "Oh, honey, don't talk like that, because it just isn't so."

Kate knew it was so, but she wasn't about to argue with Roberta. So she remained mute, her body and mind struggling to decide exactly what she was going to do.

"All right, Kate," Roberta said with resignation in her tone, "I won't push that point right now either."

"Are you going to tell Thomas?" Angie asked.

Kate lifted her head and stared into her friend's troubled eyes. "Shouldn't I?"

Angie looked distressed. "Gosh Katie, don't ask me. I—" Her voice played out.

"Of course you should tell Thomas." Roberta massaged her forehead. "After all, he's as much to blame for this as you are."

"Creep," Angie mumbled under her breath.

Kate cut her eyes in Angie's direction. "What did you say?"

Angie shrugged. "Nothing. Don't go getting bent out of shape."

"Then keep quiet," Roberta ordered, giving her daughter a hard look.

Kate stared into space until her eyes felt stretched. "I'll tell Thomas tomorrow. He's supposed to take me to church, to hear his daddy preach."

Angie looked heavenward while Roberta tightened her lips.

Kate read their thoughts. Despite their unselfish help, she felt her anger rise. They wanted to put the blame exclusively on Thomas, then label him a hypocrite. She hoped that when she told him about the baby, he'd prove that wasn't true. She had no idea how he would react, but she knew that in the end, he'd do what was right. But what was right was something she didn't want to think about, not without Thomas. They would make the decision together. He loved her. She had to cling to that.

"How's your stomach?" Roberta asked.

"I know it's there, but I don't feel like I'm going to throw up anymore." She felt tired instead, as if the blood had drained out of her.

"That's good. Go wash your face again, then I'll take you home."

When Roberta mentioned the word "home," Kate's spine stiffened. She didn't want to go home. What if they could tell just by looking that she had sinned with Thomas?

"Kate, Kate, now calm down," Roberta said, as if she could read her mind. "They won't know, unless you tell them. You won't start to show for several more months."

Hot tears ran unchecked down Kate's cheeks again. She brushed them away. "I don't know what I would have done without you . . . and Angie."

Roberta patted her hand and smiled reassuringly. "I'm glad we're here to help you."

Once Kate had washed her face and combed her hair, she felt better, more able to cope. But her eyes were red-rimmed and swollen. She could only pray that her parents wouldn't be observant enough to notice, or to care.

"Decisions have to be made about your future, Kate. You know that, don't you?" Roberta spoke those sobering words as they walked out the door to the car.

"Yes, ma'am."

"Then sooner or later, you're going to have to tell your parents."

"I know." Kate wrenched open the door, stepped inside, hunkered down in the seat and tried to ignore the block of ice around her heart.

The blood congealed in Thomas' veins. "What did you say?"

Kate's lower lip quivered. "I . . . I said I'm pregnant."

"You stupid bitch!" He loomed over her, his handsome features contorted in rage.

Fearing that he was about to strike her, Kate cowered and took a step backward.

"Oh, no you don't." Thomas' hand shot out and grabbed her. His fingers tightened around her small-boned wrist. "If you're playing some kind of fuckin' game here, it won't work."

"You're hurting me." Kate struggled to break loose.

His hold merely tightened. "Trust me, I'm going to hurt

you a lot worse if you don't quit jerking me around." He could break her wrist if he wanted to, and he just might want to if she didn't retract her words.

"Don't . . . Thomas . . . please." Kate's voice came out a pleading whisper.

"Don't, Thomas," he mimicked in a tone as cruel as his eyes.

Looking at her made his gut churn with hatred. He didn't know when he'd begun to feel this way—maybe after he'd taken her virginity and found that it hadn't been as great as he'd thought it would be. She wasn't for him, big boobs or not. As far as girls went, Kate was dumber than dirt. He liked girls who knew what sex was all about.

Thomas hadn't been able to drop her, though. His busybody daddy had questioned him about Kate, encouraged him to date her. In order to keep his old man off his back, he'd pretended he had done just that.

Still, the past week had been hell. He'd been up to his neck in trouble. His daddy had been on a rampage because he'd had another wreck. He'd ranted until Thomas wanted to puke. Although he liked his job at the country club, he hadn't wanted to work, not really. But his old man had insisted that he help pay for the increased insurance premiums.

Thomas had been tempted to use the trump card he held, tell his daddy he knew about his messing around with the deacon's wife, certain that would bring the old man to heel. Only he hadn't. Something had warned him that he should save that juicy tidbit and use it when he was in deep trouble, like now.

Sweet Jesus, how had this happened? And to think she was here in his house. He cast his eyes around the room, afraid the walls had heard her confession and would tell. He'd had no intention of bringing her to his home. Ever. But again his old man had interfered. After the church service, his daddy had sent him home to get a memorandum for one of the ladies serving on a fund-raising committee. He'd told him to take Kate with him.

Now, as Thomas took pleasure in watching fear surge into her eyes, he continued to squeeze her wrist and glower at her. "So take it back, you hear?"

"I can't, Thomas. It's the truth."

He let go of her, suddenly hating the thought of touching her, especially when she looked at him out of those sappy, love-sick eyes. Kate pregnant from that night in the car? No . . . it couldn't be true. But the thought that it might be true ripped his stomach and made the urge to puke stronger.

He turned and stomped to the window. He felt himself start to sweat. She was mistaken; that was all there was to it. His gut told him otherwise. Wouldn't you know the one time he'd been out of rubbers and hadn't taken the time to send Jackson after some, something like this would happen?

Well, it could un-happen just as easily. He had no intention of letting that bitch ruin his life; he had plans and they sure as hell didn't include her. No, he had his eyes on a real looker at the country club. She was rich, too. And she knew the score. None of this innocent crap with her.

Thomas leveled his gaze on Kate again, who stood where he'd left her, her teeth sunk into her bottom lip. God, he could barely stand the sight of her. "How do you know?"

"Angie's mother took me to her doctor and he confirmed it." She raised her chin. "You're going to be a daddy."

Two long strides brought him back in front of her.

"That's the last thing I'm gonna be, you bitch," he lashed out at the same time he slapped her across the mouth.

Kate cried out like a wounded animal, then raised her hand to find her lower lip smeared with blood.

"What is going on in here?"

Thomas cursed again. He hadn't heard his parents come in the house. The Reverend Jennings stood on the threshold and stared at Kate.

Thomas turned and followed his father's gaze. "Kate tripped over the coffee table and busted her lip, that's all. Right, Kate?"

Ruth, his mother, came farther into the room. Her eyes were devoid of warmth as she stared at her son.

"Her lip needs tending to."

"Kate, are you all right?" the Reverend Jennings asked.

Kate removed her hand from her mouth. "Yes, sir."

"Thomas, give her your handkerchief."

Thomas did as he was told.

"Kate," the Reverend said, clearing his throat. "Please, sit down. I'll send Thomas back with some antiseptic."

Nodding, Kate fell into the nearest chair and applied the handkerchief next to her lip.

"I'll be right back," Thomas said tersely, then followed his parents from the room.

Kate sat in a dazed stupor in a corner of the simply but tastefully decorated parsonage. She couldn't come to terms with what had happened. All she could think about was that Thomas had hit her.

She'd taken the abuse from Thomas, though doing so had negatively charged every cell in her body. She'd had to think of the baby, so she'd kept quiet.

Could she forgive Thomas? Yes. He was shocked by the news. That was all. When he cooled off—thought about it in the light of day—his attitude would be different.

Kate suddenly felt she was no longer alone. She looked up. Ruth Jennings' eyes were on her. She returned the stare. The woman was taller than her husband, and nicely put together, but she appeared cold from the top of her perfectly coiffured head to the toes of her stylish shoes. Kate shuddered and lowered her gaze.

"Would you like something to drink?" Mrs. Jennings asked, her tone lukewarm at best.

"No, thank you."

"Thomas should be back momentarily." She paused, as if she didn't know what else to say, then turned and walked out of the room.

When Thomas re-entered the room, Kate didn't move. She merely looked at him. He tossed a tube of medicine at her. It landed at her feet. With tears marring her vision, she leaned and picked it up. But she didn't doctor her lip; it had stopped bleeding and it wasn't even throbbing.

"You'll just have to get rid of it," he said without preamble.

This time she spoke up. "No."

"Yes," he sneered, crossing to her and towering over her again.

She cringed. "Can't we talk about it?"

"There's nothing to talk about. And if you're thinking what I think you are, forget it."

"You . . . you won't even consider marrying me?"

He laughed. "Marry you? You've got to be kidding."

Kate hung her head.

"If you hadn't been so stupid, you'd have used something. You were dying for me to get in your pants . . . "

Kate gasped. "That's not true!"

"Ah, shit. Don't act innocent with me." Thomas pounded his chest. "I know better. And there ain't but one thing to do and that's get rid of it."

Kate's already pale face turned ashen. "Please . . . I don't want to get an abortion."

"Is it money? Do you need money? Of course you do." He fished his billfold out of his back pocket and drew out some bills. "Here," he said, "take them."

Kate leaned back. "No . . . I can't . . . I won't. Please just think about it."

"*You* think about it. My mind's made up."

Her hand crept over her stomach as if to protect the baby inside. "All right, I'll . . . think about it. I . . . promise."

"See that you do. Let's go. I'm taking you home."

Nine

For days Kate felt sorry for herself. She wallowed in self-pity until she was useless.

Now that she was pregnant, she felt isolated from her classmates, even though as far as she knew no one was aware of her condition. Angie and she had tried to carry on as if their friendship hadn't been affected, but it hadn't worked.

What her peers thought, however, was the least of her worries. She still hadn't told her parents, and she lived in mortal fear that they would find out. Then there was Thomas. She had managed to avoid him at school, but she didn't know how much longer she would be able to do so. He wanted an answer about the abortion, and it was only a matter of time till he insisted she give him one.

Sure enough, that dreaded day arrived. Kate had just stepped off the school bus and was making her way across to the main door when she saw him. He was with his cohort, Wade, and if their twisted expressions were anything to judge by, they were involved in a heated discussion.

Kate willed back her sudden nausea and didn't deviate from her path. Besides, Thomas had seen her.

He said something else to Wade, then made his way toward her. He looked wonderful, Kate thought. He had on a bright red shirt and jeans. She prayed his perfectly chiseled lips would break into his breath-catching smile. They didn't.

"Hi," she said, her own smile brittle, her stomach churning.

"Well, did you take care of the problem?" Thomas stopped within touching distance.

Kate hugged her notebook against her chest and looked into his black eyes, looked for a glimpse of warmth, of love. She saw neither, and swallowed painfully. "Not . . . yet—"

"So when you gonna do it? I'm sure Angie's old lady can fix you up, her being a nurse and all." Thomas reached toward his back pocket. "The money's still yours."

Kate avoided his intent gaze, feeling cold inside. "I . . . can't."

He trailed a finger down one side of her cheek. The unexpected gesture triggered tears.

"Hey," he said in a softer, sexier tone. "It'll be all right, you'll see. Once it's over with, you and I can take up where we left off." That same finger made a path down her long neck, then back up to her ear. "It'll be better than before. You want that, don't you?"

Kate trembled and felt that familiar warmth gather between her legs. She hated the power he had over her, but she loved him. Dear Lord, she loved him and wanted more than anything for things to be like they had been before, only better. But an abortion . . .

"Do you still love me?" she whispered.

"Why, you know I do." His drawling tone ended on a smile. "You're my number one girl."

"Oh, Thomas." She wanted to believe that. She had to believe it or she couldn't keep going, especially with his child inside her.

He touched her full bottom lip with that same finger. "You take care of it." His eyes, though steady on her, were stormy. "I'm counting on you. We don't want any squalling kid messing up our lives."

As his finger continued to work its magic on her lip, his voice, his eyes, mesmerized Kate to a point that she couldn't think.

"So, are you going to take care of it?"

She gulped back the tears. "If . . . if that's what you want . . . what you think is best."

"Oh, babe, I know it's best, for both of us. I promise you won't be sorry." He bent and kissed her on the lips. "You let me know when it's done."

"Would you come with me?"

Thomas dropped his hand and snapped to attention, a menacing glint in his eyes. "Not me, baby. No way. But you don't need me. I told you, an abortion these days is a piece of cake."

Abortion. That awful word again; it lodged in Kate's brain like a sharp stone.

"But I'll be scared," she said. "I want you there."

His lips twisted with distaste. "I can't, but you're a big girl. You can handle it."

With that he turned and sauntered off. Only after a hard shudder had raked her body did Kate realize that he was whistling.

"The popcorn's ready. You girls come and get it."

Roberta's voice summoned Kate and Angie from Angie's room, where they had been trying on a new Cover Girl makeup. Following her conversation with Thomas, Kate couldn't stand the thought of going home, so Angie had taken pity on her and once again invited Kate to her house.

Roberta had left work early and fixed them a snack.

"Thanks, Mamma, that smells good," Angie said, pulling out a chair and falling into it.

Roberta turned to Kate. "Have a seat. You look like you're about to fall on your face. You all right?"

"I'm fine." Kate smiled, but it stopped short of her eyes. They remained sober. "At least most of the time."

Angie shoved the popcorn toward her. "Have some. Like I always say, it'll cure any ills."

"I wish."

Roberta sighed as her gaze swung between the girls, then stopped on Angie. "Have you told her yet?"

Kate's hand, filled with popcorn, froze halfway to her

mouth. It wasn't so much what Roberta said, but how she said it. Something was wrong; Kate just knew it. "Told me what?"

Angie hesitated, then said, "We're moving."

Kate's jaw went slack. "Moving . . . where?"

"To New Braunfels."

The popcorn fluttered from Kate's hand. "Oh, no."

"Hey, don't go nuts, okay?" Angie said, jumping up and moving to Kate's side. "You can come to see us as much as you want. It's only an hour's drive from here, for Pete's sake."

Roberta reached out and squeezed Kate's cold hand. "You'll always be welcome in our home. You know that. Why, you're just like a second daughter."

"But . . . but . . ." Kate stammered, feeling as if another rug had been yanked out from under her.

"I'm going to be the director of nurses at the hospital there," Roberta said, as if she knew what Kate was trying to say but couldn't. "It's a wonderful promotion that I simply couldn't pass up."

"I understand." And Kate did, but it didn't stop her heart from bleeding. She couldn't imagine life without Angie.

"Kate, honey," Roberta said, "you have no choice now but to tell your parents about the baby. I insist that you do."

Tears streaked Kate's face, but she didn't try to wipe them away. What else was going to happen?

"Promise me, you'll do as I ask."

Kate took a deep breath and straightened her spine, but her eyes were filled with sorrow and fear. "I promise."

"You can do it," Kate whispered. "Sure you can. You promised Mrs. Strickland."

Though Kate continued her pep talk, it didn't do any good. She knew how Daniel in the Bible must have felt when he stepped into the lion's den. She felt the same way as she made her way down the hall toward the kitchen, where her mother was cooking the evening meal. Her daddy hadn't come in from the fields.

It had been two weeks since she'd seen Angie and her mother. They were now settled in New Braunfels. Once Roberta had accepted the new position, she had turned the house over to a realtor, and she and Angie had left immediately. Angie loved the school and Roberta loved her job. Kate was happy for both of them, but she missed Angie. She'd cried until there were no more tears.

She had promised Mrs. Strickland that she would tell her parents about the baby because she knew she had no choice. In six months, she would have a child.

She'd decided to test her mother first, alone. Besides, she needed her support to confront her daddy. But telling her mother would be no easy feat. Beyond shock, she couldn't predict how Mavis would react.

Kate stepped into the kitchen, paused, and waited for her heart to settle.

"Mamma?"

Mavis stopped stirring a pot of peas and looked around. A ghost of a smile lit her plain features. "I thought you was studying."

"I have been. You need any help with supper?"

"No. It's about ready."

"Mamma, I . . . there's something I have to tell you."

Mavis' eyes narrowed. "You get in trouble at school? If you did, your daddy'll have your hide."

"No, everything's fine at school."

"Then what is it?"

"Mamma, I'm pregnant."

The spoon clanked onto the iron stove, sounding like a gunshot. Mavis grabbed her stomach with both hands and couldn't seem to make a sound other than a soft, pitiful moan.

"Oh, Mamma," Kate cried, moving quickly to her side to help her into the closest rickety chair. She dropped to her knees beside her.

Mavis lowered horror-filled eyes to Kate. "How could you?" she whispered. "How could you?"

Guilt swept through Kate. Her fingers covered her mouth

to stop her own cry. She couldn't back down now. She had to see this painful ordeal through.

"I'm sorry . . . Mamma." Kate's voice caught, and for a moment she couldn't go on. "Please . . . please don't hate me."

"Oh, child, my baby," Mavis said, rocking like a demented soul.

Kate heard the back door slam, followed by the sound of heavy footsteps. Her stomach dropped away in fear. She couldn't get to her feet; her legs had lost their substance.

Emmitt Colson's burly figure filled the doorway. His presence seemed to further shrink the room. The only sound that could be heard was the beating of hearts. Kate didn't know if it was hers or her mother's that pounded the loudest.

"Why ain't my dinner on the table? What's goin' on?"

Somehow, Kate forced her limbs to move. But once she was upright, she remained close to Mavis and stared at her daddy, her fear increasing.

His eyes had that "look," and his words were slightly slurred. Had he been drinking? Or was she mistaken? No. She knew deep down that if he was not drunk already, he was well on his way. His eyes were glazed, and his face was flushed—though if one didn't recognize the symptoms, one might think his color came from good health.

While Kate tried to beat back her panic, she concentrated on his overalls that were splattered with dirt, and part of his breakfast or lunch. Kate turned away, sickened.

Her mother rose to her feet, the fear on her face so stark that it robbed Kate of her next breath. "You're . . . early," Mavis said.

"Don't make no difference. I'm here, and I want to know what's goin' on."

"Why . . . nothing."

His eyes blazed under bushy brows. "Don't you lie to me, woman. When I'm through punishing you, the Lord'll have his turn."

"Mamma—"

"Hush your mouth, child," Mavis said, and stepped in front of her. "Kate and I was just having a little discussion."

Emmitt's face turned livid. He knocked the chair in front of him out of the way and lunged forward, his hand raised.

"No, Daddy!" Kate's muted cry stilled his hand. "It's my fault Mamma doesn't have supper on the table."

"Oh?"

His rage was still close to the surface; Kate could see it in his eyes, in the way he held himself. But she had to tell him. She couldn't let her mother take the blame.

"Daddy—"

"No, baby . . . don't . . . please." Sobs weakened Mavis' voice to a hoarse whisper. But her eyes locked with Kate's, and what Kate saw there stole her breath. She saw love.

At that instant she knew her mother really loved her. Maybe not in the way Kate ached to be loved, with hugs and kisses and kind words. But her mother loved her nonetheless. And for that unguarded moment Kate would always be grateful, because it gave her the strength to go on.

"I'm gittin' tired of this." Emmitt stepped closer, his beefy hands rolled into fists.

"I'm pregnant, Daddy. I'm going to have a baby."

His mouth worked in the silence, but no words came out. Instead he lifted his hand and knocked Kate across the room. She slammed into the wall as a ripping pain tore through her.

"Oh, my God, oh, my God," Mavis whimpered, struggling to get to her daughter.

"Stay where you are." Emmitt's roar froze Mavis midstride. "God will strike you dead if you touch her. In his sight she's filth."

Kate shook her head, even though it pounded like a drum. She struggled to stand.

Emmitt barreled across the room.

"Don't you lay another hand on her," Mavis screamed.

Emmitt stopped and swung around, shock widening his eyes. Kate had never heard her mother talk back to her daddy. She guessed Emmitt hadn't either.

"Oh, I ain't gonna hit her. That's too good for the little slut." His eyes narrowed on Kate. "Git your duds and git out." He spat on the kitchen floor. "I don't wanna see the likes of you or your bastard child again."

Mavis crumpled into the chair and sobbed. "Oh, Emmitt, no."

"Shut up, or I'll send you packin' right along with her."

Kate managed to make it to the door, where she paused, then turned. "Mamma, leave with me."

"Go on, child, do like your daddy said."

With tears streaming down her cheeks, Kate bolted down the hall. It didn't take her long to gather her belongings. She flung open her closet door, grabbed her old duffle bag, and crammed everything she could find into it.

Later, she stumbled back into the deserted kitchen. With trembling fingers, she lifted the phone and dialed. "Angie," she sobbed, "I need your help."

Ten

Two days later Thomas walked through the door of the Stricklands' home. Kate had become part of the Strickland household since her frantic call to Angie, and now she was fulfilling the one request Mrs. Strickland had made. She was meeting with Thomas in order to make a decision about the baby.

Roberta had asked if she and Angie should leave them alone, but Kate had said no. She'd wanted their support because she feared Thomas' quick-trigger temper.

Kate sat in the living room and watched Thomas halt by the fireplace. She searched his face for a hint of his thoughts, but his features gave nothing away.

He was as handsome as ever, dressed in jeans and a powder-blue shirt. His hair was mussed, as if he hadn't bothered to comb it. His sideburns were longer, which made him look even sexier, Kate thought.

She wished she looked better, although she was wearing a new pair of purple pants and a top, one of several outfits that Roberta had bought for her. Nevertheless, she felt dull and washed out.

Their eyes met for a second, and Kate's breathing went haywire. It was all she could do not to leap off the couch and throw herself into his arms. Thomas' expression, however, discouraged any advance. He leaned against the mantel, his face withered by a scowl.

Kate stiffened and tried to ignore the queasy feeling in her stomach that had nothing to do with her condition, aware only of his closeness and the invisible wall between them.

"Kate, what's going on?" he asked. His belligerent eyes darted between the three of them before coming back to her.

She could guess what was going through his mind. He sensed he was in the hot seat, and it was clear he didn't like it.

He had resisted coming here, as she'd known he would. When she'd called him, he'd demanded to know if she'd had the abortion. She had refused to answer, telling him instead that she must see him.

He had argued, but in the end, he had agreed. She figured he'd be wary of Roberta because she had made a point of mentioning that it had been Roberta's idea that they talk.

"Kate, honey, go on, tell him." Roberta's voice broke the lengthening silence.

"Tell me what?" Thomas demanded.

"I'm . . . not . . . I won't have an abortion."

The room fell silent again. Even the sounds of the cars passing up and down the busy street outside failed to penetrate their awareness.

Thomas' lips curved suddenly into a smirk. "I told my old man."

"You told whom?" Roberta's tone showed her chilly disapproval.

"Uh, my daddy."

"That's better," Roberta said.

"Told him what?" Kate asked.

"What do you think? About the baby."

Kate's eyes widened in shock. "You did?"

"Yeah."

"Why . . . I mean . . . " Kate sputtered, thinking that his father would be the last person Thomas would confide in. "What made you do that?"

Hostility blazed from his eyes. "I kinda figured you'd pull

something like this. I haven't met a girl yet who I could trust and I knew you wouldn't be any different."

"What a jerk," Angie muttered under her breath. Still, everyone in the room heard her.

Roberta swung around. "Angie, that's enough."

"Drop dead," Thomas said straight to Angie.

"Stop it, both of you." Anger shook Roberta's voice. "Angie, another word from you, and I'll send you to your room."

"Yes, ma'am."

Thomas flashed Angie a triumphant grin. Then to Kate, "I had to cover my a—" He stopped, cut his eyes to Roberta, then coughed. "Er . . . my butt, so I told him about the baby."

"And what did he say?" Kate asked, while she gripped her hands together in her lap.

"He told me he'd find it a home. There's a couple in the church who've been trying to adopt, but haven't been able to."

Kate blinked in disbelief. Roberta and Angie simply looked at each other.

"What else did he say?" Kate asked, suspicion coloring her tone, unable to believe that Reverend Jennings had taken the news so calmly.

Thomas shrugged. "He was mad at first, but then he cooled off and told me about the family."

"Well, that sounds like the perfectly obvious solution to me," Roberta said, her gaze sweeping over both Kate and Thomas.

Kate clenched and unclenched her fingers, every muscle in her body strained taut as she rested her gaze on Thomas, searching for some warmth, some passion, anything that would let her know he still cared about her.

His face showed nothing, however, and her muscles tightened that much more. Maybe when they were alone again, she could break through that wall of stubborn hostility.

"Kate, honey," Roberta said. "If you still have doubts, you should consider the counseling route. We have a special group at the hospital . . . "

Kate shook her head, then turned to Thomas. "Is adoption what you want?"

His eyes were so piercing, they seemed to dissect her. "I wanted you to have an abortion."

Kate sucked in her breath.

"But adoption's okay," he added quickly.

Kate released her breath and felt the color rush back into her face.

Roberta stood and motioned for Angie. "We'll leave you two alone, let you talk." Angie, looking mutinous, got up and followed her mother out.

"When will I see you again?" Kate asked when they were alone.

Thomas shrugged. "Not anytime soon, that's for sure." As if he sensed he'd said the wrong thing, Thomas backtracked. "Well, maybe I'll come around in a few days. Maybe we'll . . . take in a movie or something, you know."

"I'd like that," Kate responded, feeling her stomach unknot.

Thomas shifted from one foot to the other. "Look, I have to go. I gotta drive back to Four Corners," he added weakly.

"I know," Kate whispered.

Again he fidgeted, cramming his hands into his pockets. "I'll call you, okay?"

"Okay."

When she heard the door close behind him, Kate leaned her head back and let the tears flow. She had never thought of Thomas, herself and the baby as a family. But now that she'd seen him again, she realized how much she still cared. Maybe marriage was a possibility after all.

By the time the baby was born she would still be sixteen. But other girls married at that age. Why couldn't she? Then she wouldn't have to give up her baby.

She would cling to the hope that once the baby was born and Thomas saw the child, he would have a change of heart and love them both.

Angie peeped around the corner. "Is he gone?"

Kate's eyes popped open. "Uh-huh."

"Were you asleep?"

Kate struggled into an upright position and wiped at the tears.

"You want something to drink?" Angie asked in a sober tone, venturing a little farther into the room.

"Not right now. I'm fine."

"Want to talk?"

Kate smiled for the first time in a long while and patted the couch beside her. "Yeah, that sounds good."

Eleven

The October weather was perfect, with cool, sunny days and crisp, cold nights. The woods in the Hill Country flamed with brilliant colors. The faint scent of burning oak logs hung in the air.

The Strickland living room was no exception. Even though Kate sat in the swing in the back yard, she could smell the fire that crackled in the hearth. Before moving outside to the swing, she had curled up on the sofa and watched the yellow and purple flames.

Roberta hadn't thought it a good idea for her to venture outdoors, but Kate had wanted to feel the sunshine. She'd been cooped up in the house far too long.

Now, drawing her coat closer around her, Kate lifted her gaze to the tree beyond the swing where two blue jays played tag. But she found no joy in watching them nor in anything else. Her heart was a block of ice.

Today was Saturday, the day Thomas was coming for the baby. The miracle she'd prayed for hadn't happened. Thomas hadn't loved the baby girl born three days ago. He hadn't even been on hand when the doctor, assisted by Roberta, had delivered her.

Thoughts of the birth sent chills through Kate. She had always had a fear of hospitals that stemmed from her daddy's belief that one didn't get sick, much less go to the hospital.

So when her water had broken, she had begged Roberta to let her stay at the Strickland house and have the baby. Roberta had refused, saying there was always the possibility of complications.

Roberta had been right. There had been complications. Kate developed a tubal infection and as a result, the doctor had told her she would never be able to have another child.

Both Roberta and Angie had cried, but she hadn't shed a tear. She had simply been too exhausted to cope with another trauma. She knew, however, that later, when her body had healed, she would mentally saw herself into pieces.

Kate moaned, the sound coming from deep inside her chest. She wanted to sleep, and to cry. She didn't want to think about the past; neither did she want to think about the future. She couldn't, not when the present was a living nightmare.

Kate shifted positions and winced. The simplest movements required every ounce of energy she possessed. She longed to be strong again.

The phone rang. Her heart raced. Could it be Thomas calling to say he wasn't coming? She strained to hear the conversation through the raised window. When she heard Roberta say she'd be right there, her heart settled. Roberta was on call at the hospital. Already, she'd had to leave twice, and the day was still young. A flu epidemic had struck central Texas. Kate hoped that neither she nor the baby would get it.

With the sun warm on her skin, Kate closed her eyes, but she couldn't relax. For a moment, she longed to see her mother. Why, she didn't know. After fleeing the farm, she'd talked to Mavis only three times. Each time, the conversation had been strained. Her mamma loved her, but not enough to go against her daddy. Sometimes Kate thought her heart couldn't bear the pain any longer.

"Katie?"

She opened her eyes. Roberta stood beside her. "Is . . . is Thomas here?"

"Not yet," Roberta said, "but I have to go to the hospital."

"I know," Kate said. "I heard through the window."

"Reverend Jennings is coming with Thomas, isn't he?"

"He's supposed to. At least that's what Thomas told me when I talked to him and told him about the baby."

Roberta's eyes were anxious. "Well, I don't want them to leave until I get back." She glanced at her watch. "I shouldn't be too long this time."

Kate hoped for Roberta's sake that she was right. Roberta was bone-tired. Even wrapped in her own misery, Kate could see the lines of exhaustion on her face.

"You sure you'll be okay?" Roberta asked.

"I'm sure."

Roberta leaned over and kissed Kate on the cheek. "I know you're grieving, sweetheart, and I hate to leave you even for a minute." She paused. "Angie won't be here, either. She's babysitting both today and tomorrow. One of her classes is planning a trip, and she needs extra money for it." Roberta frowned. "But I . . . we can make other arrangements."

"No, don't. I'll be fine."

Roberta kissed her again. This time Kate felt Roberta's tears; they mingled with hers.

When she was alone, Kate closed her eyes again and ground her teeth together so hard that she could hear the pounding in her ears. And waited.

Kate was inside, on the sofa, holding the baby, when she heard the doorbell chime. She clutched the sleeping child to her breast. The pain inside her was so sharp, she feared her chest would burst. Still, she managed to call out, "Come in."

She peered down into the sweet, innocent face. Sara. She had secretly named her that. How could she give Sara away, the baby she'd held, kissed, cuddled, loved? She didn't think she could. She'd rather die.

Even now, she caressed the delicate features, touching, smoothing, loving. But Kate had to let her go. She'd given her word, and she had to honor it. Besides, what choice did she have? She had no way to care for her baby.

Thomas' voice interrupted her thoughts, but she hadn't understood a word he'd said. Seconds later, Thomas appeared in the doorway. He was alone.

Kate's heart scarcely seemed to be beating. "Where's your father?"

"He couldn't come."

"But . . . but—"

Thomas ignored her stammering and slowly made his way toward the couch. "Have you got the kid ready?"

Is that all he had to say? Kate agonized. No hug? No kiss? *No pain?*

Thomas stood over her. Kate looked up at him and in a choked voice whispered, "Isn't she pretty?" Sara was tiny, barely six pounds. But her features were perfect, and her eyes were big and black like Thomas'.

Thomas glanced at the child, then shrugged. "Yeah, well . . . if you say so."

"Thomas, how can we give up our baby?"

"She's not ours. Never has been."

His indifference struck Kate in the chest like a cold blade. "How can you say that?" She'd even beg if it would do any good.

Thomas shook his head. "My father's found her a home and that's that."

"No!" Kate's cry met a frozen silence.

"It's going to be all right, I promise." Thomas didn't meet her searching gaze, but his tone was cajoling. "Daddy promises. And preachers don't lie."

"Will I . . . we know who gets her?"

"I doubt it. Daddy—uh—said it wouldn't be good for us to know. And adoption is secret stuff. But I think that Daddy's arranged for a couple in El Paso to get her. They used to belong to our church."

"But I can't stand the thought of not seeing—"

"Yes, you can." Thomas' tone went from cajoling to impatient. "Because it's the right thing, for both of us."

Tears clouded Kate's vision and scaled her eyes. "Oh, Thomas."

"Look, you gotta trust me." He sat beside her and placed

an arm around her shoulders, but he kept his eyes averted. "I love our baby too." His tone was soft and persuasive. "And later when we're through with college and married, we'll have another baby."

Another baby. Another baby. Those words ripped through her. *There won't ever be another baby!* She couldn't say those horrible words; she couldn't even think about them. Right now, Sara filled her heart and soul. Kate feared she would lose both if Thomas took her baby.

Sobs forced the breath from Kate's lungs. "I do trust you, only you can't take the baby by yourself. Anyway, Mrs. Strickland said for you not to leave until after she gets back."

Thomas' face darkened, and he lunged to his feet. "I can't wait. I have to leave now."

"Why?"

"Because I just do."

"Why didn't your daddy come?"

"He was tied up." Thomas' eyes flickered past her. "I have to go to work."

"Then come back later."

"I can't."

"Then I'll go with you."

"No!"

Kate drew back. "You don't have to yell." Her lower lip trembled.

"Sorry, but you don't look like you're able to stand, much less travel."

Kate wanted to think he was concerned for her well-being, but she wasn't sure. She wished she understood Thomas better. One minute he was sweet, then the next, not so sweet. "Mrs. Strickland said—"

"I don't give a damn what she said." Thomas took a deep breath. "Just let me have the baby, okay?"

"No, not by yourself," Kate said through clenched teeth.

"Yes, by myself," Thomas responded with cold authority. "I'm taking the kid." His features turned stubborn. "And you can't stop me."

Kate knew he spoke the truth. She couldn't stop him. This

was the moment she'd dreaded, a moment she'd prayed would never happen. But it was happening; she was living its horror.

Thomas grabbed the baby's bag with all its necessities and slipped the straps over his shoulder. Then he held out his arms.

Kate edged backward; her grip on the baby tightened.

"You have to," Thomas said, then wrenched the baby from her arms.

"No!" Kate cried brokenly, her hands outstretched.

Thomas hurried toward the door. Kate opened her mouth to scream at him to please stop, that she'd do anything if only he wouldn't take her baby. But she couldn't say a word. Her throat was paralyzed.

Thomas jerked open the front door, walked out and slammed it behind him. That slam unlocked Kate's legs. She raced across the room, to the door. She reached for the knob, then yanked her hand back. "Please, bring my baby back," she sobbed. "Bring her back."

She heard the car door slam. Another sob slipped from her throat. She turned and ran to Sara's crib. The baby's imprint was on the sheets. She couldn't believe it was empty, that she would never see her child again.

Lodged in the corner of the bed was a tiny stuffed bear. She reached for it, clasped it to her chest, and squeezed. Kate hurt so badly she couldn't move.

"Sara," she finally sobbed, then sank to the floor, doubled over. She bit down on her lower lip. Only after the sound of the car's engine had faded in the distance did she taste the blood.

"Kate, honey, where are you?"

She had heard the kitchen door slam, but she didn't have the stamina to acknowledge it. Her heart lay in a million pieces.

"Kate?" Roberta called again.

Kate still couldn't respond.

Roberta walked into the living room, shedding her coat

and kicking off her shoes. "Oh, there you are," she said to Kate. "I left Angie and got here as soon as I could. Whew, I'm tired. Thank goodness, though, I beat Thomas—" Roberta's voice trailed off as her eyes went from Kate's pain-ravaged face to the empty crib.

"My baby's gone," Kate said in a dull, lifeless tone. "Thomas took her."

"And Reverend Jennings?"

Moving like a windup toy, Kate stood and faced Roberta. "No. Thomas was by himself."

"What?!"

Kate told her what had taken place, except the part about Thomas' threat to take the baby, regardless. When she had finished, Roberta released a shaky breath and eased onto the couch.

"I'd like to get my hands on that young whipper-snapper for disobeying me. Still, we can be sure Reverend Jennings will see to his end of the deal." She paused. "I'll feel better, though, if I call."

Kate didn't respond. Reliving the horror through words had started her tears flowing. She couldn't talk around the lump in her throat.

Several minutes later, Roberta hung up the receiver, a perplexed look on her face. "That's strange," she said.

"What?" Kate's eyes widened. "Has something happened to the baby?"

"No, nothing's wrong there," Roberta said. "Only the reverend wasn't home, so I asked Mrs. Jennings about the baby. She didn't respond for several seconds, then she quickly assured me that everything was all right and not to worry."

Kate wished she felt comforted, but she didn't. "The baby didn't even cry, you know." Her swollen lower lip trembled.

"Just proves she's a real trooper, like her mother." Roberta wiped a tear from her eye. "Are you all right?"

"I'm . . . fine," Kate lied.

"Is there anything I can do, anything you need?"

"No, nothing. I . . . I just want to be alone."

"I understand. We'll talk later, when you feel more like it."

"I . . . love you both, you know."

"We know," Roberta said in her kindest tone. "And we love you."

When Roberta left the room, Kate eased herself back onto the couch, buried her head in a pillow, and sobbed. She knew the agony of this day would haunt her forever.

Twelve

"How do you feel?"

Angie's question drew Kate's eyes from the windshield and back to her friend. For a moment she didn't answer as she watched Angie maneuver the car down the deserted stretch of road.

"About going home, you mean?"

Only a week had passed since she'd given up the baby. The loss was like a wound inside her that gaped with the dawning of each new day. She prayed that it would soon heal because she had no choice but to go on with her life.

It was mid-term in the school year, and she was on her way back to Four Corners, back to her parents' house, back to school.

"Yeah, that's what I mean."

"The truth?"

"Uh-huh."

"I'd rather be shot," Kate said with unusual bluntness.

Angie pursed her lips. "Well, then, why the hell are you going back? You certainly don't have to. It's not like Mamma pitched you out on your ear or anything."

"Oh, Angie," Kate wailed, "it's not that simple and you know it."

"It's that simple to me. You had a home with us and you decided to leave."

Kate sighed. "Are you purposely forgetting Mamma's call?"

"No, but I'd like to."

So would Kate. She could still hear the pain, the hopelessness in Mavis' voice. Her mamma had called the same day Thomas had taken the baby.

She had heard the phone ringing but hadn't reacted, certain that it was the hospital summoning Roberta again. When Roberta had told her it was for her, she'd been stunned.

"Who is it?" she'd asked and crossed her fingers that Roberta would say "Thomas."

"It's your mother."

Kate frowned. "My mother? Is something wrong?"

"I'm afraid there might be," Roberta said, rubbing the back of her neck, her voice as weary as her face. "I asked if I could give you a message, and she gave me a desperate-sounding 'no.'"

Kate reached for the extension phone on the nearby table.

"Mamma?"

When she hung up a few minutes later, she stared at Roberta.

"Heavens, child, you look like you've seen a ghost."

"I have to go home." Kate's voice shook. "Mamma's hurt herself."

"Oh, no. How?"

"She . . . turned a pot of boiling water over on her hand."

"How awful."

"I—"

Roberta interrupted. "There's nothing I can say to talk you out of it?"

A new onslaught of tears filled Kate's eyes, but she squared her shoulders. "No, ma'am."

Now, as she ventured another look at Angie, Kate suddenly wanted to scream. Angie's lips were stretched in a tight, uncompromising line.

"Oh, Angie, you've got to understand that even if Mamma hadn't called, I couldn't sponge off of you another day. You and your mamma have done enough already, more than enough.

"When I came to stay with you before the . . . baby was born—" every time she said the word, it felt as if someone had ripped her heart out—"I didn't intend to stay this long."

"Only you didn't have anywhere else to go, right?"

"Right."

"As far as I'm concerned, you still don't."

"Angie, please, just let me finish, will you?"

Angie shrugged and faced the highway once again.

"Mamma needs me to come back, and Daddy—well, Mamma said he wouldn't stop me."

"That's big of him."

Angie's dark sarcasm drew a faint smile from Kate. "Yeah, I guess it is."

Angie snorted.

Kate's lips burgeoned into a full smile, but the smile faded as quickly as it had come. These days smiles were at a premium.

She didn't want to go to Four Corners, but she didn't have anywhere else to go. Still, Roberta had tried to convince her to go home, see about Mavis, then come back and finish school in New Braunfels. But pride had stood in Kate's way. As she'd told Angie, she'd been a burden long enough and had brought enough chaos into their lives. It had to end. Enough was enough.

The close proximity had strained her relationship with Angie, and the strain hadn't eased after the baby had been born. It had become worse; sometimes Kate sensed that Angie didn't like being alone with her.

Perhaps the main reason she felt she must return home was Thomas. She was determined to find out once and for all where she fit into his life. Not only that, she wanted to talk to Reverend Jennings. She needed reassurance about the baby.

Once she saw Thomas again, she planned to get some straight answers. Then everything would be all right again. She was sure of it.

"Hey, are you still with me?" Angie asked after the car swished by the Four Corners city limit sign.

Kate blinked. "Hook a right at the stop light, will you?"

Angie cut her a sharp glance. "Why? That's not the way to your farm."

"I know. I want to go by Thomas' house."

"Shit, Kate. You're nuts."

Kate's features tightened. "Ang, don't start, okay? I know how you feel about Thomas."

"He's a rat, pure and simple. I just don't understand why you can't see that."

"He's the father of my child."

"Yeah, the father that wanted you to have an abortion, then when you didn't, couldn't wait to give the baby away."

"Please, Angie, don't," Kate whispered in a voice that held the threat of tears.

Angie took a hand off the steering wheel and squeezed one of Kate's, curled in a ball in her lap. "Sorry, but you know me and my big mouth."

This drew a watery smile from Kate. "Boy, do I ever."

"Still love me?"

"Yeah, but I don't know why."

" 'Cause I'm so loveable, that's why."

"Oh, Ang, I'm going to miss you."

"Yeah, me too."

They were silent a while, both lost in their own thoughts. The silence lasted until Angie pulled up in front of the Jennings' house.

"We're here." Angie shut off the engine, sat back against the door and looked at Kate. "Now what?"

Kate licked her lips. "I'll only be a minute."

"You-know-who's standing in the door."

"Oh." Kate fumbled with the handle while trying to combat the flutter in her stomach. Finally, she got out and started up the sidewalk. Thomas met her halfway. She caught the firm set of his jaw, the glint in his eyes. Her heart stumbled.

"What are you doing here?" he demanded in a taut voice.

She didn't back down. "I wanted to talk to you."

Sweat beaded on his face, and his eyes skidded back toward the house. "Over here," he said. "I don't want my parents to see us."

He pulled her with him behind a huge oak. "So talk," he

said, blowing back a stray lock of hair that had fallen to his forehead.

Kate's courage dwindled. This wasn't going to be as easy as she'd hoped. He was acting as stubborn as one of her daddy's mules. But when she told him why she was here, he'd change his attitude.

"I've come home, to stay. I wanted you to know."

"Okay, so you've told me."

Kate pushed aside her skyrocketing fear. "I also want to know about the baby." She was hungry for the tiniest crumb of information.

"Daddy's taken care of everything."

"I know, but I still want to hear what the people are like."

Thomas looked away. "They're nice, I'm sure."

"Do they have money?" Kate pressed.

"Uh, I don't know. Actually, my old man didn't tell me much."

"Maybe I could talk to him, then."

"Forget it," Thomas snapped. "And don't think about going to him behind my back either. If you do, we'll be finished."

"Oh, Thomas, how can you say that? After all, we made that tiny creature."

Thomas' face drained of color. "I don't want you to ever mention that again, you hear?"

"You can't deny the baby," she said gently, and reached for his hand.

"I'm not denying it, okay? But you've got to drop it." He played with her hand while his voice once again took on that mesmerizing tone. "It's time we both got on with our lives, thought about our future."

"But—"

"The baby's gone." His eyes were brooding. "You've got to understand that." He pushed away from the tree, then glanced at his watch. "Look, it's getting late. I have to go, but I'll call you soon." He leaned over and pecked her on the cheek.

As Kate watched him make his way back to the front steps, a pain struck her so deep inside that she almost doubled over. Her baby was gone forever. Thomas had faced that fact; now it was her turn. For her, though, it wasn't that simple.

She ached to run, to nurse her wounds in private, but Angie was waiting for her. If she didn't return to the car soon, Angie would come looking for her.

Kate composed herself, as best she could, and walked back to the car.

Life at home settled quickly into the same old pattern.

Kate's first day back, her mother had asked her about the baby. Kate had told her what had taken place, but neither had been comfortable discussing that terrible time, so Kate vowed not to talk about it again. Of course, Emmitt hadn't asked, and she had known why. She was sure he was drinking again. She had only to look into her mamma's bleak, sad face to know. At least Mavis' hand was healing.

She still found it hard to believe that Emmitt had allowed her back into the house. Maybe he had softened somewhat under that bulldozing facade, or else her mother had stood up to him for once and won. Kate suspected it was the latter, but she didn't probe too deeply. Her mother needed her and that was what counted.

Kate had found a job at the local pizza place and was happy about that; but Thomas remained unfinished business. She'd been back in school three days without having seen him.

Now as she walked out of her last class of the day, her mind churned. Where was he? She peeked at her watch. Maybe she should go by his house. It would be out of her way, but she didn't have to be at the pizza parlor as early as usual today. Maybe she would even see Reverend Jennings. Yet she hesitated, remembering Thomas' warning.

Her hesitation was short-lived. Regardless of whether or not she encountered Reverend Jennings, she had to know about Thomas. She had conjured up too many terrible things that might have befallen him not to check.

She started across the school grounds, only to stop short.

Wade Jackson blocked her path. She detested him. Not only was he repulsive to look at, she thought, taking in his shirt stretched so tight around his fat belly that she expected the material to split, but he was equally repulsive to talk to. The way he *looked* at her was even more disgusting.

"Why, if it isn't the high-and-mighty Miss Colson."

She ignored his dig. "Have you seen Thomas?"

"Who wants to know?"

"Jackson, you're a real jerk, you know that?"

His features twisted. "And you think you're better than everyone, even though you ain't a bit better than me. Why, honey, we come from the same gutter."

"Go take a flying leap." With that, Kate pivoted on her heels.

"I thought you wanted to know about your lover boy."

Kate stopped and swung back around. "If you have anything to say, then say it."

"He ain't here."

"So tell me something I don't know."

Wade snickered. "Well, I betcha you don't know he's gone, as in moved out of town. Yeah, his old man got a call to another church, and they hooked 'em." He paused and scratched his chin as if to let his bombshell hit its target. "Two days ago, to be exact."

Thomas gone? No! That wasn't possible. He wouldn't just leave town without telling her. Would he?

"You mean he didn't tell you?" Jackson asked, continuing to taunt her and obviously enjoying every second of it.

Kate tried to swallow the pain in her throat before it choked her. She couldn't. Oh, dear Lord, her humiliation was complete. Add that to her misery, and she feared she might throw up on the spot. She could only remain motionless and listen to Jackson's crude, knowing laugh.

"Maybe now you'll come down off your high horse." Wade edged closer. "You don't know what you're missing by not going out with *me*." He poked his chest out. "I've always had a hankering for you, you know."

Kate cringed inside. It was true that Wade had suggested several times that the two of them should go out, that he could show her a better time than Thomas. Of course, she had ignored him. The thought of stepping out the door with the creep was frightening in itself.

As if taking her silence for acquiescence, Wade reached out and traced a finger down her arm. "So, how 'bout it? How 'bout you and me gettin' together?"

Kate slapped his hand. "Don't you dare touch me . . . you . . . you—"

Wade grabbed her arm and jerked her against his fat belly, his lips drawn in a cruel line. "So you still think I'm not good enough for you, huh?"

"Let me go!"

He did, but not before he laughed crudely. "Well, lemme tell you something else, honey. Thomas didn't think you or your brat were good enough for him."

"You . . . know about the baby?" Kate barely got the words through her paralyzed lips.

"Sure do. Yeah, Thomas couldn't wait to get rid of you both."

"That's a lie!" Kate cried. "You're just saying those horrible things because I won't go out with you."

"Oh yeah?" Wade moved in close to her face, his anger visible in his bulging eyes. "Wanna know the real kicker?" He grinned. "There wasn't no adoption."

"Stop it!" Kate cried again and lifted her hands over her ears.

Wade jerked them down and laughed outright.

"Just shut up!" Kate was screaming, but she didn't care.

"Not yet, honey, not until you hear the truth."

"Just shut up, you hear!" she repeated.

Wade paid her no heed. "Yeah, your lover boy not only dumped you, but he also dumped your brat in a ratty motel room like it was a sack of garbage."

Thirteen

Austin, Texas. Spring 1993

Kate Colson maneuvered her Cadillac Seville into the parking space marked JUDGE KATE COLSON. Once she had switched off the motor, she sat unmoving for a moment and stared at the sign, her gaze focused on the word JUDGE.

She had slaved nineteen years to earn that prestigious title, and she aimed to hold on to her appointment by getting herself elected. It wouldn't be easy to hold on to her job. Several qualified men wanted to unbench her. But whenever Kate's stamina faltered for a second, she recalled all the years of drudgery and heartache she'd left behind.

The days, weeks, and months that followed the nightmare of losing both her baby and Thomas had proved too much for Kate. The day she'd graduated from high school, she'd left Four Corners, but not before she'd learned a valuable lesson. No matter what the consequences, she vowed to stand up for herself and her rights, especially when it came to men. From that day forward, she'd taken charge of her life.

Kate had held true to her vow. Through scholarships and part-time jobs, she had worked her way through the University of Texas in Austin. Her stomach rumbling and her heart aching, she'd crawled into bed each night denying her hunger for food and love because she had sacrificed both for a future. Finally help had come from a wealthy and kind friend, Marlo Price, who had the kind of father Kate had always dreamed of.

Patient and giving, Richard Price had stood in sharp contrast to Kate's own father, who had plunged deeper into alcohol after her mother had died of a stroke during Kate's first year at the university. Price respected Kate's intelligence and drive and had hired her as a legal secretary at one of his companies. She had worked for him for four years and had earned a good salary, but her savings had shrunk after her father suffered a cerebral hemorrhage and had to be put in a private nursing home.

After he died, Kate had decided to become an attorney, having felt the need for a new challenge. Her intelligence, past scholastic achievement and a terrific recommendation from Price had won her admission into law school.

Three years later she graduated and became an associate in the most prestigious law firm in Austin; Johns and Strassberg. It was there that she met Harlan Moore, the firm's number-one client, a man who basked in the power and success his real estate empire brought him. Dave Nielson, who had handled Harlan's business in the firm had asked Kate to help him straighten out a problem with Harlan's taxes, but he hadn't been pleased when Kate had found ways to decrease Harlan's tax bill by thousands of dollars before he could. Dave had been out of town when the firm had called upon Kate to present Harlan with her findings, and afterwards Dave had blamed Kate for his embarrassment and loss of prestige in the firm.

Dave's loud objection to her, however, hadn't stopped Kate from advancing. Everyone in the firm recognized her intelligence and commitment. She soon became a senior partner and only a few years later was appointed to the bench.

Harlan, who liked to have the brightest people on his side, had backed her one hundred percent—until she'd refused to use her influence with another judge to guarantee that Harlan would win his court case on a large land deal. He'd been livid and had vented his feelings with a vengeance that even now had the power to make Kate's legs go weak.

He'd charged into her chambers after everyone else had gone. Kate had been sorting through her case load for the next day when the door had burst open. Startled, she'd looked up and watched as Harlan barreled across the threshold.

"What the hell happened?"

He wasn't yelling at her, but he was close to it, so close that Kate pressed her lips together, deciding to let him have his say before she did.

He finally halted in front of her desk. "I thought we had an understanding."

Kate took in his flushed face and drawn mouth. Until now she had always thought of him as a good-looking man, who, in his sixties, had taken care of his body. Though short and stocky, he carried himself as if he were six feet tall. His neck and shoulders were thick with the muscles of age rather than the hard muscles of a younger man. Still, that flaw failed to detract from his mane of thick, silver hair and his ice-blue eyes. All together, he made a commanding figure and stood out in any crowd. He was shrewd, ambitious, and polished. The latter had gotten him where he was today.

"Well?"

His sneering tone caused Kate to narrow her eyes. "I told you up front that I wouldn't intercede for you."

"But I thought I explained why you had no choice but to do just that."

Kate shrugged. "I don't take orders from you, Harlan, not now, not ever."

"Dammit, Kate, you're where you are because of me!"

Kate didn't raise her voice, although she longed to tell him to get the hell out of her office and never come back. Her hands began to shake; she clutched them together, refusing to let this man intimidate her. But she couldn't burn any bridges, either. She had to make him understand how she operated, how her code of ethics worked.

Kate leaned back in her chair, but she kept her eyes on

Harlan. "Not entirely," she said with quiet authority, "although I will concede your influence helped. And you know how much I appreciate what you've done for me." She paused, letting her words sink in. "On the other hand, I never asked for your help; it was volunteered. And at no time did I ever indicate to you that I would compromise my principles for you or anyone else."

Harlan balled his hands into tight fists. "Winning that land deal case was important to me, and you could've helped me, goddammit!"

Kate stood. "Apparently you didn't hear a word I—"

"Oh, I heard you, all right!" he shot back, mimicking her tone. "But that still doesn't right a gross wrong. You and your holier-than-thou attitude got me fucked real good, lady."

Kate noticed the rapid pulse in the thickening vein that stood out on Harlan's neck as he fought for control. She had never seen him in such a state before, and for a moment, she fought off a sense of uneasiness. But when she spoke, her tone belied her fear. Her voice was icy cold. "I'm sorry you feel that way."

Harlan slammed a fist down on the desk. "Sorry! Is that all you can say?"

The situation suddenly seemed so absurd that Kate almost laughed. "Don't you think you're blowing this out of proportion? After all, you're the one who put yourself in an untenable position with the state land board, not me."

"And I resent you for not coming to my rescue!" he snapped. "Where I come from friends look out after friends. And you owe me!"

"Not if it means compromising my principles."

"We'll see about that!"

Without saying another word, Harlan stormed out of the chambers, slamming the door behind him.

Kate remembered sinking back into her chair with a burning throat and a dry mouth.

That incident had taken place two months ago, and although she'd seen Harlan several times since, he'd made no mention of it. But if he hadn't been an enemy before, he certainly was now.

The smell of fresh coffee, mingling with the scent of peach potpourri, greeted Kate as she opened the door to her chambers. She silently blessed her thoughtful court coordinator, Leslie Stringer, and walked to the tiny bar in the corner of the room, where she poured herself a cup of coffee, then slipped out of her jacket. Although it was only the middle of June, it was already hot.

Kate's eyes scanned the room. For a judge's chamber, it wasn't half bad, she conceded, but only because she'd worked at making it that way.

When she'd first walked into the room after the previous judge had vacated it, she'd been appalled. It had been cold and austere. That hadn't daunted her, however, and she had set about immediately to make it her own. Now, it was tastefully, though not elegantly, decorated, with the small bay window as its focal point. The window, overlooking a busy intersection, was covered with teal-colored mini-blinds.

Several watercolor prints adorned the walls and a bookcase dominated one side of the chamber. In front of her desk two leather-and-wood chairs were arranged on a teal and blue area rug that added an extra splash of color to the beige carpeting.

Kate turned to her desk; a thick folder beckoned. Instead of sitting down, she walked to the window, drawn by the noise from outside. She watched as an old car chugged down Guadalupe Street, leaving a trail of exhaust fumes behind. Such was life in the city, she thought, shaking her head.

Situated on the Colorado River and labeled the gateway to the Hill Country, Austin thrived. And Kate loved living there. She'd felt that way from the very first moment she'd seen it. Nothing could surpass the belts of rolling plains and rugged hills, hills that were covered with oak and hickory forests.

She often thought of the city as a fairy land, especially when it was ablaze with lights. Only it wasn't night and she had work to do. Still, Kate didn't move. She attributed her mental unrest to the fact that she was about to hear a case that involved a child.

Kate always took pride in her ability not to let anything personal bear on her rulings. Today, though, she found she couldn't steer her mind in the right direction.

The defendant, Wayne Jordan, a soft-spoken computer engineer, had been found guilty and placed on probation a year ago for sexually molesting his adopted daughter. Now, he had violated that probation on a repeated offense, and was due back in court.

Kate hadn't wanted to hear this particular case, but neither did the senior judges. Because she was new, she ended up with the case.

Still, cases involving children, especially abused ones, unnerved her. Today's hearing weighed heavy on her mind, bringing to the surface all her old feelings about her own child. She thought about that day so long ago when Wade Jackson had told her that Thomas had left town—but not before he'd dumped her baby like a piece of garbage.

Kate couldn't remember how long she'd stood in front of a jeering Wade before she'd broken into a run, not stopping until she'd reached a clump of trees. She'd grabbed hold of one, while hot, searing fury had washed through her.

Wade hadn't meant what he had said about the baby, she'd told herself over and over. His cruel words had been pure rubbish coming from someone who was jealous and vindictive.

Yet later that evening, as she'd stood at the window in her drab, tiny bedroom and watched sleet slash against the pane, she'd felt sickeningly guilty, foolish and more alone than she'd ever been in her life. Most of all, she'd felt scared. What if Wade had told her the truth? If so, she should track Thomas down through the new minister and try to find Sara.

But everything inside Kate had rebelled at the thought that Wade had spoken the truth. The idea that Thomas could be that cruel was so horrifying that it couldn't be true.

She convinced herself that Wade's warped mind and hurt pride had forced him to make up the story.

Wade aside, she had still lost her child and her boyfriend

and her grief had been raw, straight from the soul. Rage had simmered inside her, heated her blood. She'd known then as she knew now that Thomas had never loved her, that his pretense of loving her had merely been a ploy to have sex. His promise of a future had been the ultimate betrayal.

"Kate."

The unexpected sound of her name brought Kate back to the moment at hand. Shaking her head as if to clear it, she swung around to see her coordinator standing in the door.

"Sorry, I didn't mean to startle you," Leslie Stringer said in her soft tone.

Kate waved her hand. "No apology necessary. I'm glad you did. I was woolgathering, which never accomplished anything."

Leslie smiled at the same time she lifted a loose strand of hair off her cheek and shoved it behind her ear. "I didn't know you ever woolgathered."

Kate shifted her gaze. "As a rule, I don't."

Leslie looked at her curiously as if waiting for her to explain further. When Kate remained silent, she said in a business tone, "Well, it's time for you to be in court."

Kate reached for her robe. "I'll be glad when this one is behind me."

"I know you will." Leslie paused. "That s.o.b. ought to be castrated."

Kate's eyes widened, then she laughed. "Why, Leslie Stringer!"

Leslie blushed but made no apologies. "Well, he should."

"That would certainly solve a lot of the court's problems, but unfortunately I don't have that kind of power."

The room fell silent while Kate slid into her robe and snapped it closed. She looked up and stared off into space for a moment, a grim tightness to her full lower lip.

"Are you all right?" Leslie asked.

Kate gave her a weak smile. "I'm fine. Let's just get this over with, shall we?"

Fourteen

"All rise!"

The loud, nasal voice of the bailiff, Ben Applegate, brought the courtroom to life.

Kate opened the door, moved deliberately into the courtroom and walked up the steps to the chair behind the bench.

"District Court 165 is now in session, the Honorable Kate Colson presiding," Ben said. "Please be seated."

The few scattered spectators did as they were told, then focused their eyes on Kate.

"This is Case Number 14,432, the State of Texas versus Wayne Jordan. This is a hearing on revocation, application to revoke probation. What says the State?"

Prosecuting attorney Frank Parnell lumbered to his feet. As usual he was wearing too much cologne, Kate thought, the offensive smell reaching her. Maybe he thought it might in some way mask the fact that he was short, overweight and bald. Yet she found no fault with his work. He was a crackerjack assistant D.A.

"Ready, Your Honor," he said, mopping his brow with a white handkerchief.

"What says the defendant?" Kate asked.

The defense attorney, Albert Loftin, stood. In appearance he was the opposite of Parnell. He was young, tall, blond,

100

and good-looking. And cocky, Kate reminded herself, listening to his smooth but oily voice, "Ready, Your Honor."

"All right." Kate's gaze included both attorneys. "Do you desire reading the allegations of the application to revoke probation?"

"No, Your Honor," Mr. Loftin said.

Kate turned her attention to the defendant. "You're Wayne Jordan?"

"Yes, ma'am."

"Mr. Jordan, do you understand why you are here?"

"Yes, Your Honor," Loftin said, speaking for him. "He's on probation and the State's seeking to revoke it."

"And Mr. Jordan, you know the State's allegation, which says that you violated the terms of your probation." Kate's voice was firm but soft as her eyes rested on the defendant. He was a large man, with stooped shoulders and a drooping head. Never had he looked her in the eye when she'd talked to him. "Do you understand?"

"Yes, ma'am."

"How do you plead to this allegation?"

"Not guilty."

Kate's brow furrowed. "Do you plead true or not true? You plead not true to this—is that what you mean by not guilty? You're pleading that this allegation to revoke your probation is not true?"

"That's correct," Jordan said.

"Do you understand that this is an application to revoke probation?" Kate asked, fighting a mounting frustration. "This is not what we call a new trial."

The defendant's gaze remained shifted. "Yes, ma'am."

"You understand that. And yet you're saying that the allegation, which maintains that you violated the terms of your probation on a repeated offense is not true. And you're requiring the State to prove this? Is this correct?"

"Yes, ma'am."

"Do you have any questions about the proceedings?" Kate asked.

"No, ma'am."

"It's my understanding that your attorney has been appointed by the court. Are you satisfied with him?"

"Yes, ma'am."

"I'm ready for the witnesses to be called."

"I'm ready, Your Honor," Loftin said.

"Is the State ready to proceed?" Kate asked, turning to Frank Parnell.

"State's ready."

"Other than your first witness," Kate said, "let's have all the witnesses stand and be sworn. All witnesses who may testify in this case, please stand and raise your right hand."

Once the witnesses were sworn in, Kate continued, "Witnesses please wait outside. You'll be called to testify. You may not discuss your testimony with other witnesses, and they may not discuss their testimony with you."

Wayne Jordan's attorney stood. "Your Honor, the young man in the back, Wayne Jordan, Jr., who may be called to testify, may not realize why he is here. He didn't stand up and wasn't sworn in. I don't mind if you swear him in later, but he may be called as a witness."

Kate's gaze targeted the ten-year-old boy. "You may be called as a witness. Stand and be sworn in."

"I don't want to," Wayne Jr. said.

"It doesn't make any difference whether you want to or not," Kate said. "You're here in the courthouse. Hold up your right hand. In the testimony you give in this case, do you swear to tell the truth, the whole truth, and nothing but the truth so help you God?"

"No, I ain't—"

"Son, this court means you no harm," Kate interrupted, her tone sympathetic. "I'm sure you want to do what's best for your sister. Now, please, let's try again. The testimony you may give in this case, do you swear to tell the truth, and nothing but the truth so help you God? Do you promise to do that?"

"I don't know nothing," Wayne, Jr. said.

"You may not. I don't know. But you must try to cooperate." Kate kept her tone soft and sympathetic, trying to calm the boy's fear so that he would trust her.

"Yeah, all right," Wayne Jr. said, albeit reluctantly.

The room was quiet while the belligerent youngster was sworn in, then sauntered out the door.

"Ready, counselors?" Kate asked. Both nodded. "Then proceed."

The assistant district attorney stood. "I call Elsie Jordan to the stand."

Kate listened as Parnell questioned Jordan's daughter as to her name, place of birth, residence and so forth.

Elsie was a lovely child, Kate thought, watching the various emotions play across her face as the attorney questioned her. But it was when Parnell pointed to the defendant and asked if Elsie knew that man, that her facade crumbled. Tears welled in her eyes, then trickled down her thin face.

"He's . . . he's my daddy," Elsie said with a gulp.

"Did Wayne Jordan ever live in your home with you and your mother?" Parnell asked.

"Yes, sir."

"How long has he lived in the home with you and your mother?"

"Ever since I was born."

"Now, has Wayne Jordan ever touched you or done anything to you that you didn't think was right?"

"Yes, sir."

"And when was that?"

"He did it twice. A year ago and then two months ago."

"Are you sure about the two months?"

"Yes, sir."

"Why are you so sure?"

" 'Cause it was my thirteenth birthday."

"Were you home alone?"

"Yes, sir, at least that's what I thought. But I think my brother might've been home."

"And what's his name?"

"Wayne Junior."

"Will you please tell the Court what happened that day, Elsie?"

"Well, I . . . er . . . was in my room on the bed looking

through my picture album when he . . . he came in and sat on the bed."

"What time was this, Elsie?"

She shrugged. "About ten at night."

"How was your daddy dressed?"

"In his drawers."

"His drawers? You mean underwear?"

Elsie nodded.

"What did you have on?"

"My night gown."

"Go on," Parnell encouraged.

"He . . . didn't say nothing . . . just told me to take off my gown and lie back down."

"And did you?"

Elsie hung her head, then mumbled, "Yes, sir."

"Why?"

" 'Cause he'd hurt me if I didn't."

"What happened next?"

"He . . ." Elsie took a deep, faltering breath. "He . . . touched me all over, then . . . he . . . got on top of me."

"Then what did he do?"

"He . . . stuck his thing inside me."

"Is that what you understand his penis to be?"

"Yes, sir."

"Go on."

"He started doing it."

Elsie was weeping now. Frank Parnell handed her several tissues. When she was again composed, he said in a low, calm tone, "What happened when he finished?"

"He . . . burned me with his cigarette."

Wayne Jordan lunged to his feet. "That's a goddamn lie! She burned herself!"

Kate slammed down the gavel; it sounded like a bullet through a plate glass window. "Sit down, Mr. Jordan. Another outburst like that, and I'll cite you for contempt of court." Kate's voice was cold. "Is that clear?"

"Yes, ma'am," he said in a sullen tone, while glaring at his daughter.

Kate turned to Jordan's attorney. "Mr. Loftin, see that

from now on, you control your client. This Court will not tolerate another outburst."

Red-faced, Loftin stood. "I'll see to it, Your Honor."

"Proceed then."

Parnell picked up a stack of photographs. "I'd like to enter these pictures as evidence, Your Honor."

"So ordered."

For the next three hours, and without further incident, Kate listened as the witnesses both for and against Wayne Jordan gave their testimonies. The testimonies were followed by the summations from both attorneys, to which Kate listened carefully.

The time finally came when she made her ruling. "After hearing the evidence, the Court finds the allegations to be true in Case Number 14,432 and the Court hereby revokes your probation and sentences you to ten years in the Texas Department of Criminal Justice, Institutional Division, and further the Court assesses a fine in the amount of ten thousand dollars."

A murmur went through the courtroom

Wayne Jordan lowered his chin into the vee of his shirt.

Kate stared at him a moment longer, then stood while the bailiff said, "This court is adjourned. All rise!"

Fifteen

She couldn't put the case behind her. The bastard deserved a life sentence without parole, Kate fumed as she stared at the copies of the pictures submitted as evidence. They were scattered on her living room floor where she'd flung them.

She'd left the courthouse a short while ago and was now in her fifty-year-old refurbished home with its exposed beams and gleaming hardwood floors. She had found the house southwest of downtown in an area called Terrytown. Most of the homes were old, but nearly all had been renovated. Kate felt that her home was located on the loveliest street in the neighborhood, the corner of Poquonick and Woodlawn.

Here, she could be herself, drop her composed facade, putter with her plants and bake her favorite pastries in the large kitchen, which was the heart of the house. But she loved the living room, too, with its large skylight and wide hearth and antiques that she'd lovingly collected from around the world.

This evening the pleasure she coveted eluded her, however. The pictures, showing the physical abuse of the child, were unnerving her; she couldn't concentrate on anything other than the case.

Kate made her way to the French doors that opened onto a terraced patio where, on the weekends, she enjoyed sipping her coffee and watching the birds. Feeling the tug of the night air, she thrust open the door and walked out. The lovely smells of a rambling rose bush in bloom and fragrant honeysuckle swamped her senses. She lifted her thick mane of hair and felt the breeze caress her moist skin.

"Let it go, Kate!" Speaking aloud had little effect on her heavy heart. She wished she could let it go, but she couldn't. The hearing had reaffirmed her desire to find her daughter.

She turned, walked back inside, and then made her way upstairs to her bedroom. She didn't pause until she reached the attached bath with its sunken bathtub big enough for two. Peach carpet, a skylight and a dressing room with an antique full-length mirror added to the room's charm.

A short time later, Kate climbed out of the tub, smelling like lilac body wash. She then slipped into a robe and padded downstairs to the living room. The pictures, still strewn across the rug, seemed to mock her.

Averting her eyes, she plopped onto the couch and hugged a cushion to her chest, remembering the sage advice that an old and wiser judge had given her after she'd been appointed.

She'd been in Andrew Pearson's office one afternoon, and his twinkling eyes had rested on hers. "Would you take offense, my dear, if I offered you some good advice?"

"Of course not." Kate had smiled with eagerness. "Anything you can tell me that will keep me from looking like a fool will be appreciated."

Andrew had chuckled. "I'm not worried about that. But what does concern me are the pressures you're going to be under when you perform your duties. I guess what I'm saying in a roundabout way is that it's damn hard to pass judgment on others. Does that make sense?"

"I'm afraid it does. Working in a law office insulates you from actually playing God."

"Exactly. But when you walk into that courtroom in that robe, you're on an entirely different playing field. And the rules change."

"Put like that, it's frightening."

"It's worse than that," Andrew had responded bluntly. "It's mind-boggling. Most of the time the people you're judging deserve what they get. Regardless, though, it won't be easy to look them in their baby blues and sentence them to life behind bars, or worse, to death." He had paused, then continued, "Despite how you feel personally, if it's the right thing to do, you'll do it. But the real kicker is living with that decision."

"Which means living with myself," Kate had said in a small voice."

"And letting it go. If you take it home with you, the job will take its toll, and you won't be worth a damn."

Kate had let out a slow breath.

"So, are you sure you're up to the challenge?"

Kate's answer had come readily. "I'm sure."

Remembering that conversation, Kate laughed without humor. She'd been so sure that day, only to have that confidence slowly fade.

She'd had every intention of taking Andrew's advice and making it a rule that when she shed her robe at the end of the day, she'd shed the problems as well. For the most part, she'd remained committed to that promise, if for no other reason than to preserve her mental well-being.

But cases like this one got a hold on her emotions and wouldn't let go. She squeezed her eyes shut. Nothing would be accomplished by dredging up the past, but she was so vulnerable when it came to children who were adopted by a family of "good standing." Despite Wade's cruel words to the contrary nineteen years earlier, Kate had clung to the belief that Thomas' father had indeed placed her baby with a loving family. Yet lately she'd begun to question whether what had happened to Elsie Jordan could have happened to her Sara.

A soft, pained moan escaped Kate's lips. For nineteen years she hadn't felt whole, despite her success. Although she had functioned well behind a professional facade, the pain, the need to know what had become of her child, had never entirely left her.

Early on, she had kept from surrendering to those yearnings of the heart; she'd had nothing to offer her child, not even enough food to eat. Then, after she had acquired the necessary resources, Kate still hadn't tried to locate her daughter.

Apprehension had shackled her as if she were a prisoner with chains around her feet. What right did she have to interfere in her daughter's life, to disrupt it? Kate had known that if she had ever located Sara, she wouldn't have been able to stay away.

Now, she wasn't so sure she'd made the right decision. What if her daughter was in the same situation as this other teenager? It was improbable, but not impossible. That chilling thought made Kate's mind reel, and while she still didn't have the right to charge into her nineteen-year-old daughter's life and say, "Guess what, I'm your mother," she wanted reassurance that Sara had been raised in a safe environment.

Feeling as if her head was going to burst, Kate stood, only to feel her stomach flip-flop.

Clapping her hand over her mouth, she raced from the living room into the nearest bathroom. She knelt over the commode and was sicker than she'd ever been.

Angie Strickland Gates parked her Honda in the garage next to Kate's Cadillac and got out. Her steps were heavy as she made her way onto the porch.

The second she let herself into the double-wide front door, she called out, "Yo, Kate."

Kate had left the bathroom and was now back on the couch sipping a cup of tea, hoping to keep her stomach from further revolt.

"In here, Ang," Kate answered, setting her cup on the coffee table and watching as her friend strode into the room. At thirty-five, Angie's face bore no signs of aging. She was lovely, with curves in all the right places, especially her breasts and hips. She wore her auburn hair in a stylish bob that highlighted her green eyes and olive skin.

Yet Angie's looks had bought her little happiness. In fact, her beauty had lured her into poor choices where men were concerned. Angie had moved to Austin several months earlier after a messy divorce that had left her depressed and in financial ruin. Because of both, her ex-husband had managed to get temporary custody of her three-year-old daughter. He then had taken the child to Boston on a job transfer, making it difficult for Angie to honor her visitation rights.

Kate had paid back a longstanding debt by letting Angie move in with her until she could get back on her feet. So far, the relationship had worked, mainly because both were gone a good deal of the time. Angie worked as a secretary for a very demanding boss, whom Kate suspected took advantage of her. Angie would have to learn to stand up and fend for herself, just as Kate had learned to do.

"Geez, you look like something the dogs drug up and the cats wouldn't have," Angie said.

"Thanks, I feel like it, too."

"Bad day, huh?"

Kate laughed, but there was no humor in it. "That's putting it mildly. I'd say it's the worst day I've had since taking over the bench."

"Whoa." Angie flopped down beside Kate on the couch and threw her a sideward glance. "Anything you want to talk about?"

Kate's lower lip trembled. "I'm not sure I can."

"Want to give it a try?" Angie kicked off her flats, then curled her feet under her. "I have all night."

Kate didn't say anything for the longest time, trying to collect her thoughts. Maybe if she talked, some of the demons would disappear, and she would be able to put things back in perspective.

"Was it a bad case?" Angie pressed softly.

Kate rose and walked to the French doors. After a moment, she turned around, a tortured expression on her face. Angie frowned but waited for her to speak.

"I had to rule on a child abuse case today."

Angie's lips tightened. "I admire your courage, but I couldn't do that. I don't have the stomach for it."

"Sometimes, I'm not sure I do either."

"Yes, you do. You're the strongest woman I know. In fact, you've got more balls than most men I know."

Kate's mouth turned down. "I'll take that as a compliment."

"It was meant as one."

If Angie only knew how Kate's insides felt like warm putty she wouldn't say that.

"Go on, tell me about it," Angie pressed. "It might help relieve that pressure building inside you."

Kate sighed. "Maybe you're right." She began talking then. When she finished, the room was eerily silent. Finally, Kate whispered, "Ang, do you think I did the right thing?"

They both knew she wasn't referring to the case she had just described. Instead she referred to that day when she had let Thomas take her baby, a day that hadn't ever been discussed between the two of them.

Angie shifted her gaze. "Over the years I've asked myself that same question; I never trusted Thomas."

Kate couldn't help but hear the bitterness that crept into Angie's voice when she mentioned Thomas.

"Tell me something, will you? What made you hate and distrust Thomas so much?" Kate had longed to ask that question of her friend many times, but never had had the courage for fear Angie's answer would turn her against Thomas.

Again Angie shifted her gaze.

A crease suddenly marred Kate's otherwise unlined forehead. "Angie?"

Angie lurched off the sofa and paced the floor. Kate tracked her with her eyes, remaining silent. Suddenly Angie stopped, spun around, and blurted, "Thomas and I were lovers."

Kate blinked. "What?"

"It's true," Angie said in a dull tone.

Kate struggled to come to terms with what her friend had just told her, but she couldn't. Her mind refused to accept the admission. "But . . . but . . . " Her voice failed.

"Now you know why I never told you. I knew you'd react this way. You would've thought I was a tramp who slept with her best friend's boyfriend."

"Oh, Angie, I'd never think that about you." Shock had

settled in and Kate found it difficult to even talk. "You . . . were my best friend."

Angie hung her head. "That's why I couldn't tell you. I was too ashamed." Her head came up. "But to set the record straight, I slept with Thomas before you ever started going with him. The s.o.b. used to hold it over my head; he threatened to tell you if I didn't do what he wanted." Angie paused and let out a pent-up breath.

"Ang, what a mess." Kate's voice cracked.

Angie clamped her lips together.

Kate tilted her head, a premonition urging her on, "There's more, isn't there? You're holding something back. I know you almost as well as I know myself. Tell me. It couldn't be any worse."

For the first time, tears glistened in Angie's eyes. "Believe me, it is."

Kate swallowed against an unknown fear. "I'm listening."

"Thomas bragged to me that he hadn't taken Sara to his parents after all, but rather had left . . . left her at a motel on the south side of Austin." Ignoring Kate's horrified gasp, Angie went on, as if she couldn't control her tongue now that she had started. "He'd thought by leaving her there that someone would find her and take her to the proper authorities."

Kate struggled to speak through her numb lips. When she failed, Angie continued in that same hyper-driven voice, "I didn't believe him, of course. I just thought he was blowing off steam. So why add to your pain and heartache by coming to you with such a far-fetched tale?"

Kate flinched as if Angie had physically struck her. "My God, if only you'd told me."

"I came close a couple of times. But then Wade told you," Angie responded a trifle defensively, "and you didn't believe him."

"But that's different," Kate cried, rebounding from the blow. "Wade was a first-class creep who never told the truth. But if you'd told me Thomas had said it, I'd have had second thoughts."

Angie rubbed her forehead, giving Kate a sad, pointed look. "Would you really?"

The grandfather clock on the wall chimed ten strokes.

I can't stand this, Kate cried silently. I don't want to hear any more. Yet she heard herself ask, "In your heart of hearts, do you believe that Thomas was telling the truth?"

Seconds ticked by. Kate's heart sounded like a gong inside her chest.

"Yes. Years ago I didn't see it, but as an adult, I believe the sonofabitch was telling the truth and that his mother covered for him."

Rage froze Kate's body. Then just as quickly, feeling returned, bringing with it repercussions that even her imagination couldn't have conjured up.

The saliva dried in her mouth; she couldn't so much as swallow. Her vision blurred. Her mind hammered with pain sharper than any headache she'd ever suffered.

In that moment, the anger she felt toward Thomas was so intense that she wanted to kill him. But the anger was nothing compared to the panic that threatened to squeeze the very life from her heart.

"Please, don't hate me," Angie pleaded.

Kate didn't move a muscle or speak a word.

"Kate . . . please, say something," Angie begged. "Anything, for heaven's sake!"

Kate hugged her arms around her chest and rocked back and forth.

"God, I'm so sorry," Angie murmured. "I wish I'd never said a word."

Kate's eyes sprang to life. "You know I don't hate you. Nor do I hold you responsible. I'm the one who's responsible for not having done something."

"Pray tell, what could you have done? You didn't have a pot to piss in or a window to throw it out of. Besides, you were so infatuated with Thomas that had you confronted him, he'd have convinced you otherwise."

"Maybe not," Kate whispered, feeling her insides coming apart. "But then we'll never know, will we?"

Angie didn't respond. She lowered her head again and pawed the edge of the rug with a foot.

"If you don't mind, I'd like to be alone," Kate said in a dull, lifeless tone.

Angie didn't argue. Instead, she kissed Kate on the cheek, then quietly left the room.

Once the door closed behind Angie, Kate sunk to the floor. She'd known that sooner or later, pay day would come. A preacher had once said that we suffer and pay for our sins on earth. She believed him. Yet out of the excruciating pain that had flayed her heart open, she felt a resurgence of strength. She knew what she had to do. Regardless of the consequences her actions might have for her career as a judge, she had to find her daughter. She must face and resolve the past once and for all. She had to mend her soul.

Kate stood up and straightened her shoulders. She walked over to the telephone table and reached for the directory. On many occasions, Harlan had bragged about employing the most discreet private detective in town. After two attempts, she finally dialed Sawyer Brock's number and waited for the answering machine to kick on. She told herself she couldn't let her hunger for revenge toward Thomas interfere.

The bastard would get his comeuppance, only later. What mattered now was finding her daughter.

Sixteen

Harlan Moore eased back in his padded desk chair and inhaled his Camel deeply and joyously. Rarely did he smoke; it was no longer socially acceptable, especially in public. But old habits were hard to break, even if he wanted to, which he didn't. Sucking nicotine into his lungs gave him a high that nothing else could, except maybe a sexy, twenty-year-old beneath him in the throes of climax.

Dream on, he mused silently, taking another drag. While a twenty-year-old was a little young for him, a thirty-year-old wasn't. He had one waiting in the condo he'd set up for her, though she wasn't the one he really wanted.

"Damn," Harlan muttered, his thoughts taking a direction he didn't want them to take. He bolted upright in his chair, stood, then walked to the small designer bar in one corner of his large office, where he helped himself to a cup of freshly brewed coffee. While he sipped it, his eyes surveyed the premises—or his empire, as he liked to refer to it.

The office had been recently redecorated. He had used a top-notch decorator from New York with whom he'd gambled in Vegas on several occasions. He enjoyed the opulence that surrounded him. It was meant to impress visitors and prospective clients. Black leather furniture rested gracefully on plush salmon-colored carpet. The stark white walls were splashed with priceless paintings that he had acquired over the years. The wall unit behind his desk was filled with books and other mementos he'd picked up in foreign countries.

He was proud of the real estate empire he had built from nothing. If only he hadn't had to take on a partner. Harlan sighed deeply, not liking the direction of that thought either.

What he should be thinking about was his business, if he intended to hang on to it. As if business were the magic word, his financial advisor suddenly appeared in the open doorway.

"Ah, Joe, come on in. I was about to buzz your office."

Joe Ward sauntered toward the desk. He was slender, deeply tanned, and had thick brown hair sprinkled with gray. His flared nose aggravated an off-center smile and an upper front tooth that had been broken and never capped.

Despite his physical imperfections, Harlan trusted him and that was all that mattered.

"Have a seat," Harlan said, pointing to the chair positioned directly in front of him.

Joe complied, then asked, "Is there anything special on the agenda this morning? If not, I need to fly to Tampa and meet with those prospective clients."

Harlan thrust a hand through his gray hair, a grim expression on his face. "How does that deal look?"

"So far, so good." Joe shrugged. "But you never know."

"Well, we need to know. I need this deal, Joe. Make it happen."

It *had* to happen. Harlan had his balls in a vise, and the only way he could get them out was to sell that tract of land. So what if everything wasn't exactly on the up-and-up? If he played his cards right, he and his company would come out untainted. He'd also make a bundle of money. And if there should be trouble, he had the man who could fix that, too.

Joe batted the folder he'd brought with him against a muscled thigh, then stood. "I'll do what I can."

"Call me the minute you have anything, and if I need to, I can fly down."

"Have you heard anything from Wallace?"

Harlan's grimace returned. "No, but rest assured that bastard's getting ready to make his move."

Wallace Grimes was his soon to be ex-partner. At least that was what Harlan hoped. When Wallace had continued to question his method of doing business, Harlan had told him to clean out his desk drawer and get the hell out. He'd gotten out, all right, but not willingly and not without promising to have Harlan's head on a silver platter.

"We'll handle him when the time comes," Joe said, "just like we do everything else."

"Just make sure we have the funds to do it with."

"I'm doing all I can, boss." Joe walked to the door, only to swing around and walk back toward the desk. "Oh, I almost forgot." He reached into his folder, pulled a section from the newspaper, and laid it in front of Harlan.

"What's this?"

"The article speaks for itself. Read it."

Harlan's eyes dipped to the highlighted column. The headline glared out at him: DISTRICT JUDGE KATE COLSON NOT AFRAID TO TAKE ON TOUGH CASES. After scanning the article, he looked up and muttered, "Bitch."

Joe raised his eyebrows. "And a tough one at that."

"That remains to be seen."

"I think she's a cinch for the job, at least from the gossip I hear."

"Not if I have anything to do with it, she isn't."

"It seems that Judge Colson is one of those poor misguided souls who believes in our justice system."

Harlan sneered. "Oh, she does that all right."

Joe grinned. "Well, you have to admit, the lady's a good-looking broad."

"She's cold and vicious, and I don't want her anywhere near me."

"With a tight ass like hers, I'd have thought . . . "

"I know her ass," Harlan cut in tersely, "and it's mine. Count on it."

Joe looked confused. "Why the hell don't you just offer her so much money she can't turn you down? Money talks, my friend, and it can buy you out of another court debacle."

Sounds good, Harlan agreed silently, only he didn't have bribe money, even if he thought she'd take it—which he knew she wouldn't. Joe didn't know that Harlan's wife had drawn considerable amounts of money from their personal savings before he'd stopped her. Right now, he was short on cash, but if this land deal in Tampa came through, he'd be solvent once again, or well on his way.

"She hasn't officially got her campaign off and running yet, has she?" Harlan asked.

Joe brushed a piece of lint off his suit coat. "Not that I know of. After all, the election's still several months off."

"Which is good."

"Why? You have something up your sleeve?"

"Sure do."

"Care to share it with me?"

"Not yet. It's still in the preliminary stages."

Joe's off-center smile deepened. "I can't wait to hear about it."

"Call me," Harlan said by way of a dismissal.

Joe took the hint and walked out, closing the door behind him.

Harlan peered down at the article again, then with a curse crumpled it into a tight ball and tossed it in the waste basket. Even so, he couldn't get Kate Colson out of his mind. He stared out the window, hoping to dispel her image. He couldn't. He remembered the first time he had seen her.

Johns and Strassberg had thrown one of their famous parties. That one, however, had been in honor of Kate, who had recently joined the firm.

She'd been wearing a short, black silk dress that molded her body perfectly and teased the onlookers with the curves hidden beneath. Her hair had been parted down the middle and pulled back in a twist at the nape of her neck. On anyone else such a harsh style would have been unattractive. On Kate, it had looked terrific, outlining her profile to perfection.

He'd assessed the entire package and felt his loins stir, vowing on the spot to have her in his bed. He hadn't made his move, however, until a month after she'd been appointed to the bench, mainly because she'd come to represent him in the firm and had saved him mega-bucks in taxes. Still, the entire time they had worked together, his appetite for her had grown, while he had bided his time.

Johns and Strassberg had thrown another party in Kate's honor, this time celebrating her appointment to the bench. Although they had regretted losing her expertise, the firm had been proud of her. It was near the end of the party when he had noticed that Kate was still there, surrounded by several men. Harlan had approached her with the sole intention of asking her out.

"Ah, Harlan," she had said in her beautiful voice, giving him a polite smile.

For a moment, Harlan didn't say anything, feeling himself drown in her deep-set eyes. Then, recovering, he returned her smile and said, "Nice party."

"Yes, it is—was." Kate paused with a soft laugh that included everyone. "But it's been a long day, and I'm ready to call it an evening."

Ignoring the other men still present, Harlan said, "I'm about to do the same. Why don't I call you tomorrow. I'd like to take you to dinner." He grinned with confidence. "Call it a personal thanks, if you will."

Kate's facial expression didn't change, but her voice did. A coolness laced her words. "Thank you, but I already have plans for tomorrow evening."

Harlan felt his face flush. Cancel them, you bitch, he'd been tempted to say, but hadn't. Yet the rebuff had infuriated him, especially when he'd noticed the mocking ridicule in the other men's eyes.

However, he had managed to hang on to his cool. Now that she was a judge, he needed her. Later his coolness had backfired; she'd refused to use her influence to help him win his lawsuit.

Well, no one crossed Harlan Moore, not twice, anyway. Nor did anyone get away with making a fool of him in front of his business cronies.

She'd gotten too big for her britches too quickly and she had to be brought to heel. He might be in a bit of trouble at the moment, but he had confidence in his ability to get out of it as he'd done so often. He'd take on his partner and win. He'd best his wife also. He expected to be sued for a divorce any time now, which was just fine with him.

More important than either, he intended to make Kate Colson pay. Somehow, in some way, he'd engineer her downfall.

Rechanneling his thoughts, Harlan reached for the Rolodex and thumbed through it to the Bs. He'd put Sawyer on it. Sawyer would know what to do. He smiled a satisfied smile and punched out the number.

For sure, that bitch would pay, and then some.

Seventeen

Sawyer tapped the end of the pencil on the paper in front of him and continued to read for a few more minutes. Then, with a grunt of frustration, he dropped the pencil and leaned back in his chair, the squeak further grating on his nerves. He promised himself again to get the can of WD40 and quiet that noise once and for all.

What the hell was the matter with him? It wasn't like him to be so uptight. He got out of his chair and walked to the window. The sun was already high in the sky, glowing like a pot of gold.

The perfect spring day was made for jogging, not holing up in some office. But holed up was exactly where he was and where he would stay. He had enough work pending to choke a horse.

He knew what had raised his frustration level: Judge Kate Colson. He'd just finished reviewing her dossier and was now questioning the soundness of his judgment. Again.

Why had he taken the case? He hadn't needed it or wanted it. Hell, he'd long ago stopped taking cases of missing persons unless it was a high-profile one where the bucks were higher than the stakes. He'd have to admit, though, what the judge was going to pay him wasn't exactly chicken feed. Still, he didn't need the headache.

He'd reached a point in his career where he could afford to be selective and was. He'd accomplished what he'd wanted to. Well—almost. It hadn't been easy, not by a long shot. But he was proud of his accomplishments, and in rare moments, he paused and patted himself on the back. Yet he never took his good fortune for granted. The pain-riddled years of his youth were never far from his conscious mind, and if nothing else, they kept him humble.

At age ten, he'd lost his father, who had been a cop. Wayne Brock had been one of those caring, conscientious officers who had taken his job more seriously than most. He'd been patrolling his beat late one night when a gang fight had broken out. He'd radioed for backup, but his fellow officers had been too late. A bullet had struck Wayne Brock in the head, killing him instantly. The gang member had finally been captured and brought to justice. Several years later, following numerous appeals, he'd been put to death by lethal injection.

While Sawyer had cheered the end result, it had done little to improve the downward spiral of his life. His mother, who was totally unsuited for marriage to a cop, hadn't been able to cope with her husband's violent and senseless death. Shortly afterward, she had died of heart failure.

Having no other family, Sawyer had been whisked off to live with an aunt and uncle. Suddenly and unconsciously, a shudder shook his large frame.

"Damn," he muttered, turning his mind off. The last thing he wanted to do was rehash those years under his aunt and uncle's roof. They were years he wished he could surgically remove from his brain so that he wouldn't have to think about them again. But since that wasn't possible, he could only keep them buried and play the hand that had been dealt him.

Yet out of that pain came a brutal determination to survive at all costs. After a few years of struggling on his own, he'd joined the Marines and traded service for an education. He then had worked his way through college. With a degree in criminal justice, he had followed in his father's footsteps and become a cop. He soon had climbed from street patrol to a high-ranking detective.

Only after he met Harlan Moore had his luck really changed. Ah, Harlan. Sawyer smiled a grim smile, knowing he'd have to give the devil his due. Harlan was some piece of work. His house had been burglarized. Sawyer had been put in charge of the investigation. Harlan had been impressed with Sawyer's hard-nosed aggressiveness and offered to set him up in his own private detective agency, assuring himself of Sawyer's help and allegiance.

Sawyer paused in his thoughts and reached for his daily calendar. Speaking of business dealings, Harlan was due in his office any minute now.

"Great," he said, trudging back to his chair, only to suddenly stop mid-stride when he heard the knock on the door.

"Come in."

His secretary, Jane Saunders, opened the door, a smile on her attractive face. "Mr. Moore just phoned and said he was tied up and would be late."

"Figures."

Jane chuckled. "Some things never change, do they?"

"No, I'm sorry to say, they don't."

Harlan was almost always late for his appointments, chronically late, Sawyer thought, a chronic pain in the ass.

"I'll buzz you when he arrives."

"Thanks, Jane."

She nodded, then closed the door behind her.

Knowing that he'd dallied long enough, Sawyer returned his gaze to the dossier on Kate Colson and asked himself the same question he'd asked moments before. Whatever had possessed him to take this case? He suspected that her loveliness somehow had boggled his senses. Behind that cool facade, he had seen the pain in those large brown eyes, and the vulnerability. He was curious enough about the judge to run a background check on her. He'd found no smoking gun, but his gut instinct, which he trusted completely, told him she was hiding something. And he'd stake his life on the hunch that the young girl she had asked him to find was her daughter.

All he needed now was more information. She'd been stingy at best with what she'd given him. He needed more and that was all there was to it.

"Mr. Brock."

Sawyer jerked his head up and waited for Jane to speak. "It's Mr. Moore. I'll send him in if you're ready."

" 'Bout time."

Jane closed the door, but not before Sawyer saw her smile.

"Well, son, how're you percolating?"

Sawyer didn't know which irritated him more, Harlan's habit of referring to him as "son" or his "good-ol'-boy" talk, which was so uncharacteristic that it made Harlan look like a fool.

Standing, he extended his hand to meet Harlan's. He purposely kept his face devoid of emotion. When dealing with Harlan, he'd found that was best.

"Have a seat," Sawyer said.

As usual, Harlan was impeccably dressed in a blue pin-striped suit, white shirt, and a blue-and-silver tie that matched his hair. Sawyer almost smiled at his friend's obvious attempt to be perfect. Such a waste of time and effort, Sawyer thought.

"I'd like a cup of coffee."

"Help yourself," Sawyer said, sitting back down in his chair.

"How 'bout a little bourbon to chase it with?"

Sawyer frowned. "This early? Jesus, Harlan, when did you start that?"

"As soon as things started going to hell in the proverbial hand basket."

"Care to explain?"

"All in good time. First things first. Where's the bourbon?"

"Under the cabinet."

After Harlan had generously laced his cup with the hooch, he crossed to the chair in front of Sawyer and sat down.

Sawyer didn't say anything while Harlan took a generous sip. Instead, he averted his face to hide his disgust. Something was terribly wrong. He'd never seen Harlan so splattered.

"Ready to tell me what the hell's going on?" Sawyer finally asked in the mounting silence.

Harlan sat his cup down on the table beside his chair. "I have a job for you."

"I figured that."

"What you haven't figured is that I need you to get right on it. Drop whatever else you're doing."

Sawyer sat up straight; his lips formed a thin line, but his tone remained even. "That's a tall order, my friend."

"I know, but that's how important this is to me."

Sawyer had heard statements similar to this one in the past. Everything Harlan wanted was urgent. But he rarely turned down a request from Harlan. He owed him that much. Sawyer was careful never to lose sight of the fact that he wouldn't be in business for himself if it hadn't been for Harlan Moore.

He also liked the good life, and the majority of his good life could be attributed to Harlan's business. Sawyer was as ambitious as he was determined. The only goal he hadn't reached, careerwise, was his plan to expand his agency abroad. A plan to do just that had been germinating in the back of his mind for some time now. He wanted to get into anti-terrorist work for the challenge and the money.

He had vowed when he left his aunt and uncle's house with only the clothes on his back that he'd never be poor again. He'd rather be dead. His philosophy hadn't changed. And if that meant catering to a rich client and bending the rules slightly, then so be it.

"Well?" Harlan asked impatiently.

"You haven't said yet what it is you want me to do."

"I want you to get someone and get them good."

Sawyer lifted thick eyebrows. "Oh, and just who might he be?"

"It isn't a he, my friend."

Sawyer's eyebrows rose higher. "Oh?"

"It's Judge Kate Colson. I want you to get that bitch."

Eighteen

Sawyer's mouth fell open. "What?"

"Damn, son, you aren't getting hard of hearing at the ripe old age of forty, are you?" When Sawyer didn't respond, Harlan went on, "I said I wanted you to get Judge Kate Colson." His voice took on an impatient edge. "Surely you know who she is?"

Sawyer snapped his mouth closed. Rarely did anything or anyone catch him off guard, but this had.

"Sawyer, what the hell's the matter with you?"

Harlan was staring at him angrily. Sawyer shook his head and let out a slow sigh. "Of course I know who Kate Colson is." The impatience in his voice rivaled that of Harlan's.

"Is there something I'm missing here?"

Unable to sit another minute, Sawyer walked to the window. The sky had filled with clouds. A dark one seemed to hover over the building. He remained silent a moment longer, playing for time. Keeping his back to Harlan, he asked, "Like what?"

Harlan laughed suddenly. "Let's cut the bullshit, shall we?"

Sawyer swung around. "What's that supposed to mean?"

Harlan slapped his palm on one knee. "Something tells me you're holding back. Do you by any chance know her? I'll even go an additional step and ask if you're dating her? After all, it's feasible that you two would run in the same social circles." Harlan paused and rubbed his chin. "Yeah, that's sure a possibility."

"You're a barrel of laughs, Moore."

"Well, that last laugh won't be on me, I can tell you that."

Jesus, Harlan was certainly wound up, Sawyer thought. What had Kate Colson done to Harlan to make him go after her with such vindictiveness?

Turning his thoughts into words, Sawyer asked, "So why are you out to get this particular judge?"

Harlan's face flushed. "I asked her to do me a favor, and she turned me down."

"Is that all? Don't you think you're overreacting?"

"No, I don't," Harlan snapped. "She made me look like a fool, and no one does that and gets away with it."

Sawyer's eyes narrowed. "How do you two know each other?"

"For a few years she was an attorney at Johns and Strassberg, then she got appointed to the bench." Again Harlan paused; he reached into his pocket, pulled out a handkerchief, and mopped his brow.

"Go on," Sawyer said, though he knew exactly what Harlan was going to say next. After all, he'd memorized all the known facts about Kate Colson. Still, he wanted to hear Harlan's version.

"Anyway, to make a long story short, she was my attorney there and a damn good one, too. It's only after she became a hotshot judge that she got too damn big for her britches. And I do mean britches." Harlan mopped his brow again. "The only reason she's where she is today is because of my help and influence." He smirked. "Yeah, I actually helped her and then she turned on me."

"Exactly what did she do?"

"She refused to put in a word on my behalf."

"Explain. Details, Harlan. I need details."

"I asked her for help in settling that land deal that went to court."

Sawyer walked back to his desk and sat down. "And she refused."

Sawyer's flat statement of fact was not lost on Harlan. "You don't sound surprised." His tone was accusing.

"I'm not." Before Harlan could respond, Sawyer added, "What specifically did you ask her to do? Use her influence with another judge?"

"Right, and the bitch lifted her nose about an inch higher and said no, and I lost a bundle."

"Anything else?"

Harlan averted his gaze. "No."

"Are you sure?" Sawyer pressed, knowing that Harlan was lying.

"Yes, I'm sure."

Sawyer wasn't convinced, but he let it slide. "So how can I help you? Colson is squeaky clean. She has an impeccable record and a reputation as one tough cookie."

"I don't want her to win that election. It's just that simple."

"And just that complicated."

"Maybe so, but that's what I pay you for," Harlan said. "So cut through the complications and give me what I want. There's bound to be dirt behind that goody-goody facade."

Sawyer rubbed the back of his neck, then looked Harlan directly in the eye. "What if there isn't?'

"Get real," Harlan said sarcastically. "No human is lily white. We all have skeletons hidden in the closet."

The room fell silent. The cars swishing past on the busy intersection below offered the only relief from that hostile silence.

"And if I refuse," Sawyer said at last.

"You won't do that. After all, your ass belongs to me."

"Nobody owns my ass."

It wasn't so much what Sawyer said as the way he said it. Cold, controlled fury punctuated every word. This time the color faded from Harlan's face as the two men stared at each other, wills battling.

Harlan backed down first and in a much more conciliatory tone said, "There's no reason for us to disagree, now is there? You scratch my back, and I'll scratch yours." He grinned. "Isn't that the way the system works?"

"Harlan—"

Harlan waved Sawyer silent, then stood. "Check her past, talk to people at the firm. There's been a lot of rumors associated with how she rose so fast."

"Are you suggesting that she slept her way to the top?"

"That's my best guess. Find out who has it in for her, then sweep it to the press. Do you know a reporter by the name of Mick Presnall?"

"Yes," Sawyer said tersely.

"Well, if there's a worm under a rock, he'll find it, then report it."

"Only because he's a worm himself."

Harlan threw back his head and laughed. "My kind of man."

Sawyer merely grunted, knowing there was no reasoning with Harlan. He was hell-bent on revenge and nothing would change his mind. So the only thing Sawyer could do was keep his mouth shut, then decide later what to do about Harlan's request.

When Sawyer didn't answer, Harlan stomped toward the door. Once there, he pivoted and snapped, "Call me."

The door slammed behind him. Sawyer pounded his fist on the desk. "Shit!"

Thomas Jennings stretched his legs on the sofa and stared at his surroundings. Not bad, he mused, not for a hotel in Moscow, that is. Not quite as opulent as the Ritz Carlton in New York City; but he had no complaints. It was the best money could buy, and the Russians treated him as if he could walk on water. He laughed out loud. Maybe one of these days he'd be able to do just that.

Ah, yes, he thought, inching his back deeper into the cushions. He couldn't think of a thing he wanted that he didn't have. His crusade was going better than expected; the money had poured in. His life was perfect, except for one thing: the I.R.S..

A dark scowl transformed Thomas' face. He sat up straight, then rose and walked to the center of the room.

From where he stood, he could see the Kremlin skyline. Sunlight bounced off the gold-domed buildings. Now, that was an ironic sight, he thought, when more than half of the Russian population was starving. Who was he to criticize, when it was the poor who donated most of their money to his ministry?

He intended to hang on to that money, despite the Internal Revenue Service. They had called again before he had left for Russia. And if they continued to probe, the Reverend Thomas Jennings could be in deep trouble. Of course his father-in-law had bailed him out of tough jams in the past. He didn't see any reason why he wouldn't do it again, if need be. After all, his darling daughter was the apple of the old man's eye.

Suddenly Thomas felt the need for a stiff drink. He walked to the well-stocked bar in the suite and mixed a martini. By the time he'd sucked it down, he was feeling much better. In fact, the day looked promising once again. Screw the I.R.S. Screw his daddy-in-law. But most of all, screw the past.

The future was all that counted. By preaching the Word, he'd amassed a fortune, most of which he'd managed to keep hidden from his wife and father-in-law. He had plans for a future without either of them and no one was going to undermine him.

He'd worked hard to get where he was today. Standing in the pulpit, shouting and sobbing until he tapped his congregation's emotions, wasn't easy. The rewards, however, were worth it. Money was the biggest motivator. Adoration scored a close second. If he'd let them, many of his followers would kiss his feet.

But then that kind of hero worship had been his due as far back as his school days. Even in that one-horse town where he'd grown up the girls had been love-sick for him, especially one girl, Kate Colson. She had adored him. The thought of it all made him sick.

The jarring ring of the phone broke his train of thought. "Yeah?"

It was his secretary. He had brought an entourage with

him, determined to have all the comforts of home and more.

"Reverend, you have a call," she said. "It's your wife."

Thomas thought for a moment. "Tell her I'm busy, Madge. I'm working on my sermon for tonight."

"Yes, sir, but—"

"But what?"

"Well, sir, it's just that she sounds really agitated—"

"Tell Annette I'll call her later."

"Yes, sir."

"Oh, by the way, why don't you close up the office and do some sight-seeing? I won't need you anymore today."

"Why, thank you." Madge's voice brightened and she gushed, "Why, that's real nice of you."

Thomas fought the urge to slam the receiver back on the hook. If Annette called one more time today, he—Hell, he didn't know what he'd do. Just the thought of her was repulsive. Yet he had to be careful because of her daddy.

He made himself another drink, then went back to the couch and lay down. Contentment overcame him again. He had one more important meeting before he went to the stadium, one he'd been looking forward to all day. Another smile broke across his lips.

As if his mental telepathy was at work, he heard a soft tap on the door. "It's open." He watched as a lovely young girl crossed the threshold. Her breasts, with their jutting nipples, beckoned him as she shut the door behind her and walked slowly toward him.

"Hello," she whispered.

Thomas swallowed hard, then managed to croak, "Come here."

She moved quickly and didn't stop until she reached him.

He unzipped his pants. "Get down on your knees."

Without saying another word, she knelt, then surrounded him with her lips.

"Ah, yes, yes!" Thomas cried, giving in to the pleasure that darted through him.

Nineteen

A twenty-minute dip in the Jacuzzi had thoroughly relaxed Kate. As she patted herself dry with an oversized towel, the exhaustion in her limbs seemed to disappear along with the dampness. Yet she feared the tiredness would return once the effects of the bath wore off.

The morning had begun with the re-trial of a man convicted years ago for the fatal late-night stabbing of a woman in a small grocery store. The woman had been a single mother of four children, a fact that had stirred public opinion that much more. Still, after serving several years on death row, the man's defense attorney had managed to get the conviction overturned on grounds that the jurors hadn't been allowed to consider the accused's mental retardation.

Today the evidence had been presented by the defense, but the state had been just as adamant that the defendant had only borderline retardation and that he had known what he was doing at the time of the murder. Emotions had run high, with both attorneys throwing as many accusations at each other as they had toward the witnesses. Kate had spent her time refereeing in addition to sorting through the legal entanglements. It wasn't over yet. She knew the case would take all of tomorrow, and maybe part of the following day, before the jury could deliberate.

Kate sprayed herself with a scented body oil spray, then

slipped into a light terrycloth robe. She padded into the living room, but not before detouring into the kitchen, where she made herself a cup of French Vanilla Café coffee.

Once she had sat down on the couch, she curled her feet under her. She planned to tackle a mountain of work that lay hidden from sight in her briefcase.

The grandfather clock in the corner chimed four o'clock. She had at least a couple of hours before Angie came home from work, and she planned to savor this time alone.

Kate sipped her coffee and tried to sort through the multitude of things on her mind. Not only did she have briefs to study, she had campaign material to evaluate as well.

Ginger Anders, who had worked at the law firm before taking a lucrative job with a long-distance phone carrier, was her campaign manager. Ginger was insisting that Kate take an active role in her run for the judgeship. Kate thought it too early, with the election still eight months away, but Ginger didn't.

A sudden frown marred Kate's unlined forehead. Many more days like today and she just might think twice before making this job permanent. She knew better than that. She loved the challenge—the more difficult, the better. Besides, she wasn't a quitter. When circumstances toughened, so did she.

The campaign would be yet another fight for the fittest, and when she was feeling less tired, Kate would welcome it. But not right now. All she wanted to do was put her mind in neutral and not think. Just then words of warning echoed in her ears.

"Remember, my dear, that an idle mind is the devil's workshop."

Even after all these years, Kate had to smile; the professor had spoken directly to her. If she hadn't stayed busy to the point of total exhaustion every evening, she would not have survived. The dark fingers of past regrets would have choked the very life out of her.

But now, having made her decision to put the past to rest, a part of her was well on its way toward finding peace. She could only hope that when her daughter was found, her heart would once again be whole.

Turning to her work, Kate reached into her briefcase and pulled out a stack of papers. A newspaper was on top, and her eyes stopped at the bold headline:

SAWYER BROCK CRACKS THE BREMOND ESTATE CASE
IN HOUSTON

"Damn," she muttered, slamming the case shut with force. Her mind raced.

Although she was purposely collecting articles on the detective, she hadn't wanted to think about them or *him* this evening. Resentment welled up in her. This was Friday, and she shouldn't even have to work. But Sawyer Brock wasn't work, she reminded herself; he was personal. And he couldn't be ignored.

With a resigned sigh, Kate tossed the top article aside and looked at the one underneath. It was equally complimentary of Sawyer, citing several cases in which his playing hardball had solved a seemingly impossible case.

Had she made a mistake in hiring him? He unnerved her; she would admit that. It was as if he could see through her, see that she hadn't told him the whole truth. So what? She'd given him enough information to get started, and that was all that mattered.

Kate had no idea why he both frightened and intrigued her. The picture in the *Wall Street Journal* showed him looking polished and sophisticated. But that highly polished image was completely opposite from the tough, hard-nosed man she had met. Family background material was practically nonexistent, except to say that he'd been orphaned at an early age. Whatever that background was, it lacked wealth and social standing.

The articles did, however, give her insight into his education and work background. He was forty and had worked his way through college and into the police academy. From there, he'd gone into police work, which had paved the way for his private detective agency.

He had a reputation for tenacity; he was very capable of going for the jugular if that was what the case called for.

The phone jangled beside her. Kate jumped.

Squelching her irritation at being disturbed, she reached for the receiver. "Hello."

"Ms. Colson?" a Spanish-accented voice asked.

Kate was hesitant. "Yes."

"This is Julio Sanchez."

Julio? She didn't know any Julio. But he had her phone number, which was unlisted.

Before she could respond, the man spoke again. "You forget to come for your plants? Sí?"

Kate went weak with relief. She'd had very few crank phone calls during her time at the firm, and since becoming judge, even fewer. But it paid to be cautious, especially with all the crazies walking the streets these days. After all, she did make enemies daily.

"Oh, Julio, of course. Sorry, it took me a minute to collect my thoughts." He was the assistant manager at the nursery where she bought her plants.

"Sí," he responded.

She'd ordered a large number of plants, and this was the second time he'd called her about them.

"Julio, what time do you close?"

"Eight o'clock."

"Good. I'll be there shortly to pick them up."

"If you want us to, we can deliver."

"I know, but I want to see them. And, I might want to get more."

"Sí, ma'am."

Kate replaced the receiver, dumped the briefcase on the cushion beside her and scrambled up from the sofa. So much for work and Sawyer Brock. After scribbling a note to Angie, she made her way into the bedroom.

Minutes later, she was dressed in jeans and a tank top and was on her way to the nursery.

"If there's anything else I can do for you, let me know."

"Thanks, Julio, but if you've loaded the plants in the trunk, then that's all, unless I get more." Kate grinned.

Julio answered her grin, revealing a string of perfect white teeth. "Look all you want."

Kate did just that, ambling among the tables filled with colorful containers of annuals that no artist, however talented, could capture. Puttering with plants, she guessed, was her true passion. She loved to put on grubby cutoff jeans, hat and gloves and dig in the flower beds. Somehow that manual labor, that feeling of being one with nature, released the kinks from her muscles and her mind. The labor of love even managed to purge the sadness from her soul. But only for a little while.

Pausing, Kate breathed in the heady smell, glad that she had made the effort to come. She could look forward to getting up early in the morning and planting her purchases.

The evening was picture perfect, another scene an artist would have trouble capturing on canvas. Springtime, in all its fickle glory, had arrived in force. A warm, teasing sun still dominated the horizon. A red-headed woodpecker banged his beak into a tree before flying to the bird feeder and helping himself to sunflower seeds. Sweet-smelling buds covered various bushes while the smell of new grass mingled with the aroma of the plants.

Kate inhaled again just as Julio approached her, a frown on his face.

"Señorita Colson, there's a gentleman to see you."

"A gentleman to see me?" she repeated inanely. "Here?"

"Sí."

Kate swung around and stared. Sawyer Brock returned her stare. Her heart dropped to her toes.

"Did I do something wrong?" Julio hovered anxiously. "I didn't know what to tell him."

Kate swallowed hard. "You did just fine, Julio. Thanks."

Julio didn't look fine, but he turned and left. Kate, however, was oblivious to everything about her. Her vision and thoughts were filled with Sawyer Brock.

She hadn't forgotten how roughly good-looking he was. Nevertheless, when she saw him thread his way through the maze of plants toward her, her breathing became more difficult, especially as he stared at her with cool interest.

If he was surprised at how she was dressed, the shock was mutual. He had shed his suit for a pair of jeans, a green open-neck shirt, and boots. The only thing missing was the Stetson, but she bet he had one.

She knew better than to let his casual attire fool her. The man himself represented danger. From the first moment she had seen him in his office, he had affected her in ways she didn't want to acknowledge. He was a disturbingly attractive man, who was like no other man she'd ever met. Again she was struck by the differences he posed. Outside, he still wore that polished, cool look. But inside, she sensed an unpolished power in him, a mean streak perhaps.

"What are you doing here?" she finally asked, feeling unsettled. Her voice shook with repressed anger. She resented this invasion of her privacy.

"Doing the job you hired me to do." Though his tone was low and even-keyed, a muscle sprang to life in his cheek, showing his displeasure at the way she spoke to him.

"How did you find me?"

"Your friend Angie told me you were here."

Kate was aghast. "You mean you went to my house?"

"Yes." His tone dared her to make something out of it.

She accepted the challenge. "My home is off-limits to you," she lashed out.

He bowed slightly. "Yes, ma'am."

Kate ignored the mockery behind his words. "Do you make it a habit of working after hours?"

"Always. And I'll wager you do, too."

"What I do is beside the point."

"Wrong. That *is* the point. We need to talk."

"How about Monday at my office?"

"I was thinking about now."

"Now?"

"Look, Judge, do you want me to find the young woman, or not?"

"Of course I do."

"Then it would be best if you'd cooperate."

"I am cooperating," Kate lashed back, while trying not to

notice that the top buttons on his shirt were undone and droplets of sweat had collected there. She shifted her gaze.

"Couldn't prove it by me."

Kate looked back at him. "Exactly what do you want from me?"

For a moment, he didn't say anything. His gaze traveled over her. "Enough information to do the job you're paying me to do. If not, I can't take the case."

"Fair enough."

"So can we call a truce?"

"Truce? I didn't realize we were at war."

"Oh, yes, you did," Sawyer said bluntly.

Kate sighed as she looked around. Other customers were milling about the plants. She and Sawyer were drawing curious stares. "This is hardly the place to do business."

"I kinda thought that myself," he drawled.

"What's the matter, Mr. Brock, are you shocked?"

He didn't pretend to misunderstand. "Shocked that you like to play in the dirt?" He gave a lopsided smile. "Yeah, as a matter of fact, I am."

His smile caught her completely off guard. Kate felt something leap to life inside her, only to then remind herself that it was crazy to trust that smile, regardless of how it affected her.

It wasn't that she didn't have needs or wants like any other woman. She did, only she refused to give in to them. This man, or any other man, for that matter, was off-limits.

A personal relationship was something she shied away from because the pain of the past was a grim reminder of the price of love. She'd had her share of men friends, had even had a brief affair; it had been unsatisfying and unfulfilling. Nor could she forget that she could never have children. While she had made peace within herself concerning that loss, she couldn't expect a man who wanted children to do the same. With that in mind, she had decided long ago that a loving relationship with a man was not for her.

So she had best recognize Sawyer Brock for what he was: hired help, nothing more, nothing less. She'd do well to remember that.

"I guess we all have our little idiosyncrasies, don't we, Mr. Brock?" she said into the mounting silence.

"I guess we do at that," he said, another smile edging his lips. "Don't you think we could dispense with the formalities? Call me Sawyer."

Kate hesitated. "All right." Yet she couldn't bring herself to say his name.

"So back to the reason I'm here." He gave her a pointed look. "Information. The hospital provided no clues, except I did learn that no baby was adopted during the time frame you gave me."

"I know," Kate said softly.

Sawyer's features came alert. "You know? Then why—"

"I think maybe the baby was abandoned in a motel room," Kate rushed to say.

For a moment he looked dumbfounded. "Motel? Jesus!" When she didn't respond, he continued, "Surely there's more."

"Not at the moment. I've only recently learned about the motel part myself."

He swore. "Doesn't the motel have a name?"

"Of course it does, but I don't have it."

"Are you sure?" he pressed.

"Yes," Kate said tautly.

"But you can get it, right?"

"I hope so."

"Well, you should know that there's nothing more I can do unless I know where to begin."

Kate planned to confront Thomas, but on her timetable, not Sawyer's. Through the years she'd made it a point not to see Thomas, to not even read or watch anything associated with him or his ministry. Shame and pride had kept her away, but not any longer. With or without Sawyer to prod her into action, she had to know the truth, although she suspected that Thomas had indeed left Sara in a motel as if she were a small sack of garbage. If that proved to be the case, then Thomas would pay dearly. Either way, she still had to find her daughter.

"Kate."

The sound of her name on Sawyer's lips sent a tingling sensation through her. To make matters worse, he was staring at her. She turned away, finding it impossible to feel completely at ease in his presence. Maybe it was the way he looked at her with an expression in his eyes she couldn't quite decipher. Was it admiration? Or contempt? Or desire . . . ?

"Look," she said, "as soon as I get more information, I'll pass it on to you."

"Who's the child's mother?"

That sudden, loaded question came out of nowhere and sliced her to the core. Kate glared at him. "That's not relevant."

"Let me be the judge of that. Besides, at this stage everything's relevant."

"If you don't mind," she said in a pointed dismissal, ignoring his last remark, "I should go and pay for my plants."

"Fine. I'll wait and walk you to your car."

Kate wanted to scream her frustration at his uncanny ability to ruffle her composure, but she found it easy, comfortable even, to maintain calm and keep the upper hand.

"Suit yourself," she said, turning and walking toward the check-out counter, her head held high.

Twenty

Sawyer leaned against the side of a fountain and watched as Kate walked off, caught up in the way her jeans rode low on her hips. She did not resemble the businesswoman who had come to his office. In that casual getup, she looked more like a teenager than a judge. Some lucky women could wear tight-fitting jeans without looking cheap. Kate Colson was one of them.

Her hair was free of its usual confines and swung loosely about her face. In the waning sunlight, it reminded him of spun gold. Her voice had a raspy quality that became more noticeable when she was agitated. He found himself liking everything about her.

Yet he enjoyed needling her. He wasn't proud of his unprofessional tactics, but he damn sure wasn't going to apologize. He knew why her attitude rubbed him the wrong way. Like him, she'd come from humble beginnings. But unlike him, she didn't want to remember, while he made it a point never to forget.

He had to give her credit. Under fire, she kept her cool. He had purposely thrown that question to her about the girl's mother to test her reaction. Kate might have balked, but not so that anyone could see. But he'd seen it. A flicker. Sawyer's gut instinct continued to tell him that the child was hers.

He straightened suddenly and thought again how beautiful she was, a genuine pleasure to look at. Other men thought so, too. Several turned and stared at her in appreciation, and he realized that he was gawking in exactly the same way. He cursed silently.

By the time Kate reached him, her flawless skin was flushed and she wouldn't quite meet his appraising gaze.

"All done?" he asked.

Still keeping her eyes averted, she lifted her shoulders in a tiny shrug. "For now."

Her less than enthusiastic response hit a nerve. His mouth pinched. So much for the truce he'd hoped for.

"Is there anything I can carry to the car?" he asked out of the desire to once again break through that self-assured facade.

"No, thank you. It's all been taken care of."

This time his irritation burgeoned into anger. He didn't need this kind of grief, not from Harlan, certainly not from her. What he ought to do was wash his hands of the entire affair, tell them both to go to hell and then walk away.

As if she sensed she'd gone too far, Kate looked up at him. Their eyes met. Only a few inches separated them, but it might as well have been a continent. He felt the tension build and wanted to defuse it. But he couldn't. He couldn't stop looking into those lovely brown eyes.

Her deep steadying breath snapped the tension. "Okay, so the information I gave you is a bit paltry. I'll concede that."

Sawyer brightened. "Ah, now we're getting somewhere."

Kate smiled, but it seemed forced. "Do you always push this hard, Mr. Brock?"

"Sawyer."

She still couldn't call him by his first name. Instead she held up her hand. "Don't answer that last question. I already know."

"Sure you do. That's why you hired me. I'm as ruthless as the next fellow in my business. Maybe a little more so. You see, I dig for the bone even if there's only a scent."

"I'll keep that in mind." Kate's words come out sounding more raspy than usual.

"So I guess I'll be hearing from you." His green eyes held their intensity. "Soon."

Without responding, she turned and began walking toward her car. Sawyer fell in step beside her and matched his gait to hers.

At the car, she faced him. For a moment, he thought she was going to extend her hand. "I'll call you," she said. "Soon."

"Getting information out of you is like pulling an eye-tooth."

"You've made your point, Mr. Brock."

He didn't bother to correct her again. He merely opened her car door and breathed in her seductive scent, until it made his senses stir. He backed away. If she was aware of his abrupt motion, she didn't show it.

"Later," he said.

She hesitated, then nodded.

Sawyer walked to his own car and climbed in. He sat there unmoving until her car disappeared around the corner, then turned the key in his Jaguar and listened a moment while the engine purred to life. What the hell had he gotten himself into? *Why* was more to the point. Before now, no one had led him around by the nose. He laughed cynically. Maybe he was getting soft in his old age. Or maybe he'd just never met a woman like Kate Colson.

Yeah, she was something: smart, tough, and sexy as hell in that carefully composed way. He wondered what it would be like to shake that rigid control.

"Give it a rest, Brock," he muttered, then shook his head to clear his thoughts. There were more productive, if less intriguing, ways to spend his time.

Once his mind was back on track, Sawyer had to map out his game plan. The best place to start was with Kate Colson herself.

If there was any dirt associated with Judge Colson, as Harlan swore there was, then he would find it. But not for Harlan. He'd already decided he was not going to do Harlan's bidding. He intended to piece the puzzle of Kate Colson together, all right, but for himself.

Ignoring the uneasy feeling prompted by that decision, Sawyer swore, then tore out of the parking lot.

Lloyd Silverman pulled his nondescript pickup truck onto the street behind Sawyer. He'd almost made his move, but had decided against it. For now. When he confronted Sawyer Brock, he wanted all the advantages. There had been too many men inside the nursery, both hired help and customers, which meant the odds were with Sawyer. Not that Silverman thought he couldn't best him on any turf, because he could. Still, this was his show, and he wanted to be the star, the one who took the ultimate bow.

He gripped the steering wheel tight with one hand, while he dug in his rear pocket with the other and yanked loose a stained white handkerchief. He swiped the handkerchief across his upper lip and forehead, removing the sweat that threatened to impair his vision. He had to be careful. Sawyer was no easy prey. As an ex-cop, Silverman knew that Sawyer would sense a tail regardless of whether he suspected one or not. That was the sonofabitch's nature.

Silverman mopped his forehead again. He wished he could wipe his entire body as the sweat trickled through the thick hairs under his arms and saturated his shirt.

Thrusting aside his discomforts, he kept his attention on Sawyer until the detective turned into the Brock Building parking lot. Silverman veered his truck next to the curb across the street, jammed the gear into park and twisted the key. The engine didn't quit, however. It continued to clank and chug, then saturate the area with gasoline fumes.

Silverman grunted loudly, then lowered his head for fear the noise would attract Sawyer's attention. It didn't. Sawyer sauntered up the steps, his walk as cocky as Silverman remembered.

"Bastard!" he mumbled, jerking upright in the seat.

He remained there for the longest time, thinking about getting out, rushing into the building and tearing Sawyer Brock limb from limb.

As a valve for his anger and frustration, he suddenly beat

his palm against the steering wheel. The assault didn't phase him; he felt no pain, only the expanding pressure in his chest.

God, he missed Emily. How long had she been dead now? Six months? That didn't seem possible. How he had loved her. Still loved her.

His features suddenly twisted and the tears dried as quickly as they had started. A crazed glint appeared in his eyes as he stared at the upper window he knew to be Sawyer's office.

"You killed my wife, you bastard! And if it's the last thing I do, I'll make you pay."

With those words, Silverman started the truck and drove off, leaving behind a trail of toxic fumes.

Twenty-one

Kate dressed with steely determination. She had to look her best. After she finished her work, she planned to confront Thomas.

Suddenly, weak trembles attacked her legs. She eased down onto the stool at her dressing table and took several deep breaths. She wasn't afraid to meet the man who had brought her so much pain, but neither was she looking forward to it. No one in her right mind wanted to look the devil in the face. And the Reverend Thomas Jennings was the devil in disguise.

Kate thrust thoughts of him aside and resumed the task at hand. She'd already showered, put makeup on, and pinned her hair into its usual chignon. However, unruly wisps were determined to escape around her face.

Swallowing an agitated sigh, Kate stood and slipped into a beige linen dress. The rounded neckline and belt were outlined in fuchsia. Over it she wore a matching jacket with a stand-up collar and folded-back cuffs that were also trimmed in fuchsia. The bold color was striking on her, but she hadn't chosen the attire because it complimented her. She'd chosen it to bolster her morale and give her needed confidence.

She was also scheduled to hear closing arguments on the murder re-trial. Following that, she had to rule on two cases of possession of controlled substances. She had promised her campaign manager that she would then drop by the head-quarters. But once that was done, then she would find Thomas and hear the truth.

Kate smiled with no humor. She wasn't sure Thomas knew how to tell the truth, and yet he preached the gospel to millions of people. If only his adoring flock knew just how despicable their idol was.

If he had abandoned their baby, his followers would know. The entire world would know; she would see to it. First, she had to make him tell her what happened to her baby on that fateful day. Then she could give the information to Sawyer Brock.

Kate's heart gave a lurch. Sawyer. Thinking about him was unsettling. She dreaded facing him as much as she did Thomas. Since their encounter at the nursery, Sawyer had been on her mind.

She kept seeing him walk toward her with the gait of a graceful, but predatory, animal. Her pulse had responded with a purely female reaction, something she hadn't wanted to feel then or now.

But even as she berated herself, her pulse accelerated, frightening her. That easy-moving private detective with his forceful eyes and his magnetic body was exactly the type of man she dared not trust.

She vowed to control her absurd reaction to him if it was the last thing she did.

"Kate."

With the timely interruption, thoughts of Sawyer fled. "Hi, Angie. Come on in."

Angie Gates cracked the bedroom door just enough to get her head through. "I was hoping I'd catch you before you left for the courthouse."

"You barely did. I'm about ready to leave."

Angie pushed the door back farther and leaned against the frame.

Kate studied her old friend carefully, thinking that she looked wearier than usual. On the other hand, Angie seemed animated and less unkempt. Kate could think of only one thing that might account for that subtle difference: a man. Was Angie involved with someone?

"What's on your mind?" Kate finally asked.

Angie shrugged. "Nothing much."

Kate didn't push the point. "Since you're here, there's something I need to talk to you about."

"Oh?"

"Remember a man by the name of Brock?"

Angie wrinkled her forehead as if trying to concentrate.

"Sawyer Brock. He's a private detective." Kate strove to keep the impatience out of her tone. "I'm sure he showed you his I.D."

Angie's eyes suddenly sprang to life. "Oh, yeah. Good-looking dude, too. Said it was urgent that he talk to you."

"Urgent? He said it was urgent?"

"That's what the man said."

Kate gritted her teeth to keep a curse from escaping. What he'd wanted certainly hadn't been urgent. And as she'd told him, he could have phoned her.

"Apparently I goofed."

"It's not your fault." Kate thought for a moment. "Only, please, from now on don't tell anyone my whereabouts, no matter who it is."

Angie shrugged again. "Sure, if that's what you want."

"That's what I want."

Angie's eyes burned with curiosity, but she didn't ask the question that Kate knew she longed to. It was just as well because Kate wasn't up to discussing Sawyer with her. "So did you mind that I left and didn't come back until this morning?"

Kate's head came up with a start. "For heaven's sake, Angie, you don't have to justify your actions to me. If you choose to stay out all night, that's your prerogative. When I gave you the key to my house, I didn't attach any rules, other than the one we just talked about."

Angie thrust a limp strand of hair behind her ear. "You aren't even the least bit curious?"

"About what?" Kate looked at Angie at the same time as she reached for her briefcase.

"About where I was?"

"Do you want to tell me?"

Angie chewed on her lower lip and averted her gaze. "I don't think so. Not right now, anyway."

Kate sighed. "Look, Angie, we need—"

"But I will tell you this," Angie cut in. "I'm happier than I've been in a long time."

Kate's features softened. "I'm glad. You're long overdue for some good luck."

"So maybe we'll talk later, huh?" Angie asked with child-like enthusiasm.

Kate smothered a pang of guilt. "I'd like that, but right now I've got to run. I'm due in court."

"Sorry," Angie said, that pinched, uncertain look covering her face again.

Kate gave Angie a smile, then skirted past her to the door.

By that afternoon; Kate longed to be on her patio watching her flowers grow and sipping a cup of coffee. The day's docket had been cleared earlier than she had anticipated so she headed for her campaign headquarters on Guadalupe Street, just a short walk from the courthouse.

Ginger Anders looked up with a start, then spoke exuberantly. "You made it. That's great."

"Wonders never cease," Kate said as she took in her campaign manager's excited grin, thinking again how attractive she was with her pixie-like features, curly dishwater-blond hair, and light brown eyes that had a habit of sparkling.

Kate felt lucky to have her as a staunch supporter to direct her campaign. Ginger had worked part-time at the law firm and had a reputation as a top-notch worker.

When Kate had made the decision to run for district court judge, she hadn't known how to get started. She'd had some ideas of the type of campaign she wanted to run, and she'd also had a list of issues and concerns that were important to her and, she hoped, to her constituents. It was organizing her efforts that wasn't easy. She'd been lamenting that fact when

Ginger had approached her and offered to organize her campaign.

Ginger wrinkled her nose. "I was hoping you'd show up, but I wasn't going to hold my breath."

Kate's smile widened. "Don't. Where I'm concerned, it could be lethal."

Ginger chuckled.

Kate plopped her briefcase on a desk next to the one at which Ginger sat. Both were cluttered with newspaper clippings and sundry other papers.

"What on earth are you doing?" Kate asked, sitting down.

"I hope I'm mapping out your platform."

Kate rolled her eyes. "Hope it's good."

Ginger giggled. "It's good, all right. From now on, the public is going to know you as the broad with balls, no less."

"Ginger!"

Ginger wore a deadpan expression. "You mean you don't like it?"

Kate opened her mouth, only to then burst into laughter.

"I only spoke the truth! You do have more balls than most men. Too bad there's not a more delicate but forceful way to say that." Ginger grinned. "Never fear, I'll find a way. You just wait and see."

"That's what I'm afraid of," Kate muttered under her breath.

If Ginger heard her, she didn't respond. Instead she scrambled for an article and thrust it at Kate. "This piece said everything but that, citing your toughness on crime and your penchant for sending convicts to death row."

"That sounds awful." Kate sounded out of breath.

Ginger looked incredulous. "You mean you haven't seen this?"

Kate wrinkled her nose in distaste. "As a rule, I avoid reading about myself."

"Well, you sure should've read this one," Ginger said with another quick grin. "This fellow hit the nail on the head and I couldn't agree more. Don't you see that being tough on criminals, especially drug and child abusers, along with giving citizens back their rights, is what's going to get you elected?

And what's going to do your opponent in?" She frowned. "Geez, he's such a Milquetoast."

Kate merely shook her head.

"Well, he is," Ginger said stubbornly.

"Okay, okay, but just make sure the campaign doesn't get nasty."

"Oh, all right, but you do agree that we should stress your record?"

"By all means."

"And from the looks of things, we won't have any trouble with money." She reached for a stack of envelopes. "These are all checks."

Kate's eyes widened. "That's great."

"I thought so, too. First thing I'm going to do is hire some help and get this god-awful place fixed up."

Kate's eyes roamed around the stark room with its bare walls and tiled floor. "Whatever you think best."

"Good, now let's talk about TV and newspaper ads."

Kate leaned over Ginger's desk, and for the next thirty minutes they discussed business.

Finally, Kate pitched down her pencil and looked at her watch. "Time's up, I'm afraid. I have another appointment."

"Fine. I understand."

Kate grabbed her briefcase and walked toward the door.

"I'll call you tomorrow."

"All right," Kate said.

"Meanwhile, get some rest!"

"Yeah, right."

Ginger rolled her eyes.

Ten minutes later Kate was driving toward the Hill Country.

The campaign was forgotten. Her work was forgotten. She was focused on one thing: getting the truth from Thomas. Whatever it took, fair play or foul play, she intended to have her way.

Twenty-two

A security guard met her at the gate. Kate eased the car window down and smiled pleasantly.

The guard tipped his hat as he peered into the car. "Good evening, ma'am."

"Good evening."

"Are you expected?"

Kate reached for her identification card, then held it for him to see. "I'm Judge Kate Colson." She hoped her credentials would be enough. They were.

"I'll buzz you through, Judge." The guard tipped his hat again before ambling to the control box on the fancy black wrought-iron gate. Kate watched as he picked up the phone, then entered the security code.

The gate slowly opened, and Kate maneuvered her Cadillac up a long, winding drive that was lined with tall oaks. When the house appeared in front of her, Kate wasn't at all stunned by its opulence. It fit the Thomas she'd known perfectly: large, gaudy, and full of braggadocio. She wasn't surprised by his success, either. She'd expected it. After all, he'd always had a way with words, charming young and old alike.

Thank God she was no longer susceptible to that evil brand of charm. Once Thomas had left Four Corners, Kate had survived by pretending he no longer existed. Even though she'd known that he had followed in his daddy's footsteps and had gone to seminary before setting up his ministry in San Antonio, she had never sought him out. Still, she had heard news of him from time to time. Like many of the big-time evangelists, he had his name bandied about in the newspapers and on television. He was said to be one of the largest moneymakers in the business today. Her stomach revolted.

He was a fake, pure and simple.

Now, as she turned off the engine and stepped out of the car, her nerves seemed made of steel. She hadn't even bothered to call to see if he was home; she'd wanted to catch him off guard. The only preparation she'd made was to call his ministry office and find out where he lived. When she had reached the city limits of San Antonio, she'd stopped at a convenience store and asked for directions.

Kate took a long, deep breath as she walked up the front steps onto a verandah that ran the length of the house. The house itself could fill half a city block; she was sure of it. The outside was constructed of white brick with tall columns that seemed to reach the sky. The setting reminded her of Tara.

Kate pressed the buzzer and waited. She expected a uniformed maid to open the door. Instead a woman who looked to be in her late twenties or early thirties yanked it back.

"Yes," she said in a rude, slurred tone.

The woman was either drunk or well on her way to it, Kate thought. Was this Thomas' wife? If so, she looked to be one unhappy lady.

She was tall and thin to the point of gauntness. Her chestnut-colored hair was short, the ends tipped with silver. The parchment skin on her face was too tight over her bones.

"Hello, I'm Kate Colson." Kate kept her tone formal but polite.

"So?"

"I'm here to see Thomas."

The woman's lips tightened even more. "What do you want with him?"

Kate ignored her question and asked one of her own. "Is he home?"

"Look, lady, get lost."

Kate stiffened. "Are you his wife?"

The woman laughed, but it had an eerie, hollow sound that chilled Kate's blood. "You might say that."

"Your name?" Kate didn't expect an answer, so when she received one she was shocked.

"Annette Jennings," the woman said with a shrug, leaning against the frame as if she could no longer stand on her own.

Encouraged, Kate asked again, "Is your husband at home?"

"Why do you want to know?"

The distrustful sullenness had returned to her voice. Kate's heart faltered, but only for a moment. She wouldn't let this woman, however much she pitied her, keep her from her mission. If Thomas was in this house, she would find him.

"We're . . . we're old friends."

"Sure you are."

Kate flushed. "Please, tell him I'm here."

"Now, why would I do that?" Annette's narrowed eyes traveled the length of Kate. "You don't look like my husband's type." Her mouth twisted. "But then, who knows what his type is anymore?"

Despite her contempt for this woman's lack of control, Kate felt a twinge of pity for her, having picked up on the pain interlaced with bitterness. "It's business."

"Yeah, right."

"Trust me, it's business." Kate spoke in a firmer, cooler tone.

Annette slouched deeper against the door frame. "Well, I can tell you that if it's about a payoff, you're at the wrong door." She giggled, then leaned forward and whispered in a conspiratorial tone, "You see, Daddy takes care of that sort of thing." She winked. "Get it?"

Kate backed away from the boozy breath, thoroughly repulsed.

Annette giggled again before crossing her arms and hugging them to her chest.

Kate didn't stop to consider her actions. She brushed past the drunken woman and crossed the threshold into the house, where she pulled up short. The interior rolled past her eyes like the quick slide of a camera: spectacular was the word that came to mind. Pickled oak hardwood floors led to a curling peach-carpeted staircase in the distance. To her left were French doors that led to a small room full of books. On her right was a formal living room with paintings, mirrors, and a huge stone fireplace. Beautiful, but icy cold. Like its master.

Kate shuddered just as a woman in a maid's uniform rounded the corner. She stopped mid-stride when she saw Kate. Then her eyes crossed to the doorway to Annette. Ignoring Kate, she went to Annette's side.

"Come on, let's get you to bed."

Annette slumped against the woman with her eyes closed.

The woman paused again and finally studied Kate. "May I help you?"

"I'd like to speak to Thomas."

"He isn't here."

Kate's heart sunk. She hadn't believed Annette, but she believed this woman, who spoke with quiet, dignified authority. "When do you expect him back?"

The housekeeper frowned. "I'm not sure. He's in Russia, holding a crusade."

The air deserted Kate's lungs. "Russia!"

"Yes, ma'am."

Annette hiccuped loudly, then giggled. The woman patted her on the back. "Now, now, Mrs. Jennings."

Anger roiled through Kate with such intensity that she thought she might be sick. She balled her fingers into tight fists while stifling the urge to make this woman the scapegoat.

It wasn't fair, she told herself savagely. She'd built this moment of confrontation up in her mind—what she would say, how she would behave—and now it was not to be. Damn you, Thomas. Damn you. She should have known it wouldn't be easy, especially as she'd been determined to surprise him. Still, she had been hopeful . . .

So, she'd been dealt a setback. She could handle that.

After all, jumping hurdles was her expertise. This was simply one more in a long line. She wouldn't let it stop her.

She would return to Austin and regroup. Then the moment Thomas set foot on American soil, she'd meet him face to face and demand her answers. Thomas would have his day in court with her as both judge and jury.

She smiled inwardly. She didn't plan to argue the case either. She already knew what the verdict would be. She'd show him no mercy. That thought alone gave her the strength and courage to turn and walk toward the door. Once there, she swung back around.

"Tell him Judge Kate Colson came calling."

Sawyer bolted upright in his bed. His breath came hard and his body oozed sweat.

It was happening again, that same god-awful dream that placed him in that dark, locked closet. He'd been so young, but he would never forget it, nor his aunt's evil face as she'd shoved him inside.

When his heart ceased its pounding, Sawyer tossed the sheet back, got up and strode naked into the kitchen of his condo. Using the moonlight that poured through the kitchen window as his guide, he removed a glass from the cabinet, filled it full of cold water and swigged it down.

He wiped his mouth with the back of his hand before walking to the breakfast nook, where he peered into the darkness. He knew dawn was near, almost time to go to the office.

Hell, he was in no shape to work. His body continued to shake, and he slammed his fist onto the counter. He was a grown man, for god's sake, not a little boy. He should have been able to bury the past. He had done everything else he had set his mind to do. He'd learned to confront and he'd learned to win. His adversaries would attest to both.

Only in the darkest hours was he prone to give in to the pain that forced him to tear the past out of its hiding place within his soul and look at it in the light. He didn't like what he saw, remembering always that those closest to him had wished him dead.

Suddenly Kate Colson came to mind. She had suffered, too. He didn't know how or why—yet. But the heart-breaking pain was there. He had seen it behind that facade of cool aloofness that she had worn like a shield.

Sawyer cursed out loud. He didn't want to think about Kate Colson. That was trading one nightmare for another. For Kate Colson was just that: a threat to his peace of mind. What was it about this woman that had him so strung out? Was it because she reminded him that he, too, had buried past demons? He didn't want to think about that. He didn't want to think about *her* either.

So was his problem sex? Had he stooped to such a level that the mere sway of a woman's hips had the power to arouse him?

He rattled off another string of curses even as he admitted that she had indeed jump-started his sexual drive. He hadn't felt that ache in years, since he'd confused lust for love, a mistake he had vowed never to repeat. Still, he'd like to have a kid someday, but that would never happen. The entanglements of matrimony were simply not for him. He wondered what Kate . . .

What the hell. Granted, she had a great body. Big deal. Practically all the women he went out with could make that claim. So that didn't explain why Kate kept coming to mind. But she did, and he couldn't stop the ache.

Sawyer broke out in a cold sweat again, thinking about her jutting breasts visible in that tank top she'd had on. He wasn't even sure she'd had on a bra, now that he thought about it.

Why wouldn't he allow himself to seduce her and be done with it? He could imagine himself lifting that top over her head and exposing those breasts, then putting his tongue . . .

"Face it, Brock, you've got a rusty nail digging in your head!"

With that, he stomped into the bathroom, where he showered and dressed. Thirty minutes later he was sitting at his desk, having come to the conclusion that there was too much at stake to blow it because he had a hard-on for a woman who wouldn't piss on him if he were on fire.

With that cold thought, Sawyer reached for the nearest folder and started to work.

"You look like someone stomped the shit out of you."

Sawyer smiled in spite of himself. "That bad, huh?"

"Worse than bad." Ralph's eyes narrowed on his boss. "Did you tie one on last night?"

"I wish to hell I had."

"Want to talk about it?"

"Nope." He and Ralph Hutson were friends both in and out of the office. But there were some things that Sawyer wouldn't discuss even under the umbrella of friendship. His past was one, his sex life another. The former was much too painful while the latter was currently nonexistent, accounting for much of his testy attitude.

Ralph held up his hands. "Fine. Let's get down to business, then."

"I hope we've heard from that overseas job. I don't intend to let that slip through our hands—if we can hang on to it, that is."

Ralph grinned. "The way I figure, we're close to nailing it."

"Close isn't good enough."

Ralph's grin disappeared. "Well, all I can say is that Uncle Sam has asked for our expertise in training twenty diplomats against terrorist attacks. Of course, we don't have a signature on the dotted line nor do we have any money."

Sawyer's eyes turned flint-like. "Don't lose this contract, Ralph. Even if we don't make the kind of money we'd like to, ink it. It's the chance I've been waiting for."

"But—"

"Forget the buts." Sawyer stood. "Just think of the potential for making mega-bucks in the future, what with Libya, Iran and Iraq still nibbling at the U.S.'s ass constantly."

"It's not so much the money with you, is it? It's the challenge."

"It's both," Sawyer said flatly. "With government contracts under our belt, we'll be set."

"I may need to bring you in on this deal, then."

"I'm ready."

"Another pressing matter is 'Current Affair Magazine.'"

Sawyer frowned. "What?"

"You know, one of those TV shows that rehashes the sleaze of the day."

Sawyer laughed. "Great. Just what we need."

"Actually they're interested in when and if we solve that missing person case we took on last week."

Sawyer looked blank.

"Surely you remember—the deputy sheriff that's been missing for twelve years."

"Oh, right." Sawyer frowned. "Why would they be interested in that?"

"They suspect foul play, as does his wife. She says she wants to know what happened to her husband once and for all, and she doesn't care how much it costs to find out."

"How did 'Current Affair' get hold of it?"

"Don't know that, not yet anyway."

"Well, get on it. Publicity's publicity, any way we can get it."

"I'll take care of it. So, anything you want me to do on the Colson case?"

Sawyer felt himself stiffen. "I'll take that one myself."

Ralph shrugged. "Whatever you say."

"Anything else on the agenda for today?"

Ralph checked the notes in his briefcase. "That's it."

The minute his assistant left, Sawyer grabbed Kate's file. But he didn't open it; he stared at it while toying with the idea of calling her. No, he couldn't do that. First, he had no reason. He certainly wasn't going to ask her to confirm the rumor Harlan was determined to believe—that she'd been promiscuous in order to get what she wanted.

Harlan was entitled to his opinion. He was entitled to his, and he didn't believe that about her. Still, he didn't know well enough to make a personal judgment. Not yet, anyway.

He was so deep in thought that he didn't recognize the

noise for what it was, until he heard it again. He frowned. Someone was screaming. *His secretary was screaming!*

Sawyer's blood turned cold. "What the hell?" Three long steps carried him to the door. He yanked it open.

"Don't move," a shaky voice demanded. "Stay right where you are."

Sawyer stared into the barrel of a gun pointed straight at his heart.

Twenty-three

Sawyer froze in his tracks. He recognized Emily Silverman's husband right off from the photographs she had given him. And despite the man's warning, he couldn't have moved. The gun pointed at him was all the incentive he needed to stay put.

Jane remained at her desk, quietly shaking. Sawyer's eyes skirted to her, then back to Silverman. "Let her go, okay? She doesn't have any quarrel with you."

"She's dead, you know," Silverman said in a remote tone, as if he were in a trance.

"Who?" Sawyer asked, while his mind worked on a way out of this highly explosive situation. Silverman, he could tell, was close to the breaking point. If the situation wasn't quickly diffused, the idiot would most likely put a bullet in him, then Jane. No way was Sawyer going to allow his secretary to pay for something that involved only him.

"My Emily's dead, that's who, and it's your fault, you bastard." Silverman spat the last two words.

"I'm sorry, I didn't know," Sawyer responded in a soft but controlled tone.

"Of course you didn't know," Silverman sneered. "You're too busy digging up dirt on other people so you can throw it back in their faces."

"Look, Silverman, I'm truly sorry about your wife."

"Don't you dare say that!" Silverman hissed, inching closer.

Sawyer remained rooted to the spot, but his eyes never wavered from the bobbing gun. "Silverman, put down the gun, and we'll talk this out. I'll listen to anything you have to say."

"Yeah, I just bet you will. Only it's too goddamn late." His voice suddenly cracked. "She's dead. My poor Emily's dead."

"Silverman . . . "

"Shut up! You should've stayed out of my private life."

Sawyer released a trapped breath. "She hired me to do a job."

"You didn't have to show her the pictures of me screwing another woman, for chrissake!"

I didn't, Sawyer wanted to shout back. He'd turned the dirty work of tailing Silverman over to another department in his agency. Still, he was ultimately responsible for what went on inside this office complex. He would accept full responsibility. Besides, he had taken the case, then turned it over to someone else. He wished now that he'd held firm to his promise not to take any more domestic cases. Emily Silverman had obviously caught him at a weak moment.

It hadn't taken the investigator long to get the goods on Silverman. It was Emily who had insisted Sawyer show her the pictures. He had done as she'd asked.

"Look, Silverman, my agency only did what we were hired to do. Your wife was convinced you were having an affair."

"Damn you!" he cried, waving his gun.

Jane screamed.

Silverman kept his eyes on Sawyer, but he spoke to Jane. "Shut your mouth, lady!"

"Silverman, let her go."

"No! Do you know what my wife did after she left your office?"

Sawyer shook his head.

"She killed herself, that's what. She took a bottle of pills."

A sick feeling washed through Sawyer. What a frigging mess. "Look, I'm sorry . . . "

"Sorry." Silverman's lips curled. "That's not good enough. You're going to pay for what you did to her."

"Not what I did, Silverman, what you did."

"No, my affairs didn't mean nothing." His voice broke. "I loved my Emily."

"Give me the gun, Silverman. Killing me won't bring back Emily."

"No." A maniacal light burned in his eyes. "Your life for her life."

Suddenly the doorknob behind them rattled, followed by a voice mumbling, "Why the hell is the door locked?"

At the unexpected commotion, Silverman's eyes skidded off Sawyer. In that split second, Sawyer sprang forward and knocked the gun from his hand. Before Silverman could react, Sawyer backhanded him across the face, sending him flying against the wall.

Whimpering like a baby and nursing a bleeding lip, Silverman sank to the floor. The doorknob continued to rattle.

"Get away from the door!" Sawyer yelled.

For a moment, complete silence followed the harsh command.

Then Sawyer said, "Get up, Silverman."

Silverman, with tears soaking his face, inched upward while staring at Sawyer through stricken eyes. When he reached an upright position, he turned and shuffled toward the door.

"Silverman."

He turned and looked back at Sawyer.

"Don't ever come near me again." Sawyer's tone was even, but the violence he held in check was evident. "If you do, you'll be real sorry." He paused as if to let that sink in. "Now get the hell out of my sight."

Silverman's Adam's apple bobbed, then he hung his head.

"Out!"

Shaking, Silverman fumbled with the lock on the door. When he finally got it open, he ran out.

Sawyer crossed to the gun and picked it up.

Immediately Jane's low-keyed shaking burgeoned into full-fledged sobs. "He . . . he could've killed you." She gulped down another sob.

"He could have, but he didn't." Sawyer crossed to her desk and patted her awkwardly on the shoulder.

"Do . . . do you think he'll be back?"

Sawyer's lips tightened. "Who knows? Crazies like him are unpredictable."

"Shouldn't you call the police?" Another sob racked Jane's slender frame.

"No. Right now, his conscience is eating him alive and that's punishment enough." Then, changing the subject, Sawyer said in a gentle tone, "Hey, if you don't stop crying you're going to make yourself sick. Tell you what I want you to do. Call Harry and tell him to come get you. Your car will be fine here overnight. I want you to take the rest of the day off."

Jane looked up at him with wide, frightened eyes. "But . . . "

"Not another word." Sawyer smiled, taking the edge off his voice. "Who's the boss around here, anyway?" He raised his hands, his smile widening. "Don't answer that."

Jane smiled in return, albeit a wobbly one. "If . . . you're sure."

"I'm sure. Now, call your husband."

A short time later, Sawyer was once again behind closed doors in his office. He hadn't bothered to alert his other employees. Thank goodness Silverman had locked the door behind him. If whoever had tried to get in had succeeded, Silverman might have lost what little control he had and blown them all away. But, like Sawyer figured, Silverman was a coward, all talk and no do.

He was about to call Ralph when the phone rang.

"Yeah."

"What's got you so pissed?"

It was Harlan, the last person he wanted to talk to. "You don't want to know. What's up?"

"Just checking to see how you're progressing on the Colson case."

"I'm progressing." But not in your behalf, Sawyer declared silently. Of course, Harlan didn't need to know that, not right now, anyway.

Harlan's sigh was clear even through the unclear phone line. "What kind of answer is that?"

"Look, Harlan, do you want me to do my job?"

"Of course, but—"

"Then let me do it, in my own way and in my own time."

"What you're telling me is that you haven't got a god-damn thing."

"What I'm telling you is to let me do my job."

"I want you to get on this case, you hear? And stay on it."

Sawyer held the receiver away from his ear while Harlan raved on. Only when the old man paused did Sawyer speak again. "Gotta go."

"Damn you, Brock."

"Talk to you later."

With that, Sawyer replaced the receiver, none too gently either. He stared into space for the longest time, again wondering what kind of hornet's nest he'd gotten himself into.

Thomas Jennings, wagging his briefcase, walked to the back door of his mansion. The evening breeze rustled his hair as he inserted the key, then stepped inside. Silence greeted him. He knew Florence, the housekeeper, was already in her living quarters. Annette's car was in the garage, so he knew she was here.

He walked through the kitchen, then weaved his way into the glassed-in den that ran nearly the entire length of the house. He stopped in the doorway and watched his wife move to the bar and mix herself a drink.

"Drunk already," he said to her back.

Annette shrieked, then swung around, her glazed eyes roaming over him. "Ah, so the great one has returned. Should I bow and kiss your feet like all your followers?" She giggled, sloshing the drink on the floor. "Oops, see what you made me do." She giggled again.

Thomas walked farther into the room. "God, you make me sick."

She laughed. "Not nearly as sick as you make me, you hypocritical swine."

"You look awful. How long's it been since you fixed your hair or put on makeup?"

"What do you care?" Annette lashed back. "You're either out of town or out with one of your women. Or both."

Thomas stared at her another long moment, his handsome face registering his disgust. "I don't have to take this shit off you." He pivoted, then stamped toward the door.

"Who is Kate Colson?"

He stopped mid-stride, then jerked back around. "What did you say?"

"You heard me. Who is she? Somehow I don't think she's one of your whores. She has too much class."

Thomas closed the distance between them. "Don't play games with me." He clenched and unclenched his fists while his nostrils flared. "You know what'll happen."

Annette didn't so much as flinch. "You won't hit me again. If you do, my daddy will kill you."

"How do you know Kate Colson?"

As if suddenly tired of the game, Annette said in a bored voice, "She came here, to see you."

Thomas' tanned face went deathly pale. "She came here?"

"That's what I said."

"What did she want?" There was a tremor in his voice that he couldn't control. Kate Colson in his house. Christ! That bitch could ruin everything.

Annette shrugged her too-thin shoulders. "She just said to tell you that she came calling."

Thomas was sweating now, from every conceivable pore on his body.

"You're afraid of her, aren't you?" Annette laughed again. "Why, that woman has you by the short hairs."

"Shut your filthy mouth."

"I will, but only after you tell me who she is and what she means to you."

Thomas' body suddenly throbbed with suppressed fear.

"Tell me," Annette spat. "If you don't, I swear I'll walk

out on you and tell Daddy all your nasty little secrets, like how you tie me up, then beat me. Need I say more?"

"All right, you bitch!" Thomas exploded. "I screwed her back in high school." He reached in his back pocket and drew out a handkerchief. He wiped the moisture from his face. "She got pregnant and had a brat."

"What happened to the child?" she asked in a dead tone.

"I don't know. It was adopted or something."

"Oh, my God."

A silence fell while Thomas watched a myriad of emotions play across her face. How could this be happening, now, when he had everything going his way? Whatever Kate Colson wanted with him couldn't be good. His insides shook. He'd just have to handle it, like he'd always handled everything else that got in his way.

Her features twisted in pain, Annette broke the silence. "Why, you bastard, you made a baby with her. And here I've begged and pleaded for you to let me have a child."

"Only because dear old Daddy wants a grandchild."

"That's not true," Annette denied. "I want one."

Thomas looked her up and down insolently. "Why? You couldn't take care of a baby." He laughed a cruel laugh. "You'd be feeding it booze out of a bottle instead of milk."

"You bastard!"

Thomas gave a tired sigh. "Name calling isn't going to get you anywhere. Besides, I'm not to blame. You're the infertile one, not me. Go tell your daddy that."

"Maybe I'll tell Daddy about Kate Colson instead."

Rage contorted Thomas' features. "I wouldn't do that, if I were you. After all, I have a few secrets concerning Daddy's little girl that he wouldn't like to hear. It might even bring on a heart attack."

Annette raised her hand. He grabbed her wrist and glared down into her face. "Don't even think about it." He pushed her away, then turned his back.

"I hope you burn in hell, you bastard!" Annette cried.

Thomas never looked back. He just kept walking.

Twenty-four

The law office of Johns and Strassberg in downtown Austin was an institution. It had been founded by William Johns in the late 1800s, and the building contributed to the historic charm of the city.

The firm hired the most prestigious attorneys. Anyone on the team felt highly honored.

Kate most assuredly did. Even now, as she pulled into the parking garage attached to the building, that same sense of awe overcame her. She'd been overwhelmed when asked to join the firm a few years ago, despite the fact that she'd had to start at the bottom and work her way up. She hadn't minded; the climb had been challenging and exhilarating.

Even so, her tenure hadn't been all a bed of roses. She had experienced her share of heartache and frustration, the debacle with Dave Nielsen and Harlan Moore perhaps the most memorable.

Kate seldom visited the offices, as there weren't enough hours in the day to warrant indulging herself. Today, however, she made it a point to take the time. Her ex-boss, William Johns III, who ran the firm, had called and all but demanded she stop by. She suspected he was going to support her in the upcoming election.

She had dressed with care in a chic topaz silk suit, the skirt just above the knees. A simple gold chain hung around the neck of her white silk blouse, with matching pearl-and-gold earrings. Her hair was wound into its usual chignon at the nape of her neck.

With that old feeling of excitement coursing through her, Kate got out of the car. The sun, sitting low in the sky, beamed down on her. She paused and looked up, squinting against its brightness. She couldn't have asked for a lovelier day, she told herself, yet the spring had been rather dry, which meant the farmers and ranchers were getting a little antsy.

Kate shifted her mind back on track and made her way into the building, determined to enjoy the freedom of this un-expected visit. The afternoon court docket was crowded with several drug-related cases and another child custody hearing. And at the top of her "Do List" was a reminder to call Thomas' headquarters in San Antonio to see if he had re-turned from Russia.

She had already called twice, each time refusing to iden-tify herself. Both times, she'd been told that Reverend Jen-nings was expected back sometime within the week.

Underneath Thomas' name was Sawyer Brock's. She would have to call him after she had gotten some informa-tion from Thomas. Then Sawyer would find her daughter.

A sudden jolt passed through Kate's body. The thought of actually seeing Sara in the flesh, and not just in her heart, was mind-boggling. If Sawyer Brock could accomplish that, then she could put up with anything, even the unwanted physical attraction she had to admit she felt for the man.

Kate walked into the main foyer. It was exceptionally lovely, rectangular in shape and furnished with two stately maroon leather sofas and four or five leather-covered wing chairs. There were copies of several business and popular magazines on one of the glass-topped coffee tables. The ceil-ing was slightly domed and open, spilling light on the nu-merous live plants and valuable paintings on the walls.

Kate paused for just a moment, spoke to the receptionist and several employees, then entered the elevator and rode to the top floor where the offices of Bill Johns were located.

His secretary greeted her with a broad smile. "Good morning, Judge. You're looking wonderful, as usual."

"Thanks, Brenda. So are you."

Brenda stopped what she'd been doing and propped her chin on the back of one hand, her eyes filled with curiosity. "How are things at the courthouse?"

Kate smiled. "Booming, unfortunately."

"Lots of bad things happening, huh?"

"Some days I think I'm watching feeding time at the zoo, it gets so hectic."

Brenda laughed, shaking her overweight frame and head full of curls. "It sounds like a different world."

"It is, but I miss this place."

"And we miss you," Brenda said warmly, "especially Mr. Johns."

"I miss him, too. Is he available to see me now? If not, I'd like to run down to my old office and see my secretary." Kate laughed. "Guess I should say ex-secretary."

"Now, that's someone who really misses you."

"The feeling's mutual."

The buzzer sounded on Brenda's desk. She punched a button and said, "Yes, Mr. Johns."

"Is Kate here yet?"

"Yes, sir."

"Send her in."

Kate reached the massive door just as it swung open.

"Kate, my dear, it's so good to see you."

"Same here," she said, extending her hand. Bill Johns shook it warmly before gesturing toward a chair.

After Kate was seated, she studied her old boss. He was a tall man with thinning blond hair and a developing paunch. While not handsome, he had a presence that commanded attention. Also, he was one of the most intelligent men Kate had ever known.

"Is this the first time you've been back?" he asked, still standing.

"No, actually I came by a month or so ago and you were out of town."

"How 'bout a cup of coffee?"

Kate smiled. "That sounds good."

While Bill went to the bar, Kate looked around. She had always felt comfortable in this office despite the fact that it was essentially male. And opulent. A large oak desk dominated one end of the room and massive bookshelves housed hundreds of books. Personal photographs, along with more priceless paintings, graced the walls. A bay window behind the desk was framed with blue drapes and looked out onto a majestic view of the city and the Colorado River.

Bill handed her a cup of coffee, then went back to his desk and sat down. "I'm sure you're wondering why I asked you to stop by." He smiled. "Demanded would be the more appropriate word."

Kate looked at him over the rim of her cup and grinned. "I didn't mind. I've been wanting to see you, but my work keeps me so busy, I don't have time to do the fun things anymore."

"But you like your job?"

Kate's eyes brightened. "Oh, yes. I wouldn't trade it for anything."

Bill angled his head. "Not even to come back here?"

"Is that what this visit is all about?"

"No, it isn't, but make no mistake, I'd love to have you, only I know you're doing what you ought to do." He paused. "And that's what brings me to the reason I wanted to see you." He paused again and sipped his coffee. "Have you got your campaign off and running?"

"I'm working on it."

"Would a contribution help?"

Kate sat up straighter in the chair. "Of course it would."

"Good, then consider it done." Bill Johns reached into his desk drawer, pulled out a check and handed it to Kate.

Kate glanced down at the sum, then raised widened eyes back to him. "I'm honored, and very grateful."

"I'm proud that I can help. I believe in what you're about, my dear. Your toughness on the criminals is what I've advocated for a long time. The fact that you're a woman makes it even better."

Kate toyed with her lower lip. "Well, I don't know what to say. Thank you seems so inadequate."

Bill waved a hand. "I know you're grateful. Just take it and make me prouder of you than I already am."

Kate stood, feeling the sting of tears. "Again I—"

"Don't say anything else. Just make the money count."

"Thank you, I will," Kate said, swallowing the lump in her throat.

They chatted for a while longer, and then Kate left his office and headed for Brenda's to say goodbye. It was shortly afterward, when she walked into the hall, that the door opened directly across from her and Dave Nielsen's frame filled the doorway.

"Well, well, well, look who's here," he said, his smile sparse. "The Honorable Judge Kate Colson, no less." He closed the door behind him and stepped into the hallway in front of her.

"Hello, Dave," Kate responded with cool politeness, when she longed to slap his smug face.

For someone who was so full of himself, he wasn't all that good-looking, though she suspected he didn't realize that. He was of medium height and medium build with longish sandy-colored hair. His eyes were dark blue and cold. His mustache was so perfectly groomed, it looked as if it had been painted above his upper lip. All in all, he looked cold and calculating.

"So how's it going? Have you stepped on anyone's toes at the courthouse yet?"

Kate's lips twitched. "Don't you think you're being a bit heavy on the dramatics?"

"Not at all," Dave said, his smile still intact, although his eyes were cold and his tone sarcastic.

Kate bristled. "Look, it's not my fault Harlan fired you. You're the one who asked me for help in straightening out his taxes."

"Right. But you didn't have to tell him *you* came up with a way to save him thousands of dollars."

"Why not?" Kate lashed back, "That's exactly what I did."

"The way I see it, it was a joint effort, only you took all the credit."

Kate released a tired sigh. "Look, I have to go."

He shrugged. "I'll see you around, I'm sure."

Her exit from the building was quick. That run-in with Dave had left her feeling slightly on edge and the fresh air did little to bolster her spirits.

Kate shivered, despite the sun's warmth.

Twenty-five

"This is what you've been waiting for," Kate muttered as she shoved the gear into park, then stared into space.

The moment of truth had finally come. Ignoring her pounding heart, Kate got out of the car and walked toward the building in downtown San Antonio that housed Thomas' ministry. She had to know. If by some chance, Thomas had indeed taken the baby to his father and the older minister, in turn, had found it a loving home, then she would walk away and never bother Thomas again. If he had lied, he would pay.

The dread inside Kate was real. The wound that Thomas had inflicted with his flagrant disregard for her feelings had never healed. It lurked in a dark part of her heart, waiting for an excuse to poison her entire system.

"Well, here goes." She spoke aloud again, hoping the sound of her voice would give her the needed courage to take that final step. It did. Moments later, she stood face to face with Thomas' attractive secretary, who eyed her with blatant curiosity.

"Is the reverend in his office?" Kate asked, forcing a smile.

"Yes, he is. Do you have an appointment, Ms—?"

"No, no I don't." Without saying another word, Kate turned and made her way toward the door marked with a brass nameplate: Reverend Thomas Jennings.

"Hold it, M—," the secretary sputtered. "You can't just barge in—"

Kate disregarded the order, thrusting open the door and walking inside. Once there, she closed the door, then leaned against it and stared at the man behind the desk.

For the longest time, a pulsing silence filled the room.

Thomas finally stood, his eyes narrowed. "Kate?" His voice was low and raspy.

"That's right, Thomas," she said with rigid control, though she was sure her stomach had settled somewhere around her knees.

He had aged a little, but that process had been minimized, probably due to modern cosmetic surgery. After all, he couldn't afford to let his television audience see his crow's-feet.

Dressed boldly and sharply, he was still pretty-boy handsome. Cold black eyes accented his perfectly chiseled features and smile, which she knew masked a reptilian soul.

Now, as Kate settled her eyes on his face, she saw the surprise and revulsion reflected there. And something else: fear.

"What the hell are you doing here?"

Before she could answer, Thomas came from behind the desk, his eyes stony. "Better yet, how did you get in here?"

"It's simple, I walked in."

"Well, just walk the hell back out. I don't want you here."

"That's too bad," Kate said coolly, "because I'm not going anywhere until you answer some questions."

Thomas' throat rippled in a swallow. "You can't just come waltzing in here like you own the place and expect me to jump through your hoop. Besides, I have a meeting in approximately five minutes."

"Cancel it."

"What? You're crazy!"

"Cancel it," Kate repeated. She didn't raise her voice, but the cutting edge made him back up a step.

"Are you threatening me?"

"Yes, I guess I am."

"I wouldn't advise that."

"What you advise or don't advise is no concern of mine. This is my party, not yours. And we'll play by my rules."

Thomas laughed suddenly, a hollow-sounding laugh. "My, my but the little starry-eyed virgin has developed a sharp tongue and a lot of class." He paused while his gaze ran insolently over her. "Mmm, who knows? If circumstances were different, I might like to have another sample of your delectable body. After all, it wouldn't be like I haven't tasted it before."

An icy loathing clutched at Kate's heart. This time she wouldn't let him get the upper hand or rile her, which was exactly what he hoped to do, as he'd always been able to do. No longer was she the frightened, love-sick teenager who had soaked up his every word with worshipful eagerness and expectation.

"I didn't come here to talk about old times," Kate said with deliberate softness. "You know that, don't you?"

Thomas was beginning to sweat. She could see the fine sheen on his forehead, and she reveled in his discomfort. If it weren't for the fact that she might become contaminated if she stayed around him for long, she would extend this verbal torture to the maximum.

"Money. Do you want money? If you do—"

Kate's sudden movement away from the door stopped him short. She walked toward him. "No, money's not why I'm here."

"Then goddammit, what do you want?!"

Kate's eyes mirrored her contempt, but her voice never wavered. "My, my, Reverend, such foul language from a man of God. What would your followers think if they could hear you now?"

Blood rushed into his face while he closed his fists into tight balls. "You leave my followers out of this." His voice shook. "I wouldn't take this little game of yours much farther. I can make you sorry."

"Not as sorry as I'm prepared to make you."

"You don't scare me."

Kate's contempt deepened. "Oh, no? You can't cover your sins any longer." She stepped closer. "Pay day has come."

He backed up again. "I don't know what you're talking about."

"Yes, you do. Our baby, Thomas. The child we created together."

His lower lip trembled, but he clamped down on it to hold it steady. "Damn you, I told you never to mention that again."

"I want the truth."

"About what?!" he said savagely, his eyes shifting from one side of the room to the other.

"Our baby! You d—" Kate broke off, unable to bring herself to say that vile word. After composing herself, she went on, "You abandoned her in a motel." Her last statement was cold statement of fact.

"That's not true."

Kate bit back the hot words she wanted to say. Instead she spoke with deadly calm, "It is true. The time for lies has passed, Thomas. If you don't tell me where you left our baby, I'm going to see your mother."

"It won't do you any good," he fired back with cocky self-assurance.

"Oh, I think it will. Your mother definitely knew about the baby because Roberta called your house to make sure you had gotten home safely."

A sneering grin reshaped his lips. "What my mother knew about that brat died with her."

Kate felt as if she'd just had the breath knocked out of her. But she didn't let him know that.

He laughed an ugly triumphant laugh. "And if you're thinking about my father, forget him, too. He never even knew a baby existed. So what now, Judge?"

"Nothing's changed. I'm not budging until I get what I came for and that's the name of the motel."

"Oh, all right!" Thomas exploded. "So I dumped the brat at a motel. Big fuckin' deal."

A single cry erupted from deep inside Kate. Although she had known it was coming, hearing the unvarnished truth actually put into words was more devastating than she had thought possible. While she wanted to scream at him not to open his filthy mouth again, she couldn't. She needed the details, all of them, no matter how heart-wrenching.

"What motel and where?" Kate's voice came out a gravelly whisper.

Thomas' face cleared somewhat as if he realized the momentum had swung and that he had the upper hand. "She got what she deserved, what you both deserved." With each word he spoke, a cockiness was building. "I dumped her in an empty room at the Shady Oaks in Austin while she was yelling at the top of her lungs. Then I turned, ran like hell, and never looked back."

His admission left Kate feeling as fragile as glass. She feared that if she so much as moved, she would shatter into a million pieces.

The hate raging inside her came to her aid. She came back to life, longing to reach down his throat and tear out his heart. "Why, you bastard! You're nothing but a piece of garbage." Oh, God, no! The pain was killing her, all over again. She'd thought she wanted to know, but now she wished she didn't. Her insides were a mess; she felt as though she had swallowed a handful of razor blades.

Kate hadn't planned to do what she did next. It just happened. With hate pouring from her eyes, she reached out and slapped Thomas across the face, so hard that he fell backward against the desk.

Shock changed Thomas' expression. Then he retorted, "Why, you little bitch! No one slaps me and—"

Kate slapped him again. "The first one was for me! The second one was for our baby!"

A murderous glint appeared in Thomas' eyes, but he didn't retaliate. "I didn't have that brat, you did." His nostrils were open and flared. "Consider yourself fortunate that I don't return the favor of slapping *your* face. But you'd do well to forget you ever came here. More than that, you'd best forget about the brat and leave well enough alone."

"I'll see you in hell first!"

With that Kate turned and walked out of the room, not stopping until she was in her car. She couldn't go any farther. She didn't even have the strength to turn the key. She lobbed her head against the steering wheel and took deep, gulping breaths. They didn't help.

The wound that had once lain hidden now gaped open, like an incision in her heart. She tried not to think about Sara, how her baby had suffered, left alone and screaming. Kate concentrated instead on the monstrous wrong that Thomas had inflicted upon them both.

Tears streamed from her eyes and burned her cheeks. Her stomach knotted as she fought a desire to kill him. She wished she had a gun. She could picture herself charging back inside, aiming the barrel at his head and pulling the trigger.

No, that would be too easy.

First, she would make him suffer.

Blinking back the hot tears, Kate looked toward the building. "You'll pay, you bastard! I swear on my mother's grave, you'll pay."

Thomas had no idea how long it took before his head stopped its violent pounding. How dare that bitch threaten him? How dare she *hit* him?

His chest heaved while his mind turned into a cyclone of images that had Kate on her knees begging his mercy, babbling that she was sorry, that she'd leave him alone.

He shook his head and cursed, as one of his trained underlings opened the door and walked in.

"Good," Thomas said. "You're just the person I wanted to see."

Twenty-six

Sawyer pinched the bridge of his nose, then pushed his chair back. He peered at his watch and sighed. It was seven o'clock. The office was quiet. Everyone had left for the day, even Ralph, who usually worked late, too. But tonight was Ralph's wedding anniversary, and his wife had demanded that he be home on time.

The phone jangled beside him. For a second he ignored it, thinking that Jane would pick it up. Then it dawned on him that Jane was gone. Still, he hesitated. It might be Diane. He had seen her at a client's art showing and she'd made it plain that he could climb back into her bed anytime he chose. He didn't choose.

When the phone didn't stop ringing, he muttered, "To hell with it!" and reached for the receiver. "Brock."

"Mr. Brock?"

He would recognize the smoky huskiness of that voice anytime, any place. His pulse rate jumped a notch. "Hello, Kate."

He deliberately used her name, and though he couldn't be sure, he thought he heard an intake of breath. If so, it was so thinly disguised that it could have easily been his imagination.

"Look, I know it's late—"

"No problem. What can I do for you?"

"I—we need to talk."

He was instantly alert. "Now?"

"Yes, now, but if it's not convenient," she said in a breathless voice, "tomorrow will be fine. I know it's late, but I just got through myself and—"

"Hey, no problem. Now's fine."

"Thanks," Kate said, and if he wasn't mistaken, there was a tremor of relief in her voice.

Or was this imagination, too? Hell, Brock, give it a rest, will you? Stop looking for hidden innuendoes. He wasn't in a habit of doing that with his other clients.

"I was about to leave and grab a bit to eat," he said.

Silence.

"Kate?"

"Why don't we make it tomorrow then?"

"Look, have you eaten?"

"No, but I'm not hungry."

"Well, I am," he said flatly. "If you don't want to eat, that's fine. But you can at least drink a cup of coffee."

Still, she hesitated. "Why are you concerned about us being seen together?"

"I have my reasons. But I'll make an exception this time," she added hastily, though without any added warmth.

Sawyer wanted to retort, don't put yourself out, sweetheart. He didn't. "Meet me then in fifteen minutes," he said in a crisp tone.

After telling her the name of the restaurant, he hung up and walked out, slamming the door behind him. *Women!*

Kate didn't know how long she held the receiver in her hand, her thoughts in turmoil. Finally, she eased the phone back into its cradle and stood.

Since she'd walked out of Thomas' office several days ago, she'd been a crazed person. Outwardly, she had functioned as if everything were all right. Inside, she had felt hollow and violated.

She had longed to pour out her sorrow to Angie, but

couldn't find the words. Angie had sensed that something was terribly wrong last evening.

After giving Kate a close look, she had said, "You look like hell. Did something bad happen in court today?"

"Something bad happens in court every day."

Angie's lips turned down. "Don't give me that. You know what I mean."

Kate averted her gaze. "Don't mind me. I'm just tired, that's all."

Angie stared hard before saying, "Have it your own way. But if you want to talk, you know where I am."

The minute Angie had left the room, Kate had longed to call her back, but she hadn't. It was a burden she had to bear alone, a problem she had to take care of herself.

While she hadn't been able to talk about it with Angie, Sawyer Brock was a different matter. She would have to tell him.

Now, as Kate disrobed and made ready to keep her appointment with him, dread built inside. She wanted Sawyer to find her daughter, yet the man himself was turning out to be more of an aggravation than an asset.

Twenty minutes later, when she walked into the Chinese restaurant and saw him, the thought of firing him resurfaced. Sawyer was already seated at an obscure table next to a wall of glass that bordered a tiny garden. She had never been to this quaint, out-of-the-way restaurant, but then Chinese food was not one of her favorites.

She counted only a dozen tables, covered with red tablecloths. The carpet was chocolate brown and the walls were painted an off-white. Only two other couples were in the room.

Sawyer saw her and stood. He was dressed in a pair of jeans with a solid yellow sport shirt and boots. She decided that his suit must have been a fluke. He seemed to prefer a much more casual mode of dress. She'd have to admit that the image fit, but then, she'd have to admit that he would look good in anything.

As she made her way among the tables, toward him, she took in the solid, angular bones of his face with the high cheekbones and slightly pointed chin. It was a strong face, she thought again, strong and confident.

It was only after Kate reached the table that she realized he'd been watching her through green eyes that reminded her of shiny emeralds. Their intensity was almost tangible. They stared at her as if she were the only one in the room. To be the center of such scrutiny was both frightening and exhilarating. Her steps faltered. For a moment, she felt tempted to turn and run.

"Hi," he said.

The simple word was enough to dispel the tension. Kate smiled briefly, then sat down in the chair he pulled out for her.

"Have you decided to eat?"

"No, a cup of coffee will do fine."

A waitress hovered at Sawyer's left shoulder. He gave her their order and was quiet until she left. "Ever been here before?"

"No, but I can see why you come here."

"Oh?"

She smiled again. "Well, it's quiet and I suppose the food's good. After a hard day, it's probably a great place to relax."

"You hit the nail on the head." Sawyer's lips curved slightly. "So do you feel better now?"

She took a breath, trying to ease her taut nerves. "What do you mean?"

His gaze never wavered. "About this place. I doubt anyone who matters will see us here, together."

He stressed the word "together" in a mocking tone, but she didn't care. Her job was the one in jeopardy, not his. "This is fine."

Sawyer nodded, just as the waitress appeared with his food and her coffee. A silence fell between them while he ate with a fevered appetite, and she sipped her coffee. Only after there was nothing left on his plate did he push it aside.

"You don't know what you missed," he said.

Kate's lips twitched. "Apparently not."

For a moment a twinkle lit his eyes. "What can I say? I told you the food was good." He took a sip of his beer. "So how's your campaign coming along?"

She paused before answering, looking for some hidden meaning behind his innocent question. When his eyes remained as neutral as his question, she answered. "It's just getting off the ground, actually."

"Well, you shouldn't have any trouble getting elected."

"What makes you say that?"

"You're a cop's dream judge. Actually, everyone in law enforcement feels that way."

"Do you, Mr. Brock?"

"Yeah, as a matter of fact I do."

"That's nice to know."

"Wrong."

She looked startled. "Pardon?"

"You don't give a damn what I think."

In spite of herself, Kate flushed. Damn him. Damn her for letting the conversation get off track. She had to get the upper hand and keep it.

"You're entitled to your opinion," she said in a frigid tone.

Sawyer laughed, but it was only fleeting. "Yeah, I'll have to hand it to you. You do things your way, regardless, and let the chips fall where they may."

Again Kate was caught short by the laughter that was as unexpected as it was disruptive. His whole expression had changed, strengthening her opinion that this man was indeed dangerous. "Isn't that the way you do business as well?"

"Yep, I guess it is," he drawled. "So I guess we're a lot alike, in that respect."

She turned away and didn't respond.

"You don't much like men, do you, Kate?"

The personal comment rankled. She swung her head back around only to realize that he had edged closer. She felt his breath mix with hers, creating a closeness that should have unnerved her. She stiffened and waited for the urge to flee to take over. That urge never came.

Her senses sprang to life, not out of fear, but rather of excitement. She was near a man she found attractive, and that scared her.

"That's none of your business," she said at last, her voice low, almost husky.

He pulled back and shrugged. "Whatever you say."

"I say that we need to take care of business." Kate couldn't quite meet his eyes. "It's been a long day."

Sawyer crossed his arms over his chest. "Shoot. I'm listening."

"I have the name of the motel where the child was—"

"Great," Sawyer cut in. "That's the big break I've been waiting for."

Kate cleared her throat, hoping to keep her voice from wavering.

"So which motel?" he asked, watching her closely.

"The Shady Oaks, here, in Austin."

Sawyer stared at her in stunned disbelief. "What?!"

Kate looked away for fear of what he would read in her eyes.

His loud breath came out sounding like a whistle. "Lord have mercy. Years ago, that was a rat-infested hole. I can't imagine it's even still standing."

"I pray that it is."

"You mean someone actually deserted a baby in a place like that?"

"Yes," Kate said tersely, which drew another curious look from Sawyer.

"I've come across some sickos in my time, but whoever pulled that one is a first-class piece of shit."

"Find her, whatever it takes."

"Have you known this all along?" His tone was accusing. "No."

"Don't suppose you want to tell me how you found out?"

"That's right, I don't."

"Fine," Sawyer snapped, then stood. "We'll play it your way for now, Kate. But you'd better enjoy it while it lasts."

Again she didn't respond. They remained silent even after they had walked out of the restaurant into the night awash with moonlight.

"I'll call you," Sawyer said roughly.

Again he was too close. Startled, Kate peered up at him. Their eyes met. In that moment the air seemed to crackle with a tension that was as consuming as it was dangerous and daring as it was sudden.

Kate's body turned rigid. She wanted to withdraw her eyes for fear he could read her thoughts. But what about his? What was he thinking? He suddenly turned away, but not before she saw the uneasiness in his expression.

The moment was gone, but the attraction had been there. And it had been mutual. It hit her then exactly what was happening. Her job and mission were not the only things in jeopardy. Her heart could easily become involved as well.

"Good night," she said in a panic-stricken tone, and got into her car.

He slammed the door shut, then pushed back. "Drive carefully," he said thickly.

With hands wrapped around the steering wheel, Kate drove off, but she looked into her rear-view mirror. The streetlight illuminated Sawyer. She couldn't see his eyes, but Kate knew that he was watching her. She faced the street and shoved down on the accelerator.

You're walking a thin line, Kate Colson, she told herself. Her conscience didn't talk back.

Twenty-seven

"Mr. Simpson, tell me one good reason why I should grant you a continuance. The court is prepared for trial. Are you telling me you aren't? I want to know, too, why this sudden desire for more time?"

Kate folded her arms across her chest and stared at him. She knew what prompted this request. She also knew that the prosecution had the winning hand. She didn't need this lazy defense attorney trying to postpone the case.

Simpson's client, a young woman, had been accused of inflicting injury on a patient at a nursing home. While the evidence did not place the nurse's aid on the premises at the time of death, it certainly pointed to her as the last person in attendance.

The bottom line was that Simpson was never prepared no matter how much time he had. But that wasn't a valid reason to grant a postponement. The trial would take several weeks to hear, and to postpone it would further clog the docket.

"Your Honor." Simpson stood and toyed with his pen. "I beg the court's indulgence, but I can't give you the specifics as to why I need additional time. What I can say is that if you'll allow the defense team this extra time, it could have a tremendous bearing on the case."

"Your Honor." The prosecuting attorney sprang to his feet, a contemptuous expression on his face. "Mr. Simpson is way out of line here. Enough is enough. Since when does a weak case warrant wasting the court's time and taxpayers' money?"

"I'm sure it happens often, counselor," Kate said, not bothering to mask her sarcasm. "Only not in my court. So, Mr. Simpson, your motion for continuance is denied."

"But Your Honor," he sputtered.

"Mr. Simpson," Kate said tersely, "don't whine. Any further attempt to sway this court will put you in contempt."

Simpson gave her a mutinous glare but refrained from saying anything else.

Kate waited a moment, then said clearly, "Call your first witness."

Her legs cramped, and her upper body felt numb. Kate had been sitting for hours. But now the work day was over, and she was on her way home.

She couldn't wait to soak in the Jacuzzi, to wash away the aches and pains of the day. The testimonies given in the nursing home trial weighed heavily upon her. Such meanness in the world never failed to amaze her, even though she'd been on the receiving end of some herself. While she had never forgotten the pain of the past, she didn't dwell on it either. Then she would hear a case like the one today, and her feelings of despair and anger would resurface.

Kate hoped Angie wouldn't be at home this evening. She wanted her house to herself. Following her bath, she planned to settle on the chaise longue in her bedroom and work. She had briefs to go over as well as campaign decisions to make.

A short time later, Kate turned onto her street. The sight of her lovely home sitting atop a hill never failed to thrill her. She often pinched herself to make sure she wasn't dreaming, that she actually owned it—well, she and the mortgage company. Would the day ever come when her daughter ... Kate stifled that thought. She couldn't afford to think about that. If she never found her daughter, she would be setting herself up for more heartbreak.

Kate reached her long drive and was about to turn in when

she braked suddenly. A car was parked in front of the garage. She frowned. The vehicle was a black Lincoln. Her frown deepened. Dave Nielsen had one exactly like that. Could that be Dave? At her house? Impossible. Yet . . .

She stopped at a distance behind the Lincoln and was about to get out when a couple came around the side of the house.

Kate sucked in a startled breath while the blood drained from her face. It was Dave, all right. And Angie. She placed a hand over her mouth to keep a stunned cry from erupting. Not only were they together, they were arm in arm and laughing.

Kate blinked several times as if to clear her vision. The blinking didn't help. They did not disappear. They were actually walking toward her.

Somehow Kate managed to gather enough composure to ease out of the car. The couple stopped in front of her Cadillac. For a long moment, no one interfered with the awkward silence that fell between them.

Kate looked beyond Angie's shoulder and watched as the delicate breeze ruffled the tree leaves. In a nearby oak tree, two frisky squirrels scampered from branch to branch. She tried to focus her mind on the animals in order to search for something sensible to say.

Angie was the first to break the silence. "Sorry Dave blocked your way."

"No problem," Kate said, her voice sounding odd even to her own ears.

"We . . . thought we'd be gone before you got home," Angie added lamely, apparently trying to defuse what she thought could turn into an explosive situation.

"So how's the campaign shaping up?"

Kate jerked her gaze off Angie's sheepish face and onto Dave. A smirk tipped the corners of his lips. Don't let him see that you're aching to slap that smirk off his face. Keep your cool. "Fine. Just fine."

"What are your chances for getting elected?" Dave pressed.

"Do you really care?" Kate snapped in spite of the lecture she'd just given herself.

Dave's face tightened, then he laughed. "You really are a cold bitch, you know."

"Hey, you two," Angie cried, her gaze flitting from one to the other. "Time out, okay?"

"I'll move my car so you can leave."

"Kate, wait."

Kate looked into Angie's pinched features, noted that her arm remained securely linked with Dave's.

"I'm waiting," Kate said on a sigh.

"I was going to tell you. Really I was."

"Were you, Ang?" It was a complete mystery to Kate how her friend could be romantically involved with a low-life like Dave Nielsen. Once she thought about it, the answer was clear. Dave was a successful attorney, with old-family money behind him. To Angie, he must seem like the perfect catch. The only problem was, Kate knew that Dave wasn't about to marry Angie.

"Kate, please don't be mad. I did *try* to tell you once, but you were due in court and . . . "

"To hell with her," Dave cut in sharply. "Who gives a shit if she's mad or not. You don't have to apologize for us."

"He's right, Angie. You can see whomever you please."

Angie cocked her head and peered closely at Kate. "I hear what you're saying, but I don't believe a word of it."

Kate smiled lamely. "It's okay. We'll talk about it later."

"Come on, baby," Dave urged, pulling on Angie's arm. "Let's get the hell out of here."

Angie looked as if she wanted to argue, but she didn't. Instead she gave Kate a bleak, helpless look, then followed Dave to his car.

If only she hadn't introduced them, Kate told herself. Kate had taken Angie to a firm party a few months ago, and when Dave had wandered up to their group, Kate had had no choice but to introduce them. She hadn't thought any more about it. Until now.

So what was Dave up to, she wondered as she cranked her car and backed out of the driveway. When Dave's car disappeared around the curve, she drove back in and parked. What was his ulterior motive for seeing Angie? Not for one second did Kate think he didn't have one. Revenge would be her guess.

With a heavy heart, she walked inside the house, the pleasure of returning home tainted.

"Wait up, Sawyer!"

Sawyer heard the shout from a distance and hesitated, though every nerve in his body told him to jump into the Jag and escape.

"Damn!" He didn't have time to fool with Harlan, not now, anyway. Through dark sunglasses, Sawyer watched as the real estate tycoon hurried up to him.

"I'm glad I caught you," Harlan said, sounding slightly out of breath. "Your secretary told me you'd just left. We must've missed each other by seconds."

"So?"

Some of Harlan's good humor vanished at Sawyer's obvious displeasure. "So, dammit, I wanted to talk to you," he ground out, his face red.

"What's so urgent? I'm already late for an appointment." Sawyer wasn't, but if he didn't tell Harlan a little white lie, no telling what he'd con him into doing.

"I have some information I thought might help."

"With what?"

"Your investigation of Kate Colson."

Sawyer went still. "Oh?"

"I was at Johns and Strassberg's yesterday where I learned something very interesting."

"Really," Sawyer said impatiently. His gut told him that for a reason he didn't wish to examine too closely, he wasn't going to like what Harlan was about to say.

Harlan's lips thinned. "Her ex-boss just gave her a hefty campaign contribution."

"So?"

Harlan's face turned redder. "So! Is that all you can say?"

"Well, I would say more, only I fail to see why that's any help in my investigation."

"She's sleeping with the man, for god's sake!"

"Can you substantiate that or is it just rumor?"

Harlan's blustering confidence faltered. "It's just rumor, but I'm sure it's the truth. I told you already how fast she shot to the top of the firm. And I still think that happened because she slept her way there." His sudden laughter twisted his features. "She's smart, all right, but she isn't that goddamn smart. She just knew which buttons to push, and I'll bet you ten to one, she's pushing those same buttons with one or more of her fellow judges."

"I'll keep that in mind."

"What the hell's the matter with you?" Harlan angled his head. "Has she gotten to you, too? By god, are *you* having visions of getting a piece of that—pussy?"

"I'd watch what I said, if I were you."

Sawyer's deadly tone seemed to have the desired effect on Harlan. "Sorry," Harlan muttered.

"If you'll just get off your soap box, I'll get to work." Sawyer paused pointedly. "On Kate Colson."

Harlan's eyes lit. "Why didn't you say that in the first place?"

"You never gave me the chance. You were too busy letting your mouth overload your ass."

Harlan slapped Sawyer on the shoulder. "I knew you wouldn't let me down. Go after her, son."

Sawyer climbed into the Jaguar, switched on the engine and drove off. No matter how far or how fast he drove, he couldn't get the bad taste out of his mouth.

Twenty-eight

The neon sign was there, a bit askew and faded, but there, nonetheless. **Shady Oaks Motel.** Underneath the lighted words was another word: **Vacancy.** Memories of the nights Sawyer had spent in dumps like this rushed to his mind. A feeling of helpless disgust charged through him.

He climbed out of his Jaguar and made his way up the sidewalk. His eyes shifted from right to left, taking in the surroundings. He imagined what this place must have looked like years ago when that tiny baby had been abandoned here. Not much different than it looked today, he told himself, his thoughts centering again on the maniac who would do such a thing.

An air of neglect hovered over the place like a smothering blanket. Not only did the building need painting, it demanded a complete renovation. He'd bet the rooms slanted downhill and wouldn't support a glass on the wobbly table that would occupy each of the cubbyholes.

Sawyer paused on a narrow porch and squinted through the battered blind that was half open and half closed. No one was at the front desk, but he was sure someone was close by.

He opened the door to a loud clanging sound. Almost instantly, a greasy, pot-bellied man appeared through a door to the right of the desk.

He eyed Sawyer closely while he dug between his teeth

with a toothpick. "We only have one room left," he said. "Take it or leave it."

For a moment Sawyer didn't respond. He was busy surveying the lobby. If possible, it was in a sadder state of disrepair than the outside. The floor was covered with a green carpet that at one time probably had matched the green-plaid upholstered furniture. Now both were worn and filthy. The strong smell of food almost choked Sawyer. He fought the urge to turn and get the hell out of there.

Instead he squared his shoulders and faced the man who was eyeing him with bored curiosity.

"Well, Mister, what's it gonna be? I ain't got all day, you know."

"I don't want a room," Sawyer said.

The man's expression tensed. "What do you want?"

"Information."

His expression went from tense to ugly. "You a cop? 'Cause if you are—"

"I'm not a cop, but I am a private investigator."

The man spat the toothpick out of one side of his mouth. It landed next to Sawyer's elbow. "Well, now, I don't like them any better than I like cops."

"You don't have to like me. You just have to talk to me." Before the man could reply, Sawyer reached inside his coat pocket and pulled out two twenty-dollar bills.

The man's eyes lit up, and his tone became conciliatory. He grinned and rubbed his T-shirt-clad belly. "Well, I guess the cat just turned loose of my tongue." His grin spread. "Git it?"

"Yeah, I get it," Sawyer said, handing him a twenty.

"So whatcha' wanna know?" The man slouched on the counter and waited.

"How long have you worked here?"

" 'Bout ten years. Me and the missus bought it from a fellow and his wife."

"Do you know where he might be right now? The other fellow, I mean?"

"Yeah, he's pushin' up."

Sawyer released a controlled breath. "You mean he's dead?"

"Yep."

"What about his wife?"

He belched. "She's pushin' up, too."

"You didn't by any chance hear either of them mention a baby that was left here about nineteen years ago?"

"Left in one of the rooms?"

He didn't seem at all shocked, Sawyer thought. In this dump, he probably saw and heard even worse. "That's what I mean."

"Naw, don't recall it."

Sawyer's anger rose. "You're going to have to do better than this or you ain't gonna earn that money I gave you." His gaze narrowed, and his voice hardened. "You wouldn't wanna have to give that back, now, would you?"

The man backed up slightly as if he was suddenly afraid of Sawyer. "No, I don't wanna give it back."

Sawyer smiled. "Then I suggest you dig deep in that brain of yours and think of something, anything, that might help me."

"Well, there was an old man who'd worked here ever since the motel was built."

Sawyer felt a surge of hope. "Where can I find him?"

"Well—" He scratched his head again, this time sending white flakes to his shoulders. "I don't rightly know. Lemme see, we might still have somthin' with his address on it."

"Would you please check," Sawyer said tightly.

"It's gonna cost you more money."

Sawyer slapped down another bill. "Find it."

The man eyed Sawyer another long minute as if he wasn't sure he should turn his back on him. Finally, he shuffled back into the room where he'd come from.

Sawyer jammed his hands into his pockets and cursed silently. He hadn't done this type of investigative work in years, not since his agency had expanded. His expertise lay in the field of industrial espionage and insurance fraud investigations. So why was he doing this tedious job now? It wasn't because of Harlan. He readily admitted that. What he wouldn't admit was that he was here because of a woman with sad, chocolate-brown eyes.

Suddenly Sawyer thought he saw something move. Snapping his gaze to the left, he watched a giant cockroach stroll across the desk, then disappear.

Another curse singed the air just as the man came back to the front, a grin on his face. "Got it, his home address."

Sawyer all but snatched the paper from the man. "Much obliged."

With that he turned and walked out into the sunshine, taking his first deep breath since he'd arrived.

Ten minutes later, Sawyer pulled up in front of another sad, neglected structure. The small frame house, with it peeling paint and warped porch, stood on a corner lot in a neighborhood that had gone from good to bad to worse. Some of the homes to the right and to the left were deserted, while others, still occupied, were in the same state of neglect.

Yet this particular house where the janitor, Matt Roscoe, lived, or so Sawyer hoped, had a different look. The grass, what little there was of it, was mowed. Curtains hung at the windows and an aroma of bacon hung in the air.

Sawyer walked to the front door and knocked. A gray-haired woman responded to his knock. She dried her hands on her apron and gave him a tentative smile.

He felt encouraged. "Good morning, ma'am. I'm sorry to disturb you, but I'm looking for a Matthew Roscoe. Does he by any chance live here?"

Her smile disappeared, and her features returned to their pinched dullness. Sawyer's hopes deflated. Still, he held out his identification badge.

"Detective?" The wrinkles in the woman's forehead deepened. "I don't understand."

"I just need to ask him some questions, that's all." Sawyer's smile was warm. "Is he here?"

"No . . . no, he isn't."

Damn! His face showed none of his inner frustrations. He held his smile in place. "Do you expect him back any time soon?" He knew he had to be gentle with this woman. While she was pleasant enough, she was the type who would slam the door in his face if he pushed too hard.

"No, actually, he doesn't live here anymore."

"Can you tell me where he does live?" He'd forgotten just what a pain in the ass investigative work was. It would try the patience of a saint, and he was no saint. "Look, Ms.—"

"Myers," she said in a less suspicious tone. "Im his daughter."

"All I want to do is ask Mr. Roscoe some questions about a baby that was supposedly left at the Shady Oaks Motel some years back."

The pinched dullness eroded into a frown. "I don't recall him ever mentioning that."

"That's why it's important that I speak to him." Sawyer stressed the *him*.

She paused as if to consider telling him any more or not. Sawyer could see the war waging on her features. Apparently, he passed the test because she added, "He's in a nursing home in Houston where my sister can look after him. But he's in poor health. He don't always get things right. You know what I mean? He's not crazy, just a little confused."

"I understand, Ms. Myers. But I'd still like to talk to him, so if you'd give me the address of the nursing home, I'd sure appreciate it."

"Just a moment, and I'll write it down for you."

Moments later she handed him a piece of paper. Sawyer smiled as he slipped it into his coat pocket. Something told him not to offer her money. She was a far cut above that sleazy motel operator, and he wouldn't insult this woman for anything.

He held out his hand and said, "Thanks for your time and your help."

She placed her rough one in his and smiled shyly. "I hope he can help you."

"Me, too," Sawyer said, before turning and ambling down the steps.

He had a bona fide lead now. All he had to do was find the time to get to Houston. First, though, he had to see the client.

He didn't stop to ask himself if it was wise, because he already knew the answer. It damn well *wasn't* wise.

Kate paused and stared out a window of her campaign headquarters. What a lovely night, she thought. The sky was on fire like a box full of precious stones. She was sure there weren't enough numbers to count the stars. Only God could do that, the same God that she hoped was taking care of her child.

Shaking off the melancholy feeling, Kate left the window and returned to her desk. The headquarters was a beehive of activity. Ginger was rushing around like a drill sergeant, giving orders to the numerous volunteers. They merely smiled in a good-natured fashion and saluted her.

The noise and the organized bedlam got to Kate. She could only get here at the end of a full day in court. The nursing home case had gone to the jury early that morning. The afternoon had been filled with one case after another until her legs had cramped from sitting for so long.

She had felt obligated to stop by the campaign headquarters because Ginger had more television ads for her to approve. Right now she was deciding what the campaign posters would say and where they should be put. Many of the volunteers that Ginger had rounded up had been asking friends and businesses alike if they would display Kate's signs when they were ready.

"Kate."

She swung around to find Ginger staring at her with eyebrows drawn together in a frown. "There's a man to see you."

"Who?"

Ginger shrugged. "He didn't tell me his name, just said he was a reporter."

Kate shoved her disheveled hair back from her face, leaving her frown visible. No way was she going to answer a bunch of questions from a snoopy reporter.

"Tell him to make an appointment."

"I figured you'd say that."

Kate's stomach lurched, even as she snapped her head around and fastened her gaze on Sawyer. Somehow she managed to hang on to her poise, certain that anything less would be perceived as weakness.

Sawyer rested against a desk, his arms crossed over his chest. It had been a week since she had seen him. Too bad; his attraction hadn't lessened any. As usual, he looked intense in a pair of jeans, silk shirt and boots. Kate felt extremely uncomfortable—and furious under the scrutiny of those piercing green eyes.

"This way," Kate said into the silence, her tone terse.

Sawyer nodded to Ginger, who didn't bother to mask her curiosity, then said, "Yes, ma'am."

Once they reached a deserted room, Kate closed the door, whipped around, and glared at him. "How dare you show up here?"

The anger in Sawyer's eyes quickly sparked to match hers. "I needed to talk to you."

"That's not good enough."

"Well, that's just too damn bad," he said, his voice low, barely controlled.

"You assured me you were discreet."

"This is business."

Her face flushed. "What do you want?"

"Actually, I have something to report, but if you don't want to hear it—" He let his words play out in a tight voice.

Kate got the message, and her tone became much more conciliatory while her heart jumped a bit. "Sorry. Let's hear it."

"The motel's still there."

Relief made Kate weak. "Thank God. I was afraid it might've been torn down."

"Me too."

"I have a lead on an old janitor who used to work there." He was careful not to mention the gory details of the hovel.

"And have you spoken to him?" she asked a trifle breathlessly.

"Not yet, but I'll be going to Houston soon to do just that."

They were quiet for a moment, as if both lost in their own thoughts. Sawyer was the one who broke the silence. "I've been forthcoming, now it's your turn."

"Fair enough. What do you want to know?" Kate asked, though she knew she would regret her generosity.

"The mother's name, for starters." He raised his hand when she would have spoken. "I know, I've asked you that already. Twice, in fact. Both times you've said it's irrelevant. Only it's *not* irrelevant."

A chill spread down Kate's spine. "Yes, it is."

"Again, let me be the judge of that."

"I'm not at liberty to divulge that information. The mother's wish is that her name be kept out of this."

Sawyer stared at her for a long moment. Was he going to tell her he was no longer going to work for her? Her stomach twisted in knots from the highly charged atmosphere.

"Was she the last one to see the child?"

"Yes."

"And?"

"She thought the baby was being adopted. So you see, the mother couldn't help you because she doesn't know anything else."

"Who took it?"

"Her boyfriend," Kate admitted reluctantly.

"He's the father, I presume."

Kate could feel the pulse working in her throat. "Yes."

"Then I sure as hell need to talk to him."

"He doesn't know anything. He's the one who dumped the baby in the motel and left."

"Like I said, a real piece of shit."

Kate agreed wholeheartedly with Sawyer's assessment of Thomas, but she didn't share her thoughts. "When you return from Houston, let me know what you found out immediately."

He laughed, but with no warmth. "Yes, ma'am," he said in that same mocking tone.

"Good-bye for now, Mr. Brock." Her voice was flat, distant.

"Not good-bye, Kate, just good evening."

He turned and made his way to the door. She waited until he got there before she said, "Don't ever come here again."

He spun and, without warning, cut the distance between them. He stopped just short of touching her. "What is it with you, huh?"

Kate hid mounting anxiety behind firm words. "I'm trying to avoid unfavorable publicity. The press is always lurking. Under no circumstances can they know about this investigation."

"What are you hiding, Judge?" Sawyer took a step closer, taking a perverse delight in unnerving her. "Seems to me like you're taking all this mighty personally."

She looked up just in time to meet his gaze. And for a moment, the atmosphere between them crackled.

"I'm not hiding anything," she said, desperately trying to keep the tremor out of her voice.

"I find that hard to believe, especially after rumors I've heard."

Both anger and curiosity raged a battle within Kate. Curiosity won. "And just what were they?"

"Oh, that you slept your way to the top of the law firm and that you're doing the same thing at the courthouse."

Stunned by the attack, Kate sucked in her breath and fought back the rage that threatened to render her useless. Then without conscious thought, she reached out to push him as far away from her as she could, only to regret that impulsive action. The contact with his hard body, through the silk, knocked the breath out of her.

The contact affected him, too; she heard *his* sharp intake of breath. But she managed to defuse the lethal situation with her sharp words, "You can take what you heard and go to hell!"

He stared hard at her, while a complete silence filled the room.

Kate stood still, and with every nerve exposed, waited for his verbal retaliation. None came. He merely looked at her, his face bloodless and tight. Then he turned and walked out of the room.

Trembling, Kate leaned against the desk for support. Her mind raced. She felt like she was on a roller-coaster ride. Before she lost complete control, before she did something she would be sorry for, she had to get off. Now.

Twenty-nine

"Another lawsuit?"

Ralph quirked his lip. " 'Fraid so, boss."

"Sonofabitch," Sawyer mumbled.

"Ditto." Ralph hitched his pants and plopped down on one corner of Sawyer's desk. His right leg began swinging in time to the miniature grandfather clock that chimed the hour.

"I might as well add this one to the list," Sawyer said, shuffling through a stack of papers on his desk.

"This one is compliments of Ernest Grimes, the investigator that wouldn't work because of illness." Ralph harrumphed. "Yet when the little weasel brought in those doctor's slips, they were phony as hell."

Sawyer peered steadily at Ralph. "You're sure about that?"

"Damn sure, about all but one, that is. It was legit, but trust me, that was the only one because I checked them out personally."

Sawyer rubbed the bridge of his nose. "I'll call both attorneys this morning and see where we stand. It's getting so that you can't even fire an employee who refuses to work."

Ralph stood. "I don't see it getting any better, either. Meantime, I'm burying myself behind closed doors, hoping to tie up all the loose ends on that government proposal."

"Fine." Sawyer's face lost some of its brooding darkness.

"I'm still counting on landing that plum. Don't let me down."

"You know I'll do all I can, but like I told you the other day, the ball may end up entirely in your court. You know what a pain in the butt Uncle Sam is to deal with."

"We'll take it one step at a time."

"Check with you later."

Long after Ralph had quietly shut the door behind him, Sawyer continued to stare at the pile of papers on his desk. He simply could not concentrate.

Kate Colson.

He longed for a drink, only it was too damn early. He got up from behind the desk and went to the bar, where he poured himself a cup of coffee. When the first sip hit his stomach, he felt instantly better even though this was his first cup of the day.

He sat back down, but still he didn't return to the job at hand. He should have stayed away from her. He should not have gone to the nursery or to the campaign office. She had hired him because he was discreet, because he knew how to conduct himself.

Discreet, hell. He'd gone charging into both places like a bull in a china shop. From now on, though, he wouldn't conjure up excuses. It would be legitimate business or nothing.

In defense of himself, he'd wanted to get this job over with. Thanks to Harlan, it had become distasteful.

Sawyer gripped his forehead as if to banish Kate's face. Why hadn't he kept his big mouth shut? He wished he could retract his cruel words. She wasn't anything like Harlan had painted her.

Still, Sawyer had wanted to believe the worst. Now, he wasn't too sure about anything, much less Kate Colson. When he had accused her of having slept her way to the top, she hadn't reacted as expected.

For one unguarded moment, her carefully composed facade had cracked. Her rage had been genuine and her pain obvious. It was the vulnerability that had gotten to him, that had dammed the breath in his throat.

At first, Kate had been a challenge and a nagging irritant.

No longer. Now he felt a different emotion altogether—a desire to protect her from Harlan. But most of all, from himself.

Badly shaken by her pain, he would have given anything to pull out a magic wand and pass it across her face, removing the pain he'd put there.

He couldn't shrug off the haunting memory. He wasn't used to feeling this way. He was always in control, the one in charge. And he would be again.

To hell with his morbid thoughts and to hell with *her*. The complications that she could bring to his life simply weren't worth it. As long as he kept that in the forefront of his mind, he'd be okay.

He supposed loneliness had brought on all this soul-searching. Was he at the crossroads in his life where he wanted more than his job offered? No. However, he would admit that loneliness did gnaw at his gut, leaving him raw and unfit for the human race.

He could overcome that, too, just as he'd overcome his other weaknesses.

Sawyer strode to the door and yanked it open. His secretary stopped what she was doing and looked at him wide-eyed.

"Jane, I need you to take dictation," he said through tight lips.

"When will I see you again?" Angie heard the desperate note in her voice and hated herself for it. But when it came to Dave, she couldn't seem to help herself. He had become an addiction that she couldn't get enough of, offering her the same high that cocaine had once provided.

"Soon, love, soon," Dave cajoled.

Angie's heart upped its beat. "I hope so. I'm counting on it."

"I'll call you."

"Dave, look, I—" Angie couldn't finish the sentence. The words just dried up in her throat.

"What?"

She heard the impatience in his voice, though she tried not to let it upset her. After all, it was time for him to be at the office. "Nothing. Forget it for now."

"Whatever you say."

"Bye," she whispered, blinking back tears.

Angie didn't realize that she was trembling until she tried to fit the receiver back on the hook. It took her three tries before she made it.

"Damn!" she said, bouncing off the bed and slipping into a pair of cut-offs and a T-shirt. She hurried into the bathroom, where she attempted to make up her face. Her hands shook so that the task was almost impossible.

Her deepening sexual involvement with Dave Nielsen, as unexpected as it was exciting, had her nerves on edge. Remaining in Kate's house only exacerbated it. She had to leave. Not only did Angie feel as if she was imposing, but she knew Kate disapproved of her continuing relationship with Dave.

With tears burning her eyes, Angie went back into the bedroom, walked to the closet and grabbed her battered suitcase. For the first time in a long while, a man excited her. She wasn't about to give him up. Not for anything or anyone.

By the time she finished packing, the tears were dried on her cheeks and her lips were set in determination.

Maybe Dave would ask her to marry him. That would certainly solve all of her problems. To her way of thinking, such a thought wasn't an impossible dream. If it was the last thing she did, she'd make it come true.

She would.

Despite the face that it was Saturday, Kate awakened much later than she intended. When she got a chance to sleep, she took it because it had eluded her for so long.

The case Kate was due to hear soon preyed on her mind. A mercy killing—a case guaranteed to be both depressing and difficult. She and the other judges had all talked it over and somehow she'd ended up with it on her docket.

"You're the right one to take the case, Kate," Mike Ashburn, the senior judge, had told her.

"Oh, Mike, I don't know. You've had so much more experience than I have."

"That doesn't make any difference, not in your case, anyway. In the short time you've been on the bench, you've garnered a reputation of being tough but fair."

"Flattery will get you nowhere."

He grinned. "It's not flattery and you know it. Besides, the defendant and his attorney asked for a non-jury trial and requested you as the judge."

"Really?" Kate asked in awe.

Ashburn's lips twitched. "Really, and you ought to be pleased."

"Pleased? I'm scared to death."

"That's good. That's what keeps us human."

"I guess you're right," Kate said, "but somehow that doesn't drive the butterflies out of my stomach."

The butterflies were still playing havoc with her stomach. And Sawyer Brock's last visit wasn't helping any.

Her heart skipped a beat. When she had placed her palm against his chest . . . No. She wouldn't replay that foolishness in her mind. She wouldn't give in to the emotions this man evoked in her. She had her life planned; a man simply did not fit into those plans. Even if she were interested, she wouldn't choose a man like Sawyer; he would always remind her too much of her past.

Kate's rumbling stomach suddenly made her realize that she hadn't eaten nor had she had a cup of coffee. She left the bedroom and walked toward the kitchen.

She didn't see the suitcase until she'd stumbled over it.

"Ouch!" she cried, leaning down and covering her big toe with her hand. Kate looked at it to make sure she hadn't drawn blood. She hadn't.

When she lifted her head, Angie stood staring at her. Kate's eyes widened.

"Sorry," Angie said, shifting her gaze.

Kate pushed her hair out of her face and squinted at her

friend, who reminded her of a lost puppy. Angie was long-faced and maybe a little cowed.

"What's this all about?" Kate asked, incredulity in her voice.

"I thought it would be best if I left."

"Why on earth would you think a thing like that?"

"I thought the reason was obvious."

"Oh, Angie," Kate cried, her heart heavy. She should have suspected something like this, only she'd been too preoccupied to pay any attention.

"I've imposed on you long enough."

"You know better than that," Kate responded, her voice a bit shaky.

"Oh, Katie, I don't know better than that," Angie wailed. "We both know that—"

"I don't approve of Dave," Kate finished for her.

"That's right."

"Well, that's not the end of the world, you know." And it wasn't. Granted, she thought Dave was a rat, pure and simple. Angie just hadn't seen that side of him yet, but given time, she would.

Meanwhile, Kate couldn't bear to see her back on the street, possibly living in some hovel. Angie's job as a secretary didn't pay much. That aside, Angie was her friend; she always had been and always would be. Nothing would change that, especially not Dave.

Finally, Kate said, "Go unpack. You're not going anywhere."

"I won't stop seeing Dave." A look of defiance appeared in Angie's eyes as well as her voice.

"I think you're making a big mistake." When Angie would have interrupted, Kate raised her hand and stopped her. "Hear me out. Like I told you when you moved in, you're free to do as you please. I still mean that. If you think Dave is right for you and that you need him in your life, then who am I to pass judgment?" She paused and took a deep breath. "Just be careful. That's all I ask."

"Are you sure?"

"I'm sure." Kate forced a smile. "Go unpack while I fix us some breakfast."

Angie's chin wobbled. "Thanks, Katie. I owe you."

"No, you don't," Kate said softly. "Remember, I'm the one with the debt."

Thirty

"Mmm, I could stay like this forever," Angie murmured as she snuggled closer to Dave's nude body.

With his arms around her, Dave trailed a finger up and down her back. But his mind was miles away. He knew he ought to get his butt up and get dressed. He had a tough day in front of him. His lips suddenly stretched into a thin, tight line. He couldn't afford to make any more mistakes, at least not noticeable mistakes. It seemed that Bill Johns watched him constantly and was ready to pounce on him like a hungry dog on a bone if he should make one wrong move.

"What's the matter?" Angie asked, pulling back and peering up at him through rather dazed eyes.

"Nothing. Why?"

She sighed, her lips grazing his chest. "You tensed up all of a sudden, as if you were having a bad dream." She smiled. "Only you weren't asleep."

Dave wished his problems were only bad dreams. But he wasn't about to discuss his work or anything with this woman. Angie was a good lay, and that was all. Right now, his efforts were concentrated in keeping his ass away from the firing squad.

Since the Harlan Moore tax debacle, his life hadn't been the same. When Moore had raised hell and transferred his business to Kate Colson, Johns had gone berserk. The boss

210

rarely tolerated what he called critical mistakes. In Johns's estimation, Dave hadn't just made a mistake, he had screwed up royally, and he hadn't forgotten the incident.

And it was all that bitch's fault.

"Are you sure nothing's wrong?" Angie whispered, her lips close to his ear.

Dave shivered.

"You're still strung too tight to suit me."

"I was just thinking about your buddy, actually."

This time it was Angie who tensed. "Kate." She made a flat statement.

"Yep."

"What about her?"

Dave lifted an eyebrow, her petulant tone grating on his nerves. "Surely you're not jealous of her?"

"Of course not," Angie snapped.

"Yeah, right."

Angie kissed him on the lips. "All right, I'll admit it. I'm jealous of any woman who looks at you."

"That's a mistake," Dave said brutally. "I see who I damn well please."

Angie's lower lip trembled before she bit down on it. "Sorry, I didn't mean to get possessive." She paused as if to regain control, then spoke again. "What about Kate?"

"She made me look like a fool."

"You're kidding. How could anyone do that? Why, you're so smart and have so much on the ball."

"Just trust me, she did."

"I . . . didn't know."

"Well, it's not something I talk about to just anyone."

"Gee, she must've really done something terrible. I can't imagine—"

"It was bad."

Angie wrinkled her forehead. "I know how ambitious Kate is. Still—"

Dave's eyes merely darkened, and he remained quiet for a long moment. "Enough about that bitch. Let's fuck."

Angie flicked her tongue across his button-hard nipple. "I thought we just did, all night, in fact."

"So? What's wrong with doing it again? Then I got to split."

"You're a randy s.o.b., aren't you?"

"Are you complaining?"

"Not on your life."

"Didn't think so."

By now Angie's lips and tongue had moved from his nipples to his belly. Her tongue dipped into his naval.

"Ahhh, yeah, baby."

"Like that, huh?"

"Oh, you bet," Dave wheezed.

As his words encouraged her, Angie grasped him and massaged him. His breath caught in his lungs. "Suck me off," he ordered, his breath coming in short spurts.

"Whatever you want," Angie said eagerly, and replaced her hands with her mouth.

Dave thought he might not survive the aggressive attack on his organ, it was so exhilarating. He didn't know how long Angie would suit his purpose, but until he kicked her out of his bed, he was going to enjoy the ride.

He grabbed a handful of her hair and was about to sink into oblivion when the phone rang.

"Damn!"

Angie groaned. "Don't answer it."

"I have to. I'm working on an important case."

Angie lifted her head and watched as he reached for the receiver. "Yeah," he grunted.

"I need to see you."

Dave raised himself. "Harlan?"

"You mean you didn't recognize my voice?"

Dave pushed Angie away, all business now. "Sorry, I was sleeping."

"Sleeping? At this time of the morning?"

Dave had to bite his lower lip to keep from saying that it was only six o'clock, for chrissake. What he did say was, "I was about to get up."

He would like nothing better than to get back in Harlan's good graces. He knew for a fact that since Kate had left the firm, Harlan wasn't happy with the attorney who was handling his work. Dave yearned for the chance to prove that he could do every bit as good a job as Kate had, if only Harlan would give him another chance. The weight it would pull with his boss—well, that went without saying. For Harlan to call him, something must be up.

"So what can I do for you?" Dave tried to keep the eagerness out of his voice, but knew he failed.

"You can get your ass out of bed and to my office."

Dave felt an adrenaline high shoot through him that had nothing to do with sex. "Now?" he asked inanely.

"Yes, now," Harlan said with thinning patience. "Is that a problem?"

"No, sir, it's not." Dave's reply was as hasty as his lunge upright in the bed.

"Good. I'll expect you shortly."

Dave sat holding the receiver, listening to the obnoxious buzz while his insides quivered with excitement. Angie had scooted back to his side and was caressing his shoulder.

"No," he said, thrusting her aside. "I gotta go. Put your clothes on and beat it."

Angie lowered her eyes. "Will you call me?"

"Yeah, soon," Dave replied, his mind already on the possibility that this was the chance he'd been waiting for. Yet he knew in his gut that second chances were rarely free. He wondered as he headed for the shower what the price of this one might be.

It didn't matter. He'd gladly pay, whatever the cost.

Harlan Moore was pissed—about everything. Nothing seemed to be working in his favor. His misfortunes, once sparked, seemed to have multiplied. But he intended to remedy that situation.

While he would love to cast all the blame on Kate Colson's shoulders, he knew he could not. Some of it sure as hell could be placed there, and he intended to use that to his advantage. First, though, he intended to have her in his bed.

Harlan's heart thudded suddenly and sweat popped out on his forehead. He didn't know how he was going to accomplish that feat, but accomplish it he would. The "how-to" merely needed careful planning and deep thought.

Where the hell was Dave Nielsen? Harlan walked to the door of his office. He opened it to see his secretary standing near a filing cabinet, a raft of papers in her hand.

"The minute Nielsen gets here, send him in and hold all my calls."

"Yes, sir."

Once Harlan was back in his office, he sat down, only to get up again. He was too edgy to stay in one spot for long, although he had plenty of work awaiting his attention, work that even his able assistant couldn't handle.

He had just laced his coffee with a shot of bourbon when he heard the knock. "Come in."

Harlan eyed Dave closely, thinking he looked slightly unkempt, as if he'd dressed in a hurry. But then he guessed he had, as Harlan's phone call had roused him out of bed. His tie was slightly askew and his hair not quite in place. His suit, however, was of the best quality and fit his frame as if it had been tailor-made.

"I'm glad you called," Dave said with a smile.

"Are you now?"

Some of Dave's confidence seemed to fade like a balloon with a fast leak, but he faked it well. Harlan would have to hand him that.

"You bet I am," Dave said.

Still, it was obvious that Dave was uncomfortable. Good, Harlan thought. He had him exactly where he wanted him, on edge. He hadn't forgiven Dave for costing him money, but Dave didn't have to know that. Besides, Dave owed him, and Harlan was determined to make him pay. But he'd learned over the years that one caught more flies with the right words than with honey.

Harlan gave a curt jerk of his head. "Sit down."

Dave did as he was told, an expectant, yet controlled, look now on his face.

"How would you like to work for me again?" Harlan asked from behind his desk.

Dave's eyes sparked. "Are you serious?"

"I don't make idle offers," Harlan said coldly.

Dave flushed. "Of course you don't. And, yes, I'd like that very much. But why? I mean—" His voice played out.

"For one, I'm not happy with Riley. He's not hungry enough."

"I understand."

"My partner and I are splitting—or rather we *have* split."

Dave looked shocked. "Why?"

"He's turned out to be a liability rather than an asset."

"What do you want me to do?" Dave sat on the edge of his chair.

A hard, cold kernel of anger shone in Harlan's eyes. "Get me everything. I don't want the bastard to get one red cent."

"I'll do what I can."

"That's not good enough."

"Okay, so I'll nail his ass."

"Just do it. Whatever it takes."

"You can count on me. I won't let you down this time."

"I wouldn't advise it."

Dave swallowed visibly. "I appreciate your giving me a second chance."

Harlan nodded curtly, not in any mood to hear Nielsen's babbling gratitude.

Dave stood, as if sensing the meeting was over. "I'll get started on it as soon as you give me the information I need."

Harlan waved his hand. "Ask my secretary. She'll give it to you."

"I'll be in touch, then." Dave sauntered to the door.

"Oh, by the way."

Dave swung around and waited.

"How do you feel about Kate Colson?"

A flush covered Dave's face. "Why are you asking me that?" His tone was cautious.

"I want to rain on her parade, that's why."

Dave seemed at a loss as to how to react. Harlan smiled at the confusion written across Dave's face. "You thought I'd be Kate's champion, didn't you, thinking that after all, she'd saved me bundles of money on my taxes?"

"That's exactly what I was thinking."

"Well, you thought wrong."

Dave shrugged. "She's not my favorite person, either."

That was what Harlan wanted to hear. Yet he shouldn't have to depend on this jerk to help him. Sawyer was supposed to be getting the goods on Kate Colson. So far, Harlan wasn't pleased with Sawyer's performance. Harlan smiled inwardly. He knew there were other ways to skin a cat. Dave Nielsen had probably been trying to do the same longer than he.

"Think you can help me?" Harlan purposely kept his voice bland, as if he were asking the time of day.

Dave, on the other hand, held nothing back. He stepped forward, a strange light in his eyes. "I not only can, but will."

"How?"

"I've been seeing Kate's best friend."

Harlan lifted his eyebrows. "Seeing?"

"Sleeping with her."

"Ah, now, that's more like it," Harlan replied with a smile. "Think she'll talk to you?"

Dave didn't hesitate. "I know so. In fact, we discussed Kate this morning."

Harlan rubbed his chin. "That's interesting."

"Right now, I have Angie where I want her."

"Keep me informed."

"Will do."

Dave nodded. When the door closed behind him, Harlan's eyes narrowed, his mind already switched off Kate and onto his soon-to-be ex-partner.

No one fucked over Harlan Moore and got away with it. No one.

Thirty-one

Kate was nervous, nervous to the point that her stomach was queasy. She was meeting Sawyer. He had something to tell her.

Hoping to calm herself, she took deep breaths. They helped somewhat, enabling her to freshen her makeup and recomb her hair. Finally ready to walk out the door, she paused in front of the full-length antique mirror in her bedroom and stared at her reflected image.

Not bad, she thought with a grim smile, especially as she had dressed early that morning, then worked all day. She'd chosen a rich rose-colored linen dress, with a matching jacket. Her hair was pulled back at the nape of her neck, coiled, then clipped with a gold barrette.

Another sigh escaped her. Why did she care how she looked? Determined not to dally, she walked out the front door and got into her car, only to realize her hands were clammy. Ignoring that, she started the car and backed out of the drive.

As Kate pulled into an empty parking lot adjacent to the building, a feeling of apprehension completely overtook her excitement. What if the news Sawyer had for her wasn't good, what if . . . No! She wouldn't let her imagination run wild. Her fears were usually worse than life's hand.

Once she was out of the car, Kate noticed that dark clouds

had formed. At the last minute, she grabbed her umbrella out of the front seat and made her way across the street to the out-of-the- way café Sawyer had chosen.

By the time Kate had opened the door and crossed the threshold, her mouth was cotton-dry.

The café was small, dark and dank. She shivered, glad she had on a jacket. On closer observation, the place was immaculate, and the aroma coming from the kitchen was quite tantalizing. Her stomach gave a decided lurch, reminding her that she hadn't eaten since breakfast.

"You can have a seat anywhere."

At the sound of the voice, Kate turned. A woman behind the cashier's stand was smiling at her, almost as hard as she was chewing a piece of gum.

"Thanks, but I'm supposed to meet someone."

The woman gave her a conspiratorial look. "It wouldn't by any chance be that gentleman over there?"

Kate turned in the direction the woman indicated. Sawyer sat at a table tucked in a corner, a bottle of beer in front of him.

She flushed, knowing exactly what the woman thought. Without looking at her, Kate said, "Thank you."

Sawyer didn't see her until she reached the table. "Ah, you made it. Good." He stood and held out her chair.

"You knew I'd come, surely?"

He shrugged. "No, I didn't, not here anyway. You made it plain you didn't want to be seen with me in public. So—"

"No problem. This place is fine."

A faint smile lifted Sawyer's lips. "Good. I'm glad you approve."

Kate expected to hear that familiar mocking edge in his tone, but if it was there, she failed to pick up on it.

"Well, it's different, to say the least."

Sawyer sat back down and took a swig of beer. "It is that."

Kate looked around. The tables were made of brown Formica and had a candle burning in the middle of each. There was no one eating, but several men were sitting at the bar.

Suddenly a clap of thunder rattled the building. She jumped.

"Hey, take it easy," Sawyer said.

Before Kate could respond, the waitress appeared at Sawyer's side. "What'll y'all have?"

"Only coffee for me," Kate said, watching Sawyer. He was dressed in a pair of dark slacks and had apparently discarded his tie. The collar of his silk shirt was unbuttoned and hinted at the wiry, dark hair underneath. She swallowed hard, then turned away before he caught her staring.

"I'm fine for now," Sawyer was saying to the waitress.

Once the waitress had gone, the silence between them stretched. Sawyer seemed content to sip on his beer, his brows drawn together in concentration.

Kate wanted to shout at him to say what he had to say so that she could get out of there, away from him.

The waitress brought Kate's coffee and set it in front of her. "If y'all want anything else, just holler," the woman said, then shuffled off again.

Kate lifted the cup to her lips just as another clap of thunder rocked the building. Sheets of rain slammed against the windowpanes. Her slender frame shook visibly.

"You always this jumpy?" Sawyer asked. "Sure you wouldn't like a glass of wine?"

"Yes, I'm always this jumpy when the weather's bad. And no, I don't care for any wine."

Sawyer faced the window. "I'll have to admit, Mother Nature's raising some kinda hell."

Kate felt herself relax somewhat. Maybe this encounter wasn't going to be so bad after all. She took a sip of her coffee, then made a face.

"What's the matter? The coffee taste bad?"

"It's a toss-up as to which is stronger—the coffee or the weather."

Sawyer laughed. "Then don't drink it. Come on, have a glass of wine. It'll do you good."

When he laughed like that, causing the brooding darkness to disappear from his face, Kate realized she could easily forget why they were here and who he was. They could have

been a couple who had met for a forbidden liaison, savoring
with anticipation what was to follow, reinforced with intimate conversation, heady drinks, *warm touches* . . . She almost gasped aloud at the path her thoughts had taken.

Some sign must have escaped because he asked, "Is something wrong?"

"No," she said quickly, striving to put things back on an
even keel. "It's just that I don't normally drink wine," she
added.

"Why not? They say it's good for the blood."

"That might be true, but it's not good for my control."

"Losing control every once in a while might not be a bad
thing."

"For you maybe, but not for me."

For a moment, their eyes met and held.

"I gotta hand it to you, Judge. You're something else."

Kate turned away, knowing his words weren't complimentary. But she couldn't help how she felt. For nineteen years,
control over her emotions and her activities had been tops on
her list. Yet each time she was around Sawyer, that control
slipped a little more.

She blamed that on her physical attraction to him. Even
the fresh scent of his cologne tantalized her senses, as did the
way the hard lines around his eyes and mouth eased when he
smiled.

"Well?"

She shook her head. "Well, what?"

"You figured out what makes *me* tick yet?" he asked
bluntly.

Kate's breath caught. "You flatter yourself."

"Oh, I don't think so," he said with lazy ease. "But it
doesn't matter. I'll answer anything you want to ask. Almost
anything, that is."

"All right. How come you never married?" The minute the
question popped out of her mouth, Kate wished she could recall it, mortified at her impulsiveness.

A smile flirted with Sawyer's mouth, as if he realized how
uncomfortable she was. Then his face turned serious. "No

reason, except I never found a woman who I thought could or would put up with my bad habits or my hectic life-style."

Despite the flippancy, his eyes revealed a vulnerability she never would have suspected.

"That's understandable," she said for lack of anything better to say, kicking herself all over again for asking the question in the first place.

"Still, I'd like to have a kid."

Kate's jaw dropped in disbelief.

He chuckled. "It's obvious you weren't expecting that."

Kate ignored the twinge of pain inside her and said, "No, no, I wasn't."

He shrugged. "Sounds crazy, I know, but—" He broke off, then added, "Enough about me. How 'bout yourself? Why haven't you married?"

She shifted in her chair. "My career has always been the most important thing to me." She knew she came across sounding like a prim old maid. But again, this man seemed to bring out the worst in her.

"Ah, sounds like we have more in common than we care to admit."

The way he said that, combined with the intensity of his gaze, set off another warning bell inside Kate's head. But she couldn't ignore the tingle of excitement it brought as well. Yet flirting with this type of danger was suicidal. That dose of reality forced her to steer the conversation away from anything personal and back on business.

"If you don't mind, I'd like to get to the point of this meeting." The word "like" was a far cry from what she really felt, but she had to keep her emotions hidden. Maybe that was why she allowed the conversation to drift, so that she could postpone any crushing blow he might deliver.

"Sure thing," he said flatly. "I talked to the janitor."

Kate held her breath. "And?"

"He came through."

"That's great news."

"The old man couldn't tell me today's date, but he could tell me everything that happened years ago."

Kate's tongue was stuck to the roof of her mouth. She couldn't say a word.

"Anyhow," Sawyer went on, "around nineteen years back, he said he remembered a baby that had been found in one of the rooms."

Kate had difficulty in containing her excitement. "Go on."

"He's pretty sure a convent was called and a nun sent to pick up the child."

Kate's heart was drumming so hard inside her chest that she was sure Sawyer could hear it. Maybe her daughter was all right, after all. She licked her dry lips before saying, "That sounds like good news."

"I thought so, too."

"So what happens next?"

"The obvious. I track down the convent."

"Of course."

His eyes held hers in close scrutiny. "Is there anything you'd like to add?"

Kate had the feeling that if she were in court, he'd be the one found guilty, but guilty of what she wasn't sure. A cover-up, perhaps? He was as reluctant to share his secrets as she was hers. Still, she had a compelling urge to confess everything to him.

Suddenly she felt the urgent need to get away from his probing eyes and intimate questions. She refused to make a complete fool of herself.

"If there's nothing else, I should go." She forced herself to look at him, as if by doing so she could prove that she was once again in control of the situation.

"No problem," Sawyer said in a normal tone.

Kate noticed, however, that his lips were drawn tighter than usual as he stood, then walked around to her chair. It happened then, what she had feared most, only at the time she didn't realize it.

She reached for her purse, which was hanging on the back of the chair, at the same time Sawyer reached for the chair itself. Their hands touched.

With color in her cheeks, Kate stood abruptly. Instead of

releasing her hand, Sawyer tightened his grip and steadied her. For a long, frozen moment, his eyes settled on her face. Kate licked her lips and watched as his gaze drifted to her throat, then to her breasts, lingering for a split second. Just long enough for her to wonder what it would be like to kiss him. She suspected it would be an experience far beyond her imagination. He would exhibit control, but not at the cost of pleasing himself or her.

Those crazy thoughts forced Kate to withdraw her hand, but she was very much aware of the lingering warmth on her skin. "Sorry," she whispered.

"Me too," he responded in a gruff voice. Then without looking at her, he added, "We'd better get going."

The walk to the cars was made in silence. Even with distance between them, the power he exuded was attacking her nerves.

She was careful not to look at him until he had opened her car door, and she was behind the wheel. Later, she didn't know why she had chosen that moment to become careless and gaze at him, but she had found him leaning toward her, his face and lips only inches from hers.

She was startled, and her lips parted.

"Kate," he groaned at the same time he grasped the back of her neck and sank his mouth onto hers.

For an instant, the world seemed to falter around her, and she couldn't respond. But when his tongue broke through the barrier of her teeth, her entire body awakened.

The sweet assault was as hot as it was brief. Sawyer jerked back with a shattering expletive, directed at himself, she was sure. Yet his next words canceled any remorse he might have felt. "I won't apologize."

Her mind reeled beneath the implications of what had just happened. "I . . . didn't expect you to," she said weakly.

He rubbed the back of his neck.

"Look, I—"

"I have to go," she said, cutting across his words.

"I'll be in touch," he muttered, slamming her car door shut and stepping back.

It wasn't until Kate pulled up in her driveway that the truth hit her. She had known that searching for her daughter could present insurmountable difficulties. She had prepared herself for that.

What she hadn't expected was Sawyer Brock.

Thirty-two

Kate removed her gloves, then swept an unruly tendril of hair off her forehead. She wished the weather would change; it was too hot to suit her.

"Anything else, Señorita Colson?"

Kate turned and faced the man who ambled toward her. She smiled. "I can't believe you'd ask that, Carlos."

"Whatever you need, I'll do." He rubbed the mustache that seemed to grow with his grin.

"Well, I need for you to go home." Kate's eyes swept the yard. "We've done more in one afternoon than most people do in a week."

"But what about the flower beds?"

Kate shook her head. "I'll finish up there. You don't worry about them, okay?"

"Okay."

"I'll expect you again in a couple of weeks, though. Give my best to Juanita."

After Kate heard Carlos' pickup truck chug to life, she mopped the perspiration from her forehead and pulled her cotton shirt away from her bra.

She had taken the afternoon off, a rare turn for her. She had at last cleared her docket, and though she'd had numerous briefs and motions to study, only one was pressing, and she had already prepared for it. So it was with a clear conscience that she played in the dirt. If only she could simplify the rest of her problems as easily.

Feeling that tightness threatening to invade her chest again, Kate hurried to the long flower bed in front of the house, dropped to her knees, and started digging. Weeds and nut grass were plentiful. It was only after she'd yanked out two pieces of the grass that she realized she didn't have on her gloves.

"Darn," she muttered, and looked at the dirt that bordered each of her long, painted nails. "You're losing it, Kate Colson."

The damage was done; gloves would do her no good now. She sank her hands back into the ground and fought the soil with as much fervor as she fought off thoughts of Sawyer Brock. When it dawned on her that she was using her favored pastime, flower gardening, as a whipping post for her frustrations, she stopped.

Working in her yard usually gave her the mental space she needed to solve tough problems. Even when she hadn't had a yard, she had still puttered with potted plants.

But today, the gardening was no solace. No matter how hard she tried to purge him from her mind, Sawyer Brock continued to intrude where he wasn't wanted. Maybe if she thrashed it out, didn't try to fight thoughts of him, she might be able to put the matter to rest once and for all.

Perhaps when she saw him again, she would admit how ridiculous the whole thing was. Then again, what if she didn't? What if she was deliberately deceiving herself. Fear charged through her.

If only he hadn't kissed her.

In desperation, Kate cast her eyes toward the sky. The few clouds that floated reminded her of puffs of cotton candy. The sun, thank goodness, was hidden behind one of them, making the moment much more bearable. Nothing, however, could alleviate the high humidity.

Kate lifted her head higher and let the coolness of a sudden breeze play over her. She unhooked several buttons at the neck of her shirt and held it open to catch as much air as possible. While the gesture relieved her hot flesh, it did nothing to cool her mind.

Down the block she heard the screech of brakes. She looked up and watched as a convertible full of teenagers pulled against the curb several doors down from her. She suspected they were visiting the new teenager who had just moved there with the rest of her family.

Kate made a mental note to visit them, even as her mind's eye pictured the family unit. A husband, wife, and child—a real family, something she would never have.

An ache filled her heart. Was her present life-style no longer enough? Was that why she suddenly felt the need for a man? But the need wasn't for just any man. Only Sawyer Brock could fill that hole inside her.

Unconsciously, Kate dug back into the freshly turned earth, and for a moment its rich texture and musky odor soothed her. She held up one hand and let the soil trickle through her fingers and thought about him and how the feel of his callused hand against her soft one had nearly devastated her.

But thoughts of him were no longer enough. She wanted more. Not only did she want to feel his lips against hers again, she wanted to feel his entire body. She wanted to make love to him, have their bodies come together in an erotic collision.

Panic seized her. What if she gave into these desires, and they got in the way of finding her daughter? She couldn't take that chance, not for a few days, weeks, or months of sexual gratification, and not with a man who could not offer her any more permanency than she could offer him.

She would instead get hold of her tattered emotions and depend on the inner control that had never let her down. The pain of the past had helped mold her into a headstrong, competent woman who seldom let her heart overrule her head.

Despite this alien feeling inside her, tempting her, she would not give in. Not now, not ever.

"Yo, Kate!"

The unexpected sound of Angie's voice startled Kate. Her

hand flew to her chest, though the intrusion came as a blessed relief. She'd been saved from the hangman.

"Sorry, didn't mean to scare you."

"That's all right. My mind was on another planet."

Angie smiled tentatively. "Well, your hands certainly weren't. The flower bed looks super."

Kate brightened. "You think so? I've been out here all afternoon."

"I can tell. And *you* look like you could use a drink. How about I fix us a margarita?

Kate shook her head. "No margarita for me, thanks. But I could use a strong glass of iced tea."

"I'll holler when it's ready."

Kate collected her tools, then lifted her shoulders several times to remove the kinks. Did she feel better for all her soul-searching? Not really. She only hoped to remain strong enough to fend off any man who might undermine her determination to find her child.

"Tea's ready," Angie called from the porch.

With a resigned sigh, Kate made her way inside the house.

Harlan read the headlines in the morning paper and couldn't have been more pleased. In fact, he chuckled out loud, as he continued to read: PUNISHMENT PHASE OF CONTROVERSIAL MERCY KILLING NEARS END.

Kate Colson's courtroom promised to supply the goods he needed to launch his smear campaign against her. He took a sip of his coffee, while his eyes dipped back to the paper that was spread across the dining room table. The article beneath the headlines read as follows:

> There is much speculation as to how Judge Colson
> will rule on the killing. Her dissenters fear that
> she'll rule for the defendant, thus giving the
> flagrant disregard for life another boast. Her
> loudest dissenters at the moment are a Right To
> Life group that's gathered in the city to protest a
> new and innovative Planned Parenthood Center.

They have connected the possibility of her ruling to that of the unborn child. If she rules in favor of the defendant, they vow to see that she's not elected to the bench.

On the other side are Judge Colson's backers, who don't seem to care what decision she renders. They are rallying around her for the duration and vow in turn to fight anyone who tries to oust her from office.

There was more, but he decided not to read it, not now anyway. He had something he had to do. He reached for the phone directory on the buffet behind him. Moments later, he punched out a number and waited.

Mick Presnall whistled as he threaded his way through the newspaper room toward his office. It was a cubbyhole, but he didn't care. He couldn't have been prouder. To have his own office meant status. And status was the most important thing to him at this juncture in his life. Lord knows, he had sucked hind tit long and hard to get where he was today. Nothing or no one was ever going to nudge him from his present position, except maybe to kick his butt higher up the ladder.

He'd made that promise to himself after he'd fought in Nam and come him to find his fianceé living with another man. He had tossed aside the rose-colored glasses and immersed himself in his work, doing the only thing he knew how to do—and that was write and report news. How he did it, or who he hurt in the process, was of no consequence. He had done and would continue to do anything, even sell his soul to the devil, to uncover a hot story.

"Hey, Presnall, answer your phone, for chrissake! It's been ringing all morning."

Mick upped his pace. "It wouldn't hurt you to answer it for me, you know," he muttered, passing the cluttered desk of another reporter.

"Hey, I'm not your goddamn secretary."

Mick threw his coworker a scathing look before racing to his phone and lifting the receiver.

"Mick Presnall here," he said in an out-of-breath rasp, only to instantly straighten as he listened to the crisply spoken words on the other end of the line.

"Yes, sir. I'm leaving now."

After slamming the door shut to his office, Mike raced through the maze of desks and chattering employees to the exit.

Fifteen minutes later he reached his destination, a park on the south side of town. The man he was to meet was already there, pacing in front of an out-of-the-way bench.

As Mick approached him, the man stopped and stared through piercing eyes. "I have a job for you. Actually, two."

Even Mick was taken aback by the man's bluntness. Hell, he'd never even met him before. "What kind of job?"

"I want you to damage someone's reputation."

Mick was intrigued. "Whose?"

"Judge Kate Colson."

Mick whistled, then asked, "What else?"

"How good are you at playing detective?"

" 'Bout as good as most newspaper hounds." Mick paused. "Snooping is the way we get out of work." He paused again. "Tell me something, will you? How did you get my name?"

"I know your work. You don't seem to mind whose toes you step on or how hard."

"True, but—"

"Does the name Sawyer Brock ring a bell?"

Mick scratched his head. "Nope, can't say that it does."

"Well, I'd like for you to acquaint yourself with him. Will you do both jobs?"

"I'll do anything, if the price is right."

The man looked at him with contempt, which made Mick want to belt him one. Who the hell did he think he was? Mick knew he behaved like scum at times and made no apologies for it. It was guys like this one, who wanted someone else to smear their shit, then pretend their hands were clean, who irked him. But like he said, if the price was right, he'd do it.

"How much?"

Mick told him.

The man swallowed hard, but reached for his wallet and took out some bills. "Keep me posted," he said, thrusting the bills in Mick's hand. "You'll get the rest when I'm satisfied."

Mick shrugged. "You're the boss."

"And don't you forget that."

Mick merely grinned, then saluted the man's back as he walked off.

Thirty-three

To Kate, yesterday's headlines were nothing more than today's garbage. Before she entered the courtroom following the break, she had reached for the newspaper article on her desk, wadded it into a tight ball, and tossed it in the trash.

The mercy killing case was the most difficult one of her career thus far, and the continued scrutiny of the news media didn't help. Testimony in the guilt/innocence phase of the trial had just ended.

However, Kate felt in no way pressured to hand down her ruling. She had much to mull over, much to study before she would attempt to make a decision. If either or both counsels expected her to take a short recess and then come back with a verdict, they were fooling themselves.

Kate stared at the stack of papers on her desk that related to the case. A few minutes later, she walked back into the courtroom, her chin a notch higher.

"All rise!" the bailiff called out.

They did as ordered. Kate, from her position behind the bench, stared into the faces of the two men: one young and confident, the other old, but equally as confident.

"I'll take what's been said here today under advisement and render my decision accordingly." Kate's gaze swept the courtroom, then she stood.

The bailiff followed suit. "This court is now adjourned. All rise!"

Kate didn't linger to hear the buzzing that commenced the instant she'd spoken, but she didn't have to. She had been aware of the hostile climate in the courtroom. Those for and against mercy killing had been present in numbers. For the most part, though, they had behaved with decorum. Only once had she threatened to empty the courtroom following an outburst by one dissenter.

Now, as she reveled in the silence of her chambers, Kate breathed a deep sigh, but not necessarily of relief. She slipped out of her robe, hung it on the hall tree behind her desk, then sat down. The defendant's folder lay open in front of her. She sat back in her chair and massaged her forehead, her mind churning underneath her fingers. Wrestling with a decision was the worst part of her job, but since that *was* her job, she had no choice.

Paul Bronson, a seventy-five-year-old man, had taken a gun, placed the barrel next to his wife's temple and pulled the trigger. He swore that he and his wife, Eleanor, had made a pact that when the pain associated with her terminal cancer reached a certain level, he would put her out of her misery.

"She made me promise," he had sobbed from the stand. "And I kept that promise."

His broken words had touched off emotion in the courtroom. Not all had been moved, however. The couple's two children were devastated and blamed their father for what they labeled an inhumane act. That sentiment had been echoed by the opponents of mercy killing and the pro-lifers who were in town.

Kate lowered her hand, removed the defendant's folder and picked up the defense attorney's memorandum of law in which he cited cases from the Court of Criminal Appeals. That high court had heard and rendered decisions that were both different from and similar to his client's case. He had also cited cases from the Fifth Circuit Court of Appeals.

She reviewed the cases again, noting carefully how the judges had viewed mercy killings and the discretion the

judges had used in giving or not giving leniency, whichever
the case was.

Kate hadn't wanted to hear this case. It just so happened
that the case was next in line on her docket, and the defendant had waived his right to a trial by jury. Because the
killing wasn't capital murder in the eyes of the law, it had
been the defendant's decision to make.

"But murder is murder," she said aloud, hoping the sound
of her voice would somehow reassure her that she had the
knowledge and the courage to make the decision. As to
whether it would be the right one, she had no way of knowing. Either way she would offend certain factions, not to
mention the fact that she had a man's future in her hands, a
man who by many accounts had already suffered the maximum.

People often accused judges of playing God. While that
thought never entered Kate's mind, it was cases like this that
made her more painfully aware of the responsibility she
bore.

Unable to sit still another minute, Kate rose and walked
around to the front of her desk. She leaned against it, her
brow drawn in concentration. Her mind grappled with the
evidence. After a moment, she reached behind her for the
pre-sentence report that had been done by probation. The officer had talked with the defendant. He had also talked with
his family, friends, and acquaintances.

Although the officer had testified at the punishment hearing and given his recommendation, the final decision was
hers alone to make.

Should a man who was seventy-five years old spend the
rest of his life behind bars? It was in her power to assign
punishment anywhere from five to ninety-nine years in
prison or five years probation and no fine.

Her thoughts were chaotic as she once again reviewed the
information at hand. By the time Kate reached her decision,
both her head and her heart felt battered and bruised. She
forced her weary body to walk out the door, hearing the hall
clock chime twelve times.

What a day. She knew her decision would evoke further

controversy. While she didn't necessarily feel good about it, she felt at peace.

For now, that was enough.

The phone rang.

Harlan Moore welcomed the interruption. He and his wife had been fighting about money during breakfast for the past thirty minutes and he needed a break.

"Let it ring," she ordered bitterly.

"No." With that Harlan got up from his place at the dining room table and crossed to the desk, where the phone continued to ring.

"Hello," he said, clearing his voice.

"Have you seen the paper?"

It was Dave Nielsen. Harlan took his eyes off his wife, whose face was lined with bitter accusations. They had been arguing ever since he'd come downstairs. She wanted a divorce. While that was fine with him, as he'd been unfaithful to her for years, her terms were not. Like his partner, she wanted much more than he was prepared to give. Yet with his wife, he'd have to be more careful. If he got the wrong judge, one like Kate Colson, his wife would likely come out the winner.

"Yes, as a matter of fact I have," he said, forcing his mind back on track.

"Well, she's played right into our hands with this decision. It could very well be the end of her career." He paused. "If not, it could deal it a severe blow, especially with those right-to-lifers raising hell."

"My thoughts exactly," Harlan said, warming to the conversation, despite his wife's cold stare.

"Have you figured out a way we might use this to our advantage?" Dave asked.

"You bet I have."

"Oh?"

"Look, I can't talk now. Stop by my office the first chance you get, and we'll talk some more."

Without giving Dave a chance to respond, Harlan replaced the receiver."

"Who was that?" Val asked. "One of your playmates?"

"No, but what if it was?" The instant the words slipped out, he wished he could withdraw them. He knew he was playing with fire by antagonizing his wife, but he couldn't look at her without feeling contempt. She could spend more money than he could ever hope to make, or so he had convinced himself.

"You think you're untouchable," she said quietly, "but one of these days, you're going to get what's coming to you."

Once she'd left the room, and he was alone, Harlan reached for his napkin and wiped his brow. On his plate the uneaten egg, which had once looked so appetizing, now turned his stomach. Cursing, he thrust the plate aside.

One thing was for sure: if he lost everything, he wasn't going to be the only one. He intended to drag several people down with him.

That thought remained with him as he left for the office. His steps were lighter than they had been in a long time.

"Hey, Presnall, wait up, will you?"

"Can't," Mick said to a fellow worker, whose head seemed to hang in space as it appeared around his door. "Gotta go."

"Chasing a big story, huh?"

"Yep."

"Thought so. You got that shit-eatin' grin on your face."

Mick scowled.

The guy laughed. "Later, buddy."

Mick didn't even bother to answer as he grabbed his camera and his notebook. The time was right to pay a visit to Judge Colson. He'd been waiting for a good reason; he knew from checking around that she rarely gave interviews.

He wasn't about to be put off. Somehow, he'd get in to see her and question her. The potential here was too good to pass up. Besides, he had taken money to do a job, and he intended to do it.

Before adding the newspaper to his notebook, he peered at the headlines once again: JUDGE RENDERS DECISION IN MERCY KILLING CASE. *The defendant, Paul Bronson, receives a five-year probated sentence . . .*

If the rumblings he had heard were anything to go by, and he assumed they were, Judge Kate Colson's ruling was not a popular one with the majority of Americans. Many said it was a dangerous precedent to set.

Mick looked up, his eyes narrowed in thought. There was more, but he didn't bother to read it. With that decision, the icy judge had placed a knife against her own throat. His job was to make sure she *cut* that lovely throat.

He whistled all the way down the hall.

Thirty-four

Kate had just taken off her robe when the knock sounded on the door.

"Come in," she said, and watched as Angie walked into her chambers.

"I bet I'm the last person you expected to see, right?" Angie smiled, but the smile didn't quite reach her eyes.

Kate didn't hesitate. "Right. So what bring you down-town?"

"I have a meeting, then—" Angie broke off and shifted uncomfortably. "I'm supposed to meet Dave, only I'm early."

Kate forced a smile. "So have a seat."

Once Angie had plopped down into a chair in front of Kate's desk, she said without preamble, "You knew I went to see Mamma?"

Kate frowned in confusion. "Yes, but—"

"Mamma found this and wanted you to have it." Angie half rose, her hand outstretched.

Perplexed, Kate reached for the tattered envelope. "What on earth?"

"Open it. You'll see."

Kate should have guessed something was wrong because of the hesitant tone in Angie's voice, only she didn't.

Silently, she lifted the tab and slipped out a small snapshot. At first, the face didn't register; then it hit her like a blow.

"Oh," she moaned, clutching her stomach.

Angie took another anxious step closer. "Are you all right?"

Kate waved her back. "I'm . . . I'm fine. It's just that I wasn't expecting . . ." She couldn't go on. The last thing she thought she would see was the tiny face of her child. Over the years, she had yearned for a photograph of Sara.

Kate's hand trembled as she peered into the sleeping face. Her baby was even more perfect than she remembered, with her full rosy cheeks, rosebud-shaped mouth, and thick lashes that fanned those cheeks. In spite of her efforts to remain in control, Kate began to shake visibly.

"For heaven's sake, sit down," Angie said, reaching as if to catch hold of Kate.

Again Kate put her off. "I'm fine, really I am. It's just that seeing the . . . picture was such a shock."

"I was afraid it might be, but Mamma said you would want it." Angie looked uncomfortable. "To tell you the truth, I debated whether to give it to you, no matter what Mamma said."

"Of course I want it," Kate said, unable to take her eyes off the child. The weight on her chest was so heavy, she thought it might explode from the pressure. Tears stung her eyes, but she dashed them back while Angie stood silent.

Finally, Kate looked up. "Please, I'd like to be alone."

Angie's relief was apparent. "I need to go, anyway."

"Thanks," Kate whispered.

"Kate . . ."

"Not now, Angie, please."

When Kate was alone, she sank into her desk chair, no longer certain her legs would support her. She fought for enough breath to get past the bitter fury filling her heart, fury that mercifully overrode the blinding pain.

"Damn you to hell, Thomas Jennings!"

Kate didn't know how long she sat there before she got up and went into the bathroom. She stared in the mirror to make sure the torn fragments of her emotions didn't show. There was no containing her thoughts; they were on fire. Still, Thomas' comeuppance would have to wait a little longer.

The picture of Sara had deepened Kate's desire and only one person could turn that desire into reality. On shaky legs, she made her way back to her desk and was about to pick up the phone when the door burst open.

"I told him he couldn't come in here!" Leslie cried, only two steps behind a man Kate had never seen.

Kate bristled. "What's the meaning of this? Who are you?"

"Mick Presnall, Judge."

"You're a reporter." Kate said with disgust.

The insult didn't take. "I've been trying to get an interview with you for over an hour now, and this woman—" he pointed at Leslie, "refused to even tell you I was here."

"I—" Leslie began.

Kate held up her hand. "It's all right, Leslie. I'll take care of Mr. Presnall."

Leslie didn't look at all sure, but she didn't argue.

When the door closed softly behind Leslie, Kate balled her fists while rage of another kind rose inside her. "I'll have your job for this."

His face, tanned and square as a building block, didn't so much as change. The same insolent expression remained. "You can try, Judge, but that's about as far as you'll get."

"Get out of this office before I call security."

He shifted his camera. "If that's the way you want it, Judge, then I'm prepared to play it your way."

"Get out," she repeated through clenched teeth. "And I don't ever want to see you again."

"I'm going, but as far as not seeing me again—" His voice gave way to a cocky grin. "Only in your dreams, lady, only in your dreams."

Kate looked him up and down, slowly. The expression on her face registered her reactions. Contempt, revulsion, and boredom.

Mick's face flushed and his mouth spread into an angry line. "You think—"

"If you don't leave right now, I'm going to have you thrown out."

He laughed as he swaggered toward the door and then out.

Kate barely noticed, her insides shook so. After several deep breaths, she was once again in control. Ordinarily she would have been better prepared to deal with scum like Mick Presnall.

Her eyes strayed to the picture on her desk. Her baby. She closed her eyes and ignored the building pressure. She had been strong for so long. Now was not the time to let her defenses down.

Sawyer Brock remained her only hope of finding Sara. She punched out his number.

Sawyer walked into his office to the ringing of the phone. He hitched his leg on the edge of his desk and reached for it.

"Brock."

"This is Kate Colson."

For a second he seemed at a loss for words. The sound of her soft-spoken, honeyed voice went straight to his gut. He shook himself, then cursed silently.

"Are you still there?"

"I'm here," he said, much more sharply than he intended.

There was a moment's hesitation. "Have you found out anything about the convent?"

"As a matter of fact, I have."

"So you do have some information?" she pressed, sounding almost breathless.

Yet underneath that breathy sound, he heard an eagerness in her voice that struck another chord deep inside him. "Yes, only—" He paused, hating to tell her that the news wasn't all that great.

"Can we meet?" she was saying. "I have something for you, too."

"Where?"

"I was about to walk to the park."

Again he was caught off guard. "Park?" he repeated.

"Yes, park."

He heard the smile in her voice. He gripped the receiver, trying to keep a tight rein on his emotions. "Whatever you say."

"You know which one I'm talking about, don't you?"

"Since you're walking, I assume it's the one by the courthouse."

"Right. I'll meet you by the gazebo."

"Till then."

He replaced the receiver and stared out the window. The sky looked like it was going to erupt. Park? He shook his head and headed for the door. Who the hell was he to second-guess a woman?

Kate didn't see him at first, which gave him a moment to study her. She sat stoically straight on the bench inside the gazebo as if lost in deep thought. He was struck by how incredibly sad and lonely she looked.

Still, nothing could disguise her haunting beauty. Despite the lack of sunlight, her silver blond hair looked shiny and sleek. Her perfect features were the classic sort that photographers yearned to capture on film, but quite often could not.

She was dressed in a suit; its soft lilac color seemed to enhance her vulnerability. The sight intensified that ache deep inside him. He shifted to the other foot.

She turned, and their eyes met and held. He saw something flicker in hers. Fear? Curiosity? Desire? The latter almost made him choke.

Sawyer closed the distance between them. She stood, then, keeping her gaze averted, asked, "Is this all right?"

"Sure. Why not?"

They both sat back down on the bench, far enough apart that they could turn and face each other comfortably. But there was nothing comfortable about the silence that hung between them.

"You look tired," Sawyer said suddenly, bluntly.

Her head jerked up, and for a moment he felt he had overstepped the boundary. Again.

"I'm more angry than tired," she said. Then as if she'd been too forthright, she turned away.

Sawyer sensed that something had happened. He didn't know what, but something. He believed her when she said she was angry, but at the same time, she seemed far less sure of herself.

"Tough decision you had to make."

She almost smiled. "So you saw the papers?"

"I think the world's seen the papers."

"Or TV," she said ruefully.

"I'm sure you made the right decision."

She frowned. "Are you?"

"You did what you thought was best." He lifted his shoulders in a shrug. "That's the way I work, and to hell with what anyone thinks."

"Unfortunately, that's not my way," Kate said, lifting a hand and replacing a strand of hair that the wind had loosened from the knot at the nape of her neck.

Her words barely registered as he caught the way her movement caused her blouse to conform to her full breasts. Sawyer turned away, feeling heat, but not from the sticky climate. He wanted her, and the fact that he couldn't have her added to his misery.

"No, I guess it's not," he forced himself to say. "After all, you're running for an election."

"Do I detect some censure there?"

He smiled. "Actually, I kinda admire your tactics, Judge."

She lowered her head sideways. "Why is it that I don't believe you, that I think you're merely offering lip service?"

His lips twitched. "Now why would I want to do that?"

"Why would you?" she said, peering at him closely.

He shrugged again, then looked up and watched as the clouds thickened overhead. Damned fool idea to be here in the park. It was soothing, he guessed, if one thought of it that way.

"What did you have to tell me?"

He brought his head back down. "I located the convent."

"That's exactly what I wanted to hear."

"Only it's not good news."

The life went out of her face. "Why?"

"The convent's no longer there."

Her throat rippled in a swallow, but when she didn't comment, he went on, "An apartment building's there now."

He could have told her that over the phone, but the phone was not the place to conduct business. He had found that in dealing with clients or suspects it was better to look them in the eye. Old habits die hard.

"I was afraid that might be the case," she said, despair in both her voice and her eyes.

Sawyer acted before he thought. He reached out and covered her hand. She lifted her face to his and for a moment their gazes held; the force of the unexpected contact created a smothering tension.

She pulled in a hard breath, but didn't remove her hand.

"Look," he said thickly, "don't worry. I'll find the young woman." Suddenly he didn't care why Kate wanted to find that person. He just wanted to find her—for Kate. "I'll be looking into what happened to the convent records. You'll trust me, won't you?"

Without responding, Kate reached into her purse and pulled out an envelope and opened it. "Here's a photo of the child. I didn't give it to you earlier because I've only recently acquired it." She forced her hand not to tremble as she handed it to him. "I thought you might find it useful."

Sawyer took the picture and stared into the tiny face. "She's a real beauty," he said, looking back at Kate.

Kate swallowed. "Yes, she is."

Sawyer's eyes narrowed on her and for a moment, he swore he could see her heart pounding.

The sudden drop of rain shattered the spell. Kate jerked her hand out of his and shifted her gaze.

"Damn," Sawyer muttered, standing.

She followed suit, her eyes raised heavenward.

Sawyer couldn't help himself; he gazed at her long, swanlike neck, aching to trail his lips along those delicate bones . . .

He stretched his lips into a tight line and said brusquely, "Come on, I'll drive you back."

While Kate looked up at him and nodded assent, he tried to come to grips with this sexual pull that seemed to influence everything they did or said. He'd had many women in his life, but none had affected him like this one.

Now was not the time to try to figure out why he lusted after her, not when they had to run like hell to get out of the rain.

Once they were inside his Jaguar, he faced her. "Where to? Your car or your chambers?"

He tried to ignore the delicate smell of perfume. It was impossible. With no distance to speak of between them, it wrapped around him. All he wanted was to bury himself inside her. When it came to Kate, he was a walking stick of dynamite with a lighted fuse.

He gripped the steering wheel and stared ahead, furious with his lack of self-control.

"I'm not sure where I want to go," she finally answered.

He threw her a strange glance.

"Actually, I think I'd just like to ride around for a while."

"No problem." Sawyer cranked the car and tried to ignore the excitement roiling in him. He'd been loathe to leave her.

"Thanks," Kate murmured.

He pulled out into the ongoing traffic. "Any place in particular?"

"No." Then, as if she realized that she might be infringing on his time, she faced him, her brows puckered. "I didn't even ask if you had something else to do." She paused as if struggling to overcome her embarrassment. "It's not like me to—"

"Forget it. I have plenty of time."

She watched him for another moment, then turned away.

They rode in silence. It took all of Sawyer's willpower to keep his eyes off her. But he didn't have to look at her. Her image was imprinted on his mind. Still, he found himself sneaking glance after glance.

That was why he didn't see the car following him, until it was too late.

"Shit," he said under his breath, increasing the speed of the Jaguar.

They were on the open highway now, headed for the Hill Country. He hadn't asked her, but he knew a quaint out-of-the-way restaurant where he'd like to stop. He'd had every intention of simply cruising along until they reached that destination.

The car behind him changed all that. Sawyer upped the Jag's speed even more.

"What's wrong?" Kate asked, pressing the palm of one hand against the dashboard.

Sawyer flung her another quick glance. "We're being followed."

Her face went pale.

"It's nothing to worry about. I'll lose him."

"Are you sure the car's following *us*?"

"I'm sure. Have you forgotten I'm an ex-cop?" Before she could respond, he went on, "Don't turn around, whatever you do."

Kate swallowed. "Do you have any idea who it might be?"

"I sure as hell do."

That seemed to satisfy her, and she fell silent again as he maneuvered the Jag smoothly in and out of the traffic. The blue sedan followed his exact pattern.

Sawyer looked at Kate again, wondering what she was thinking. Most women would be hysterical or close to it. Not Kate. She sat straight, and though not relaxed, she remained perfectly poised. She had guts, he had to admit. It would take a great deal more to shake her than a persistent tail.

Again, he wondered just what it would be like to get past that barrier. To stoke the fire beneath the ice.

Forcing his mind back on the pressing business of losing the bastard riding his bumper, Sawyer stared into the rearview mirror. The blue sedan was gone.

He was patting himself on the back when a flash in the

rearview mirror caught his attention. Sawyer cursed, just as the Jag was hit hard from behind.

"Sawyer!" Kate's eyes were stark with terror.

"Hold on tight. The sonofabitch is trying to run us off the road!"

Thirty-five

Sawyer couldn't make out the driver's face. The vehicle had a highly tinted windshield that reduced the driver to a menacing silhouette. Sawyer could only make out fingers around the steering wheel.

He flung another quick look at Kate. The color had receded from her face, and she gripped the dash as if she expected the situation to get worse.

It did. Another slam from the rear shook the Jag.

"Are you all right?" he asked without taking his eyes off the road.

"I'm fine, except that every time he hits us, it jars every bone in my body."

Sawyer's response was to put his foot down harder on the gas pedal.

It was a long, curvy highway and the farther they went, the less traffic they encountered. But twilight was approaching, adding to the danger.

Large oaks and other trees lined the highway, their branches thick with leaves. The summer rain that had forced them into the car had stopped moments before, leaving the pavement wet and slippery.

Now, however, the dreary sky was parting like a curtain and letting in a weak sunlight. But the man who was trying to either scare the hell out of them or kill them remained a blur. Whatever the bastard's motive, he wouldn't get away with it.

"What are we . . . you going to do?"

"Don't worry. It's going to be all right."

"Is . . . is he still behind us?"

"Yes."

"You'd think we could outrun him, with your Jag, that is."

"I could if I didn't have you in the car."

"Do what you have to do. Don't worry about me."

Although she spoke with confidence, Sawyer caught the slight tremor in her voice. She was scared, no doubt about it. He knew she wasn't about to admit it. Again he felt nothing but admiration for her.

"I'm worried about you and me," he said flatly. "But I'm also worried about the road. At this speed, it's slippery as hell."

"Oh my God!" Kate cried.

"What the—!" The rest of the words were shoved back down Sawyer's throat. The sedan drew beside the Jag, fender to fender.

Kate cried out again.

"Sonofabitch!" Sawyer swung the wheel hard to the right, only he wasn't quick enough. The blue car swung also and banged into Sawyer's side of the car. The blow sent the Jag careening off the road toward a tree.

Sawyer downshifted at the same time he jerked the wheel. The Jag skidded and spun, but it missed the tree. He jammed on the brakes and killed the engine.

"Are you okay?" he asked, flinging a glance in Kate's direction.

She stared back at him with wide, frightened eyes. "I think so."

He kept his eyes on her for another heartbeat, then opened the door and lunged out of the car. Of course, the blue sedan was nowhere in sight.

"Shit," he muttered, and walked toward the road, where another car had pulled up.

A man got out. "Hey, buddy, you all right?"

"Yeah, thanks. Did you see what happened?"

"No, not all of it. I just saw you get knocked off the road. I was so busy tracking your movement and trying to keep my own car on the road, that I didn't get the license number, if that's what you're asking." .

"That's what I was asking."

"Want me to call the police?"

"No, thanks." Sawyer's eyes held a murderous glint. "I'll take care of that myself."

"Well, if you're sure you don't need anything, I'll be off."

Sawyer waved. "Thanks again."

The man drove off, and Sawyer turned and bounded back to the car. Kate had unbuckled her seat belt, and her head was resting against the window. When she heard him, she straightened and turned, her brown eyes filled with questions.

"Did you get a glimpse of him?"

"Nothing. The bastard was gone by the time I got out of the car."

Kate's teeth sank into her lower lip. "Who was that you were talking to?"

"Some guy who offered to help."

"Did he see anything?"

"Just us sailing off the highway."

At Kate's shudder, Sawyer's eyes darkened. "Are you sure you're okay?"

"Just a little shaken, that's all." Kate paused, narrowing her eyes as if straining to see him in the gathering dusk. "How about you?"

Sawyer wanted to ask if she really cared, but he didn't. Nothing suited him at the moment. He was madder than hell that the man behind the wheel had gotten the upper hand. Not for long, he vowed. He had a good idea who it was. If he was right, *when,* not if, he got his hands on Lloyd Silverman, he'd tear him limb from limb.

"Sawyer."

He jerked his head around and stared at her for a moment. "You said it."

She gave him a perplexed look. "What?"

"My name."

Their eyes held for another moment. "Oh."

He smiled. "And it didn't kill you, did it?"

"No, no I guess it didn't."

She turned away from him, but that didn't stop Sawyer from continuing to look at her. What was she thinking? What was churning behind those huge brown eyes? He would give anything to know; she continued to be a complete enigma. The few times they had been together had given him no insight, no new understanding of her being. Still, she'd totally captivated him.

"You said you knew who was responsible."

Her voice broke into his troubled thoughts. "Yeah, a guy by the name of Lloyd Silverman. He pulled a gun on me at the office. Swore he'd get even."

Kate's face lost its remaining color. "That's awful."

"It was worse than that, but I took care of it."

"Well, I hope you're right and it is him."

"Why is that?" he asked, his tone suspicious. There was something odd about her statement. His gut instinct kicked in and alerted him.

"No reason," she said at last.

"I don't buy that. You sounded like you knew someone who might have pulled this crazy stunt."

"Well, I don't." The words came out in a rush.

"You're lying."

Her body stiffened. "And you're out of line."

"Is that all you can say, after what we just went through? This isn't some kind of goddamn game."

"I'm aware of that," she said tightly.

"Well then talk to me." When she continued to sit mute, Sawyer's blood pressure rose another notch. "Look, dammit, we could've been killed." His patience had run out. "If you know something, then I suggest you tell me."

She seemed to mull over his words for a minute. "Oh, all right. There are people who don't want this baby found, but that's as much as I can say."

"Were you threatened?"

When she kept silent and didn't deny it outright, he knew in his gut that he'd guessed right.

"Jesus!"

"Look, I can handle whatever happens."

Sawyer snorted.

"It's probably that Silverman guy, anyway."

"I gather you're *not* going to tell me who threatened you."

She pursued her lips. "That's right."

He cursed. "Sometimes I'd like to—" Sawyer broke off with another stinging curse. "Oh, what the hell. I'll take you back to your car."

It took him a minute, but he managed to crank the Jag and get it back out on the road, all the while aware of Kate sitting stoically beside him.

He quashed the urge to stop the car and shake her until she told him what was on her mind. Instead, he gripped the steering wheel and headed toward town.

The aftershocks of the collision had begun to take their toll. Kate's skin felt clammy and cold and her stomach nauseous.

Could Thomas have been trying to kill her? If so, then he was running scared. On the one hand that made her feel good, but on the other, it sent darts of fear through her. Or, had it been Sawyer's disgruntled client?

What about Harlan? She couldn't forget about him. Yet she couldn't conceive of him trying to harm her.

Then there was Sawyer. He was equally as dangerous, though for a different reason, a reason she very much wanted to ignore. She looked at him out of the corner of her eye. His jaw was bunched, and his lips were drawn tight. He looked mad enough to kill. She knew the brunt of that anger wasn't Silverman. Kate shivered. He was mad at her.

She kept her eyes turned away even after they pulled up beside her car. Darkness had fallen, but the moon was out and the parking lot was well lighted.

Before she could say anything, Sawyer was out of the Jag and around on her side. Once he opened the door, she slipped out and was surprised to find that her legs would still carry her weight. But it wasn't her legs she worried about. It was her heart and its erratic beating.

Sawyer stood in front of her. Close. Too close. She peered up at him and, to her dismay, tears pricked her eyes. Her voice even sounded weak and thready as she said, "Thanks."

"For what?"

Did his voice sound thick or was it her imagination? She breathed deeply, and when she did, she inhaled the rich scent of his cologne. Her senses clamored, and for a brief moment she shut her eyes. When she opened them, tears stained her cheeks.

"Kate."

Her name seemed to be dug out of him. Suddenly she had to get away from him, from the need to fling herself into his arms.

"I . . . have to go." She turned, but not quickly enough. He clasped her arm and turned her back around. His hands then circled her shoulders.

"Don't," she whispered, not looking at him.

He tipped her chin. "Don't what?"

She opened her mouth to respond, but no words came out.

"Touch you," he said thickly. "Like this." His finger traced the side of her cheek.

"Sawyer." Her cry was broken.

"Shh, don't talk."

"I have to. And you have to listen."

That finger moved to her trembling lips where he outlined them. The trembling increased under his gentle tutelage.

"I can't," he responded in a tortured tone, slowly pulling her against him. "It's too late."

Oh, please, no, not again, she cried within, but it didn't do any good. It was as if another person had invaded her body and was commanding her to act in a manner totally foreign to her.

His eyes seemed to take on a special glint in the semidarkness as his face lowered to hers. An unidentifiable sound, half whimper, half moan, escaped her throat.

As before, their lips met with such suddenness, such heat that she felt as if she'd stepped on a live wire. The rough brush of his day-old beard against her skin, combined with the heat of his darting tongue, proved to be too much. She sagged against him as the kiss deepened, relentlessly, fiercely, taking possession of them both.

Sawyer was the first to pull away, though she could tell it hadn't been easy for him. He was struggling to regain both his control and his breath, as was she. A frenzy of sensations had reduced her self-control to mere remnants.

Only after he searched the depths of her eyes did he say in a shaken but rough tone, "Don't you think it's time you told me the whole story?"

She folded her arms across her chest, confused and wary. "I've already told you—"

"I'm not referring to the threat."

Kate's eyes shuttered. "What are you talking about, then?" She knew, but she would do anything to protect herself. She wasn't up to any more confrontation tonight. Both her heart and mind were too embattled.

"How are *you* involved with this missing girl?"

A fine sheen of perspiration moistened her forehead while the lie flowed from her lips. "She has to do with a case I'm working on."

"Uh-huh. I know you wouldn't compromise yourself like that. Nor would you go beyond the boundaries of the law."

An icy feeling of fear gripped Kate's insides and wouldn't let go. "Then let's just say it's none of your business."

"How can you say that after the way you kissed me both—"

"That doesn't mean you own me," she said, cutting across his words. "Besides, those . . . kisses were mistakes that I don't intend to repeat."

He recoiled as if she'd slapped him. And for the second time since she'd met him, his carefully placed facade slipped, allowing her to see his naked emotions. He was furious, but there was something else reflected in his eyes. Contempt. She wanted to cry. But she didn't. She couldn't. If she ever started, she knew she wouldn't be able to stop.

Without breaking the silence, Kate unlocked her car door and got inside.

Before she could close the door, Sawyer grabbed it and held it open. "Please," she whispered.

Her plea seemed to have no effect on him. He stared at

her, his expression harsh and unyielding. Kate wanted to turn away, but she couldn't. She was tangled in a web of her own making.

"This thing between us, whatever it is, isn't over."

"Get out of my way," she said tersely. "I'm going home."

Thirty-six

Kate felt she had the audience exactly where she wanted them: interested and attentive. She had been asked to speak to the Chamber of Commerce at their anniversary luncheon, and now she was having as much fun as her audience seemed to be.

"So ladies and gentlemen, it comes down to the fact that the new composition of the U.S. Supreme Court will force the state courts to decide more 'thorny social issues,' such as abortion, civil rights, and school funding.

"I want to leave you with the firm commitment that I, as a District Court judge, will be on the side of the law and not on the side of special interest groups as one of my opponents is."

Enthusiastic applause rocked the room.

Kate smiled, feeling she was on a roll; her speech was nearing an end. One final time, her eyes swept the room. That was when she saw him. Her heart almost stopped beating. Sawyer stood at the rear, leaning nonchalantly against the door. How long had he been there? Not the entire time, surely? Damn him!

Her smile widened. She wouldn't let him unnerve her, but it was hard to stand there and pretend that she wasn't affected by his unexpected presence.

"My opponents apparently think it's their role to resolve

political issues based on their philosophy," Kate said. "You all expect your courts to be impartial, unbiased—an institution that doesn't take sides.

"I'm a Republican, but the Democrats can be assured that when I walk through the courthouse door, politics is left outside. I represent all of you, and I'm not beholden to groups who promise large campaign contributions.

"Thank you so much for allowing me to share my views with you today on yet another anniversary of your worthwhile organization."

She waved her hand to another resounding round of applause, careful to keep her eyes off Sawyer, who continued to stand relaxed, hand in one pocket of his dress slacks, as if he didn't have a care in the world. What was he doing here? Then it dawned on her that he was most likely a member of the chamber. After all, he was an astute, influential businessman, with strong ties in the community. Yet somehow she didn't feel reassured by that reasoning. She couldn't help but suspect ulterior motives

"Judge, you were marvelous," the president of the chamber said, holding out his hand.

Kate cleared her mind and grasped his hand. "Thank you so much for inviting me."

The president's compliments were seconded by other dignitaries.

She shook several hands, basking in the crowd's support of her.

"Nice speech, Judge."

Kate stiffened, that low, raspy voice sending a tingling through her. She swallowed and turned around slowly, wiping her features of all emotion. "Thank you, Mr. Brock."

That faintly mocking smile tipped his lips, but he didn't say anything else because a man whom he apparently knew slapped him on the back. "Hey, Brock, where'd you disappear to? Haven't seen you at a meeting in Lord knows how long."

"Hello, Wiley. Been busy. You know how it is." Sawyer's eyes rested on Kate for a minute before going back to the man.

Wiley chuckled. "Well, glad you came today." He winked at Kate. "This lady made one hellava speech, didn't she?"

Kate flushed as she felt Sawyer's eyes deepen on her. "Yeah, she did."

"Thank you both, gentlemen," Kate said, making a point to shift her gaze away from Sawyer. "If you'll excuse me, I really must go. I'm due in court."

"Later then, Judge," Sawyer said, his voice devoid of emotion.

The look in his eyes were a different matter. They'd glinted with that same fierceness just before he'd hauled her into his arms. Kate licked her dry lips, then forced them into a smile. "Thanks again."

She made her way out of the building into the bright sunlight before she realized just how shallowly she was breathing. Still, she didn't stop until she reached her car.

Once inside the Cadillac, Kate lay her head back against the seat, aware that when Sawyer had crossed the line and touched her after the incident on the road, the underpinnings of her secure life had been severely shaken, if not torn down entirely. She felt somewhat winded and a little desperate, not quite certain how to cope with this latest development.

She was not a person who did things in halves. For her, it was total commitment or nothing. That was the only way she'd been able to survive. She had been content, if not happy. Lonely, sure, but not unbearably so.

How dare he keep intruding upon her personal life? How dare he look so good and smell so good? The way his silk-blend suit hugged his tall frame, just enough to hint at the powerful muscles underneath, was not fair.

He shouldn't have come to that meeting. Kate released a pent-up breath, then massaged her head against the sudden pounding at her temple.

It had been a week since they had last met, since he had kissed her. During that time, she'd vacillated between firing him and not firing him. And the kiss—well, she couldn't even think about that without shame and remorse. And anger. At herself.

In one short moment, Sawyer had awakened her body, set

it on fire with his sucking mouth and hot tongue. When had things gone so totally beyond her control? When had their relationship veered so sharply off the business track and onto the personal one?

She couldn't pretend that she had been blindsided by the kiss. The attraction had been between them from the beginning. She had ached for him to kiss her, to touch her.

She had to pull herself out of this quagmire. She was willing to risk her career to find her daughter, but she wasn't willing to risk that part of herself that she had kept under lock and key. Thomas had taught her well, and she wasn't ready to experience that kind of pain again, no matter how good-looking, how charismatic, or how intriguing Sawyer was.

So why did she find it so difficult to heed her own advice? She still wanted Sawyer. Dear Lord, she wanted him. Worse, he knew that she wanted him.

Nothing had changed. She was still scared to get involved with any man, even one who made her body vibrate. She was afraid that if she cared, if she caved in to her needs, it wouldn't last and she'd be alone again.

She didn't want to be torn, didn't want to be sidetracked. She wanted to find her daughter and win an election. Both would require all the strength and stamina she could muster.

And it required Sawyer Brock; he was still the best man to find Sara.

Her car phone buzzed. She jumped. After several rings, Kate reached for it. It was her court coordinator.

"Tell counsel I'm on my way."

Thomas patted a strand of loose black hair back into place as he continued to stare at himself in the mirror. Were new wrinkles appearing on his face? Should he consider a facelift? He peered closer into the mirror. His panic subsided. His face was as wrinkle-free as a baby's butt, he thought. Well, almost.

It was a miracle, though, with all the pressure he'd been under recently. He'd even found himself neglecting his ministry. It was damn hard to concentrate lately. Kate Colson was responsible.

Nothing he did seemed to vanquish her from his mind. He never knew when or where she might walk back into his life, and he was tired of sweating over her. He had to know what she was up to.

She hated him, and as he well knew, hate was a powerful motivator. Thomas had no choice but to seize the upper hand. He flashed his cocky smile into the mirror and let out his favorite slogan. "Do it unto others before they do it unto you."

Even now, the thought of his humiliation at her hand made his blood pressure rise.

He walked quickly to his desk, where he unlocked a drawer and retrieved a small black notebook that contained private numbers he didn't share with anyone. He located the number he wanted and reached for the phone. The call was answered immediately.

"Frost here."

"I need a favor."

"Favors cost, even for you, Reverend."

"That goes without saying. I need some information."

"That's my expertise."

"Don't brag too soon," Thomas snapped.

"I'll brag; you pay. Deal?"

"Deal."

"So gimme a name."

"Judge Kate Colson."

There was a moment of silence on the other end of the telephone, then, "That's heavy stuff. *She's* heavy stuff."

"So?" Thomas felt his temper rise.

"So, okay, I'll do it."

"Follow her. I think she's hired some private dick, and I want to know why, especially if he's following me. In fact, I want to know everything she does."

The man on the other end of the line laughed. "You're out to put her in a world of hurt, huh?"

"Exactly," Thomas replied, then hung up.

He straightened the collar of his silk shirt. He could not afford to let Kate Colson disrupt his life any further.

Even if he had to kill her.

The bed covers were a mess. Sawyer had shoved them off, leaving him naked. He didn't care. He was alone. Alone. For the first time in a long while, he allowed that word to penetrate through his subconscious.

"Shit!" Now was not the time to turn his thoughts to the past. These days he seemed no more able to control his thoughts than he could his compulsion to see Kate.

Torturous images flashed through his mind: Kate's lovely features in the candlelight at the cafe; Kate moving sensuously among the plants at the nursery; Kate's rare smile; Kate standing proudly before the chamber members; Kate's expressive eyes.

And her moist lips—the way they had trembled under his, the way they had tasted, the way her breasts had dug into his chest. At that moment, he had been sure the top of his head was going to come off.

He'd been on a high and hadn't wanted that sweet torture to end. He had wanted to loosen her hair, thread his fingers through it, then touch her all over: her breasts, her belly, her hips . . . He wanted to watch her face as he thrust deep and long inside her.

When he lay in bed at night, staring at the ceiling, he would think about her on top of him, watching his face, as she rode him wildly. Now that same image triggered an erection that was so painful, it drove him onto the side of the bed.

He wished he found his randy condition amusing, only he didn't. It frustrated him, made him think of his teenage years when he'd gotten his first hard-on.

He couldn't recall ever having such radical fantasies about a woman. Did that mean he was in love?

Hell, no.

Long ago, love had ceased to be a part of his vocabulary.

His daddy and his aunt had shown him that love was a farce, something to be used to break one's spirit.

To this day, Sawyer flinched against the stinging pain of the belt as his aunt lashed it against his back, his buttocks, and his head. When she had finished her evil deed, she would tell him she'd punished him because she loved him.

That was when love had become a meaningless, empty word.

No, love was not what this was about with Kate. Yet she awakened something inside him he had never felt before, something as frightening as it was exciting.

So where was he headed in these uncharted waters? He'd like to think he was headed for her bed. He laughed a sudden, bitter laugh. Hell, he'd be lucky if she didn't fire his ass.

She hadn't been happy about that kiss. She hadn't been happy that he'd shown up at the chamber meeting. He had made no apologies; he'd needed to see her. And he knew that until he'd made love to her, he would never get her out of his system.

The alarm sounded. He shut it off, got up, and trudged into the bathroom and into the shower.

Sawyer rode up in the elevator, stepped off on the eleventh floor, and made his way to Harlan's office. He dreaded this meeting and could think of other places he'd rather be and other people he'd rather see. It was one of those rare days when the temperature and humidity were in sync, which called for a day at the beach—if not to swim, then to jog. Or make love. To Kate.

Again his body responded, and again he cursed out loud. Sawyer didn't even realize he'd walked into Harlan's office until Harlan's secretary questioned him.

"What were you saying, Mr. Brock?"

"Nothing your sweet ears should hear."

She giggled. "Mr. Moore's waiting for you."

The instant Sawyer crossed the threshold, he stopped. Harlan wasn't alone. A man Sawyer had never seen before was staring at him as if he resented the interruption.

"Ah, Sawyer," Harlan said, standing behind his desk.

"Good to see you." He faced Dave. "You know Dave Nielsen, don't you?"

"No, can't say that I do." Then he faced the stranger and nodded slightly. "Nielsen."

Dave tugged at his mustache. "Hello, Brock."

Sawyer tensed his jaw, but that was all the emotion he allowed to show. He wasn't happy. For some reason, Nielsen bothered him. Sawyer couldn't put his finger on that reason, but it was there nevertheless. Maybe it was because he was too goddamn arrogant and prissy to suit him.

"Gentlemen, be seated, please," Harlan said.

Sawyer slouched against the wall. "I'll stand, if you don't mind. I can't stay long."

Harlan gave him a hard look. "This meeting's important."

"So is my time," Sawyer said drolly.

"If he feels that way," Dave said, "let him go. We don't need him."

"Shut up, Dave, and sit down."

Dave flushed, then glared at Sawyer, who smiled at him with pity. Dave's flush deepened, but his eyes were filled with venom.

"What's going on, Harlan?" Sawyer asked. "Why is Nielsen here?"

Harlan grinned suddenly, like a cat who had just devoured a canary. "I want you to be the first to know that Dave is now a candidate for District Judge." He paused. "He's my choice to run against Kate Colson."

Sawyer's jaw dropped, then he threw back his head and laughed. "You're joking, surely?"

Harlan's face paled while Dave's turned flaming red.

"I don't joke about something this important," Harlan responded in a heated tone. "If you had done *your* job and found something on Kate, I wouldn't have to resort to this."

Sawyer felt his stomach sour with disgust. "Look here, Harlan, I—"

"Well, I won't procrastinate," Dave put in, standing and glaring at Sawyer. "I have an inside track."

Sawyer crossed his arms over his chest. "Oh? And just who might that be?"

"Angie Gates."

"So what can she tell you?" Sawyer asked, suddenly bored with the whole charade. Listening to these two clowns was a waste of time.

"A lot, I'm sure," Dave said with confidence. "If anyone knows Kate's secrets, it's Angie."

Sawyer's eyes hardened as they went from Harlan back to Dave. "What if Angie won't talk?"

Dave smiled. "Oh, she'll talk all right. One of these times when I'm banging her hard and fast, she'll tell all."

Sawyer shrugged, instead of smashing Dave's conceited face like he wanted to. "All it means to me is that you're a cocky bastard who thinks he has stainless-steel balls."

"Damn you, Brock!" Harlan's face was blustering red. "You'd best get a handle on your mouth and your attitude. And just because Dave is helping, it doesn't mean you're off the case. I'm still counting on you to do your job."

Sawyer stared at Harlan, all the while biting his tongue to keep from telling Harlan where he could stick it. But now was not the time. He simply shrugged and said in a mild tone, "Whatever you say."

"Good, now we can get to some strategy planning."

"Count me out," Sawyer said. "I've got work to do."

With that he turned and walked out of the room, thinking that both his personal and professional life had gone down the drain real fast.

Thirty-seven

"Don't answer it, please," the brunette beside him purred.

Thomas ignored her demand and reached for the phone. "Hello," he said, trying to make his tired brain work.

"I got the information you wanted."

Thomas sat up straighter in the bed.

"Come on, honey, lie back down."

Thomas held his hand over the receiver and glared at her. "Either shut up or get up. I don't care which."

The woman flounced out of bed. "Go to hell."

"Sorry," Thomas said back to the detective. "Now, what were you saying?"

"I got the information you wanted. Or at least part of it."

"Great. Let's hear it."

Kate rarely worked until after dark, but this evening was an exception. She had several cases to rule on, but there was one in particular that demanded thought and deep concentration. Didn't they all? she reminded herself ruefully.

Maybe she should take Bill Johns up on his offer to return to the law firm. She had thought about it. But that was all it was, a thought, and a fleeting one at that. While she had enjoyed her work at Johns and Strassberg, she had needed a new challenge, not that her work there had been boring. It hadn't. It was that she'd felt stymied, that she wasn't getting anywhere with all the traveling, the late nights, and endless meetings.

She had purchased her home and longed to enjoy it, only she never seemed to find the time. She guessed the truth was that she had become suddenly selfish, wanting more time for herself. So when the opportunity had presented itself for the judgeship, she had taken it.

Now, Kate set her pen down, turned away from the glare of the desk lamp, and rubbed her tired eyes. She had made a lot of headway in her work, so she wasn't complaining. Besides, tomorrow was Saturday, a day she planned to spend in the yard, working with her flowers.

Her gaze rested suddenly on the telephone. Why didn't he call? She chewed on her pencil. What if he didn't call at all? She wished it didn't matter that she hadn't heard from Sawyer in several day. She had told herself that she only wanted an update on the case. The process of tracking her daughter was taking much longer than she had expected, but then she wasn't an expert on missing persons. Deep down Kate knew that her impatience didn't stem entirely from Sawyer's lack of progress, but also from the fact that she hadn't heard from him.

She still harbored the need to see him, hear his voice, *touch* him. Feeling her eyes sting and her shoulders burn from sheer fatigue, Kate thrust her worrisome thoughts aside and lowered her head into her hands.

She heard it then. An unidentifiable noise. Her heart quickened. What was it? She heard it again. A door opening and closing? Had someone entered the outer office? If so, who? She glanced at her watch. Her heart settled. Pete, the janitor, more than likely. Even if it wasn't him, it was probably another judge just stopping by. She wasn't the only one who worked late.

She looked up and waited for the knock on the chamber door. Nothing. Frowning, she stood. "Anyone there?" Kate called, feeling an unwanted chill feather up her back.

Still nothing.

She took two steps toward the door, only to suddenly halt

in her tracks as the door burst open. Thomas Jennings walked in and slammed the door shut behind him.

Kate's breath caught, then expanded in her throat until she thought she might choke.

"Hello, Kate."

The triumphant, yet cold tone of his voice proved the catalyst that unlocked her voice. "Get out! Now!"

Thomas laughed. "Not on your life. Not until I've had my say."

"We have nothing more to talk about."

"Tut, tut, Your Honor. I can't believe such a prominent judge would stand there and lie to an old acquaintance—or should I say past lover—this way."

"You're despicable."

He laughed again. "If name calling is the best you can do, then I'm in good shape."

Kate had the sudden urge to hurtle herself at him and claw his eyes and face. He had a lot of nerve making demands on her. She shook so hard inside that she feared her bones might shatter, but she'd be damned if she let on. No matter what it cost her, she must maintain control. After all, what could he do to her? Nothing, she assured herself. She was perfectly safe. Or was she? The accident on the slippery road came to mind.

"We need to have another little talk, you and I."

"Get out!" Kate said again.

Thomas ignored her and inched forward, close enough for his cologne to fill her nostrils. She almost gagged. He smelled as if he'd bathed in the stuff. Yet she was sure he thought he had on just the right amount, just as he thought he was perfect in every other way and maybe to some he was. His suit was custom made, as was his tie, and possibly his shoes. Everything about him suggested perfection, except his face. Behind that smile and glint in his eyes, evil lurked. He was a vile creature in every sense of the word, and she loathed even being in the same room with him.

As if he sensed what she was thinking, his features contorted. "You think you're untouchable, that you can interfere in my life without any consequences. Well, I'm here to tell you that you can't."

"I don't know what you're talking about."

Thomas stepped closer. Kate backed up. "Oh, I think you do. How about Sawyer Brock?"

Kate closed her eyes against a sudden chill that shook her body. "What about him?"

"You hired that dick to investigate me, didn't you?"

"Why would I do that? I already know your dirtiest secret." She paused and looked him up and down, her face showing her contempt. "Besides, I'd pay more attention to a piece of garbage than I would you."

Thomas' face turned purple with rage. "Then why did you hire Brock?"

"That's none of your business."

"I'm making it my business. If it's not to investigate me, then it must be to find that brat you bore."

"I despise you, Thomas Jennings."

He laughed his trademark ugly laugh. "Call him off, you hear?"

"And if I refuse?"

"You'll be sorry."

"Like I was the other day when you ran us off the road?"

Thomas' expression didn't change. "I don't know what you're talking about."

"Of course you don't," she vented with skepticism. "But it doesn't matter. I never expected you to admit it, anyway."

That evil gleam in his eyes sharpened. "Seems like lots of people don't like you, Judge, and want you out of the way."

"Now that you've had your say, get out and don't come back."

"Not until I'm satisfied that we understand each other. Don't fuck with me or you'll be sorry. Forget about that brat and forget you ever knew me."

"Don't you dare tell me what to do."

"I *am* telling you," he said in a vicious tone, "and you'd better listen."

He was closer now, and Kate was as far back as she could go. Her back grazed the wall. She was trapped.

Thomas loomed over her, his teeth bared. "Consider this your last warning."

"You don't scare me," she said at last, staring him down.

Thomas gripped her wrist suddenly and yanked her against him, his hot breath accosting her face.

"Let go of me!"

"Not until you do like you're told."

"I'll see you in hell first," Kate railed. "I'm going to make you pay for dumping my baby. You understand? I'm going to make you pay!"

"You bitch!" Thomas shook her.

Kate twisted in his grasp. "Let me go!"

"Shut up!"

"No!" Kate screamed, but this time it wasn't the voice of a pathetic teenager begging for him to love her. It was the red-hot anger of a woman fighting back, someone determined never to be a victim again.

Thomas' hold on her tightened. He raised his hand.

"I wouldn't do that, if I were you."

Both Kate and Thomas went still as if in a freeze-frame.

Kate's mind grappled to sort out what was happening. Sawyer? She couldn't believe it. but he was there, behind Thomas, in the flesh. Her heart soared.

"Get your hands off her," Sawyer said, his voice as threatening as the edge of a razor.

Thomas ignored him and kept his tight lock on Kate's wrist. "You go to hell!"

With the quickness of a hungry dog vying for a bone, Sawyer closed the distance between them, grabbed Thomas by the shoulder, and spun him around.

Thomas bellowed, "You can't—"

Sawyer slammed him against the wall. For a moment Thomas seemed stunned. Like an angry bull he recovered and charged Sawyer. Sawyer was ready. As Thomas lunged, Sawyer grabbed him by his shirt, jerked him upright and hit him twice. The blows snapped Thomas' head, then sent him reeling to the floor.

Sawyer, his breathing still even, peered down at the crumpled form. "Crawl if you have to, but get out of my sight!"

"You'll pay for this," Thomas sniveled, struggling to rise.

"I wouldn't count on that, if I were you." Sawyer's eyes were frigid and held no mercy. "Tonight better be the last time I see your sorry ass because if you ever touch her again, I'll kill you with my bare hands."

Kate figured Thomas must have realized he was in a no-win situation because he actually staggered out the door. Sawyer snapped the lock behind him, then turned around. Kate, leaning against the desk for support, stared at him, all the while trembling.

Sawyer crossed deeper into the room, only to suddenly stop, as if unsure of what to do next.

Kate's eyes welled with unshed tears.

Sawyer's face had lost its color and turned hard in a different way. "Did he hurt you?"

"No. I'm just a little shaken, that's all."

"I meant what I said. If he ever touches you again, he'll regret it."

Kate knew he meant what he said. While she wouldn't be opposed to Thomas' getting what he deserved, in the end she wanted to be the one who gave it to him.

"I owe you a big thanks," she whispered.

"I don't want your thanks." His voice was low and brusque.

Kate wet her dry lips. "What do you want?"

Silence filled the room.

"You," Sawyer said in a strangled tone. "I want you."

Thirty-eight

Kate's breath stuck in her throat while his words, *I want you,* melted her defenses.

"Don't," Sawyer muttered in an agonizing tone and rushed toward her.

She turned away, ashamed of the weakness she knew resulted from the showdown with Thomas.

From behind, she felt Sawyer's palms on her shoulders, warm and tender, so different from Thomas' brutal touch. She turned blindly and buried her face into his chest. His arms encircled her. The pressure of his hard, warm body jolted her like a current. He felt it, too. The rapid beat of his heart matched hers.

This was insane, she told herself frantically. She shouldn't let him hold her because she feared it wouldn't stop there. His strangled groan, *I want you,* continued to ring in her ears. Yet he seemed content just to hold her.

Kate bit down on her lower lip to stop its quivering.

"Don't . . . please," he said again. He bracketed her cheeks with his big hands. "I promise he won't hurt you again."

It's not Thomas I'm worried about, *it's you,* she wanted to say, only those words wouldn't come. "I'm sorry that you got involved in this mess," she whispered instead.

"Hey, you don't worry about me. That sonofabitch didn't

get near what he had coming." Sawyer's face and eyes were as hard as a piece of stone.

Kate shuddered.

His arms encircled her again, but this time loosely. "Want to talk about him?"

"No." She lifted her head and looked into his face. "Please . . . I just want you to hold me."

"Oh, God, Kate, you don't know what you're asking." His voice sounded rusty, unnatural.

Kate moved, then, just enough for their mouths to actually touch. She whimpered softly. He groaned; it sounded as if it were pulled from deep in his throat. She tightened her hold as his lips pressed savagely against hers, and she kissed him with a fever that matched his own. It was as if her empty heart had opened to let him in.

If she could have spoken, she would have told him that this wasn't supposed to happen, that she hadn't meant for him to kiss her again. Now that he had, it was too late to stop the madness.

Sawyer dragged his lips away. "If we don't stop now, I won't be able to."

"Don't . . . stop."

His mouth came back to hers, hotter than before, more devouring. His lips left hers again to nip at her neck, leaving his hot trail there, while his hands were busy kneading her buttocks.

Her thighs quivered against his erection as emotion after emotion charged through her. She had never experienced anything like this. No man had ever touched her with such intensity, knowledge, or certainty. Sawyer knew what he wanted and took it.

"I want to feel you without these goddamn clothes on," he ground out against her lips.

"We . . . can't," she croaked. "Not here."

"Yes, we can. The door's locked."

Excitement at doing something so totally crazy and forbidden shot the blood through Kate's veins in pounding force.

He said nothing while he discarded his clothes, then

slowly removed hers. Only when he pulled the pins from the back of her hair did he make a sound.

The silky strands framed her face and shoulders like a cloud. He drew in a sharp breath and wound his hands through the silken mass. He reached over and flicked off the light that sat on her desk. Her body was now illuminated by the moonlight that poured through the window. His eyes roamed freely over her.

"Lovely. You're so lovely," he whispered.

Kate stood transfixed by the intoxicating look in his eyes. All she had to do was say no, and he would stop. She could walk away with her body intact. What about her heart? It couldn't take the pain of wanting him inside her.

As if he read her mind, Sawyer moaned, lowered his head and took a nipple in his mouth. He tongued it, until it was moist from saliva and sweat. Then he moved to the other breast. The raw heat that gripped Kate made it impossible to breathe.

He gave a muted cry as she closed a hand around him, stroking and rubbing him into full hardness. She wanted him to take her, fueled by the emotions of excitement and danger.

"Oh, Kate, Kate," he muttered. They tumbled to the soft rug, locked together.

"Sawyer!" she breathed, arching against him. His knee parted her thighs, and he buried himself inside her, filling her completely.

Still, Kate craved more. Her thighs and belly raged with need to feel his hard thrusts, to feel his seed spill into her. Her breath came from down deep inside her as she dug her nails into the muscles of his buttocks.

"I can't wait!" he managed to get out. "I'm sorry—oh—" His head came forward at the same time his lips opened over a breast while deepening his thrusts. Her eyes widened as the incredible heat almost split her in two.

She heard his guttural cry just as her fingers once again dug into his buttocks to receive his strongest thrust. Her orgasm came instantly. She buried her lips against his shoulder, tasting his sweat, following the scent of his arousal, as her thighs tightened, then rocked against his hard flesh.

Afterward, they lay exhausted and out of breath. Neither wanted to move, so they remained wrapped in each other's arms. When Sawyer rubbed his leg against hers, and she felt another jolt of need shoot through her, almost too intense to bear.

"Kate."

"Mmm?"

"We have to talk about . . . us."

She panicked. She tried to lower her head so that he wouldn't see. As it was, he saw far too much. But he was too quick for her. He held her chin firmly so that their eyes were even.

"I don't want to talk about us," she said in a halting tone. There is no *us*, she wanted to shout, but didn't.

He drew a shuddering breath. "All right. Then let's talk about your visitor."

Her heartbeat kicked in faster. "I don't want to talk about him either."

Sawyer ignored her. "Who is he?"

"He's someone from my past who I . . . used to know."

"That someone has a name."

"Why do you care?" she flung back.

"You damn well know why I care." His voice shook.

"Oh, Sawyer." His name came out a sigh. "If you must know, his name is Thomas Jennings. That's all I'm telling you."

She raised her head just in time to see his face close and his eyes frost over. She couldn't let his anger affect her. It didn't matter who Thomas was, not to Sawyer, anyway. Thomas was her responsibility. Besides, she intended to take care of Thomas in her own time and in her own way.

"Jennings, Jennings." Sawyer repeated the name as if trying to remember where he'd heard it. Then suddenly, he sucked in his breath. "He wouldn't by any chance be Reverend Thomas Jennings, the televangelist?"

Kate pointedly sidestepped his question and asked one of her own. "Why did you come here tonight?" Especially when I asked you not to, she added silently. "Do . . . you have some information?"

The pulse throbbed in Sawyer's neck, and for a moment she thought he wasn't going to let her get by with switching subjects. But then he said, "Sort of. One of my investigators has been scouting the neighborhood where the old convent used to be. An old woman who lives near there gave him the name of a priest at her church who used to hold mass at the convent. I'm in the process of tracking the priest down."

"That's wonderful news," Kate said on a breathy note that had nothing to do with the fact that his leg was again moving against hers.

"We'll see what develops." Another moment passed, then Sawyer said, "Kate."

It wasn't the fact that he said her name that alerted her, but how he said it. She knew he was about to return to the forbidden subject. She couldn't let that happen.

"Shh," she whispered, placing two fingers against his lips.

His curse ended in a groan as he trapped those fingers in his mouth and began sucking on them. Every nerve in Kate's body sprang to life.

"We should go," she whispered.

"We will, only not now." His voice came out low and hoarse. "Not until I have you again."

He brought his lips down to hers. The second time was different. The frantic need to come together was absent. Since he was still inside her, she felt him harden as he began to move. He slid in and out of her wetness with gentle, hot intensity until they both cried out into the night's stillness.

Long before dawn peeped through the darkness, Kate rolled away from him while the moonlight played across her back, the crease of her buttocks.

"Are you sorry?" he asked.

She swung around to face him. "I don't know," she said in a small voice.

He looked at her for a long moment, sighed, got up and slipped into his jeans. Feeling as if something might explode inside her unless she moved, Kate reached for her clothes.

When Sawyer was dressed, Kate felt his eyes on her as she fumbled with the button on her skirt.

"Kate . . ."

She inhaled raggedly. "Please . . . I need to go."

His expression turned fierce. "You think this was just another one-time fuck, don't you?"

Her head came up in a startled jerk. "I don't know what I think."

"The hell you don't."

She winced against the cutting edge of his voice.

"I know you don't want to talk about us." He paused and took a harsh breath. "But sooner or later you're going to have to. What's happening between us has to be resolved."

Us. That word again. "We should go."

"Goddammit, Kate!"

The pain in his voice tore another piece out of her heart. For a second she almost turned and rushed back into his arms. Brutal realism stopped her. Even if a relationship was possible between them, marriage wasn't. He wanted children; she couldn't give him any. Not even love could bridge that gap.

"Let's go," she said again, ignoring the heavy weight crushing her chest.

Together, yet miles apart, they walked out the door into the darkness.

Thirty-nine

Sawyer boarded the plane at the Dallas-Fort Worth airport. He found his seat, stored his briefcase in the overhead compartment, and sat down. Although his head was reeling, he wasn't tired, which was good. As soon as he landed in Austin, he intended to drive straight to Four Corners and New Braunfels to see what secrets he could uncover there.

Excitement provided the adrenaline that rushed through him. He'd hit the jackpot, finally. He had just interviewed the priest who had held mass for the nuns at the convent years ago. The old man lived in a home for Catholic priests, which had made the interview hard to come by.

The priest in charge of the home had been reluctant to let Sawyer talk to the elderly man.

"It's a matter of grave importance to a young woman," Sawyer had said, using his most persuasive and professional tone at the same time he'd pulled his badge.

"All right," the priest said, "but only for a few minutes. Father Franklin is not well and sometimes his mind wanders."

"You have my word; I won't upset him."

The priest led the way down an austere hallway into a tiny room that reminded Sawyer of a cell. Despite its air of neglect, it was spotlessly clean and bright. There was a picture of Jesus hanging on the wall and a vase of dried flowers on a scarred table. Close to the table a white-haired man sat in a wheelchair.

"Father Franklin, someone's here to see you," the priest said, placing his hand on the old man's shoulder.

The elderly priest blinked his blood-shot eyes several times, trying to focus on Sawyer. "Do I know you, young fellow?" His voice was raspy and shaky.

Sawyer drew a rather rickety, straight-backed chair close to the man and straddled it. "No, sir, you don't. The name's Sawyer Brock, and I'm a detective from Austin."

"I'll leave you two alone," the priest in charge said, and left the room.

The old man's head nodded, then fell forward on his chest. Sawyer's hopes faded. He wasn't going to accomplish one thing by coming here. Then the man's head came back up. "What do you want, young fellow?"

Sawyer shook his head, confused. The old priest sounded totally rational now. "Did you hold mass at St. Agnes' Convent in Austin, Texas?"

"Yes," he said simply.

Sawyer leaned forward. "Do you remember a baby that was brought there almost nineteen ago, one that had been left in a motel room?"

Something flickered behind the man's eyes. Sawyer curbed his excitement.

"A baby, you said?"

"That's right. A newborn baby."

The old man picked at the threads on the blanket that covered what Sawyer suspected were paralyzed legs. "There was a child, once, a little girl."

Sawyer couldn't contain his excitement now. "Can you tell me anything about what happened to her? Was she adopted?"

The priest didn't respond for the longest time. Then his birdlike chin came up. "Seems like she was adopted."

"Can you remember any details?"

The priest's watery eyes narrowed. "The records are sealed."

Screw the records, Sawyer thought. Anyway, seals were

made to be broken. "Then the child was there and then adopted?"

"Yes."

"Can you remember the name of the church that would have inherited the convent's records?"

"Christ Cathedral," he rasped.

Sawyer fought the urge to grab the old man and hug him. But he contained himself, knowing that a humble thanks would suffice.

Father Franklin's chin dipped back to his chest and, though Sawyer waited, it never came back up.

Sawyer stood and patted him on the shoulder. "Bless you, sir," he muttered, then walked out.

At the reception desk, the priest in charge looked at Sawyer through inquiring eyes. "Was he able to help you?"

"Yes, he was. I appreciate you letting me talk to him."

He bowed slightly and smiled.

Sawyer hesitated, then cleared his throat.

"Is there something else?"

"Could you . . . I mean would I insult you if I were to make a donation to your home?" Damn, he was fumbling worse than a frightened schoolboy in front of the principal. "I'm sure there are programs for the underprivileged that you . . . sponsor . . . or maybe you could use the money here—" Sawyer's voice trailed off lamely.

The priest's smile lit up his whole face. "Not at all, Mr. Brock. I wouldn't be insulted at all. In fact, I'd be very appreciative."

Sawyer returned his smile, reached into his coat pocket, and drew out his checkbook.

That conversation had taken place only hours earlier, and Sawyer was anticipating his next move: his trip to Four Corners and New Braunfels.

He tried to scorn the feeling of guilt that suddenly passed through him, but he couldn't. Not only did he want to find proof that Kate was the mother, he wanted desperately to know more about her personal life as well. He had no business going to either place. His job was to track the young woman, not Kate. Yet he wanted to know what had made her the survivor she was, and he had given up hope that she would trust him enough to tell him herself.

Ah, Kate. Such a contradiction. Cool and unshakable on the outside and hot and tumultuous on the inside. A fascinating but lethal combination.

The jet engines buzzed in Sawyer's ears, but the noise wasn't loud or intrusive enough to pull his thoughts away from Kate. Had he actually made love with her? Or had he simply fucked her? No. Everything inside him rebelled against that thought. He'd told her she wasn't a one-time fuck, and he had meant it. Yet he couldn't call that frantic coupling making love, either.

What he could call it was a mistake. He had done something damn well forbidden. He had crossed the line he'd sworn he wouldn't cross. And now he was entangled with his beautiful and mysterious client.

Yet if he had it all to do over again, would he pull back, force himself to push her away? No, no more than he could have stopped breathing.

So what now? he asked himself, stretching his legs as far as the first-class seating would allow. Where did they go from here? If Kate had her way, they wouldn't go anywhere. She had made it plain there would be no repeat of that wild night, but he was hooked. He knew he couldn't leave her alone. And he simply had to know more about her life.

It wouldn't be easy, though; far from it. He wasn't sure what type of cooperation he'd find on the other end of the investigation. Another pang of guilt darted through him. When Kate found out, she would be plenty pissed—if she found out. He didn't hold out much hope that he could keep his search a secret. He'd like to think she would be flattered that he wanted to know more about her—but he had no doubt that she'd be pissed.

The flight attendant appeared in front of him. Sawyer blinked.

"Sir, would you care for something to drink?"

"Coffee, please."

Sawyer drummed his fingers on the table in front of him, while his mind mapped out his plan of action. He'd decided against talking to Angie again. Besides, Dave was already sniffing around her, not that it would do any good, he thought with confidence. He hadn't warned Kate of that fact because he felt certain that Angie wouldn't betray her friend, despite Dave's persuasiveness in the sack. Sawyer almost burst out laughing when he thought about that wimp. Even if Angie did talk, provided she knew something of importance, Kate could hold her own against Dave. She could do the same with Harlan and Thomas Jennings.

Unless she'd given birth to an illegitimate child.

Sawyer was convinced that that was her secret. He also suspected that that asshole, Jennings, was the father. Soon he would know everything there was to know about the reverend. He'd sent Ralph on a witch-hunt.

Right now, he was operating on gut instinct that Kate had had the child and that Jennings was its father. Sawyer's features darkened. What he needed was the proof. He'd get it, one way or the other. He had to hurry, though. If he could uncover that information, so could others. Dave and Harlan for starters.

That bombshell, in the wrong hands, could destroy Kate with the electorate. He wasn't about to let that happen.

"Here's your coffee, sir."

Sawyer nodded his thanks. Instead of drinking his coffee, he put his head back and closed his eyes. He didn't wake up until the plane landed in Austin.

Thirty minutes later, he was in his car and out of the airport proper. But instead of heading toward the highway to Four Corners, he found himself driving toward the courthouse. He didn't know what had spurred this action, except that he wanted to share the good news with Kate.

"Yeah, right, Brock," he muttered underneath his breath as he pulled into a parking spot across the street, only to look up and see Kate walking down the steps of the courthouse.

Without questioning his stroke of luck, Sawyer steered the Jag across the street. He knew she had seen him because she paused, then waited.

"Hop in a sec," he said.

Though Kate seemed a bit dubious, she did his bidding.

The instant she sat down beside him and he inhaled the smell that was all her own, he wanted to yank her into his arms and bury his lips into hers.

"Where were you heading?" he forced himself to ask.

"To the park. I just needed a breath of fresh air between sessions."

Her hair was mussed, tangled from the wind, and there were dark smudges under her eyes. He hadn't noticed them before, but instead of detracting from her loveliness, they added to it.

He gripped the wheel tighter and said inanely, "Surprised to see me?" Even to his own ears, his voice came out sounding like a rich growl.

"That's putting it mildly."

"Are you going to chew my ass out for showing up here?"

She shot him a quashing look that said she'd like to throttle him.

"I've never chewed anyone's ass out, as I recall," she said primly, only to quickly add, "Well, I take that back. I guess I have, at that."

He smiled into her eyes. They were half-wild, half-afraid as they locked with his. He knew that she was remembering the same thing he was: how they had made love, exploring each other with ravenous hunger.

"Kate . . ."

She licked her lips as if they were dry, leaving them slightly wet. He cursed and shifted in the seat.

"Did you find out anything?" she asked, averting her gaze.

She spoke so softly that her words seemed almost vaporized.

He coughed. "I just got back from visiting the old priest."

Kate swung back around. "And?"

"He told me the baby had been adopted, then gave me the name of the church that possibly had the records."

"Praise the Lord," Kate cried jubilantly.

"As soon as we track the records, we'll be in business." He paused. "So am I forgiven for showing up here?"

"There's nothing to forgive," she said softly.

Her eyes were again fixed on him and what he saw in their

depths, a complex mixture of fear and wanting, caused the ache inside him to explode. Without thinking, he moved toward her.

"No!" she cried and pressed both palms into his chest, staving him off.

He jerked back. "Sorry "

She grabbed the handle and opened the door. "I have to get back to court."

He released a harsh breath, his throat so dry he could hardly speak. Then clearing it, he added, "I'll be in touch."

He didn't know if she heard that last part; she chose that moment to slam the door behind her. He watched her walk up the steps and into the building. He fell back against the seat and closed his eyes, feeling sick with longing.

Four Corners, Texas, was even more dreary than he'd imagined. In fact, it was little more than a ghost town. The people who lived there were mostly farmers.

Sawyer's plan of attack was to find a grocery story, one that he hoped had been there for many years. If it had the same proprietor then he'd be in luck. If not, he'd try the school. Librarians were known for their longevity.

If Kate had had a child there, someone would know about it, and if he pushed the right button, they would talk. People generally took delight in other people's troubles.

Sawyer pulled the Jag in front of the only store on the main street. It looked recently repainted, but no one had bothered to jack it up, Sawyer thought with an ironic smile.

He walked in and found it deserted, except for a dark, beefy man with a thatch of white hair and a twinkle in his eyes.

"Howdy."

Sawyer shoved his Stetson back on his head, held out his hand, then said, "I'm Sawyer Brock, a detective from Austin."

The man lifted his eyebrows, but shook Sawyer's hand. "Well, now, we don't get many of your kind in these parts."

Sawyer's lips twitched. "Mr.—?"

"Elmer Sides."

"Mr. Sides, I'd like to ask you some questions."

"Can't promise I'll answer, sonny. We don't go blabbing much to strangers."

"I understand that, but my purpose is to help someone who used to live here."

Elmer scratched his chin. "And who might that be?"

"Kate Colson."

Sawyer watched his face closely. It changed from guarded to downright friendly. "Why, I'll be a sonofagun! I haven't seen that youngin' in no tellin' how long."

Encouraged, Sawyer asked, "Mind if we sit down?" His eyes had spotted the fountain and tables in a far corner.

"Sure, sure. Want something to eat?"

"No, thanks."

Once they were seated in a booth that was covered in a blue plastic cloth, Elmer said, "Tell me about Kate. She was always one of my favorites, used to sneak her candy, in fact." The light went out of his eyes suddenly. "Too bad she had such a sorry daddy. Why, that man wasn't worth taking out behind the barn and shootin'."

"Why?"

"He was a drunk, one of them mean ones. Why, he used to whip up on the missus." Elmer leaned across the table and made a face as if what he was about to say was unpleasant. "Some of us think he might've taken a hand to the girl, too, but we had no proof."

Sawyer's stomach muscles clenched. The thought of Kate enduring the same abuse he had suffered made him want to tear someone limb from limb.

"Why are you wantin' to know about Kate?" Elmer's voice now held that same guarded tone, as if he realized he'd been talking too much and too freely.

Sawyer tried to reassure him without being too forthcoming. "I'm working on a case that involves her. I'm afraid she's in trouble."

Concern darkened his eyes. "That's too bad. So whatcha wanna know?"

"Did she always live here in Four Corners?"

Sides was quiet for a minute while he rubbed his fat, whiskered chin. "Don't rightly know about that."

"What about New Braunfels? Did she ever live there?"

"Well, now that you mention it, maybe she did. Seems like when her friend Angie Strickland and her mamma moved there, Kate left and lived with them."

"What about boyfriends? Did she have a steady?"

"Nah, not that I know of. Her old man didn't cotton to that kind of nonsense. He was some kind of religious nut."

Sawyer stood and held out his hand. "Well, I guess that just above covers it."

For a moment, Elmer Sides looked at him with a flabbergasted look on his face. "You mean that's it?"

Sawyer smiled. "That's it. I've taken up enough of your time. Anyway, I think I just heard the bell jingle."

"Hope so." Elmer lifted his beefy body out of the booth and followed Sawyer. "It's damn near impossible for a fellow to make a living these days."

"Ain't that the truth," Sawyer agreed with a grin.

Sides stood beside Sawyer and looked up at him, that same perplexed question on his face. "You sure you got what you come for?"

"I'm sure," Sawyer said hastily, then held out his hand again. "Much obliged."

"Come back anytime," Elmer said.

"Will do." Sawyer nodded to the old woman who stood in the aisle eyeing him with undisguised curiosity, then walked out into the blinding sunlight.

He should've felt good about his morning's work. He didn't. He felt lousy. He had been determined, rabidly so, to find out all there was about Kate, unearth all her deep, dark secrets. But when Sides' mouth turned out to be the size of a whale, he'd felt like one miserable s.o.b.

Sawyer stomped to the Jag and got in. Now was the time to call it quits, to go back home. But he couldn't. He had to see his investigation through. Personal facts and recorded facts were two different things. From now on, he'd stick to the recorded facts.

Dammit, he hated it when his conscience got the better of him.

A man in a parked car across the street watched Sawyer get into the Jag. Only after Sawyer pulled away from the curb did the man make his move. Smothering a yawn, he stepped out of his car and stretched.

He stuffed his shirttail back into his slacks, then made his way into the grocery store, a satisfied smile on his face.

New Braunfels was the seat of Guadalupe County. Sawyer found its courthouse without any trouble. With assistance from a young woman, Sawyer located the records he needed and sat down. It wasn't long before he found what he was looking for.

There it was in black and white, documentation showing that Kate had given birth to a female child. Surely Kate must have known he would find the information. *But why would he have bothered to look?* That would be her reasoning.

Sawyer read further. When he came to father, his pulse rate faltered. None was listed. The line was blank. Cursing, he sat back in the chair and massaged his neck. He had been afraid of that, but now that he'd confirmed it, it was a bitter pill to swallow.

He was back to square one on the matter of the father. Although Kate was right when she said that information wasn't needed to track the child, *he* wanted to know.

So who would tell him? That part wasn't easy. Roberta Strickland? Angie? Getting them to talk would be damn near impossible. In fact, he would bet his entire bank account that neither would provide him with the information. He just prayed Angie would keep her mouth shut to Dave as well. So where could he get the truth?

His lips tightened. For him, there was only one source.

Kate.

Forty

The instant Kate walked through the door of Johns and Strassberg, she noticed a group of attorneys, both men and women, gathered in the reception area. Some she knew, some she did not. The minute they saw her, they stopped talking. A funny feeling stole over her; somehow she knew that she was the topic of conversation.

"Hiya, Kate," one of the men said. That greeting was echoed by two others.

Kate stared into their red faces. "Hello. It's nice to see you."

"By the way, how's the campaign going?" another asked.

"Fine," Kate said politely.

They fell silent as she walked past them and made her way to her old office. By the time she got there, Kate had decided that she had overreacted to her former cohorts.

"It's so good to see you, Kate." Babs Bishop paused and scrutinized her more closely. "You're looking great, except I think those circles under your eyes are a bit more pronounced."

Kate stuck her tongue out at her former secretary. Babs merely laughed.

She had stopped by her old firm with the excuse of wishing Mr. Johns well at his birthday party and wanting to borrow some books that would help her settle a case. But she really hadn't wanted to spend the evening alone. Only when she was around others could she stop thinking about Sawyer.

Kate had asked Angie if she would like to go to dinner and a movie with her, hoping they might attempt to have a real talk instead of the polite rhetoric they now exchanged on a daily basis. Angie had declined, saying she had other plans. Kate knew those other plans included Dave Nielsen, much to her continued regret.

"Hey, what's with you?" Babs was saying. "You look strung out or something."

Kate deliberately gave her head a shake. "Sorry. You're right, I am strung out, only I wish it didn't show."

"I see it because I worked with you so long."

Kate's mouth turned down as she walked to the window in Babs's office. "I still wish you worked with me." Babs, with her bright perky features and dedicated enthusiasm, was special. She could never be replaced.

"That's nice to hear," Babs said, perching on the edge of her desk and facing Kate. "I miss you, too. So tell me, what's been going on?"

"Work mostly," Kate said, averting her gaze.

"Me, too." Babs grinned. "Working all the time is the pits, isn't it?"

Kate laughed, then glanced at her watch. It was nearly time for the party to begin. It was for office personnel only. She suspected that Bill Johns had added her to the guest list himself. The party was being held in one of the large conference rooms upstairs.

"I guess we'd better join the others."

Babs sighed. "You're right, we better." But she didn't move. Instead she turned her head to one side and stared at Kate.

Kate felt uncomfortable and said so. "What's the matter? Do I have something in my teeth?"

Despite Kate's attempt at humor, Babs didn't smile. "No, it's just I've been trying to decide if I should tell you something."

Another funny feeling fluttered down Kate's spine. "You know you can tell me anything."

Babs shook her head. "I'm not so sure about this."

"Oh, for heaven's sake. Out with it."

"Okay," Babs said. "This office has been buzzing."

"About me." Kate's words were a flat statement of fact.

Babs' eyes widened. "You know?"

"Not really. It's just that when I came in a little while ago, I interrupted a group talking." She paused. "About me, I thought. Then I told myself it was my paranoia rising to the surface."

"Well, it wasn't," Babs said bluntly.

"What are they saying?"

Babs flushed.

"Suppose I tell you. They're saying I got where I am on my back. Right?"

Babs' flush deepened. "That's right."

"I've heard that before and believe me, it goes in one ear and out the other."

"All I know is that it makes me madder than hell." Babs waited a minute, then added, "There's something else, too."

"Oh," Kate said wearily, though not with surprise. She'd decided that anything she was involved with had the potential to go wrong.

"Yeah, rumor has it that Dave is going to announce his candidacy for judge."

"Dave? Run for judge?" Kate's tone was incredulous. "Why, that's the craziest thing I ever heard."

Babs pursed her lips. "My thoughts exactly."

"So that's why the rumors are circulating so hot and heavy. Dave's determined to divide my support here in the firm."

"Keep in mind that I haven't been able to confirm that he's definitely running," Babs said anxiously.

"Don't worry, I won't say anything. Anyway, it's too late for him to enter the race. An unknown like him will have a tough time, no matter who backs him."

"So you think some big gun is backing him, huh?"

Kate's brown eyes turned cold. "Yes," she said emphatically, and stopped there. Harlan Moore was behind this insane move by Dave. She didn't know how she knew, but she knew. Maybe it was because that combination seemed to fit. Both lacked morals and integrity.

"You're not mad at me for telling you, are you?" Babs's tone was anxious.

Kate smiled. "I'd have been mad if you hadn't."

Babs released a breath. "Good. Come on, let's go, before Mr. Johns sends the troops after us."

The decorated room was full of Johns and Strassberg employees. Not often did the firm throw such a bash. During her tenure, Kate could remember only one other. Bill Johns turned sixty-five today, which he considered a milestone. Kate agreed. Anyone who managed to live to that age in his pressure-cooker of a job deserved to be honored.

She and Babs mingled, and then Babs was abducted by a junior partner. Kate was glad. She wanted to make herself seen, then slip out. While she knew most of the people, she no longer felt much rapport with them.

"As usual, my dear, you look smashing."

Kate turned and smiled at Bill Johns. "Thanks, but you'd say that no matter what."

Johns chuckled. "You're right, I would. Maybe you look so good because you're way ahead of your opponents in the polls."

Kate waved her hand. "I don't pay attention to polls, though my campaign manager does. Ginger's the one who deserves all the credit."

He snorted. "I don't buy that at all. You're the draw. Just stick to your guns, and you'll win by a landslide. Remember, I'm behind you one hundred percent and so are a lot of the others here."

Kate felt both grateful and uncomfortable. She knew Johns was telling her in a nice way not to worry about Dave Nielsen or the ugly rumors. "I appreciate you so much," she said, a slight catch in her voice.

Johns winked at her. "Well, I do have an ulterior motive."

"You do?"

He laughed. "As soon as you get this judgeship business out of your system, I'm going to see that you return here."

"And what if I don't ever get it out of my system?" she teased.

"Then, I guess the people will be blessed with a damn good judge."

Kate impulsively kissed him on the cheek. "Thanks for everything." She suddenly felt weepy. "You're good for me."

She had barely spoken those last words when she spotted Dave Nielsen. He was slouched against the French doors, nursing a drink and watching her, a cold, sardonic expression on his face.

Kate bristled but didn't let it show as she pulled back and gave Bill a bright smile.

"I want you to mingle, have a good time," he said. "Oh, and don't let what the media said about your decision on that mercy killing get to you."

"I'm trying not to. I did what I thought best."

"'Atta girl. You hang in there."

"I intend to, and happy birthday."

The instant her ex-boss walked off to mingle, Kate didn't hesitate. She made her way toward Dave. When she stopped in front of him, he didn't so much as move. He kept his insolent stance and expression.

Kate plastered a smile on her face and spoke so softly that the average onlooker would think they were having an amiable discussion. "If you were smart, you would keep your filthy mouth shut."

His face drained of color, but his tone was ugly. "You don't scare me, Judge." The way he said *Judge* made her ache to slap him, which was nothing new. Any time she was around him, she felt that urge.

"Either prove what you're saying, or, as I just said, keep you filthy mouth shut," she snapped.

Dave laughed. "Oh, honey, you just won't learn, will you? Believe me, when the time suits me, I can prove it."

Kate refused to let his confidence intimidate her. "We'll

see about that," she said through clenched teeth. "I'd advise you also not to underestimate me."

She turned her back on him and was about to walk off when he said in a sly, mocking tone, "Oh, by the way, I don't think I ever thanked you for introducing me to Angie. Yeah, ol' Ang is quite a talker."

Kate froze, then struggled to regroup. Angie. Dear Lord, if he was indeed going to run for judge, then he would use whatever ammunition he could uncover against her. Would Angie betray her? Would she tell him about the baby? No, Kate's heart and mind rebelled on both counts. She and Angie may have their differences and their problems, but Angie would never betray that trust.

She spun back around. "You leave Angie out of this." Anger underscored each word.

Dave merely shook his head and laughed.

Forty-one

Kate expected the probation officer to arrive at any moment. The day had been hectic from the start, and it looked as if it was going to end that way.

The case she was hearing now was expected to last several weeks. A white sheriff and two deputies were accused of beating a black prisoner to death in his cell.

The sheer nature of the case called for added publicity, which Kate shied away from, even during election time. She continued to despise interviews. Her thoughts suddenly conjured up memories of Mick Presnall and his aggressive style.

Kate felt, however, that she was holding her own among her opponents, and even if Dave ran against her, she was more determined than ever to beat him. No way would she let that low-life beat *her*. As far as Dave digging into her personal life was concerned—she'd have to talk to Angie as soon as she could.

The beginning of the murder trial had been exhausting. She would have liked to have gone home, slipped into cutoffs, and worked in the yard. That was not to be.

Kate rocked back in her chair and pinched the bridge of her nose. She had another ruling pending on a case she had heard several days ago, one that was almost as unsettling as the mercy killing. Now, she had to switch her mind off the murder case and back onto the previous case and determine the punishment.

Lifting her pencil, she peered back down at the brief. Two young boys, just out of high school, who had obtained scholarships to play football at major colleges, had been stopped for a minor traffic violation that had ended in an arrest on drug and weapon possession. While there was no doubt about their guilt, there was another major factor that she had to take into consideration.

The older brother of one of the boys had tempted them with extra money to transport the drugs, saying that there was nothing to it, that it would be a piece of cake.

As far as Kate was concerned, mules were mules. The fact that the two youngsters seemed naive and gullible didn't cut any pluses with her, especially when the drug was crack cocaine.

At first both boys had refused to cooperate, but after being assured that they would be indicted, first offense or not, they decided to cooperate and work a plea agreement.

It was up to her to decide whether they received the maximum sentence or probation. She had built a reputation for her tough stance and stiff punishment on drug crimes. She didn't intend to bend the rules now. She had informed both attorneys that she would not accept a plea bargain unless it was for a minimum of ten years. With any case involving drugs in quantity, there was very little room for bargaining. A tap on the door brought Kate's head up. "Come in."

"Hello, Judge," Jim Darcy said, as he ambled through the door with briefcase in hand.

Because she would consider the report at sentencing, she wanted to talk to the officer in her chambers, off the record.

Jim was a tall, thin man with glasses and a bald spot on the top of his head, which made him look older than his thirty-odd years. Looks aside, he was thorough and fair in his job, and she never failed to consider his recommendation.

"Hard day?" he asked, sitting down.

Kate gave him a fleeting smile. "Aren't they all?"

"Yeah, guess you're right."

"So did you finish the report?" Kate asked, all business.

Jim removed it from his case, then passed it to her. Instead of looking at it, she laid it on her desk. "Suppose you tell me what you think."

Jim chewed on the side of his jaw for a moment. "I spoke with a lot of people who know and work with these kids. They have nothing but the highest regard for them."

"What about prior arrests?"

"None," Jim said. "Records are as clean as a whistle."

"Family background? How about that?"

"All right there, too, or as far as I could see. Both boys have parents who live together and who seem to be supportive. They're both from modest-income families with the same problems as the rest of us."

Kate stood, feeling her agitation mount. "Then why did they do it? They had everything to look forward to. I just don't get it."

"Well, me neither. As we know, they were both a trifle belligerent when first arrested; then when they knew they were in serious trouble, they started babbling like a broken water faucet."

"But did they give any specifics as to why they did it?"

"One of them did it on a lark, for the pure thrill of it. He seems to be the more remorseful of the two. The other one said he needed the money for his girlfriend's abortion."

"Oh, my God," Kate said, a sinking feeling in the pit of her stomach. "An abortion I bet the parents didn't know about."

"You got it."

"So what do you recommend?"

Jim tapped his pen on his knee while staring at Kate. "You're not going to like it."

Kate sighed. "Try me."

"Probation with community service. If you send them to prison, not only will it nullify their college scholarships, it will ruin their lives."

"I know, but they have committed a crime, good kids or not."

"I told you you wouldn't like my suggestion."

Kate gritted her teeth. "If I let them off, it'll just add to the court's problems. You know state courts have been looked on as a joke for our leniency in drug cases. I vowed to change that when I put on this robe; so far I've stuck to that vow."

"And I admire you for it, too," Jim said, snapping his case shut. "There's more in the report." He stood. "When is the sentencing scheduled?"

"I don't know. At the moment, I'm involved in a murder trial. I'm hoping to sandwich it in after one of the day's sessions."

"I'll talk to you later, then."

"Thanks," Kate said.

Jim nodded, then left the room.

Kate lifted the first sheet in the folder and began reading. She didn't know how long she'd been poring over the report when she heard raised voices in the outer chamber.

Frowning, she stood and was halfway to the door when it burst open. A frazzled but determined Leslie marched across the threshold. Then, closing the door behind her, she leaned against it, breathing hard.

"What on earth is going on?"

"There is a woman out there," Leslie said tersely, "who insists on talking to you, said she wouldn't budge until she did. She's a female version of that newspaper creep, Presnall."

"Just calm down, Leslie. Who is she?"

"Says her name is Annette Jennings."

Kate barely kept her features from showing her shock. Annette Jennings here? That didn't make sense. Or did it?

"Do you want me to call the bailiff and have him pitch her out on her ear? He's gone on break."

Kate shook her head. "No, it's not necessary to get Ben. If I need him, I'll let you know."

"Do you mean you're going to talk to her? I'm sure she's been drinking, though I can't smell anything." Leslie shivered. "She just has that look in her eyes."

"I'll see her." Kate's tone was clipped.

"I hope you won't be sorry. She's a bitch," Leslie added under her breath, just before she opened the door.

"Well, it's about time," Annette Jennings said as she ceased her pacing and swept into Kate's chambers.

Leslie gave Annette a scathing look, then went out and closed the door.

For a moment there was silence in the room as the two women sized each other up.

"What can I do for you, Mrs. Jennings?" Kate asked.

Annette's lips twisted, which made her look even more harsh, Kate thought. And desperate. On closer observation, Kate saw that Leslie was right. Annette had the appearance of someone who had been drinking, if she wasn't already drunk. Her eyes were glassy, and her breathing unsteady.

"What you can do, Miss Colson, is leave my husband alone," Annette spat. "Stay out of our lives!"

Kate wasn't in the least bit intimidated. "Thomas and I have unfinished business."

Annette laughed an ugly laugh, baring her teeth. "That's where you're wrong, Judge. You and *my* husband don't have shit."

Kate's eyes turned cold. "You've had your say. Now, I suggest you leave." Kate turned to walk away.

"Oh, no, you don't!" Annette cried, latching on to Kate's upper arm and swinging her around. "You're going to listen to me, you hear?"

"Take your hand off me," Kate said in an icy voice. "And get out."

Annette released her arm, but she didn't move. Her lips curled. "You think just because he fucked you and you had his brat—"

"Shut your mouth!" Kate said, whipping across Annette's crude words. "And don't you ever say anything like that to me again."

Seemingly stunned at Kate's quick and vindictive response, Annette backed up a bit. "You don't scare me. I've bested my husband's other whores with as much clout or more than you have. So don't threaten me. Besides, if you don't stop digging into the past and shoveling up dirt, my daddy has the means to ruin you."

"Well, you just tell 'Daddy' to take his best shot. But re-

member that if my dirty laundry gets aired, then so will
Thomas'. Tell 'Daddy' that, too."

"That will never happen, I assure you," Annette said, her
face contorted. "And if you think it will, then you don't
know Thomas Jennings."

Kate turned and walked to her desk. "Close the door on
your way out."

When the door banged shut behind Annette, Kate flinched,
then sagged against the desk. Annette Jennings was pitiful.
When she could think straight, she might feel some compas-
sion for her. Now she only felt violated and furious. And
scared, scared that sooner or later, she wouldn't be able to
dodge all the missiles that were being launched at her.

Tired as she was, Kate was determined to stay up and wait
for Angie. She had to know if Angie had said anything to
Dave about her past. The matter had to be settled once and
for all.

She wasn't looking forward to it. A lump had grown so
huge in Kate's throat that she couldn't swallow around it.
She had to face the fact that Angie may have betrayed her.
Just as she had to face the fact that she had made love to
Sawyer Brock.

More than a week had passed since that night, and she
hadn't seen or talked to him. Still, every time the doorbell or
the phone rang, she expected it to be him. She should have
been thinking about her daughter and not Sawyer. A sob tore
through her. Dear Lord, she was concerned about Sara, when
she could get past thoughts of *him*.

A dull ache began at the back of Kate's head. She rose
from the couch and looked at her watch. It was ten-thirty.
Maybe if she turned on the television and watched *Nightline*
with Ted Koppel, she could get her mind on the right track.
Only she didn't know what the right track was anymore.

All she knew was that she liked what she had shared with
Sawyer on the carpeted floor and wanted a repeat.

"Oh, God," Kate whispered out loud in agony.

It had been stupid, stupid, stupid to indulge herself. His

being inside her had left her aching for more. He had awakened her sleeping body and now it was screaming for more
of the same.

She bent over and rocked. She had never made love like
that, never even imagined that coupling could be like that.
He had touched her on every level, using his body to render
her senseless. The hunger of his powerful body had bordered
on the savage. She had responded in kind, giving herself totally to him as one wrenching orgasm after another had
pelted her body.

Now, she didn't know how to handle what was left of her
battered heart and body.

"Kate, are you all right?"

Startled, Kate tried frantically to swallow that lump so that
she could speak. She faced Angie. "I'm fine." She made herself smile, but she wasn't sure Angie even noticed. Angie
looked equally as agitated. "I've been waiting for you, actually."

"Me? Why?"

"I thought we might talk."

Angie shook her head, but not before Kate saw the wary
look in her eyes. "It's late. Besides, I'm bushed."

"Have you been with Dave?"

"Yes," Angie said hesitantly.

"Please, Ang, sit down. I promise this will only take a
minute."

There was a short silence while Angie walked deeper into
the room and perched on the edge of a chair.

Kate went straight to the point. "Word has it that Dave is
going to run for judge."

Angie's expression didn't change. "If that's the case, he
hasn't said anything to me. And I'm sure he would have, especially since we're—" She broke off, then clamped her lips
together.

"Since you're what?" Kate pressured.

"Forget it. It's nothing." Then, as if the strained look on
Kate's face made her feel guilty, she flushed and added,
"Maybe I'll tell you later, okay?"

Kate sighed. "Okay." She knew what Angie had been

about to say. The thought of Angie marrying Dave was untenable. Yet she didn't think that union would ever come about. She was positive Dave was using Angie for his own gain. Poor, gullible Angie . . .

"What else is on your mind?" Angie asked into the growing silence.

"Has Dave ever ask you anything about my past?"

"I can't believe you'd even ask that!" Angie sounded shocked and hurt.

Kate drew in a shuddering breath. "Under the circumstances, I had to ask."

Angie stood. "Under what circumstances?" Before Kate could answer, she held up her hand and shook her head. "Forget it. I don't care. You'll just have to trust me."

"That's your answer?"

"That's my answer," Angie said flatly. "At one time, that would've been good enough."

With that, Angie turned and walked to the door, only to suddenly swing back around. "Instead of worrying about me, you'd best be worried about Sawyer Brock."

Kate felt her jaw drop along with her heart. "Sawyer Brock?"

"Yeah. He's been snooping around Four Corners, asking lots of personal questions about *you*."

Forty-two

"Where the hell have you been?"

Annette's strident voice grated on Thomas' nerves. He couldn't even walk into his own house after a long day at work and find peace. Lately, she was always waiting for him, behaving like a fish-wife. But then, that was exactly what she was. She turned his stomach. If it weren't for her old man, he would dump her.

"At work," he said tersely, not knowing why he even bothered to answer.

She was lounging on the couch in the den, looking as though she hadn't slept in weeks. The deep tan she was so proud of made her look old and worn. As usual, she was puffing on a cigarette and drinking a martini.

"That'll be a first," she said in a nasty tone, pulling herself upright.

Thomas felt the need for a drink himself. But he wouldn't give her the satisfaction of knowing that she affected him in any way. He just wanted to take a shower and get the hell out of her sight.

"Aren't you going to ask what I did today, Tommy dear?" she cooed as she walked toward him. She stopped within touching distance. Her boozy breath saturated his skin just as she reached out and toyed with the knot on his tie.

He jerked back. "Knock it off. I don't know what kind of

game you're suddenly playing, but whatever it is, count me out."

An ugly flush covered her face. "No, you never want to play unless it's with one of your whores."

"Spare me, for god's sake," Thomas said, rolling his eyes.

"Well, even if you don't want to know what I did today, I'm going to tell you."

"Look, I don't really give a damn."

"I paid a visit to your old girlfriend—the judge."

Thomas' eyes narrowed to slits.

"Yeah, I thought it was time someone put that bitch in her place, since you obviously aren't going to. I don't want Daddy to find out that she's had your child. No—"

He didn't plan it. It just happened. His hand snaked out and slapped her hard across the face. "Dammit, stay the hell away from her and out of my business!"

Annette's hand flew to her cheek, and her eyes glazed over with shock. "You . . . hit me. How dare you . . . hit me!?" she screeched.

"Then by god learn to keep your mouth shut." Thomas loomed over her. "I'll take care of Kate Colson in my own way." He turned his back and took a step.

"Where are you going?"

"Out."

"You bastard! I hope you get what's coming to you!"

He twisted slightly, his eyes filled with contempt. "Stop slobbering. Just do what you do best. Get drunk."

Mick Presnall was about to walk out the door of his apartment when the phone rang. For a moment he was tempted not to answer it.

"Oh, what the hell," he muttered, then stomped toward it.

"Yeah," he said.

"How come I haven't heard from you?"

"Ah, Harlan, my man." Mick kept his tone light when in reality he knew he was treading on thin ice. In fact, he was in deep shit.

"Don't "Harlan my man, me.' I paid you damn good

money for information that I haven't gotten. Nor has there been any adverse publicity on Kate."

Mick's blood pressure rose. "Now, you wait just a minute. There's been two articles that put the judge in a bad light."

"Well, not a bad enough light—she's still leading in the polls." Harlan's tone was harsh.

"So," Mick said in a whiny tone, "I'm doing the best I can."

"What about Brock?"

"As a matter of fact, I followed him and he went to a very interesting place."

"Oh?"

"Yeah, he went to the judge's old stomping grounds— Four Corners—the little town where she grew up."

"Ah, now you're talking."

"I'm afraid I struck out, though."

"Dammit, Presnall."

"Hold on a sec," Mick said with more patience than he was feeling. He would've liked to have told Harlan to go take a flying fuck, but he couldn't. Harlan Moore was a powerful man and if Mick got on his bad side, it could cost him his job at the paper.

"There's not much time to hold on, you idiot."

Mick paled, then decided he didn't have to take this, especially when he was doing the best he could. "Look, I talked to the same old man that Brock talked to. He owns a groc—"

"Spare me the details," Harlan said, cutting across his words. "What's the bottom line?"

"The old man wouldn't talk to me. He looked me up and down and when I mentioned Kate Colson, his jaw clamped together like he had lockjaw."

"Damn!"

"Short of threatening him, there wasn't a thing I could do. But I'm not giving up."

"If you come up empty-handed, then be prepared to return my money."

A resounding click assaulted Mick's ear. "Fuck you!" Mick slammed his own receiver down. But he didn't leave. He stood still while his mind raced.

* * *

Sawyer looked up as his assistant sauntered into the room. Ralph's freckles seemed duller today, Sawyer thought distractedly. Maybe that was because there was no sunshine in the room; everything looked dull.

"Well?" Sawyer asked, locking his hands behind his head.

"I located the Christ Cathedral Church, but they don't seem to be able to put their hands on the records."

"Sonofabitch!"

Ralph sighed. "I hear you. In fact I feel like I'm running into one brick wall after another."

"You'll just have to go through that brick wall, if that's what it takes."

Ralph gave him a disgruntled look. "Sounds easy enough, only it isn't." He plopped down in the chair in front of Sawyer's desk. "I told them to keep looking, that it would be worth their while."

"You're damn right. I'll be glad to make a contribution."

The silence stretched as both men's minds worked. Sawyer was the first to speak. "Dammit, those records have to be somewhere in that church."

"You'd think so, boss. But I'm here to tell you that from what I saw, those people aren't very organized."

"There are ways around that."

"What if the records *are* lost? What if they were destroyed when the convent was torn down?"

Sawyer thrust his hands through his hair, then pounded his fist on the desk. "I refuse to believe that. Besides, Father Franklin, that old priest, took charge of the adoption, or so he led me to believe. That means the records have to be on the premises somewhere. Check and see if there have been any changes in the church."

"Such as?"

"Renovations, something along those lines."

"That's a thought."

"Ask about attics, storage places where records have been put and forgotten."

"Now, why didn't I think of that?"

Sawyer smiled. "You really want me to answer that?"

"Go to hell," Ralph muttered.

Sawyer laughed and, surprisingly, it felt good.

"So you want me to make those records top priority?"

"You should've been halfway there already."

"As soon as you let me outta here . . . Oh, by the way, here's the poop you wanted on that preacher fellow, Jennings." Ralph tossed the closed portfolio to Sawyer.

"Thanks."

"Anything else?"

"Yeah, I need you to get one of the guys on some of this." He pointed to the stack of folders.

For the next few minutes the two men discussed pressing work that needed to be taken care of. The most important item was the 500 guard dogs for the Emir of Kuwait, which fell under the auspices of Sawyer's anti-terrorist work abroad. When they finished, Ralph left.

Sawyer opened the file on Thomas Jennings, but after reading through it, he found no smoking gun, certainly no link to Kate, other than the fact that they had grown up in the same town, which he already knew.

His eyes hardened. There was indeed a link. Sawyer was convinced that Jennings was the father of Kate's child. Even if he wasn't, the files told Sawyer that Jennings was not the godly man he professed to be. For starters, the government was breathing down his neck for tax evasion, thus putting his television ministry in a bad light. Yeah, Sawyer thought, there had to be a dead rat around Jennings. And when he found it, he'd make sure everyone smelled it.

"Shit," he murmured, staring up at the ceiling, silently wishing away the ache in his groin. He knew that he was wasting his effort. Until he saw Kate again and made love to her, he would have no relief. Regardless of how much she pretended not to want him, he knew better. She wanted him as much as he wanted her.

Feeling like a caged lion, Sawyer shoved back from the desk and got up, then punched the intercom button.

"Jane, I'm going to be out of the office for the rest of the day. Cancel all my appointments."

* * *

Going home did nothing to dispel his sour mood. His thoughts followed him there. Even working out with weights for a while failed to calm him. To hell with this crap. He was going to see her. Still, he hesitated. He didn't have anything more to tell her about the case, except that his assistant was pushing the church to search for the records. And he certainly couldn't tell her that he'd uncovered her secret. He wanted her to tell him, not vice versa. He wanted her to trust him.

The knowledge that Kate had borne a child out of wedlock had tightened the noose around his neck. Harlan was waiting for that juicy tidbit to use against her. And the fact that he wasn't about to oblige Harlan didn't lessen his quandary.

"Ah, to hell with it!" he muttered out loud. He had put off the inevitable long enough. He headed for the door. In order to survive, a person did what he had to do.

He was halfway to the door when the doorbell chimed and stopped him mid-stride. He frowned. Who could that be? He rarely had visitors because he didn't encourage them.

Irritated at being sidetracked, Sawyer snapped the lock and flung back the door. He stiffened, then a slow smile immediately replaced the frown.

"Well, what do you know?" he drawled, feeling fire shoot through his veins at the sight of Kate.

Kate didn't respond.

"We must be on the same wavelength," he added. "I was just about to head for your place."

Only after he finished speaking did he realize that she hadn't answered his smile, hadn't answered him, period. Instead she stood reed straight, a look of cold fury on her face.

Sawyer's exuberance faded along with his smile. "Kate, what—"

She reached out and jabbed a finger in his chest. "How dare you!? How dare you probe into *my* personal life?"

Forty-three

Sawyer's eyes hardened, but his voice remained low and steady. "If you'll give me a chance, I'll explain."

"As far as I'm concerned there's nothing to explain," she said coldly, battling that sick feeling in the pit of her stomach.

She wished now she hadn't come here. When he looked at her like that, she wanted to make love, not war. Now her anger resurged and overrode her weakness.

Sawyer's eyes didn't waver. "Well, at least come in and sit down."

He closed the door, then made his way into a large, high-ceilinged living room. If she was to have her say, she had no choice but to follow him.

"I don't want to sit down," Kate said, stopping by a chair and leaning against it.

"Suit yourself. Want something to drink?"

"No, thank you."

"Well, I do," he said flatly.

Seething inside, Kate watched as he walked toward the kitchen. He had on a pair of gray athletic shorts and a white T-shirt that made him look rugged and more appealing than ever.

She closed her hands into tight fists. She wouldn't let his sexual power get in the way of her telling him exactly what

307

she thought of him. Yet she admired the way his shorts streamlined the muscles in his buttocks and legs. She had experienced the power of those muscles. She had run her hands over them . . .

Don't, she told herself, feeling the tight rein on her control slipping. She took several deep breaths and looked around. She liked his condo. It seemed to fit him. While the decor was definitely masculine, it had touches that only a woman could have added. She felt a strong twinge of jealousy and hated herself for it.

Her eyes completed the tour, taking in the thick forest-green carpet, the plush leather furniture, a large entertainment center that dominated one wall, and a fireplace that dominated the other. There were paintings on the walls that she was sure cost a fortune. Plants were positioned to get the benefit of the sun through the skylight.

From where she stood, Kate could see part of the kitchen. She assumed that beyond it were the bedrooms. She shifted her gaze.

"Sure you don't want anything?" Sawyer called from the kitchen, breaking into her train of thought. When she didn't answer, he went on. "I'm making some fresh coffee."

"No, thank you," she said again in a terse tone.

He didn't say anything else. Kate walked around the room and fought the urge to tell him to hell with the coffee. He was using it as a ploy to avoid a confrontation. Yet he wasn't the type to back down from anything.

Why had he probed into her personal life? Just because she'd slept with him hadn't given him that right. She hadn't hired him to investigate her. Her heart hammered wildly in her chest. Had he uncovered her secret? If so, what would it mean?

Stunned and angered by Angie's revelation, she had called Roberta.

"Roberta, it's Kate," she'd said with false brightness.

"Why, Kate, honey, what a nice surprise. How are you?"

"I'm fine. How about yourself?"

"Oh, all right, I guess. All I do is work."

"I hear that," Kate said.

Roberta laughed. "And eat. I'm getting fat."

"I bet you're not."

Kate visualized Roberta in her mind's eye. Her tall, raw-boned attractiveness was the kind that would be slow to fade. A sudden sadness came over her. It had been a long time, too long, since she'd seen Roberta. The woman had been a second mother to her, and in a way had saved her sanity, if not her life.

"Roberta," Kate had begun, her tone hesitant.

"I know why you're calling, and it's all right."

"Tell me what you know," Kate said.

"Not much, actually," Roberta said. "You remember my cousin, Elmer Sides, at the grocery, don't you?"

"Of course."

"Well, he's the one who talked to the detective. And you know how people are in Four Corners; they tend to nose into everyone's business."

"Did Elmer give any specifics?"

"Only that this Brock guy was asking personal questions about your life, using the excuse that he was working on a case that involved you." Roberta had paused as if waiting for Kate's input. When none was forthcoming, she had continued with a question of her own. "Kate, honey, are you in some kind of trouble? I know you're running for office—"

"No, Roberta, I'm not in any trouble, and I did hire Mr. Brock, but not to investigate me."

"Uh-oh."

"That's putting it mildly. Look, when we both have more time, I'll tell you what this is all about. I feel I owe it to you. Meanwhile, please, don't *you* answer any personal questions about me."

"That goes without saying."

"Thanks—and—I love you," Kate said softly.

"And I love you. And thanks for taking care of Angie—" Roberta had broken off as if choked up. "Sometimes I wonder what's going to happen to her."

Me, too, Kate thought silently. "Things will work out."

"Call me again soon, okay?"

"I will, and take care."

After hanging up, she had ached to confront Sawyer immediately, but her schedule hadn't permitted her that luxury. The murder trial had taken precedence over anything personal.

Today was the first opportunity she'd had. She had driven by his office first. When she hadn't seen his car, she had headed for his condo.

Sawyer suddenly rounded the corner with both a cup of coffee and a beer. "I told you I didn't want anything."

"I know what you told me, but I brought it anyway."

Their eyes sparred while the tension blanketed the room like a thick smog.

He set the coffee down on the table in front of the couch, then took a drink from his beer.

"Why did you do it?" she asked, her mind seething with resentment.

He moved to within touching distance of her. "I wanted to know about you."

"That's wasn't the deal," she snapped, her temper threatening to rise out of control, especially in light of his nonchalant attitude. "You're supposed to be doing the job I asked you to do."

"Aren't you the least bit curious as to why I did it?"

"No. I'm angry," she flung back. "You owe me an apology."

The air between them turned heavy. It was as if everything hinged on this one point, so fragile was the moment.

"Okay," he said after an eternity. "So I stepped out of line."

Kate knew that was as close to an apology as she was going to get, but it wasn't good enough. She didn't want to ask, but she couldn't seem to control her tongue. "So did you find what you were looking for?" Her tone was as nasty as she could make it so as to counteract the fear that had electrified every nerve.

"What do you think I found?" His voice sounded cracked and dry.

"Look, I'm not in the mood to play games with you. Finding the child is your only job. Understand?"

"And I'm doing that."

"So where is she? Have you found her?"

His eyes glittered now with matching anger. "No."

"That's my point. Adhere to the rules," she hammered cuttingly, "or I'll find someone else who will. And don't you ever interfere in my personal life again."

"You can trust me, Kate."

"Trust has nothing to do with this."

"Oh, I get it. You can fuck me but you can't trust me."

She flinched, but she wouldn't back down. "We had a deal. You do what I ask, and you get paid."

"Christ! Is that all I am to you, hired help?" His voice cracked like a whip across the silence.

She turned away so that he couldn't see how hard her heart was beating. Damn him! She wouldn't let him do this to her. She didn't want to trust him on a personal level. God help her, she didn't want to want him, period. She wanted to be free of that eternal ache inside her.

Sawyer suddenly swung her around. "Don't turn your back on me."

Her eyes flashed. "Take you hands off me."

She thought she saw him tremble while the blood drained from his face.

"Dammit, that's my problem," he said harshly. "I can't keep my hands off you. I can't stop thinking about you, either! You've got my body, my life tied in fucking knots!"

She opened her mouth to respond, only he stopped her words. His lips pressed savagely into hers. She moaned as she struggled to push him away, but his arms around her were unyielding.

Instantly, Kate felt the coiled readiness of his body as his tongue, hot and forceful, invaded her mouth and stroked hers to life. Then he moved a hand to cup her breast.

Her senses were on fire with unnatural heat and without conscious thought, Kate wrapped her arms around his neck. A strangled sound left his throat at the same time his hands shifted to her buttocks, pulling her against his hard length.

Shock ran through her. "No!" She jerked away. "I can't . . ." she whispered, sunken-eyed and desperate.

He gasped for breath while she struggled to right her rumpled clothes. They avoided looking at each other.

"I have to go," Kate said through stiff lips, her body shaking. She grabbed her purse and headed for the door.

He didn't say anything, nor did he try to stop her.

Ben Applegate closed the door behind him.

Kate looked at her bailiff. "Are you ready for me?"

"Nearly. Five more minutes max."

"How do you think it's going?" Kate asked, referring to the murder trial of the two white law officers accused of the death of a black inmate.

"Fair to middlin', I'd say. At least, you're doing your job and keeping the attorneys on their toes."

"I want everything to be done exactly right."

With her personal life unraveling in front of her eyes, Kate could not bear the thought of the same thing happening in her professional life. The only way she could maintain control was to not think of Sawyer and that last confrontation.

"You're doing a great job," Ben was saying.

Kate gave him a grateful smile. "You're good for my ego, Ben." And he was. His long, thin face was almost overpowered by a prominent set of front teeth that was usually visible unless someone messed with Kate. He hovered over her like a mother hen with newborn chicks.

Ben blushed. "You don't need no ego stroking. You're building a Jim-dandy reputation; you're going to tear those other whippersnappers up in that election." He paused and shifted his holster to the left. "I meant to tell you I thought you made the right decision on them two young boys on those drug charges."

Kate came from behind her desk. "So you agreed with my giving them deferred adjudication?"

"Yeah, I did. To my way of thinking, that's the only choice you had. Here's just hoping they'll behave."

"If they don't, rest assured I'm going to throw the book at them."

"You should, and with a clear conscience, too. Beats me why kids nowadays seem to look for trouble."

"I know, especially when their behavior stems from boredom."

Ben looked at the clock behind Kate. "You have three minutes."

"I'll see you shortly."

When she was alone again, Kate's thoughts turned back to the teenagers. She had mulled over that case long and hard. When she finally reached a decision, she had prayed she had made the right one. Based on their plea of guilty, she had put off judging them and placed them on ten years' probation.

If they violated that probation, however, she could and would haul them back into court and find them guilty, then sentence them to anything within the terms of years.

The advantage of deferred adjudication was that if they fulfilled the terms of the probation, she would completely dismiss the charges and clear their records. She had no way of knowing the eventual outcome and could only hope the boys would make the most of their second chance.

"Time's up, Judge," Ben said, sticking his head around the door.

Kate sighed. "I'm ready."

She didn't move, taking an extra minute to settle her mind. Then she slipped into her robe and, for a moment, stroked it, filled with a renewed sense of pride. She did make a difference. She did.

Forty-four

"Have you ever in your life seen such unmitigated gall?"

Kate shook her head, then smiled at her campaign manager. "Now, now, calm down before your blood pressure gets the best of you."

Kate had left the courthouse after work and had walked to her campaign headquarters. She looked outside and saw that dusk was near. It had been a long day. And it wasn't over yet.

"Blood pressure, hell," Ginger said, her gray eyes sparking. "Just who does he think he is entering the race at this late date? And the fact that he thinks he's going to win is worse." She paused, then added on a mutter, "Pompous ass."

"Ginger!"

Ginger looked sheepish. "Well, that's what he is, and you know it."

In spite of herself, Kate's lips twitched. "You're right, he is."

The rumor that Dave Nielsen was going to enter the race with the backing of prominent real estate developer Harlan Moore was now fact. Both television and newspapers had carried the story.

While the thought of Dave winning the judgeship was far-fetched, the damage he could do to Kate was not. She had tried not to let this latest development throw her off base.

Yet having made enemies of both Dave and Harlan, she couldn't help but wait for the ax to fall.

Kate let out a slow breath. If her past became known, her political career would be doomed. No doubt Dave and Harlan would use the child she had borne out of wedlock as a weapon against her—if they found out.

Her spirits brightened. Sawyer hadn't been able to track her child, so what made her think anyone else could? Her spirits tumbled just as quickly. Finding the child wasn't the issue: the fact that she'd had the child and given her up was the only ammunition they needed. To date, neither Dave nor Harlan knew and perhaps never would, unless Angie . . . Kate nursed her lower lip. She wouldn't think about that now.

"Hey, wake up." Ginger snapped her fingers.

Kate blinked. "Sorry. I'm out of it."

"Who wouldn't be. That jerk entering the race is enough to do it."

"You don't think he has a chance to win, do you?"

Ginger shook her curls. "Nope, but he's got a big mouth and from what I understand, he detests you."

"That about sums it up."

"So that means we're going to have to go after *him*."

Kate didn't hesitate. "I know."

"Since you worked with him, you ought to know his strengths and his weaknesses."

"I do. I know someone else who can help. Believe me, I'm capable of playing hardball with the best of them." Kate's lips tightened. "I may not beat him, but he won't come out of this without bruises."

"Poppycop. He doesn't stand the chance of a snowball in hell."

"I hope you're right."

"I know I'm right," Ginger said airily.

Kate frowned. "I wouldn't underestimate Dave. He's a cutthroat who'll land on his feet regardless of the circumstances."

"I guess we'll see, won't we?"

"I guess we will, at that."

"So let's talk about our next move and the television ads

we're going to run," Ginger said. "I need your final approval."

"Let's make it as quick as possible." Kate peered at her watch. "I have some briefs to go over tonight."

"It won't take long, I promise."

Kate lifted her shoulders in a stretch. "I'm ready. Let's get to it."

Sawyer stuffed the papers into his briefcase, then grabbed his Stetson.

"Going somewhere?"

He paused, then scowled. "I was thinking about it, unless you figure a way to keep me here."

Ralph grinned as he sauntered into the room. "What's with you lately? You got a burr up your butt about something?"

"Mind your own business."

"Sure, boss, whatever you say."

Sawyer snorted. "What do you want?"

"Thought you might like to see this." Ralph was all business now.

"It had better be important."

"Read it and see for yourself."

Sawyer's eyes scanned the sheet Ralph handed him. With each word he read, his face turned darker and harder. "That sonofabitch!"

"I knew you'd love it."

"Did you turn this over to the police?"

"Yep."

Sawyer sank his Stetson on his head. "I'm outta here. I'll talk to you later."

"What if I need to get in touch with you?"

"I'll get in touch with you."

He didn't know how long he sat across the street, the darkness hiding him and his Jag. Time didn't matter as long as the end result was in his favor. It was. He saw Dave Nielsen drive up and Angie came out of the house, bag in hand.

Since it was Friday, Sawyer assumed that the two were going away for the weekend or at least for the night—or at least he hoped so.

He knew what he was about to do was risky business, but he was going to do it anyway. He hadn't seen Kate or talked to her in several days. They hadn't exactly parted on the best of terms either. As usual, when he was around her, he lost his head and did something he swore he wouldn't do. Now he was about to do it again. Only this time he had a reason; he had something to tell her.

Sawyer made his way to the front door. Maybe she wouldn't slam the door in his face, he told himself. Not too hard, anyway.

The truth was he ached to see her. Ralph was right. He'd been in a foul mood all week. He didn't like the change in himself.

He rang the doorbell, then realized he was holding his breath. Cursing, he released it.

"Who is it?"

Kate's soft, hesitant voice sent a dart of longing through him.

"It's Sawyer," he said, clearing his throat.

She unlocked the door and pulled it back. Wide, startled eyes that reminded him of melted chocolate stared back at him.

"Before you say anything, hear me out." Sawyer heard the desperate sound in his voice, but couldn't overcome it. She was dressed only in a robe of sorts. While it was more than adequate coverage, he bet she was naked underneath. Fire licked through his veins and settled in his crotch. He felt himself grow hard and push painfully against his zipper.

He cleared his throat again. "I have some news."

"What if I hadn't been here alone?" she asked, her voice tense.

"But you are. I saw Nielsen pick up Angie."

Kate opened her mouth to say something, then closed it.

"Have you had dinner?" That desperate note again.

"No."

"Would you like to go out and eat?"

She pulled the robe tighter around her. "No."

His head began to pound. "May I come in, then?"

Seconds ticked by.

Their eyes met and held, hers troubled and luminous, his guarded and dark as he asked himself just what he was trying to prove. Why couldn't he leave well enough alone? Now was a perfect time to be totally professional, and forget that he'd ever touched her, ever made love to her.

He couldn't do it. Whatever it was that had him torn up inside, he wanted it settled, wanted it to be right between them.

Kate's lips parted. "Sawyer?"

"I had to see you," he said suddenly, harshly. "Don't send me away."

Kate was beyond rational thought. He had only to look at her and speak to her in that raspy, aching voice, and she couldn't deny him anything. The fact that he had appeared on her doorstep without an invitation was beside the point. He was here and that was all that mattered.

"Come in," she whispered.

The instant Sawyer crossed the threshold and reached the dimly lighted living room, he pulled her into his arms.

Kate heard herself whimper as he ground his lips against hers, frantically and hotly. She answered the sweet assault by giving as much as she received.

Finally, he tore his lips from hers and stared into her eyes. "I know this is crazy, but, God help me, I couldn't stay away."

"I know . . ." Her voice broke, and she couldn't go on. Words weren't necessary, just touching and being touched was all that was important, all that she wanted.

She tightened her arms around him, kneading his neck as she pressed closer to his body. She loved the way he felt when aroused. He hardened all over. This set her on fire, made her wild.

He brushed her riotous hair aside and ran his tongue along the side of her neck. That made her wilder, and she clung to him.

"God, I want you," he said thickly.

She couldn't respond, especially when his hand tugged at

the sash on her robe. In seconds, the garment lay pooled around her ankles.

He looked at her through glazed eyes at the same time she felt the gentle scrape of his fingers on her breast. The contact drove the air from her lungs, even as those same fingers trailed along the flesh of her thighs.

A gasp rent the air as she watched him slowly sink to his knees and replace his fingers with his tongue. When he reached the juncture at her thighs, her legs were quivering so hard that she thought they would buckle underneath her. Yet her thighs parted to receive his hot, lancing tongue. She draped over him, her eyes fluttering closed as she drowned in sensations that only he could evoke.

"Oh, Sawyer . . . I'm . . . coming . . . I—" Her words were lost as an orgasm, so intense, so beautiful, shocked her body. She cried out and ground her throbbing nipples into his back.

Once she was limp in his arms, he lifted her. "Where?"

"Upstairs," she murmured weakly.

Once there, he laid her on the bed and quickly shed his clothes. Her eyes were feverish as she let them travel over his superbly formed body, stopping only when she came to the apex of his thighs. He was hard and pulsating.

"I want you inside me," she pleaded.

"I want that, too—so much it's killing me." His voice was so strained she could hardly hear him.

They groaned simultaneously as he positioned himself barely inside her, then stopped, as if determined to prolong the heady torture. He edged a little farther.

She moaned at the same time she bit his shoulder.

He edged still farther. "Tight, so tight. So hot."

Kate splayed her legs more, but instead of penetrating deeper, he pulled out, then buried two fingers inside her.

Another spasm rippled through her. "Oh . . . please," she cried.

He lay down beside her and entered her. A gasp of pleasure parted her lips. Instead of thrusting deeper, he rolled over and took her with him, stopping once she lay prone atop him.

"Ride me," he whispered, lifting his hands and pushing

back her damp hair so that he could look into her eyes, eyes
that were dazed with passion.

"Yes, oh, yes." She kissed his nipples, his chest, before
lifting herself up. She gasped again as he rose high inside
her, and she began to move.

"Oh, darling, oh, yes," Sawyer muttered incoherently as
they began to move as one. "Make it last . . ."

All too soon, though, she collapsed against him, his cry of
pleasure ringing in her ear.

Forty-five

"You told me you had some news?" Kate's voice was soft and drowsy as she lay in the crook of Sawyer's arm, their legs still entwined.

"I did, didn't I." Sawyer smiled a satisfied smile. "Somehow that got pushed aside."

A flush of guilt charged through Kate, and for a minute she couldn't respond. They had been awake only minutes, both having fallen into an exhausted sleep. Before now she hadn't been capable of thinking about anything until that thirst for his body had been quenched.

"I know who sideswiped us."

Kate went rigid. She hadn't been expecting that, but rather an update on her case. Her guilt tempered somewhat.

"Yeah, and I was so sure that it was my nutcase, Silverman, only it wasn't." Sawyer's voice was as cold as marble.

"Who was it, then?"

He peered down at her. "One of Thomas Jennings' lackeys."

Kate sucked in her breath. She shouldn't have been surprised, especially after she'd suspected that herself. But when Sawyer had been so positive that it was his man, she'd stopped worrying. "How did you find out?"

"Ralph, my assistant, who's like a bloodhound, checked body repair shops until he bingoed. At first the owner had been mum, but when Ralph pulled out a roll of bills, his tongue loosened considerably."

"That bastard!"

Sawyer pulled back and looked at Kate, an incredulous expression on his face. "Why, Judge Colson, tut, tut, tut."

"I mean it," she said. "Thomas won't get away with that. He'll pay." Along with all his other sins, she promised silently.

"Count on it," Sawyer responded, his tone deadly.

They fell silent for a long moment, content to bask in the safety of each other's warmth.

"Do you have anything to report on the case? I know that's not why you came by, but—"

"Soon. We're in the process of trying to find the adoption records at the church." He went on to tell her more about his conversation with Ralph concerning the misplaced records.

"Do you think the records are there?" she asked in a small breathless voice.

"I do, but then I've been wrong before."

"You? Wrong? Heaven forbid!"

A sardonic grin twisted his lips. "All right, you made your point."

She smiled.

"Have you forgiven me," Sawyer asked thickly, "for prying into your life?"

"No."

He expelled a deep sigh. "I didn't think so."

Another long silence fell between them.

"You know, don't you?" Kate asked in a less than steady voice.

Only the loud beating of his heart answered her. Then he moved so that once again he stared deeply into her eyes. "Yes, I know."

Unexpected tears gathered in Kate's eyes as she struggled to speak. As if he felt her pain, he kissed her on the top of her head and simply held her.

"I had to know," Sawyer said finally. "I had to know everything there was to know about you. I'm a man possessed."

Kate swallowed painfully. "That day I came to your house and confronted you, deep down I knew that you weren't telling all. But I just couldn't get through my anger to think rationally."

"Believe me, I deserved your tongue-lashing." His voice was low and strained.

Kate watched him through sad eyes. "You also know that . . . Thomas is the father, don't you?"

"I figured as much, though I had no proof."

"She . . . was so tiny, so perfect, and I loved her so much." Tears darkened Kate's lashes and mixed in her voice. "But he didn't want her, didn't want me."

"You don't have to tell me this. I know how much it must hurt."

"I want to," she whispered, then went on, as if she couldn't stop herself. "Thomas wanted me to have an abortion."

"That sonofabitch," Sawyer interrupted.

"When I refused to get one, he promised that his father, who was also a minister, would find her a loving home, and I believed him." A sob ripped through Kate.

"Hey, take it easy."

"I can't."

"Yes you can. You're being too hard on yourself."

"For years afterward, when I thought of Sara, and knew I'd never see her, I wanted to go mad, to kill and destroy everything." The band around Kate's heart was so tight that breathing became almost impossible. "Thomas didn't have the right to do that to me. I was so young, so stupid . . ."

"Shh; it's going to be all right."

"Oh, Sawyer, I wish I could believe that. Yet I don't think I'm a bad person for what I did; I did what I thought was best for my baby."

He leaned down and kissed her on a wet cheek.

"Since I decided to find her, I can't get her off my mind. Part of me is out there somewhere, walking the streets of some city, and I can't touch her, hug her or tell her I love her." Feeling herself splintering apart, Kate sobbed quietly.

"I'm so sorry," Sawyer said huskily, burying her face into his chest. "So sorry."

He held her while the tears flowed, and she knew in that moment that she loved this man, that she had fallen deeply and forever in love. But instead of adding comfort, it added to her grief.

"Do you have any idea how scared I am, how inadequate I feel at the thought of maybe seeing my child?"

His arm tightened around her. "I can imagine. I've been that scared before and it's mind-boggling."

"What if . . . ?" Kate's words tangled with the huge lump that had formed in her throat.

"Don't say it. Don't borrow trouble. Let's just wait and see what happens. For now, try to get some sleep."

She snuggled closer to Sawyer, but not even his warmth could melt that cold knot of fear lodged in her heart. Only seeing and holding her daughter could do that.

Kate awoke a while later and stared into Sawyer's peaceful face. She lifted her hand and with the tip of one finger outlined his face. What had she done by falling in love with this enigma of a man?

His eyes opened.

"Are you sorry I woke you up?"

"No. I can sleep anytime," he said, stroking her arm.

Kate buried her hands in the wiry mat on his chest, felt his erratic breathing and looked into his eyes. "Tell me about you. Turnabout's fair play, you know."

He tensed. "It's not a pretty story."

"Did you have a bad childhood?"

He laughed a mirthless laugh. "What childhood?"

"Mine was pretty rotten, too." She couldn't believe she had said that, but why not? He already knew her deepest, darkest secret.

"Tell me about it?"

"You mean you don't already know?"

"I deserved that."

She was quiet for a minute, then said, "My daddy was a

drunk who was afraid that if an honest emotion got out, it might contaminate someone."

"Lots of people have that problem."

"He often used my mamma for a punching bag."

"Go on," Sawyer encouraged gently.

"There's not much more to tell except that my mamma tried to love me and did in her own way. Still, my childhood was hell, and the day Thomas ditched me, I swore no man would ever use me again."

Sawyer moved his hands through her silky hair as if to relieve some of her tension. She gave in to the feel of his stroking hands. "What about you?"

He took his hand away, and she could feel the tension in him turn his body rock hard.

"It's not any prettier a tale than yours."

The moonlight played across his face and, for a moment, seemed to smooth out the grooves, the harsh lines of regret, the hard knocks of life, that were similar to her own. "I'm sure it isn't."

"I'm surprised you didn't have me checked out."

"Well, I did read everything I could find about you," she said meekly.

He laughed. "I would've been disappointed if you hadn't."

"Your file merely skimmed the surface. I know that your father was a cop and that he died when you were five. Later your mother died. After that, there's a blank space in your life that doesn't start again until you enter the police academy."

"When my mamma died, I was taken in by my aunt and uncle, who continually accused me of not only disrupting their household, but actually bringing harm to one of their children."

Sawyer paused, and when he did, she looked at him. His face was pinched in pain.

"Their sicko son was inflicting terrible injury to his own body because he was jealous of me. The kicker was he blamed me, and his parents believed him."

"How horrible."

"After that, I was booted out of the house and into one foster home after another. It was only after I joined the Marines that my life was worth anything." He paused. "And I'll do whatever it takes to keep my status in life. Whatever it takes," he added on a bleak note.

Tears stung Kate's eyes again.

He groaned. "Oh, honey, don't cry any tears for me. I just want to hold you, make love to you."

She raised her lips to his. "That's what I want, too."

They made love again. And again. Sawyer could not get enough of her. Yet he knew what he felt wasn't all sexual. He yearned for the closeness that followed the act. When he was inside her, it was no longer just a part of his body there, but his heart as well.

Later, he turned toward Kate as she slept beside him. His eyes devoured her, the finely crafted face, the lovely eyes now closed, the graceful arch of her neck, her full, ripe lips. The intensity of her attraction for him was almost more than he could bear. He wanted her again now, so much that it caused him both physical and mental pain.

He realized then that in a matter of weeks, she had broken through the concrete that surrounded his heart. The ache of loneliness was now gone.

If this wasn't love, then it was the closest thing to it. And to pry himself away from Kate would tear him to pieces.

So what did he do now? His thoughts turned to Harlan, and he flinched. He was worried about what Harlan would do if he found out about Kate's baby. Nor could he ignore the ramifications of his having withheld information from Harlan. And he couldn't forget his relationship with Kate. If Harlan got wind of that he could definitely use it against Kate and hurt her. When Harlan wanted to, he could be meaner than a junkyard dog. But so could he.

Sawyer didn't ever remember feeling so inadequate or so torn.

Forty-six

"We struck gold, boss!"

Sawyer looked up as Ralph burst into his office, grinning from ear to ear, his freckles lit like neon.

"Halle-damn-lujah," Sawyer responded, standing.

"I thought you'd see it that way."

"So give me the details."

Ralph practically fell into the chair across from Sawyer's desk. "Well, I knocked down that brick wall."

"Where were the files?" Sawyer asked, his grin still in place.

"Would you believe in an old box in the attic?"

"Didn't I predict that?"

"Yep, and you were right. You were also right about the church remodeling some years back. That was when they carted the old records to the attic and stored them. This new priest didn't have a clue as to their whereabouts until he sent one of the janitors to look."

"So what did you find?" Sawyer's voice had changed and the grin was gone.

"The adoption didn't go through the Catholic adoption agency as happens in most cases. Apparently the priest knew of a couple who wanted the child. Therefore, the adoption was handled privately through an attorney."

"That's a relief."

"How so?" Ralph asked, scratching his head. "Attorney or agency, the records are still sealed."

Sawyer set his jaw. "But not for long."

"Figured you'd say that. So how are you planning to unseal them?"

"Remember our client Senator Dan Hemsley?"

"The fuckin' do-gooder?"

Sawyer nodded. "That's him. Well, if you'll recall, he's a champion of adoptees who want to find their birth parents."

"Yeah," Ralph said, as if a light had clicked on inside his head. "I'd forgotten about that."

"I hadn't." Sawyer punched the intercom button. "Jane, get Senator Hemsley on the line, please."

"Here's hoping he'll go for it."

"Oh, he'll go for it, all right," Sawyer said in a confident voice. "He owes us—we got the goods on his wife, and he came out of that divorce smelling like a rose."

"I'd say. If I recall, the judge not only granted him the divorce but gave him most of their assets. That's almost unheard of."

"Mr. Block," Jane cut in, "the senator's on line two."

Sawyer winked at Ralph, then reached for the receiver.

The white-columned mansion sat atop a bluff in the Hill Country. Sawyer wasn't impressed with the house's lines or symmetry. Even in the sunlight, it looked cold and uninviting.

He didn't know how long he'd been standing beside his car in hopes of finding the courage to walk to the front door. He knew a housekeeper would inquire politely as to who he wanted to see. Sweat beaded his forehead and upper lip.

Was Kate's daughter on the other side of that door? After nearly twenty years, was Kate going to have a chance to see her? On one hand, Sawyer was excited for her and for himself because his agency could take the credit. On the other hand, he was sorry that the investigation was about to end. When Kate was reunited with her daughter, she wouldn't need him any longer.

He couldn't believe he was thinking like that. He and Kate had made love a few times; that hardly constituted a relationship. But God, he wanted it to be more, only he didn't know how to make that happen.

Sawyer cleared the sweat from his brow with two fingers, then massaged the back of his neck. He hadn't told Kate anything that had taken place since their night of lovemaking. After he'd sent Ralph back to the church, the pieces had started to fall into place.

Now, three days later, he was about to take steps that would change Kate's life forever. Sawyer straightened the knot on his tie and began his trek up the long walkway.

"Hi."

The sound of Sawyer's voice, like rough sandpaper, always had the same effect on Kate. Her bones turned to water.

"Hi," she replied breathlessly into the phone.

"Can I see you?"

"Yes," she said simply. It had been several days since their marathon night of lovemaking, but she hadn't stopped thinking about him.

"Are you alone?"

"Yes."

There was a short silence, then he said in a low voice, "I've missed you."

The highly charged words made her heart race. "I've missed you, too."

"Look, I'll see you shortly."

"Sawyer . . ."

The next thing Kate knew, she was holding the receiver with nothing but a buzz ringing in her ear. She frowned. She couldn't put her finger on it, but he sounded different. Nervous? Was that it? Nah. Sawyer never got nervous about anything. He was always cool . . . except when they were making love.

The anticipation of his making love to her again this evening sent frissons of heat through Kate. She had a pizza in the freezer and some wine. They would eat that, then . . .

She shook her head to clear it, then bounced off the couch and made her way into her bedroom. Her gaze strayed to her desk piled with briefs and campaign material. She frowned, her thoughts holding on the upcoming election.

Dave Nielsen had hit the campaign trail hard and heavy, slinging mud at her at every turn. Oh, he'd shot a few barbs the other candidates' way, too, but they were minor compared to the aggressive way he'd gone after her. She was just grateful that she still remained far ahead in the polls.

Kate checked herself in the full-length mirror and decided against changing clothes. When she'd come in from work, she had put on shorts, a T-shirt, and sandals. That outfit would have to suffice. She switched off the light just as the doorbell rang.

She hurried back into the living room and opened the door. Sawyer looked larger than life as he stood on the porch and stared at her. The gathering dusk did little to hide the intense expression on his face. Kate's mind clicked. Her intuition had been on the mark. Something was terribly wrong. Or maybe something was wonderfully *right*.

"You've found her, haven't you?" Her voice cracked.

"Let's go inside." Sawyer walked past her and didn't stop until he reached the living room.

Kate swallowed hard and followed him. "You've found her, haven't you?" she repeated, hearing her voice rise.

"Yes, I've found her."

Kate's heart soared, then plummeted with terror at what that could mean.

She must have cried out because Sawyer was instantly at her side. "Are you all right?"

Kate's temples throbbed and blood pounded to the top of her head. After all these years, she was finally going to get to see her baby. Feeling faint, she weaved.

"For god's sake, sit down!" Sawyer took her by the arms and eased her onto the couch. "Put your head between your legs and take deep breaths."

She did as she was told and soon felt her body stabilize. She was mortified at her show of weakness. "I don't remember ever fainting or even coming close," she said, licking her dry lips.

He sat beside her, his face pinched with concern. "Feeling any better?"

"I'm fine."

He snorted. "You're far from fine."

"How . . . did you find her? I mean . . ."

"I know what you mean."

Kate listened quietly while he brought her up to date. When he came to the adoption papers, she interrupted, "Weren't they sealed?"

He nodded.

"Then how—?"

"I know someone who had the power to unseal them."

She jumped up, then felt her head spin. Sawyer cursed as he stood beside her. She waved him away. "I was just dizzy, that's all. As an officer of the court, I'm not supposed to know that."

"So I never told you."

"Okay, so you never told me," Kate finally whispered with only a twinge of conscience.

They looked at each other for a long moment.

Kate's mind clamored with the longing to know precisely where her daughter was and if he had actually seen her. But she hadn't been able to ask that question. Fear held her mute.

Sawyer was the first to shift his gaze. "There's something you ought to know about me."

She blinked. "About you?"

"I only took this case because of Harlan."

Kate looked perplexed, then said impatiently, "Well, after all Harlan recommended you."

"I know, but—"

"Couldn't we talk about this later? I want to know about my . . . daughter."

"You don't understand." Sawyer's face was white, and his voice was hoarse. "Harlan hired me to do his dirty work."

Kate's eyes widened incredulously. "What are you saying?"

"I'm saying that he's determined to sabotage your election."

"And you were to provide the ammunition?"

A loaded silence followed that question.

"That was the deal."

Raw fury rushed through her. "You bastard!"

"Kate—"

"So have you run to him and told him all my secrets, that I had a child out of wedlock and gave her away? Did you?!" Her voice had risen out of control, but she didn't care.

When Sawyer opened his mouth, she held up her hand. "No! Don't answer that! It doesn't matter." Her eyes were on fire. "Not only did you deceive me personally, you betrayed me ethically as well. Just tell me where my daughter is and get the hell out of my house. And out of my life," she added on a broken note.

When would she ever learn? First, her daddy, then Thomas, and now Sawyer.

"Kate, please. It's not like that."

He sounded desperate, but she ignored it. She was just as desperate in her own way. She was struggling to hold body and mind together. She placed her hands over her ears. "No!" she cried again. "I don't want to hear any excuses!"

Before she knew it, he was in front of her, lifting her hands off her ears. She jerked back. "Don't touch me!"

"Christ, Kate! You're not giving me a chance to explain."

"Tell me where my daughter is, damn you!"

As if he realized he was wasting his time trying to reason with her, he stepped back, his eyes registering defeat and pain. She ignored that, too.

"Your daughter's in Koenig Place."

Her pupils contracted with confusion, then shock. "But . . . but that's a—" She couldn't go on. The words jammed in her throat.

"A home for the mentally retarded," Sawyer finished for her in an agonized voice.

Another cry passed through Kate's lips, and she clutched the back of a chair to keep from sinking to the floor. When she had given up her baby, she had felt as if she'd lost part of herself forever. When she had learned that her child hadn't been adopted but left in a dingy motel room, she'd wanted to destroy as she was being destroyed.

Now, she only wanted to curl up and die. Instead, hard tremors shook her body. Her heart took the brunt of the pain. It felt like a piece of glass that had been stepped on and crushed.

"Kate, please," Sawyer begged, "don't do this to yourself."

"What . . . happened . . . to her?"

"She was adopted by a well-to-do couple. They named her Amber. Amber Sterling." He paused and drew a deep breath, then went on in a tormented voice, "When she was two years old, she came down with a high fever. The babysitter was with her and didn't know what to do. By the time her parents got back home, the damage was already done. The fever had damaged her brain, irreversibly."

Kate clasped her arms across her middle, rocked back and forth, and stared into space. "I refuse to believe that. Nothing is ever that final."

"Kate, darling, don't," Sawyer repeated.

"Leave me alone," she said in a dull, listless voice, then turned around. "Just leave me alone."

He stared at her back, then walked to the door and closed it behind him. That was as far as he went. He sagged against the house, his vision blinded by tears.

Forty-seven

"When do you expect him back?" Harlan's brow puckered and came together like a thundercloud ready to erupt.

"Mr. Brock's out of the office. That's all I'm at liberty to say."

"What's this liberty shit?" Harlan demanded, gripping the receiver so hard he thought it might crack. "Never mind. Just tell him I want to see him as soon as he gets back."

He slammed the phone down in Jane's ear. He knew he'd been offensive, but he didn't give a damn. The underpinnings of his once stable life were crumbling.

Harlan lunged out of his chair and strode to the bar, where he poured a shot of bourbon and then downed it in one swallow. The burn in his throat and stomach was horrendous, but it would be only a matter of seconds until the booze calmed his nerves. This time, the relief was minimal. He poured himself another shot.

When the alcohol failed to perform its magic, Harlan walked to his desk and sat down. He couldn't concentrate on work. Most of it was legal crap on pending lawsuits against him. The top folder was compliments of his partner. The second was from his wife demanding a divorce. The third and most damaging was from the client in Tampa who was suing him for selling him land with poisonous chemicals on it. If that guy won his suit, then Harlan would be ruined, professionally and socially.

Nothing was going right on the political front, either. His scheme to get Dave elected to the judgeship was backfiring. He had known he was taking a chance when he had talked Dave into entering the race. Dammit, Dave could've been a viable candidate, only he apparently didn't have what it took. He'd made one gaffe after another to the media. His aggressiveness toward Kate hadn't garnered the support that they had both hoped for, either. It had merely put Dave in a bad light.

Harlan balled his fists. He wasn't giving up. Kate Colson hadn't won the election. Yet.

"Bitch," he muttered.

Another thorn in his side was Sawyer. He'd helped mold his career, but Sawyer had changed, and Harlan was convinced he knew why. Sawyer had become personally involved with Kate.

So, did that mean that he should let Sawyer off the hook? Hell, no. Sawyer was going to do as he was told or else. Harlan didn't know what that "or else" would be, but he'd think of something. If backed into a corner, Harlan thought Sawyer would side with him.

The intercom on his desk interrupted his thoughts. "Yes," he snapped.

"Mr. Brock's here, sir."

"Send him in."

Keeping his face expressionless, Harlan watched as Sawyer opened the door and walked into the office.

"Jane said you wanted to see me."

"Sit down."

Sawyer lifted an eyebrow at Harlan's harsh command. "I'll stand."

"Suit yourself." The conversation was not starting off on the right foot, Harlan realized, watching Sawyer closely. A muscle ticked in his jaw, which indicated he wasn't as cool as he looked. Harlan suddenly felt the need for another drink.

He stood and once again crossed to the bar. Once there, he faced Sawyer. "Care for one?"

"Don't you think it's a little early?"

"Who gives a shit?"

Sawyer shrugged. "Not me, that's for sure."

Harlan helped himself, downing the liquid in one swallow.

"What's so urgent that it couldn't wait until our regular meeting tomorrow?" Sawyer asked.

"You remember some time back before this Colson shit started, I asked you to check on a client who had bought some land from me, to dig up anything you could on him?"

"Yep. I remember."

"Well, you never gave me that information."

"That's because I didn't find anything. The man's as pure as fresh-driven snow."

"I don't believe that for one minute."

Sawyer lifted his shoulders. "Why the renewed interest?"

"The sonofabitch is suing me for selling him poisoned land. My partner's in on the lawsuit."

"Sounds like you got your balls in another vise."

Harlan glared at him. "And it's your job to help me loosen that vise."

"We could've discussed this tomorrow."

"What's the matter with you? You're always in such an all-fired hurry."

Sawyer's eyes turned cold. "I'm busy. I have other clients, you know?"

"Damn few," Harlan muttered.

"I'm outta here," Sawyer said flatly.

"Don't you dare walk out on me. You haven't told me what you've gotten on the Colson broad."

"Why don't you give that a rest?"

"You'd like that, wouldn't you?"

"It doesn't matter what I like."

Harlan face twisted. "That's a damn lie."

"I'd be careful if I were you, Harlan."

Harlan flapped an arm. "Look, I don't want to argue with you. I just want you to do your goddamn job and get me something on that bitch."

"What about your lackey, Dave?"

"What about him?"

"I thought lover boy was going to get the goods on Kate." Sawyer's tone was sarcastic.

Harlan flushed. "He's working on it, which is more than I can say for you."

Sawyer shrugged again.

Harlan's face turned redder. "Well, something's going on. Dave told me that Angie said Kate was terribly upset about something and left town."

"I don't have a clue."

"Well, find one, damn you. That's what I'm paying you for."

"Not anymore, you're not."

Another silence.

"Just what's that supposed to mean?"

"I'm no longer working for you. If that's not plain enough, then how 'bout, I quit?"

"Why, you can't do that," Harlan sputtered.

"I just did."

Harlan stuck out his chest. "You won't make it, son. We both know that I'm ninety percent of your business."

"At one time that was true, but not any more."

Uneasiness jolted Harlan, but he covered it quickly. "You're lying again."

"Check it out. I've branched out far beyond my expectations, while you've been wallowing in your own financial mess." Sawyer paused, planted a balled fist on Harlan's desk, then leaned forward so that they were eye to eye. "Even if you were my only client, I wouldn't give a shit. I'd still quit."

Sawyer might as well have punched him in the stomach. The result would've been the same. Harlan clutched at his heart, but his eyes and voice were filled with hatred. "You can't do this to me. I won't let you."

Sawyer merely looked at him, then walked to the door.

"I'll ruin you, you hear!"

Sawyer turned around. "Fuck off."

"Don't you dare walk out of here!" Harlan shouted, his voice quivering with rage.

"I just hope one day Kate gets the opportunity to burn your ass in court."

Harlan didn't know which was the loudest, the slam of the door or the beat of his heart. He slumped down into his chair and hung his head in despair.

The motel sign had come unhooked and was swinging tenaciously by one metal cord. Still, the words Shady Oaks Motel were clearly visible. Kate gripped the steering wheel and let visions of stabbing Thomas in the heart play out in front of her like a horror movie.

Her next move was to get out of the car, but she wasn't sure she could walk into that place. She battled against the all-consuming pain and anger that had driven her here.

After she had learned the fate of her daughter, she had existed in a zombie-like state. Yet she had worked harder than she'd ever worked. Her job had been the buffer against the pain.

At night nothing helped. When she walked through the door of her house, heartache seemed to be waiting to sink its tentacles into her flesh.

Her first thought had been to go to the institution to see Amber, to prove that it was all a lie. But she had been too damaged emotionally to take that bold step.

What she had needed was to get away, to think about what to do with Amber and what to do *without* Sawyer. She'd gotten that opportunity. The defense attorney in the murder trial had become ill; he had asked for a few days of recess.

She had thrown a few articles of clothing into a bag and walked out, leaving Angie a brief note. She had spent one day driving around Four Corners as if searching for the answer to why her life had turned out the way it had.

She'd found no answers, nor would she at the motel.

Now, as she continued to look at that broken sign where her baby had last been seen perfectly healthy, the cruelty, the unfairness of the past renewed her pain and despair.

Somehow, Kate managed to climb out of the car and walk

inside. What she was about to do would seem certifiable to some, but she had to do it.

"May I help you, ma'am?"

The desk clerk's clothes were grossly dirty; so was his face and hair. Kate forced herself not to flinch visibly.

"I'd like a room, please."

Forty-eight

They lay in the bed, naked. Angie stared at Dave as he rubbed his leg up and down hers. They had only moments before finished making love.

"I'm getting hard again." Dave scooted closer. "Feel me."

Angie released a pent-up breath, forcing herself not to get excited again. They needed to talk, not make love. Instead of responding, she turned her back and sat up on the side of the bed. She heard Dave's startled gasp and felt his eyes bore into her back.

"What the hell's the matter now?"

Angie pushed an auburn curl off her forehead, then twisted her head just enough to look at Dave. He was scowling. She sighed inwardly. "We need to talk."

"We need to screw."

"We've already done that. In fact, that's all we do."

"I've never heard you complain before," he pointed out in a whiny tone.

"No, you're right, I haven't." Angie stood, then looked down at his nakedness and for once wasn't turned on.

As if he sensed that, Dave flounced onto his stomach. "All right. Get it over with so that we can get back to business."

"Is that all you ever think about?"

"Yeah, so what? I like to fuck." His tone had turned ugly.

"You also like to ask questions."

His eyes narrowed. "What's that supposed to mean? You never seemed to mind that either."

"Now I do. You've been grilling me about Kate because you're running for the same office, right?"

"Right." He grinned. "All's fair in love and war, baby. Politics is war big time." His grin faded, and his face turned hard. "But so far you haven't told me anything that I can use against her."

"Is that why you keep seeing me?"

Dave lunged upright. "Hey, no commitments, remember? And no promises."

"I never asked for any." Angie's voice was filled with despair.

"Oh, come on, don't go all syrupy on me now. I'm not in the mood."

"Do you love me, Dave?"

He looked stunned. "Love? Me? No way, baby." He patted the bed beside him. "Come here. Our relationship was supposed to be fun and games, no strings attached. What's all this love bullshit?"

Angie ignored his efforts to get her to lie back down. "I want more, Dave. It's that simple. I had one disastrous marriage, and I'm looking for some stability for myself and, I hope, for my daughter."

"Well, then, you'd best count me out. Like I said, I'm in this for fun and games. I thought you were, too."

With as much composure as she could muster under the pressure of a broken and humiliated heart, Angie got up, retrieved her clothes, and put them on.

"Where do you think you're going?"

"Home."

"Damn you! You can't just walk out on me. I'm not through with you yet. You haven't told me what I want to know about Kate."

Angie whirled. "Kate's the reason for this whole affair! Isn't she?" Anger shook Angie's voice. "You never cared one fig about me. You just used me, didn't you?" When Dave didn't answer, she stomped over to him and pressed her palm against his chest. "Answer me, damn you!"

Dave grabbed her hand and shoved her away, his lips curled back like a snarling animal's. "That's right, baby. I fucked you just so I could get information. But I don't need you any longer. I'm going to beat Kate Colson in the polls, fair and square. There are a lot of people who don't agree with her hard-ass tactics."

"You conceited jackass!" Angie spat. "You're not going to win anything! Kate had you pegged from the start. She tried to tell me about you, only I wouldn't listen." She paused and dashed the tears from her eyes. "But I'm tired of being used. As far as I'm concerned, you can go straight to bloody hell!"

Sawyer looked at himself in the bathroom mirror. He stared back at the image whose features had all the earmarks of one who hadn't slept for a long time. His eyes were even bloodshot.

He intended to find Kate today. After she had kicked him out of her house and out of her life, he had left her alone, hoping that in time she would heal enough to listen to his side of the story. It hadn't been easy to keep his distance. He ached to comfort her. In fact, he ached for her in every way possible.

Besides that, he felt empty; he'd been gutted. Nothing made sense to him anymore. Even his work failed to remove the cloud of hopeless depression that had settled over him.

He wanted Kate; he wanted to live with her. He wanted to experience things that he'd never experienced before. Her lacy underwear hanging in the bathroom. Her toothbrush lying next to his. The feel of her next to him all night long. The way she rose on top of him like a goddess, impaling herself on him, her eyes wide and glazed.

He'd like to see her belly swell with his child. Without her, his loss seemed to reach to the bottom of his soul.

"Shit," he cursed, leaving the bathroom and returning to the bedroom, where he dressed with haste.

A short time later he pulled into Kate's driveway. Her car was still missing from the garage. He strode up to the door and rang the bell.

Angie Gates jerked the door open.

"Hello," Sawyer said, thinking she looked ghastly. Her eyes were hollow and her features drawn. Was unhappiness a major epidemic going around? He felt terribly sorry for her without knowing why.

"I'm Sawyer Brock. Remember me? We spoke—"

"I know who you are." Suspicion brought her dull eyes back to life.

"Look, do you have a moment?" Sawyer asked uncomfortably.

"Why?"

"I want to ask about Kate."

"Why should I tell you anything about her?"

Sawyer looked at Angie while he tried to come up with a plausible explanation that would get her to open up. "Because I care about her, that's why." Then, suddenly words that he'd had no intention of saying slipped through his lips. "No, make that because I love her."

Kate stared at the main building, which looked more like a southern mansion than an institution. For those who lived there, it was home, she corrected herself mentally. It was her daughter's home.

Last night, in that dingy motel room, she had made her decision. It hadn't been easy. She had cried until she'd had no tears left to cry. Out of those tears, strength had emerged, the strength to see her daughter in the flesh.

Kate had dressed specially for the occasion, though the lighting and the mirrors had been horrendous in the motel room. Still, she knew she looked all right, having chosen to wear a turquoise linen dress. Her hair was swept back up off her neck to accent the simple strand of pearls, pearls that were the only keepsake she had of her mother's. She had hoped one day to pass them on to Sara.

Kate clutched her purse and made her way up the lovely manicured walk, pausing only for a moment to survey her surroundings. The grounds were green and covered with flowers. The scents drifted by Kate's nose, and she inhaled deeply. Behind the main building, white cottages dotted the landscape.

Did Sara live in one of those? she wondered, making her way closer to the main entrance. She was shown into the visitors' lounge by a sweet-faced young woman who told her to have a seat. Momentarily, she returned.

"Mr. Renfro is free now," the secretary said with a smile. "You may go in."

"Thank you."

A robust, gray-haired gentleman came from behind his desk to greet her. "Frank Renfro, Ms—" he held out his hand.

"Judge Colson, sir."

His eyebrows lifted as they shook hands. "Ah, yes, Judge Colson. The name's familiar. Mmm, you're running for reelection, right?"

"No. I was appointed to fill a vacancy. Now, I'm in the race for real."

"Hope you win."

"Thank you."

"Please, sit down."

Kate sat on the edge of a chair in front of his desk, while he leaned against the desk and crossed his arms over his chest. His eyes were piercing blue.

"What did you want to see me about?"

Kate cleared her throat. "It's not what, it's whom—a young lady named . . . Amber Sterling." Even as she said the name, it sounded foreign on Kate's lips. However, she could no longer think of her daughter as Sara. Legally, her name had been registered as Amber, and Kate had to honor that. Still, it hurt.

"Ah, sweet, sweet Amber. One of my favorites. But why do you want to see her?" he asked bluntly, but kindly.

"I'm a family friend," she lied.

His expression changed. He didn't believe her, but then she wouldn't have believed her either. She'd always been a terrible liar. Kate's breath rattled in her chest as she waited. If he refused . . .

"I see no harm in you seeing her."

Kate almost went limp with relief. "Thank you."

"Come, I'll take you to her."

Once they were outside, Kate forced herself to ask, "Is . . . Amber happy here?"

Mr. Renfro peered down at her. "Very happy, Judge. She'd be miserable and frightened in the real world as you and I know it."

"Is there anything more that can be done for her?"

If he thought her questions strange and out of order, he gave no sign of it. She was past caring what he thought. She wanted to know everything there was to know about her child. First, though, she wanted to touch her, hold her . . .

They had entered a garden that looked as if it had been taken out of the pages of a fairy tale. A bubbling brook ran through the middle, with park benches and flowers on either side.

A dove, fat and sleek, scooted through the grass, his beak stabbing the sunflower seeds strewn across the ground. A few of the residents were enjoying the lovely day. One was sleeping next to a tree. Two women were laughing.

"Ah, there she is," Mr. Renfro said. "There's Amber."

Kate felt a smothering sensation in her chest, and for a second she thought she might faint. "Where?"

"In the swing. See her?"

Panic licked through Kate. "Yes, I see her."

"Shall I leave you two alone?"

"Please." Kate couldn't take her eyes off the young woman in the blue dress.

"Have a good visit," Mr. Renfro said, then walked off.

Kate's legs refused to move. They felt like lead as she inched closer, so as not to frighten Amber. Reaching a safe distance, Kate paused and stared, her heart in her throat.

Amber was lovely with curly, shoulder-length blond hair and brown eyes that were very much like her own. She was humming a tune that Kate didn't recognize. She looked so normal, so like a teenager who should be in high school, marching in the drill team, laughing with her boyfriend . . .

Oh, God, the pain inside Kate's chest was so intense she

almost cried out. Instead she bit her lower lip. If she didn't handle this just right, she might not get another chance.

"Amber . . . I'm your—" She couldn't say "mother." It stuck in her throat. She was about to try again when she sensed that someone was behind her.

She swung around. Her eyes widened. "*You!*" she mouthed, shock waves shooting through her.

"I had to come," Sawyer said, staring at her through sad, hollow eyes.

He looked so good, so dear, so familiar that she wanted to hurl herself into his strong arms. But she couldn't. He didn't love her. He had merely used her for his own purposes. He was only here to absolve his own conscience.

Kate turned back around and took another step toward her daughter.

"Don't," Sawyer said in a low, strained voice. "It won't do any good. Her doctor said she would never understand, that she's happy here, in her own world, that her life shouldn't be disrupted." He paused, took in a ragged breath, then went on, "She's well taken care of. Her family is wealthy, and she doesn't want for anything."

Kate turned slowly back around, her face drenched with tears and her lower lip quivering. "But do they love her and hug her and kiss her?"

"No," Sawyer confessed. "They have never been to see her here. They're ashamed of her."

"Oh, God, no," Kate sobbed, doubling over.

"Kate, don't," Sawyer begged, and stepped closer.

When she saw his shadow looming over her, she straightened and stepped back. "Don't. Stay away from me."

"Kate, let me help you." Sawyer's voice broke. "Let me hold you."

"No!" she wailed, sobs raking her body. "Leave me alone."

Kate didn't know how long she stood there before she looked over her shoulder. Sawyer was nowhere in sight. She turned to her daughter once again. Amber stared back through empty eyes.

Kate cringed inside, as if tiny needles were pricking her

flesh. She ached to run, to hide from the truth as she had so often as a child after her daddy had hurt her mamma. Only she couldn't run now. She wasn't a child, and she could no longer do childish things.

Suddenly Amber smiled at her, a sweet, charismatic smile, a smile that was all too familiar. Thomas' smile. Hot, boiling anger surged through Kate. Damn his soul to hell, she cried silently, consumed once again with the need to make him pay, even if she had to plunge the knife through his heart herself.

Only that would be too easy. He should have to suffer. Long and hard.

With one last loving look at her daughter, Kate dragged herself away from the garden and walked back to the front. Suddenly she pulled up short. Angie was leaning against the Cadillac.

"Angie . . . what—"

At the sound of Kate's voice, Angie rushed toward her. "Kate, please, don't be mad at me for intruding like this, but I had to come."

"How did you know where I was?" Kate shook her head.

"I know. You talked to Sawyer, then he found me."

"Yes. He came to the house looking for you."

Kate drew in a shuddering breath, feeling her iron control slip a bit.

"I know how torn up you are," Angie said desperately, crying herself. "Let me help. Please. And just so you'll know, I never betrayed you to Dave. The only thing I told him was to fuck off."

In spite of herself, Kate smiled.

"Oh, Kate," Angie said, lunging into Kate's arms.

For the longest time they hugged. Then Angie said, "Come on, let's go home."

With arms tightly circled around each other, they walked toward the cars. Once there, Kate placed her hand on the door handle, only to stop. "I'll be back in a minute," she said, staring at the building.

"Where are you going?" Angie asked.

"Back inside. You go on. I'll follow shortly."

Angie looked at her strangely, but didn't argue. "All right, if you're sure."

Kate gave her a wobbly smile. "I'm sure."

She wasn't sure, wasn't sure at all. With each step, she told herself she didn't have to do this. No one knew the truth. No one ever had to know. Angie hadn't talked and never would.

After today, she suspected Sawyer hadn't talked either, despite her accusations to the contrary.

All she had to do was stop, turn back, get in her car, drive home, and pick up her life where she had left off. She had it all and she could continue to do so with no one the wiser.

"Do it, Kate. For god's sake, just do it!" she muttered tersely.

She didn't turn around, nor did her steps falter. She walked back into the building, straight to Mr. Renfro's office. He was standing in the hallway talking with a woman.

He smiled when he saw her. "Ah, Judge Colson, I thought you were gone. Did you forget something?"

Kate stopped in front of him, took a deep breath, then returned his smile. "Yes, as a matter of fact, I did."

"Oh?" Then turning to his companion, he said, "Would you please excuse us a moment?"

The woman nodded before turning and walking off.

"I'm sorry if I caught you at a bad time."

"No problem. Now, what is it you forgot?"

In a firm voice Kate said, "I forgot to tell you that I'm Amber Sterling's birth mother."

His mouth dropped open.

"That's right." Pride sparkled in Kate's eyes. "Amber is my daughter."

Forty-nine

During the next few weeks, Kate used work to soften her heartache. Yet when she thought about her daughter and the injustice of all that had happened, she would get physically ill. Still, she was determined to establish some type of relationship with Amber, though she knew it would take time and patience.

First, she had to accept the fact that this lovely young woman had the mind of a five-year-old. When Kate thought about that, her heartache intensified. She wasn't about to give up hope, vowing that even if she won the election, Amber would never be neglected again.

The institution made that vow easy. Though the Sterlings had set up a trust fund for Amber's care, they had made the institution the executors. Mr. Renfro had given her permission to see Amber whenever she wanted.

Kate wished her thoughts were that clear about Sawyer, but they weren't. She couldn't bear to think about him. The pain of their parting, combined with her daughter's plight, was too much for her overburdened heart. Work once again became her panacea.

Not only was her own docket crowded, but she had to testify herself. She was about to be called as a rebuttal witness in Harlan Moore's trial, which was under way. This was one courtroom scene she didn't want to miss. Even if she hadn't been testifying, she would've sat in on the case when time permitted.

Harlan had finally gone too far, as she'd known he would. He was being tried for duping a client into buying land that was tainted with poisonous chemicals.

Kate had slipped into the back bench the day that Harlan was cross-examined. The prosecutor had asked him about that bribery charge.

"That's a lie," Harlan had said, his face red with rage. "I've never tried to bribe anyone in my life."

Kate hadn't heard another word of his testimony. Inside she'd seethed. The bastard had tried to bribe *her*.

As soon as the trial had ended for the day, she had marched into the district attorney's office and said, "Carl, I can help you in the Moore case if you want me as a rebuttal witness."

Now, it was only a matter of waiting until Harlan's trial began, and she could testify against him. There was no doubt in her mind that her testimony would hand the state the last nail it needed to seal Harlan's coffin. He would indeed serve time. She smiled.

That smile soon disappeared, however. The only person whose comeuppance mattered was Thomas—her one piece of unfinished business.

"Ladies and gentlemen, you will now go with the bailiff to deliberate this case," she said in a strong voice.

The courtroom was unusually quiet while the jury box emptied. Then Ben stood and said, "All rise!"

Kate rose and swept out of the courtroom into her chambers. She had no idea how long it would be before the jury reached a verdict. Not anytime soon, she suspected. It had been a long, complicated trial, although the evidence had been well presented from both sides. For now, though, her job was done.

She hoped that she would have some free time, as the case with Harlan was also over. As she'd predicted, he'd gone to prison.

She sighed as she removed her robe and hung it up. Her stomach gurgled suddenly. At the same time her head pounded over her left temple. Hunger. She hadn't eaten anything this morning and now it was after noon. Food, however, didn't interest her, but then not much did these days.

It had been six weeks since she had visited Amber, and the wound inside her was still open and raw. She could never change what had happened. One didn't have the luxury of going back and righting old wrongs. However, one did have the luxury of learning from mistakes.

She had made a start when she'd confessed to being Amber's birth mother. Still, that wasn't good enough. She wanted to win the election, but she didn't intend to neglect Amber in order to do so.

Kate closed her eyes for a moment and listened to the sounds from outside. Somehow, though, the noise from the heavy trucks and the cars whizzing by didn't bother her. In fact, the uninterrupted noise was comforting. It kept her aware of a world beyond the vacuum in which she now lived.

"Judge."

Kate opened her eyes to face Leslie.

"This packet came by special delivery. I thought it might be important."

Kate frowned. "Thanks, Leslie."

Leslie laid the envelope on Kate's desk and left. Kate eyed it for a moment, then picked it up and opened it.

"Oh," she gasped, as photographs of Thomas leapt out at her: Thomas holding a woman's hand, a woman who was not his wife. Thomas with his arms around another woman, kissing her.

Other pictures, more explicit, and a video tape rounded out the packet.

Kate's hand shook and she had trouble getting her next breath. Who on earth had sent these? She saw the note then, scrawled in a bold hand, and stopped breathing altogether.

> One of my agents tailed Thomas. Use the sordid
> goods however you see fit.
>
> Sawyer

Kate stared into space. Was this Sawyer's way of apologizing for his deceit? For a moment, she allowed herself to think about him. Their affair had started out like a house afire, only to suddenly burn to the ground with only ashes to show for it.

She could blame no one but herself. Sawyer hadn't made any promises, had never come close to saying that he loved her. They hadn't even discussed what would happen when the case ended. Again, she was the stupid one, the rash one, who had fallen in love.

Kate thrust aside the pain the thoughts had brought and stared at the photos in front of her. She hadn't known how she would bring about Thomas' downfall. She had only known that one day she would. Now, the ammunition had been dropped in her lap. Those photos, along with the tape, were exactly what she needed to expose Thomas to the world as the inhumane bastard he was. But in exposing him, she would also expose herself.

Her heart quickened. Should she risk it? Could she live with herself if she took that risk? More important, could she live with herself if she *did not*?

Kate stepped out the door of her campaign headquarters into the bright summer sunlight. She knew she looked like a woman in charge of her life and her career. Her green silk designer suit was tailor-made to fit her trim figure. For once her hair was in place; few willful strands fanned her face.

Now, as she glanced over the sea of media with their cameras flashing and their microphones poking in her face, she felt good about her decision. Yet inside she trembled with fear.

Kate squared her shoulders. "Ladies and gentlemen, I'm sure you're more than curious as to why I have called you here today."

"Yeah," one reporter shouted, "especially since we're always on your hit list."

Laughter erupted. When it died down, Kate forced a cool

smile and continued, "Actually, I have a confession to make."

Immediately, she sensed she had them where she wanted them, hanging on to her every word. "When I was sixteen years old, I had a child out of wedlock."

Shocked murmurs went through the crowd. She held up her hand and quieted them. "I was talked into giving it up for adoption to a supposedly loving family. Unfortunately, that wasn't what happened. The father of the child was supposed to have taken the baby to the proper person so that the adoption could go through. Instead, he dumped the baby in a dirty motel room and walked out."

Kate paused, sucked in her breath, and watched the press's pens and pencils burn across the paper like wildfires across dry grass.

Then the questions came, all at once.

"Who's the father?"

"Where is the child now?"

"Who adopted it?"

"Was it a girl or boy?"

"Do you plan to make it a part of your life?"

"Does he or she know you're its birth mother?"

And so it went, until they realized Kate hadn't said a word in response. Suddenly the voices fell silent. "The man I hold responsible, the father of my . . . child—" Her voice faltered as the intense love for her daughter raged against the cruelty of Thomas' action.

She took a deep breath, then went on, "The father of my child happens to be a renowned television evangelist."

Shouts came from every direction. "Tell us who he is. Give us a name!"

Kate composed her features and reached for the packet that one of her campaign workers held out to her. She, in turn, held it up in front of the media. "It's all in here." She then pointed toward a table stacked with packets. "And as you can see, my assistants have enough copies for all of you."

When the noise settled, she added, "I want to thank you for coming. Good day."

Kate re-entered the headquarters, but not before she saw the media descend like vultures on the material. Once the door had closed behind her, she sagged against it. Her heart pounded. Her legs trembled. Her hands oozed perspiration. But she felt cleansed. She had promised herself that Thomas would pay for his sins. He wasn't the only one, though.

Pay day had finally come for both of them.

Fifty

The following morning Kate stared at the headlines in the newspaper.

WEALTHY AND RENOWNED TELEVISION EVANGELIST, THOMAS JENNINGS, FALLS FROM GRACE AT THE HANDS OF JUDGE KATE COLSON

The article went on to give a detailed account of Kate's confession, followed by the lurid contents of the packets, which exposed Thomas for the hypocrite that he was.

Kate sipped her coffee and read the article, word for word. When she finished, she stared out the window. Before the press conference, nervous energy had motivated her. Now, only sadness filled her. Nothing had changed; her revenge had not freed her daughter from the institution, nor had it assured her of an election win.

She was hopeful about her career, though. The phone hadn't stopped ringing. All evening, support for her had come through headquarters, especially from women's groups who heralded her for her courage and honesty. Most of the people at the firm had stood by her as well.

Nothing, however, could fill the emptiness that dogged her days and nights. She yearned to find a solution that would allow her to become a part of her daughter's life.

She also yearned to pick up the phone and call Sawyer.

Unwelcome tears burned her eyes. She blinked them back. No more tears, she told herself savagely. She had made her decision concerning him and there was no turning back.

"Why so down in the mouth?"

Kate turned. "Oh, good morning."

Angie bounced into the breakfast room and sat down. "You ought to be riding high." She grinned. "I know I am. Boy, did you grab him by the balls, then squeeze the life out of 'em."

"Angie!"

"Well, you did, and I'm loving every minute of it."

Kate's face clouded again. "I don't know. The whole thing was so ugly, so sordid, so against everything that I've always stood for and believed in."

"Sure it was, but you had to do it." Angie cocked an eyebrow. "You're not regretting it, are you?"

"No. No regrets."

"Not even if it costs you the election?"

"Not even if it costs me the election."

"Well, it was a ballsy thing you did. I couldn't have done it. No way."

They were quiet for a moment, then Kate said, "I just wish that somehow Wade Jackson would get what's due him."

"Funny that you should mention him."

Kate's eyes widened. "Why, do you know something?"

"Yep. Mamma and I were talking about him the other day. She said scuttlebutt around town is that he's been running drugs off the coast of Miami and that he got himself in trouble with some of those drug kingpins."

"If that's true, then it couldn't happen to a more deserving person."

"Oh, you haven't heard the good part." Angie's grin was a leer. "Supposedly, they got him for holding back on the cash and cut both his ears off, then slashed his throat."

Kate's stomach revolted. "Oh, for crying out loud, Angie!"

"I'm just telling you what's going around. Of course, they haven't found his body."

"Can we change the subject?" Kate asked, white-faced.

"Sure. I have some other news, anyway."

"Oh?"

"I'm leaving town."

"Isn't that rather sudden?"

Angie turned away. "No, I've been looking for another job since . . . since Dave and I split."

"I'm sorry—"

"Ah, don't be. He was a bastard and deep down I knew it. And speaking of that jerk, have you heard the latest about him?"

"No. Have you?"

"Sure have." Angie chuckled. "I'm just full of all kinds of good news today."

"That you are, my friend," Kate said drolly.

"Well, aren't you the least bit curious about lover boy?"

"Of course I'm curious. I hope he got his just desserts."

"Oh, believe me, he did."

Kate lifted her eyebrows. "Since you've split, how do you know?"

"I went to the firm, that's how. I'd left a couple of things at his apartment, and I wanted them. I'd tried to call him for days, but he was either out of the office or not at home. So I decided to camp out at his office until he came in."

Angie flapped her hand impatiently. "So to make a long story short, I walked down the hall just as he was coming out of Mr. Johns's office. Not only was he swearing hotly, but he looked as if *his* throat had been cut and all the blood drained from his body."

"My god, Ang, you're on a roll today with your descriptions."

Angie laughed. "Anyway, come to find out, the boss had just given him the ax—as in you're fired, buddy."

Kate was stunned. "Are you serious?"

"Yep. Apparently Johns proved that Dave was responsible for the malicious gossip that had circulated about you, which was something he wouldn't tolerate. Also, some of his work was found to have been unethical."

Kate let out a slow breath. "I can't say he didn't deserve it, because he did. He's been a thorn in my side on occasion, that's for sure."

"Well, needless to say, you won't have to worry about him giving you any competition at the polls. After word gets around as to why he lost his job, he'll be finished professionally and politically."

"I wish I could believe that. But the Dave Nielsens of the world don't just crawl into a hole and lick their wounds."

"You're right, but he's through at the firm."

"Don't be surprised if he doesn't rally." Kate paused. "I fully expect him to open his own business and appear in my courtroom."

Angie laughed out loud. "If that happens, I'd love to be a fly on the wall." Her features sobered. "Ah, just blow him off. I have."

"Are you sure about that?"

Angie smiled wanly. "Okay, so he was a good lay, and it was fun while it lasted. But yeah, it's over."

Kate laughed. "You're crazy, but I love you."

"Me too."

"So where are you going?"

"To Dallas, with a good job, too."

"Oh, Ang, I'm so glad."

"Maybe this time I won't screw it up."

"You won't. You'll do just fine."

Angie was quiet for a moment. "I can't thank you—"

"Forget it."

Angie stood. "I'm leaving at the end of the week, but when you win the election, I'll be back for the celebration."

"That's a big 'if,' but I'll hold you to it."

Angie reached the door, then swung back around. "You're probably going to shoot me for saying this, but I think you're nuts if you let him go."

Taken aback, Kate frowned. "What on earth are you talking about?"

"It's not what, it's who. And you know I'm talking about Sawyer Brock."

The color fled Kate's face. "He's history."

Angie shrugged. "He doesn't have to be."

"Yes, he does." A closed, mutinous expression came over Kate's face.

Angie sighed. "You're more stubborn than your daddy's old mule! I just wish I had someone who cared about me as much as Sawyer cares about you."

With that, Angie flounced out of the room, leaving Kate with her mouth agape.

Later, though, when her mind had settled, she realized that Angie didn't know what she was talking about. Sawyer didn't care about her in the way she wanted, nor would he ever.

Fifty-one

Thomas Jennings walked out of the ministry headquarters and was instantly swarmed by reporters. "Goddamn vultures," he swore, even as he tried to ignore them.

But that was impossible. They surrounded him like the vultures they were, feeding off others, until he felt his head threaten to explode like a ripe watermelon.

"Get out of my way!" he hissed.

A woman stuck a microphone in his face, "Reverend, who's the woman in your life these days?"

"Yeah, Reverend, who is she?"

Another: "Tell us her name?"

"How do your followers feel about you now, Reverend?"

"Reverend, how could you dump a baby in a motel? What kind of monster would do a thing like that?"

Thomas, breathing like a marathoner, thrust his way through the horde of media. "Get out of my way. Leave me alone. I'm not going to answer any of your questions."

He should have known better than to leave the office, but dammit, he couldn't spend the rest of his life in hiding. Yet he feared that was exactly what he would have to do, thanks to *her*. He would like nothing better than to walk up to Kate Colson and stab her in the heart, then watch her bleed to death.

Thomas finally made it to his car, where he lost no time

getting in, locking the doors, and cranking the engine. The reporters surrounded the car. "Out of my way or I'll run over you," he shouted through the glass.

He would, too. He was just that angry. And frightened. He felt his blood pressure rise even higher as he maneuvered his Lincoln out of the parking lot and onto the street.

Sweat drenched his skin and soaked through his clothes. His insides clenched in a vise. Since Kate's cold-blooded announcement, the phone hadn't stopped ringing. People were outraged, said they were withdrawing their monetary support.

His television sponsors had canceled, except for two, and he expected them to do so shortly.

When he gripped the steering wheel he heard his knuckles pop. Still, he didn't let up on that hold until he drove into his circular drive and killed the engine. He sat still for a moment and waited. Silence greeted him. No reporters.

He got out and looked at his mansion and was actually glad to be here. He mopped his face with a handkerchief, grabbed his briefcase, and walked inside. He stumbled into something heavy, almost losing his balance and falling. "What the hell?"

"I'd think it's self-explanatory."

Thomas glared first at the three pieces of luggage on the floor, *his* luggage, then up at Annette, who stood in the middle of the curving staircase.

Thomas' Adam's apple bobbed up and down. "This is my house, damn you!"

She laughed a shrill, empty laugh. "Built with my daddy's money."

"It's in my goddamn name."

"And mine. That's irrelevant; no judge in this state or any other would give it to you now."

"Go to hell."

"I'm sure I will, but I won't be alone. You'll be dancing with the devil long before I will. Now, get out. I'm sick of looking at your face. Go to one of your floozies." She paused, then threw back her head and laughed. "She really carved you a new ass hole, didn't she? I have to hand it to her, the lady judge not only has claws, but fangs, and she sure stuck them in you. And me." Her eyes turned colder and harder. "And I don't like being married to someone who's such a monster."

"You can't do this! You can't just kick me out!"

A man stepped out of a bedroom onto the upper balcony. He was a big bear of a man with a thatch of gray hair and thick jowls.

Thomas' heart thudded to his toes. Annette's father, Riley Holcomb, was the last person he wanted to encounter.

"Maybe she can't kick you out, but I can," he drawled, without raising his voice. "You're a disgrace, boy, to this family, to the Lord, and to this state." He peered down at his watch. "I'd say about now, a locksmith is changing the locks on the ministry building."

"What!?" Thomas shrieked. "You can't do that!"

"I own the building. I can do anything I please. Now, get those bags and be on your way, you hear?" When Thomas didn't move, he bellowed, "Now!"

Thomas jumped as though he'd been shot, then scrambled to pick up the luggage. He struggled to the door and finally made it outside. But he couldn't go any farther. His energy was depleted.

What was he going to do? Where was he going to go? He was ruined, disgraced. He thought about the gun in his glove compartment. Maybe hell was better than life on earth. He couldn't do it; he wished he could, but he was too chicken.

The worst part of it all was that the bitch had won; Kate Colson had outsmarted him and had him on the run with his tail between his legs.

He trudged to the car.

Sawyer read about Harlan's trial and actually smiled when he read the part detailing the guilty verdict and the number of years Harlan would spend in prison. He'd be an old, old man by the time he got out.

Other than checking out the guy in Tampa and finding him

clear, Sawyer hadn't had a part in that dirty land deal. Ol' Harlan had waded in that sewer all by himself.

While he was glad Harlan had got what he deserved, he was downright ecstatic that Thomas Jennings had got his just due, pleased that Kate had used the material he'd sent her.

Sawyer couldn't pat himself on the back, though. He was too miserable to do much of anything. Since his breakup with Kate, Ralph had practically run the company.

Kate had his guts so tied in a knot that he couldn't think straight. The only bright spot in his dismal days was that a jury had found one of his clients, accused of murdering his stepsons in a fire, not guilty. Sawyer patted himself on the back for that. He had uncovered much of the evidence that had saved the case. But the congratulations was short-lived. That hole inside him was getting bigger.

Sawyer popped a video in the VCR, then sat back on the couch. He had taped Kate's press conference. Since then, he'd lost count of the number of times he'd replayed it just so that he could look at her.

He turned on the VCR. Kate's image filled the screen. He had never seen her looking better, except for the definite circles under her eyes. Otherwise, she was perfect. The sunlight shone on her hair, making it shimmer. He knew exactly what it felt like threaded through his hands. And he knew the feel of that tiny pulse beat in the hollow of her neck.

Sawyer felt his own flesh building. He groaned. Kate was the best thing that had ever happened to him. How had he let her go? In a month's time, the election would be over and she would have won the judgeship. The response to her honesty and forthrightness had been positive. No doubt great things were in store for her.

But dammit, she cared about something other than her job. She cared about *him*. He had seen that caring in her eyes, heard it in her voice, felt it in her touch.

Then how had things gone so wrong?

He had replayed that fateful day in his mind over and over, trying to figure out why he hadn't defended himself, why he hadn't tried to make her understand that when he'd told Harlan he'd get the goods on her, he hadn't cared about her. Hell, she'd been just another client. If he had known that he was going to lose her, he would have made her listen.

He closed his eyes for a moment, breathed deeply, then lunged off the couch.

"Congratulations, Kate! You did it."

Kate grinned at Bill Johns, who held his thumbs up. Her victory party was going strong. Although she was thrilled with the win, she was emotionally drained and had to force herself to join in the festivities.

Champagne flowed freely and everyone patted each other on the back. Kate excused herself and went in search of Angie, who had told her she needed to leave soon. She had hoped that Angie would spend the night with her, but Angie was going to New Braunfels.

"I wish you wouldn't go," Kate said, finding Angie at the buffet table.

Angie finished dipping a shrimp in the cocktail sauce before facing Kate. "Mamma's counting on seeing me, and I get to go home so seldom."

"I know. It's just that I'm selfish." And lonely, Kate thought, so lonely that she couldn't stand herself.

"What's wrong?" Angie asked. "You look like you're about ready to crash."

"I had a tough case. The murder trial finally ended."

"Oh, how did that come out? I haven't seen a paper in weeks."

"The jury found the deputies guilty. Said they cold-bloodedly murdered the black prisoner."

"And you're sure that's all that has you strung out?"

Kate forced a smile. "Yes, I'm sure."

Angie rolled her eyes. "I wish I could believe that."

"Your imagination's just working overtime, my friend."

"No, it's not. It's Sawyer, isn't it?"

Kate stiffened. "I don't want to—"

"I know," Angie said, "you don't want to talk about him. But dammit, you two are crazy for not patching up your differences."

Kate leaned over and kissed Angie on the cheek. "I love you."

"In other words, butt out," Angie said with a shrug, then grinned.

Kate grinned in return. "Hurry back to see me." After she left Angie, Kate mingled for another hour; then, pleading exhaustion, she left campaign headquarters with good wishes ringing in her ears.

A short time later Kate eased onto the couch and stared into the hot cup of gourmet coffee. She should be in bed, even though she didn't have to work tomorrow. In honor of her victory, she'd been given the day off.

She was far too keyed up to go to bed and had had one too many glasses of champagne.

And, God help her, she wanted Sawyer. At one time, he had wanted her—desperately. She took a quick sip of the coffee. Somewhere in the back of her mind, she had thought he might show up at her party tonight. He hadn't, of course—that wasn't Sawyer's style.

What if she went to him tomorrow, told him she was sorry, that she'd made a terrible mistake? Would he listen? Would he give her another chance? And if he did, then what?

The doorbell rang. Kate frowned. Who would be at her door at this time of night, especially as she had left the party still in full swing? She tightened her robe around her. Angie must have forgotten something.

Shoving a tendril of loose hair behind her ear, Kate crossed to the door.

"Who is it?"

"Sawyer."

The muffled sound of his voice dried the saliva in her mouth.

"Kate . . . please open the door."

The desperate note in his voice drove her into action. She unlocked the door and jerked it back. A shaft of moonlight bathed him in its glow while their eyes met and held.

He coughed, the breath rattling in his chest. "I know it's late, but I saw your light and wanted to congratulate you."

The light sheen of sweat on his face was evidence of his emotional state.

"Thank you. And I . . . wanted to thank you so . . . so many times." The words ground to a halt, then began again in a husky whisper, "For the packet."

"You don't owe me any thanks." Sawyer cleared his throat again. "That was the least I could do."

Their gazed continued to hold.

"Would you like something to drink? Champagne maybe?"

"No, I just wanted to stop by and offer my congratulations."

"I'm . . . glad you did."

His eyes were dark with emotion. "Are you?"

"Yes," she whispered achingly, wondering how she was going to live the rest of her life without him.

"God, Kate, don't look at me like that, not if you don't mean it. I—"

"Hold me, Sawyer," she pleaded.

With a muffled groan, he reached for her, crushing her against him. "Oh, Kate, I didn't mean to hurt you." He rained kisses on her lips, her face, her neck. "But I never told Harlan a thing. Never."

Kate was equally as eager, yearning to touch, to hold, to make up for all the time lost. "Shh. I know," she murmured between wet, hungry kisses. "I'm so sorry for misjudging you."

"I love you," he said. "I love you."

"And I love you."

They held each other in a long embrace, still standing in the patch of moonlight. Finally, Sawyer held her at arm's length and looked into her eyes. "Will you marry me?"

Her shining eyes clouded, and she moved out of his arms. "There's something you should know."

"And just what is that?" he asked in a teasing voice.

"When I had Amber . . . the doctor told me I could never have another child."

His face sobered. "I'm sorry, honey, but what does that have to do with our getting married?"

"You told me once how you'd like to have a . . . child."

"Come here," he said thickly.

With a cry, she drove back into his arms.

"Hell, there are lots of kids who need a home. If we feel the urge to have a baby, hell, we'll just go get us one."

Kate pushed back and looked at him. "You really mean that, don't you?"

"It's you I want. Anything over and above that would merely be gravy."

She laughed. "Oh, Sawyer Brock, I do love you."

"And I love you."

Her features suddenly tensed again. "There's one more thing."

"Okay, let's hear it."

"There's Amber. You have to know that I'm determined to find a way to become part of her life."

"Correction," Sawyer said. "*We'll* find a way."

Fifty-two

The house smelled of Christmas. Potpourri burned in containers throughout the living room, where Kate stood surveying the Christmas tree. An ornament dangled from her hand. The tree was already perfection itself, standing tall as heaven draped in lights that sparkled like tiny diamonds and covered with ornaments of all sizes and shapes. Still, she couldn't seem to leave it alone.

She heard a noise, and thinking that it was Sawyer, she turned around. Only it wasn't her husband; a log had settled in the fireplace. Her eyes rested on Sawyer, who was sprawled sound asleep on the couch.

She smiled and simply looked at him. Gone was the tension around his mouth and the gauntness in his face. Marriage agreed with him, she thought warmly, as it did with her. She'd never known so much happiness and contentment and neither had Sawyer.

They had married three days after she won the election and since then, they had talked at length about their miserable childhoods. That was one reason she wanted their first Christmas together to be perfect. She had decorated the house herself with live poinsettias and various other Christmas decorations. She'd even baked cookies and cakes, and

368

Sawyer had teased her unmercifully because she'd burned the first batch of cookies.

Her smile widened as she remembered how he had gulped them down anyway; and she had been moved to tears when he'd told her he'd never had homemade cookies.

Moments like those were as precious as the times he went with her to see Amber. Sweet Amber, he called her, and she never failed to respond with a laugh.

Amber had become a part of their life, even though the progress was slow. They had yet to bring her out of the home. But she hoped . . .

"Just can't leave it alone, can you?"

Sawyer's husky voice claimed her attention.

He was walking toward her, wearing nothing but his underwear. "It's hard to improve on perfection."

Kate sighed and faced the tree. "It is lovely, isn't it?"

"I wasn't referring to the tree."

Before she could turn around, his arms encircled her from behind. He nuzzled her neck. "Mmm, you smell good enough to eat."

"I've never seen you when you weren't hungry or horny."

He chuckled as a hand snuck through an opening in her robe and wandered over a full breast. "I love you."

"And I love you."

"Show me," he said thickly.

She turned in his arms and offered him her lips. He groaned as he plundered them with his own. She clung to him as warm fire settled between her legs at the same time she felt his burgeoning hardness.

"I can't get enough of you," he muttered, slipping off her robe while lowering her to the floor. "If only some of those bad-asses could see you now, all warm and melting, such a change from the prim, cold judge who sits on her throne."

She pulled him down to her by the hair on his chest. "Shut up and kiss me."

He didn't speak again. Words were no longer necessary. He began to stroke her breasts, her stomach, her navel, first with his hand, then his tongue.

She quivered, then begged, "Please, I want you inside me. I don't feel complete unless you are."

"Oh, God," he groaned in a litany, then rose above her in the firelight, as if taking flight, before settling over her and easing into her.

"I'll ride." He thrust deep and high inside her. She climaxed within minutes, then again, as they both cried out simultaneously.

The constant ache was once again satisfied, and she thought how amazing it was that she'd lived all these years without knowing that loving and being loved could be so fulfilling.

Sawyer snuggled next to her on the warm rug, after pulling her robe over their nakedness. "You're so quiet. Are you all right?"

"I'm wonderful, in fact."

He pushed a damp strand of hair out of her eyes. "I love you. I don't think I'll ever get tired of saying that."

"I hope not."

They were silent for a while, content to hold each other, to bask in the beauty of sharing.

"Do you think we could bring Amber . . . home for Christmas?" Kate asked in a soft, faltering voice. Her eyes strayed to the tree, to the spot where a special box was wrapped with Amber's name on it. It contained the pearls that her mother had given her. She longed to place them around her daughter's neck.

Sawyer rested his head in the palm of one hand and peered down at her. "Of course we can bring our daughter home, if that's what you want."

A tear trickled down Kate's face. He licked it off. "When?" she whispered.

"When what?"

"When can we get her?"

Sawyer sat up and grinned. "What's wrong with now?"

"Now?" Kate's voice shook. "You mean leave now, this minute?"

Sawyer's lips twitched. "Well, maybe we oughta get dressed first."

"Oh, Sawyer!" she cried, and flung her arms around him. Then she jumped up and dashed toward the bedroom, only to stop suddenly and turn around. "Just think, if we bring Amber home, we'll be a *real* family."

"Always, my darling, always."